BOMB
SHELL

BOMB SHELL

GENEVA LEE

QUAINTRELLE

To Sophie,
Our favorite bombshell

PROLOGUE

I t doesn't make sense. I read the certificate in my hands again, my eyes skipping over the boxes where someone typed up the vital statistics. Four entries stand out to me:

Adair Anne MacLaine.

The woman standing across from me. The woman I didn't know before this moment. The woman I'm not sure I'll ever know.

November 1.

The day after her birthday. Four years ago. A day I was drunk on leave with Jack and Luca.

Elodie Anne MacLaine.

Her niece. They have a club for Sagittariuses. Sagittari? She likes hot chocolate.

Unknown.

But I know what name belongs in that box. Adair knows. More importantly, Adair *knew*, even then. It should have been my name in the box next to Adair's name—the box marked *father*.

1

ADAIR

THE PAST

We make our way back down the thickly carpeted steps of the Valmont Country Club. If I look away for a moment, my heart swells like a wave cresting at high tide when I see him again. And his eyes? They crash over me, pulling me under until there's only him and the promise of a life I was sure I'd never reach. I'm lost in him, and I never want to be found.

Thankfully, no one seems to have noticed we were gone. I'm even more thankful that I can feel my tipsiness wearing off. We practically float into the Valmont Country Club ballroom, anchored to the earth only by our clasped hands and make our way to the dance floor. Sterling's eyes glint, catching the last, dying ember of sunset streaming through the large windows

God, he's handsome. God, I love him.

"Are you ready to dance, Lucky?" he says, but before I can answer he spins me against his body, catching my hand in his and pressing the other to the small of my back.

"If you put your hand any lower, we'll have to find another closet," I tease.

The adoration on his face transforms to something darker, sending my own mind to thoughts of another stolen moment alone. He pulls me even closer to him, twirling us between two other couples, and bends down to kiss me.

Pop.

The energy in the room changes, and I sense the people around us stop dancing as though we've actually become the center of the world instead of just feeling like we are.

Pop. Pop-pop-pop.

Flashes of light fill the ballroom, and this time, even I stop. I look around, half-expecting to discover some well-intentioned, but soon-to-be-unemployed server has turned on a strobe light.

Boom!

A shower of sparks ricochets over the lake outside, and a split second later, another loud *boom* fills the room. Orbs of pale pink and champagne bloom in the night sky, the water doubling the effect of the fireworks. The ballroom lights dim above us as the next firework goes off bathing everyone in flashes of pastel light. Around us, the people *ooh* and *ahh* as the flashes keep coming, now without any big, booming explosions.

The piano in the corner, unused all night, begins playing. I know everything about the wedding plans—and this isn't part of them. My eyes scan the crowd, hoping to find a glimpse of Ginny. There's no way she okayed this. I would know.

"There," Sterling says, guessing who I was looking for and pointing to a spot by the glass wall.

Ginny's brow is crinkled, her mouth agape. For a second, I'm sure she hates the disruption, as her gaze flies around the room, from DJ to wedding planner, finally coming to rest on Malcolm's face beside her. For an anguishing second, I think she's about to widow herself until my brother gives his new wife a sly grin. She softens into a swoon, and he bends down to whisper something in her ear. As he does, a small group of violins and cellos start playing next to the piano, sending another titter through the audience. I'm not into classical music, so I can't place the composition. But it's lovely—soft and rich, with big swells that take my breath away.

"Debussy, I think," Sterling says, his face dancing almost as much as Ginny's.

It's pure magic.

A man dressed in a black-on-black suit stands in front of the musicians, cupping his hand over a black earpiece. He must be coordinating between them and the fireworks people. When the next swell hits, it reveals another surprise. An entire small orchestra has filed into the back of the room as everyone looks out on the fireworks, and they all begin playing as an incredible flurry of fireworks burns the sky nearly as bright as day.

Two huge fireworks soar above the others, and when they explode I can feel my breath catch, waiting for the sound to make its way to us. Crashing cymbals join in time with the thunderous boom of the explosions, and the surging triumph of the music sends a collective *ahh* through the crowd.

I see Ginny looking up into my brother's eyes, her face a portrait of adoration.

"Being here with you—I feel like I'm in a dream," Sterling says softly. We watch, his arms wrapped around me and his chin on my shoulder, the music rising and falling as the lights of the fireworks burn arcs in the sky before collapsing towards their reflections. They match the swell and crash of my heartbeat. With each, I become more aware of him. With each, I fall a little more in love until I no longer want to see the fireworks themselves—only how they are reflected in his eyes.

"Count on my family to go big," I say, and for once I'm nearly proud of my brother. As far as I know, he has never had to plan so much as what to eat for lunch—and this definitely took a lot of planning. Of course, he might have done it just to impress people. It's the kind of thing our father would do for a party. But I'd rather believe he did it for love. I'm proof that even a MacLaine can fall head over heels.

"I'm beginning to see what you meant when you said you wanted a big wedding," Sterling says, an easy smile stealing across his face.

"I knew you'd come around," I pull his chin towards me and kiss him, his stubble lighting my skin on fire.

The final crescendo is intense, the horn players discarding their stops and playing at full volume as the cymbals crash over and over again. Two final *booms* bring the orchestra to its final flourish, and the strings draw quickly to one last, soft run of the melody, bringing the room to silence.

By the end, my ears are ringing from the noise. I see Sterling's mouth move but can't make out what he says. Although his lips seem to form the word *champagne* before he releases me to disappear into the sea of people, all applauding with the same contented grin he wears.

"And he had a hell of a time," says a young man a few feet away, talking as loudly to his date as only the recently deafened can. I recognize him as one of my brother's friends from prep school.

"She couldn't make up her mind about the colors until just a couple of weeks ago, and he had to send them to China so the fireworks would match exactly," the man explains. His date looks rapt, like she would have his children on the spot if he promised to do something like this for her. "He hired the company who did last year's Fourth of July fireworks over the White House to deal with it. I guess he didn't dare upset the bridezilla with the wrong color scheme."

So much for romance. It seems my brother bitched about having to wait on his wife, then made a phone call. I wonder how many minutes it took him to arrange this. Five? A whole ten? Not that it stopped him from bragging to his buddies. It's just another wealthy pissing contest between billionaires. If he couldn't use it to make himself look good, it would be a bad investment.

The deejay begins playing something much softer, and my eardrums appreciate it. When another couple of minutes pass without Sterling's return, I search the crowd for him. The ten-foot-tall champagne fountain, lit with an artist's care, shows no sign of him, nor does the table holding the remnants of the wedding cake.

Just then I hear something that makes my blood run cold. It's a sound I've heard often at Windfall, and my ears catch it despite the noise all around me. No one else seems to have noticed, but I do. Somehow—even at a distance and through thick walls and carpet—the spite in my father's voice carries all the way to me. Everyone at Windfall has felt his voice cut through them. It had been that way since as long as I can remember. My body's conditioned to respond to it like a survival mechanism.

I whip around, now desperate to find Sterling.

But he's not here.

Sterling, who is in love with me. Sterling, who is completely caught up in the romance tonight. Sterling, who wouldn't leave me, isn't here in the ballroom.

And my father is spitting venom.

2

STERLING

I want to give Adair a night like this.
The thought turns over in my mind, again and again.
She deserves to be the center of attention, to have everyone
care about what she thinks and what she wants—exactly what
her family will never give her. The problem is that I can't
imagine how I'd do it. I told her earlier that I imagined a small
wedding, attended only by people we care about. But what
would that actually look like?

Me, her...and Francie? Who else is there? Maybe Poppy
and Cyrus? In a room rented by the hour from the rec center
near our place in Queens? Or maybe we could do it in
Central Park, *fast*, so no one will be able to ask if we have a
permit?

She says it doesn't matter to her, but that's a lie she's
telling herself. She doesn't know what it's like for her
stomach to grumble with hunger, or to be bone tired but
unable to sleep over worries about money. Her heart means
well, and she loves me, which is something like a miracle, but
she doesn't know what she doesn't know.

What I know.

I duck into the men's room, considering what major I should declare. Economics or business? They'd help me make the most money. But something steady, like medicine or law could give us a nice life, too. It's the only shot I have at keeping her: becoming a man who deserves her. I'm no nearer the answer when I toss a hand-drying towel in the bin by the door, and shoulder my way back into the hallway.

"I'd like to have a word," a croaky voice says behind me.

It's Angus MacLaine.

His wheelchair is almost baroque—trimmed with carved wood, upholstered with green velvet, and tasseled with gold thread. It's motorized, of course, and I can't help noticing how he sits *on* it, like it's a throne, rather than in it. He twiddles the carved marble joystick that controls his chair, already turning his back to me and making his way to an office room farther down the hall.

I hate that he thinks I'll just come along because he said so. I hate even more that I do.

I've always known this was inevitable. I had to meet him in private at some point. I've managed to avoid it purposefully mostly because I couldn't be sure I wouldn't haul off and hit him. Now? I'm not ready. I haven't thought enough about how to play it. Should I be defiant? Honest about how he treats his family? Or should I be cordial, like all that matters is avoiding the worst outcome? I just don't know. When he asks me my intentions, do I tell him the truth?

I slide into the room behind him, resolved to talk as calmly as I can, until I get a better feel for how he sees me. The room is a cheap approximation of something at Windfall, with slightly warped wood coverings on the walls, and thin, industrial grade carpet on the floor. A wood-veneered desk sits squarely in the center of the room, and Angus wheels his way behind it, his lip curling into a sneer as the sharp edge of the desk catches the fabric of his suit near his elbow and nearly ripping it.

"Fuck!" he says, he eyes flailing for someone to complain to, but there is only me. He shifts in his chair and turns a bug-eyed glare on me. "Having a nice time at the wedding, boy?"

Boy? Five seconds in and I'm already fantasizing about hitting him.

"It's a very nice wedding, sir," I say, starting with something neutral but respectful. I'd much rather tell him that he needs to treat me with some respect. But I get the sense that he doesn't take verbal orders. If I want respect, I'm going to have to demand it through actions.

"Been spending a lot of time with my daughter?"

"Yes, sir. She's very special—"

"Of course she's special! She's a MacLaine." He says it like he can't believe he has to tell me the sky is blue.

"Right, I—"

"And what do you hope to gain by seeing her?" he asks, his eyebrow raised. Otherwise, his face remains neutral and business-like. It's his poker face, but a man like him doesn't gamble. He buys, sells, and takes—that's what he's really hiding behind that mask.

This is a negotiation.

"Nothing besides her company," I say, trying to deflect his suspicions while pretending I'm not afraid of the consequences of my answer. One wrong step and the discussion portion of this chat will be over.

"Bullshit," he says casually, then sniffs.

He'll have to do better to unbalance me. "Believe me. Don't believe me. I can't change that."

His dark eyes narrow to slits, studying me like a boa constrictor regarding a mouse, his full attention on me for the first time. He takes stock of my appearance, his eyes raking my expensive tuxedo, my shiny Italian shoes. Does he see the price tags that go along with each? Does he wonder how I paid for them? Does he know she bought them for me?

"I see why she likes you," he says, drumming his fingers on the desk. "You clean up alright, anyway, and you don't mind playing the part you're given, do you?"

A pregnant pause unfolds, both of us refusing to break eye contact.

"Meaning?" I say.

"You know *EXACTLY*—" his voice roars out of his mouth, moving the air around me and making the hair on my neck stand up, "—what I am talking about! Who paid for that tuxedo you're wearing? "

I tried to tell Adair it wasn't a good idea. And it turns out we were both right. I was right to think her father—who forces everyone at Windfall to live under his surveillance—would not approve. But she was also right. Because she can't let this ugly toad's whims control everything. *We* can't.

I grit my teeth, trying to calm my temper by reminding myself of her, of the importance of salvaging as much as I can from this conversation. He doesn't like me. Now. He might not ever like me. But he doesn't get a say in how she feels about me.

"Adair paid for it," I say. There's no point in lying about it. Then, I'll just be what he wants me to be: a gold digger and a liar.

"Suddenly stupid, boy?" Angus roars again. "No. No. You're not, though, are you? If you took a swing at me—and I can tell you want to—this would all be over in a moment.

Better to play the part you know she wants: the misunder-stood pauper, the diamond in the rough. Stick to it, you think, keep yourself under control, and the door to all of this will stay open." He waves expansively, meaning the wedding, the country club, everything he has that I don't.

"I don't want anything of yours." I shrug, hoping it will get under his skin. He wants me cowed. He couldn't do it if he tried. Not after what I've been through in life.

"A lie. You've had your eye on the jewel of my fortune," he seethes, and I start to protest, but he cuts me off, "You want my daughter."

For a moment, I'm taken aback, enough to blurt out, "Adair is *not* your property."

It sounds naive, even to me.

"She *IS* mine, you stupid boy." His chest is a bellows, pumping air to fuel his hatred, and he takes a moment to right himself, out of breath from his own theatrics. "I know you. Had some of my people look into you. Orphan. Bounced around the foster system. A sealed juvenile record. What exactly did you do, boy?"

Of course, he looked into my past. I'd convinced myself that his indifference to Adair extended to me. But she came home with me for Christmas. She ran to me on Thanksgiv-ing. He might not give a shit about her emotionally, but he's paying attention to every move she makes. Why else would he put cameras up all over his grounds? Adair is just another possession to be guarded, in his eyes. He can keep her in a case and bring her out for special occasions. "I don't owe you any answers," I say, my self-control nearly depleted. If he thinks I won't hit him because he's in a wheelchair, he's sorely mistaken. The only reason I haven't done it yet is Adair.

Now, I'm beginning to think she's the reason I *should* punch him.

"I already know what's in those records, of course," he continues, and as soon as it's out of his mouth, I know things are going from bad to ugly. "You stabbed your own father—"

"After he beat my mother to death," I add in a deadly soft voice, "or was that not in your summary?"

His snake eyes blink, black and beady. There's not even a shred of sympathy in them. They're as cold as he is. "One does not bite the hand that feeds, no matter the reason."

"Lucky for you, huh?" I say with meaning. I'm not the only one hiding sins.

"Luck has nothing to do with it. Money. Connections. Adair doesn't bite, because she's been trained. She's pure-bred, unlike you."

The only thing more powerful than the hatred I feel towards this man is the disgust he provokes at every turn. Apparently, Angus MacLaine has never been in the same room as shame.

"I've had enough." He raises a bent finger. His body is obviously as warped as his mind. "You have no idea what this life takes, the sacrifices our family has to make to stay on top. You are unsuitable for such a position. Therefore, you will stop seeing my daughter. At once." He says it like a bored judge reading the same jury instructions aloud for the thousandth time.

"No."

He doesn't look surprised. Instead, he heaves a weary sigh and reaches into his breast pocket to withdraw a checkbook and pen. "How much? A hundred thousand?"

I stare at the checkbook in his hand and process what he's

offering. It takes me longer than it should. "Think what you want about me, but I have more self-respect than that."

"Two hundred," he counters, writing my name across the *remit to* line.

I lean over the desk and look down at the great Angus MacLaine, my white knuckles popping against the wood. "Adair can make her own choices."

He swallows hard, and the smallest whiff of panic flashes in the corners of his eyes before being quickly tamed. He sniffs again, his lower lip drooping to reveal a gobbet of spit. "You can't give her the life I can. You may not want to hear it. But you know it's true. You're on scholarship, which means you might have a better future ahead of you, but we both know what you are."

"What's that supposed to mean? Are you—"

He waves me away, continuing, "Let me be plain, since you seem to be confusing your self-ideals with reality. YOU. ARE. *TRASH.* A mutt. A mongrel. You're nothing to her but a sad, unwanted dog. You might get an education, maybe even a decent job, but you can't change the blood pumping through your veins."

Suddenly, I'm back in my old apartment, my hand pulling at the sheet covering my mom's lifeless body. I see my father, his mustard-stained undershirt, drenched in pit sweat and stale beer, yelling in from the kitchen. I see my sister, her toes poking through holes in the fronts of her shoes, her hair dirty and matted—exactly like animals in some forgotten zoo.

I see Angus MacLaine in front of me, too, but he is telescoped away from me, as if we're both watching my young self from opposite ends of a hallway. I feel violated. And sick. And then a bottomless rage takes hold of me.

My anger boils, pouring out of me like sweat. I want to

wrap my hands around the crepe-like skin of his neck and squeeze.

"I may be a dog," I say, and, without breaking eye contact, I grab the right edge of the desk and heave as hard as I can. The desk flips over on its end, and the look of sudden, abject terror on Angus MacLaine's face is balm for my fury. "But that's still better than a blue-blooded monster who abuses his family. Fuck you, fuck your money, fuck the sad, small cage you pretend is your kingdom."

He starts to say something in reply, but his voice catches. He clears his throat like a broken trumpet, trying to find something to turn our encounter back in his favor. After another steadying breath, his composure returns, as if he has already forgotten what just happened. Angus drums his fingers on the lacquered arm of his wheelchair, a smug, spiteful grin lighting the shambles of his face. I see myself reflected in his black eyes, and I know why he's smiling. "Enjoy the rest of the wedding, Sterling Ford."

I stumble into the hallway, feeling like I'm in a nightmare I can't wake up from, because I'm exactly what he said I was. The mixed breed dog no one wants because he never learns, he just forgets and attacks. He wasn't provoking me to wreck my chances with Adair. He did it to prove he doesn't have to interfere. I'll fuck things up all by myself. I'm not sure where to go, but I need to put distance between myself and everyone else, or I'll only do more damage.

A line of faces wait in the hall, the country club staff standing stock still. I guess disagreements over golf don't usually get so heated.

"Christ, Sterling. Are you alright?"

I realize one of the faces is Cyrus, who's coming out of the restroom.

"Sterling?"

I realize I want to punch him, too. I've got to get control of myself. I close my eyes and take a deep breath, but it makes little difference.

"I know this look," he says. "Follow me."

I let him guide me down a flight of stairs and a hallway, and we arrive at a pair of double doors with a large sign hanging over them: *The Nineteenth Hole*. Inside, the room is dark, only the outlines of high tables and chairs silhouetted by the lights outside.

"He's lucky I didn't kill him," I say, taking one of the stools at the bar, which is right next to the doors. I realize my hands are clenched into fists and force them to loosen. "I should go back up there. Let him know exactly—"

"Whoa, man. That's not a good idea." He stoops behind the bar and begins rummaging around. "I'm not saying he doesn't have it coming. I think everyone has fantasized about killing Angus MacLaine at some point. It's a Valmont rite of passage."

"Did it ever occur to you he got this way because no one ever has kicked his ass?" They're cowards. All of them. That's why he wheels around like a king on his throne. Because no one ever challenges his authority.

"Did it *seriously* occur to me to attack the most powerful man in Valmont with the kind of resources that could ruin me and my family? *No*."

"Nobody's brave enough, huh?"

"Nobody's that stupid," he corrects me.

That's what he doesn't understand. The line between bravery and stupidity comes down to success. Fail to take the crown, and you're stupid. Conquer a kingdom, and you're brave. Maybe it's a lot easier to see more than one outcome when you have nothing more to lose.

"Normally, this wouldn't be the best thing for you," he says, thumping down a bottle of whiskey, along with a crystal rocks glass, "but it's got to be better than killing your girlfriend's father."

For a moment I try looking anywhere but at the bottle. Cyrus's face is cast in just a few shades of grey, his expression a mixture of concern and, I think, condescension. Part of me knows that he's trying to help, that my anger just wants an outlet, but I can't stand the way these people look at me, like I'm a misbehaving puppy that has to grow out of this phase.

"Thanks," I say, getting up from my stool and swiping the bottle of whiskey. "I need to get out of here."

I expect him to object, but he surprises me by giving a small nod. Then again, I did just threaten to murder the father of the groom. "I'll let Adair know you left."

I don't know where I'm headed, but it doesn't really matter as long as it's somewhere I can be alone with my bottle.

3

ADAIR

My heart skips a beat, and I rush towards the ornate french doors along the opposite wall of the room. The biting snarl of my father grows closer with each step I take.

"Wasn't it wonderful?" a dreamy voice asks as a clammy hand lands on my forearm.

I turn to discover Ginny with one hand on me and the other holding the ivory silk of her dress while beaming like a spotlight from some combination of romance and champagne.

"It was, but my dad" I begin to tell her that I don't have time to listen to her moon over my brother, who doesn't actually deserve the admiration, while my father attacks my boyfriend. But it's not Ginny's fault that my family can't behave themselves for one night. Why should I be the one to ruin it for her? She'll discover the truth soon enough. She knows what it's like in my house—how could she not? But she doesn't know what it's like to live that way week after week, year after year. She hasn't developed radar for my father's fits of rage. She is happy. At *her* wedding. I don't need to take that from her. Someone else will. So I take a second, as if I'm trying to find just the right description of my brother's show, before continuing, "It was really special. You know, I don't think my brother ever planned anything before. Definitely not a symphonic flash mob. Did you like it?"

"Not at first. I mean, I was wondering why a piano was suddenly playing, you know? I mean, I didn't approve a pianist. But when I saw his face, I knew. It was..." she falters, unable to find the right words, before continuing, "beyond anything I ever dreamed."

That's one way to put it. "I have to hand it to him. I don't think anyone will forget your wedding now."

"It could still be this way for you," she says idly, but there's an anxious edge to her voice, like she's saying something she hadn't dared say before. "If you make the right choices."

"What does that mean??" I ask slowly, afraid I already know exactly what it means.

"The perfect wedding. The perfect life." She gestures behind her, at the champagne fountain, the manicured vista, the ample evidence that everyone here has conquered life. Suddenly, I'm reminded of Jay Gatsby and his parties—and I know exactly how that turned out.

"Not for me, thanks." I hope she leaves it there, but I know she won't. She's a member of my family now, so why shouldn't she tell me how best to live my life? Goes with the territory.

"Why not? You have everything you could ever need. Security. Prestige. Luxury. People would kill for your life. You just can't throw it away on bad choices."

"You don't know what you're talking about, Ginny. Let's

not do this now." My self-control is slipping, and it's the only thing keeping my temper from flaring.

Her mouth clamps shut, and for a split second, I think I've convinced her to save it for another time. She opens her mouth, and if it's to placate me, I will never know, because I hear my father's voice again and one word: *trash.* Ginny hears it, too, and when I try to move through the door she steps in front of me.

I go rigid, fighting a surge of adrenaline. Every part of me wants to push my way past her. If she doesn't get out of my way, things are going to get ugly.

"Let me go before this gets worse," I warn her.

"This is *my* wedding, Adair," she hisses, trying to keep as many of the people around us out of our conversation as she can. Propriety must be observed, especially at weddings. She's a better MacLaine than me already. "How can you be such a narcissist?"

"What the fuck is that supposed to mean?" I say, no longer checking my volume.

She leans in close to me, her voice dropping to a venomous whisper as she jabs an accusatory finger at me. "Jesus, look at you! About to go make a scene by screaming at your father at *my* wedding. Does anybody get to have a nice moment? Or do you ruin them all?"

"I was minding my own business, Ginny," I say, grasping at the last bit of understanding inside me and feeling it fray. "Unlike—"

"Like hell you were. Nothing I say can stop you, will it? Because—despite having *everything*—you still have to be a wrecking ball, don't you?"

I open my mouth to protest, but the words aren't there. I take a second to find my voice, and when it comes out I am surprised how calm it sounds. "I'm not the one who has to control everything."

"No. You're the one who has to destroy everything. Nothing can exist if it doesn't perfectly please you, right? Not Thanksgiving dinner with our families. Not even a conversation with your brother or father."

Does she think her shiny, new wedding ring gives her the right to order me around? Has she always seen behind the curtains to the ugliness we keep hidden until now? I'd always thought she was naive—maybe willfully so. I thought she was too focused on the perfect wedding and blind to the harsh reality. Now? I wonder how much she's willing to ignore in search of her perfect life.

"I understand you don't like your family, Adair. And I know your father is...very difficult—"

"—that doesn't begin to cover it—"

"—but it still doesn't excuse *your* behavior. You've never had to do chores. Never had to work for anything. You may be able to treat everyone else like that, but not your family." Her words suck the air out of my lungs. She is just like them. I can't believe I never saw it before. "You're just a brat," she finishes with an exasperated sigh.

My arm spasms toward her, and my whole body jerks from the effort of stopping my hand from slapping her.

She flinches, sending a gasp throughout the crowd that has gathered around us. I can tell at once that she is going to behave like I actually hit her, making me wonder why I didn't just go ahead and do it. Somehow, through the red haze fogging my vision, I realize hitting her would prove her point.

She flinches again as I throw my hand around her shoulder and pretend to hug her, while dropping my mouth to her ear.

"You know nothing, Ginny," I whisper coldly. "You have girlish dreams of what life in my house is like. But your dad didn't scream at you every day of your life. You didn't have to watch yours get drunk, wondering how long it would be before he went after your every flaw, real or imagined. And you didn't have to sit in a hospital, waiting for them to come out and tell you that your drunk father killed your mother."

She pulls back. I expect her to be cowed, to look sheepish, but she doesn't. It's the sorrow in her eyes that catches me off guard, making me feel the size of a pea. "I'm sorry that happened to you. And I'm sorry you're so angry—"

"But I'm ruining your perfect wedding, right?"

"What would your mother say right now?"

The weight of a boulder lands on my chest. What am I supposed to say to that? I hate her. That's what I want to say. How dare she use my mother against me? She barely knew her, never got to see all the pain my father caused her. She thinks a few wedding planning sessions gave her deep insight? It barely gave her a glimpse. A few hours into being a MacLaine, and she's already an expert. And that's just it. I don't know why I worried about Ginny joining the family. She fits in better than I ever will.

"She'd tell you to make the best of your life. To take your advantage of wealth, your family connections, and make a good life from it. She wouldn't want you to be so full of rage. Because she would see what I see—that the anger is hurting you most of all."

Her words are sharp and pointed, delivering a precise prick that deflates me like a carefully popped balloon. She's right, isn't she? I can say she didn't know my mother well enough, but that's exactly the kind of thing my mother was always telling me.

Maybe I'm so accustomed to expecting the worst that I'm seeing it now. I'm ready to forgive Ginny—admit that I'm wrong—until she adds, "Instead, you're going to burn it all down. Fight with everyone, every chance you get. You're just like your father, actually. No compromises. No consideration. You don't even realize you're lashing out. I mean, for Christ's sake, Adair, you're dating some piece of trash orphan who's only out for our money!"

Her words sting, and I recoil, stepping back from her.

That's what this is about. It *was* coordinated. She *is* a MacLaine. Even today, my family can't relax and celebrate. They have to plot and manipulate and control. She planned this with my father. How else could she know about Sterling's past? My father is having the opposite version of this conversation with Sterling, right now. I know it. Did they plan it, or is Ginny so perfect for my family that she didn't have to be told? Is this a role she has chosen, or the one she was born to play?

I don't even realize my palm is swinging toward her face until my eyes lock with her panicked ones. It's too late to stop it. I might as well enjoy it. She deserves it. She made her wedding a battle zone. She deserves a little friendly fire.

"Kindly *do not* hit my wife," Malcolm says, catching my arm an inch from her perfectly made up face.

Ginny collapses into him, blubbering and teary, a jumbled mixture of what I said and a lot that I didn't spilling out of her mouth. I see her eyes peek up at him through wet lashes, trying to gauge his reaction so she can calibrate her performance. So he will remember me as a monster who tried to take her perfect day from her, instead of what really happened. Somewhere in her babbling I hear her mention my mother again.

"Don't ever talk to me about my mother again," I snarl, gathering up the hem of my dress, kicking off my heels, and running through the doors.

There is only wait staff in the hallway, but they are stopped dead, looking at the door on the far end of the hallway. I know the look people get when my father has been truly nasty, and it's on every face I see.

The eyes in the hall turn away from me when I meet them, pointing instead at a door down the hall. I hold my chin as high as it will go, and march through the door, gasping at the sight of the overturned desk, its lamp casting light upward from the floor, throwing my father's form into a strange, demented relief.

"What did you do?" I demand.

"I told your boyfriend what I thought of him." My father looks at me coldly, his voice breaking in a way I've never quite heard before.

I can see beads of sweat on his forehead, and that his hand shakes if he doesn't continuously grip the arm of his chair. Whatever happened, Sterling scared my father—something I thought no one could do. But whatever satisfaction it might have given me—I'm still a MacLaine, after all—I know it will come with a cost. "You don't know him enough to judge him."

"I know more than you. Do you know his record? What he came from?" Inflicting psychological pain is my father's true joy, and some of his wicked glee seems to return as he hangs on my answer.

"I know what happened to Sterling as a kid," I say, hoping he doesn't catch the quiver in my voice. "Hate to break it to you."

"It's worse than I thought, then."

"Meaning?"

"I've never understood how someone so smart could also be so stupid." His eyes dart towards the ceiling, as if he is talking to the heavens. "It means you find all his red flags charming, daughter mine. How you disappoint me. You're as beautiful as your mother and as headstrong as me, but the second you find a stray dog, you want to bring it home, fleas and all."

I flinch, not surprised by how he sees Sterling or me. But a cut still hurts even if you see it coming. "And I've never understood how you find so much ugliness in everyone else, but not in yourself, *father*."

"He is unsuitable for you. A criminal record? A violent temper? I won't have it. End of story."

"You don't control me!" I scream the words at him and instantly regret it. It only serves as proof that I'm some hysterical, weak creature, which is exactly what he wants me to believe, so I measure out what comes next carefully. "I'm not interested in what you think. Sterling gives me what I need, which is more than you've ever given me."

"You're confusing your wants with your needs. He treats you like you want—but I take care of your needs. Which he cannot."

"What do you know about my wants and needs?" My father doesn't recognize other people's desires unless it suits him. It always reduces to his money. He equates it with everything. He pays for things, therefore no one can complain about him.

"I know he's gotten you so twisted that you snuck off to screw him at your brother's wedding. Did you *need* him then?"

Heat blooms on my cheeks as I remember our perfect

tryst, then a knot forms in my stomach as I realize someone must have seen us. A flicker of realization hits me. "It was Ginny, wasn't it?"

"She saw you hustling down the stairs, looking like you just stumbled out of a hotel room—and she knew."

"So, she came to you?" The betrayal stings even after my fight with her.

"Of course not. She told her husband." My father thinks he has me now, so he leans forward, goading me with a smug grin.

For a second I wonder how he got to Sterling, but I push it aside because I'm not finished telling my father what he needs to be told. "If you have something to say about *my* choices, then take it up with me, not my boyfriend. Stop screwing around with my life. You've taken enough from me."

"Taken? What have I taken? I've given you everything you have." His voice is cold rage. His chest swells, and for a second I swear he will get up out of his chair and try to strangle me.

"You know exactly what I mean. You killed Mom." I don't care if he does strangle me. It's worth it to see his goggling eyes, his suddenly fish-like mouth. "Should I go and get you a nice brandy, *father*? You can drink the whole bottle and then have a temper tantrum until you feel better. Or at least make everyone as miserable as you are. At least, we don't have to worry about you getting behind the wheel anymore."

"You—you *cannot*," he splutters, his lips curling away,"*SPEAK TO ME LIKE THAT!*"

I don't wait around for his rage-filled tirade to end. I walk out the door, slamming it behind me.

· · ·

I CAN'T FIND STERLING ANYWHERE. I CHECK THE BALL room, the halls upstairs, even ask a few of the staff—but there's no sign of him. And every time I don't find him, my panic grows, until I realize I'm both cold and sweaty. My earlier tipsiness has worn off entirely, leaving a vague, throbbing headache in its place. Tears smart my eyes as each second unravels me a little more.

"There you are," says Poppy, who bobs into the room trailing Cy behind her.

I didn't know how much I needed to see a friendly face. I take one look at Poppy and burst into tears, burying my head against her shoulder.

She shushes me gently. "Hey, we're here now. You're okay."

Slowly, my body stops shaking, my anger and fear seeping out of me. I have friends here. We'll all be able to find him. My father hasn't won.

"We heard your father yelling. Are you okay?"

Half the wedding probably heard that fight.

"My father cornered Sterling, and they argued. Now I can't find him."

"Well, there are three of us. We can split up and look for him. We're here for you, Adair." Poppy gives me one of her patented, bright smiles.

Before it can cheer me up, Cyrus clears his throat, kicking the carpet with the toe of his shoe. "Actually, I think he left."

"You've seen him?" I ask. Poppy looks as surprised as I do.

"Cyrus Eaton, we've been trying to find Adair for ten minutes, and you didn't mention this? I thought they might be together! If I'd known he'd left..." Poppy's brow furrows dangerously. It's so rare to see her angry, Cyrus doesn't quite know what to say.

"It's not like I wasn't hiding it. It's just..." he trails off, a little anxious.

"What?" Poppy demands.

"He told me he needed to get away from everyone. He swiped a bottle of whiskey from the bar downstairs and left." His eyes dart to mine, looking guilty for ratting out his friend.

"Cyrus!" Poppy gasps. "Why didn't you try to stop him?"

"No—it's not his fault, Poppy," I interject. "He probably didn't want to get Sterling into trouble."

"Exactly. I tried to talk to him," Cyrus says. "Look, if he's on foot, he can't have gotten far."

"I have to find him. How long ago did he leave?"

"About fifteen minutes, I think. But I haven't really been checking the time."

I go to the dressing rooms, where I left my purse and keys, and Cyrus and Poppy follow after me, offering helpful suggestions about where Sterling might have gone.

I call his phone, but it goes straight to voicemail, meaning it's probably switched off. I call again, just in case, but the result is the same.

"I don't think Sterling knows much about this area," I say, feeling increasingly anxious. The Valmont Country Club is huge, and backs up against a state park, meaning Sterling probably didn't wander into the woods. "He'll stick to the main access road, I think. I'll go that way. You two can check wherever else you think he could be. As soon as anyone finds him, we call to let each other know. Alright?"

"Yes. Now go," says Poppy, giving me a quick hug and a look that reminds me of my mother: all empathy and love.

Which is probably why I pull her into the world's worst hug. "Thanks."

THE JAGUAR SPINS ITS TIRES AS SOON AS THE SECURITY guard opens the gate, and I fishtail onto the main road. I quickly realize the car's biggest fault: headlight power. There are no streetlights along the wide, manicured drive leading to and from the country club, and tall trees line the shoulder of the road, blocking most of the moon and starlight. The Jag's high beams don't seem brighter than the normal ones, and I have to force myself to slow down as I go around bends—or else drive straight into darkness.

The main road branches off about a mile down from the gate, but I leave it for Poppy and Cy to check. If Sterling walked at a normal pace, that would leave him somewhere between here and the highway another mile farther down.

My heart leaps when I catch sight of someone walking along ahead of me, and I slam on my brakes. It's Sterling, holding a bottle in one hand. He holds his other between my headlights and his eyes, and when I turn them down, I see a look on his face I've never seen before.

His eyes are somehow wild and frozen at the same time, and when I turn on the dash light so he can see me, too, his look doesn't brighten. His bowtie is undone, hanging loosely around his neck. His manic eyes fade to a dull grey, and suddenly he looks tired, like he doesn't have the energy to deal with me.

I've seen that look before: in the eyes of the staff at Windfall, or my mother's eyes even looking back from the mirror. I want to scream at him—ask him how dare he scare me like this—but that's not what someone needs after dealing with my father. And so, I take a deep breath and do my best to put my feelings aside.

"Hey there, sailor," I yell, hoping he'll find it funny.

Sterling doesn't reply. Instead, he starts toward the passenger seat of the car, which I lean over to unlock for him.

He sinks into the bucket seat with a grunt, not meeting my eyes.

"Are you okay?"

Sterling holds the bottle of booze in his lap protectively, his face a mixture of revulsion and anger.

"Yeah," he mutters. "I'm not sure I want to talk about it."

"I won't make you." I'm not quite sure where to go, with the conversation, or with the car, but I turn on the engine anyway. "Where to?"

"I don't want to be around people," Sterling says through gritted teeth.

"Does people include me?" I ask, trying to keep my tone neutral, but praying he doesn't say yes. Does he know how much it would break me for him to say yes?

He stays silent for an unnervingly long time, and I start driving towards campus. I'll drop him off and wait for this to blow over. I have some experience avoiding the storms my father causes. After a couple of minutes he finally responds. "It's not your fault. I just...don't want to be reminded of how all those rich assholes look at me. And where the fuck can I get away from that in this fucking town?"

"I know a place," I say absently, thinking of Little Love.

We drive in silence for about ten minutes, and by the time the Jag's tires begin crunching along the gravel drive leading to the Little Love parking lot, Sterling has stopped staring at the bottle. I park as far down the lot as I can, about 50 feet past the nearest car, right in front of a log barrier designed to prevent cars from sliding down the steep slope behind it.

"This is Little Love. When I was in high school, and no one had parents out of town, this is where we had our parties. There's a bigger version in Nashville, but this one is closer." I pause to see if he wants to say anything, but he just looks out at the campus, dotted with its beautiful old buildings. I can't even tell if he hears me. "Anyway, no one will bother us here. Do you want me to leave?"

"How do you *not* kill him?" Sterling says, and I'm still not sure he has heard anything I said.

"My father has a way of pulling you into his world. He owns everything, controls everything. And he uses all of it, all of the time, to get what he wants. You either let him, or you learn how to break out of his world."

"I don't want to break out of his world. I want to destroy it."

If it had been said by someone else, or without so much sincerity, I might not take it seriously. But I've never seen Sterling like this. For the briefest of moments I wonder if he should get drunk, just for tonight, just to help him let go of whatever happened. But I know that's the cheap way out, that it will just create more problems.

"I know that feeling. Believe me."

He looks at the bottle in his hands and twists off the cap. My heart sinks as I wait for him to take a swig. Instead, he inhales deeply, savoring the smell.

"You haven't tried to stop me from drinking," he says, somewhere between confusion and accusation.

"Part of me wouldn't blame you," I murmur. "You have to remember, I've been dealing with Angus MacLaine my whole life. So I know the last thing you need is for me to tell you what choices to make."

He nods. "You're right about that."

"But I also know drunk Sterling isn't the best Sterling. And isn't that what my father wants?"

"He offered to buy me off. Six figures," Sterling says, pausing to savor the whiskey's aroma again. "I don't even warrant a million from a multi-billionaire. Doesn't he know that's how it's supposed to work?"

I force myself to laugh, but it falls in hollow peals between us. It's not funny to either of us.

He screws the cap back on the bottle, setting it down on one of the posts holding up the log barrier, and I breathe a sigh of relief.

"I'll make him regret fucking with us," Sterling says, turning to me with the same wild look he had on his face when I caught up to him on the road.

"I'd like to see that—but it's probably not going to happen tonight." I put as much smile behind it as I can and reach for his hand. "Let's go back to your dorm. Forget my father. He can't control us if we don't even think about him."

Sterling lets me take his hand, but he doesn't grasp it, then gives me a weak smile.

"You win, Lucky. Let's go."

We get back in the car, and I back up in the silent dark, wanting to put this behind us. But as I shift into drive, the headlights glint off the full whiskey bottle reminding me that there's a difference between wants and needs and sometimes knowing the difference between the two is as hard as walking away from the answers at the bottom of a bottle.

4

STERLING

The spring air is crisp and cool as Adair drives us down the switchbacks leading away from Little Love. She shivers slightly, ducking toward the dashboard in an attempt to stay away from the air rushing overhead. A rumble of thunder sounds in the distance, and by the time we reach the bottom we're being pelted with rain.

Stupid, Sterling.

I shouldn't have left her at the wedding. Now she's here, driving a convertible in the rain, freezing cold, and wondering if I'm going to go off the reservation and start drinking again. Am I trying to prove Angus MacLaine right?

We're in a full-on thunderstorm by the time we pull into the dorm parking lot. Adair screeches to a halt in the first open space, then jumps out and begins trying to get the roof of the Jag up before the rain completely soaks the interior. I pull off my jacket and hold it over her head, doing my best to keep the rain off her.

"Thanks," she says, and when she struggles to get the roof in place I leave the jacket over her and go around the other side of the car to help. It takes a few minutes, and by the time we're standing inside the entrance of the dorm, we're both soaked to the bone.

"You really love that car, don't you?" I say.

"Yeah. It was my mom's, remember?" she says, her teeth chattering.

We take the elevator to my floor, and I can't help wondering what would happen if her father disowned her because of me. Does she move in with me, somewhere off campus? We both work—but she can't afford school, of course. I can see it so clearly: the Jag breaks down, but the repair bill costs more than either of us makes in a year. She has to sell it. I have to see her heart break when she does it.

As soon as I unlock the door to my room, Adair darts inside. "Need a warm shower," she says, throwing her small purse and keys on the table beside my bed and going to lock the door leading from our suite-mates' room to the bathroom before someone over there does the same to us.

"You need help removing those wet clothes, Lucky?" I call in to her, pulling off my own wet shirt and pants. I'm not sure what kind of fabric this tuxedo is, but I'm sure it's never supposed to be this wet.

"I got it, thanks," she says, her tone more guarded than I expect.

I've fucked up. Bad. Some rational part of my brain reminds me this is her father's fault as much as it's mine. It doesn't really help though, because that bastard is in my head. I keep hearing his words. *You are trash. You are trash. You are trash.* Is she starting to see it, too?

She closes the door to my room, and I hear the shower start, the curtain slide open. Suddenly, music starts playing, and it takes me a moment to realize it's Adair's ringtone. I pull it out of her purse to look at the screen, but it's gone to voicemail. Then it starts again, flashing Poppy's face.

"Hey, Lucky?"

"Yeah?" she calls over the shower.

"Poppy is calling—"

"Shit!" Adair yelps. "I was supposed to call her when I found you!"

"Wait, do you mean there's a search party out looking for me?" I know it's stupid—that she was trying to look out for me—but I fucking hate the thought of a bunch of rich kids stooping down to my level to help me out. I didn't fucking ask them to.

Adair did.

"Just Poppy and Cy," she says. "Can you answer and tell her everything is fine?"

I swipe the icon on the phone, and as soon as the clock begins ticking, I hear Poppy's voice, "We checked all the service roads around the club. There's a big party on Greek row, so I'm heading there. Cyrus went by their room, but—"

"Poppy, it's Sterling," I interject.

"Oh," Poppy says, and I can picture her furrowed brow.

"We got caught in the rain in the Jag, we just got to my place. That's why Adair hasn't called. She's in the shower, trying to thaw herself out."

"I see," Poppy says, and it reminds me of how Francie used to talk when she chose to leave her feelings on whatever stupid thing I had done unsaid.

And I guess, from the outside, she has her reasons. Her best friend had to leave a wedding because it looked like I went on a bender. But isn't that the whole fucking problem to begin with? Poppy—an extremely nice person—sees more to complain about from my behavior than Angus MacLaine's.

That's how much money has warped these people. I'm a lesser being because my net value is in the negative. Poppy is nice, but she's not asking if I'm okay. She was looking for Adair. She doesn't give a shit about me. I'm Adair's lost puppy. A stupid mutt they're all putting up with.

But I don't want her pity. I don't want to explain myself to her. If she doesn't get it, she can fuck off. An awkward silence hangs between us, and I decide I've had enough of talking to Poppy. "Do you want me to have her call you when she gets out of the shower?"

"Just tell her to call me if she wants," Poppy says brusquely.

"Will do."

I end the call as the water shuts off in the shower. I move closer to the door, placing my palm on it. One piece of wood separating me from her, but a world between us. Where do we go from here? How do I show her she needs to get away from everything she's ever known? How can I even be sure she really wants to?

"I have some boxers and an undershirt when you're ready," I say, putting on the same ensemble myself.

"Just leave them by the door."

I wish I knew the answers. I don't. I just know I'm lucky to have her, and that—if she really means it when she says she'd give up everything to be with me—I need her to open her eyes about her family. Her friends. Her world.

She comes out of the bathroom looking as tired as I feel. The corners of her eyes are red and puffy, and I can't tell if it's because she's been crying, or if that's what it looks like after a girl takes off makeup with one of my cheap washcloths.

"Feel better?" It's a stupid question. Of course, she doesn't.

She hugs her waist, inadvertently stretching the thin fabric of my shirt until it's nearly sheer. "Much better. I didn't think I'd ever stop shivering."

"You're still cold," I say, noting how pert her nipples are beneath my undershirt. There's something I can do about this. "I can warm you up some more."

"I want you to promise me something first," she says, giving me the sense she has been screwing up her courage to tell me whatever it is she's about to say.

I brace myself. "What would that be?"

"Promise me you won't let anyone come between us." She puts her palm on my chest, and looks up at me with eyes like a full moon. The bright hope there leeches away my anger. "I need something real, Sterling. *Someone real.* Someone I can count on. And it's going to be hard. We both know that now."

I pull her to me, wrapping her in my arms.

What did I ever do to deserve her—the girl with everything, who somehow wants me more than all the rest? I can't pretend I understand everything about how she works yet, but there is no doubt in my mind she means what she says.

"I promise," I say, and tension melts from her face. "Can you promise me the same?"

"Of course," she says, her eyes closing, her lips waiting for my kiss.

"Then show me," I say, covering her lips with mine.

She opens to my touch, tilting her head back to help me explore more of her. I lift her by the buttocks, smashing her body into mine. We continue to search for answers with our lips and hands, our skin and our teeth. My mouth finds her earlobe. It takes her breath away, and she stops kissing my shoulder, burying her face there, clearing the path for me to take the lead.

I need her to understand she is mine. What did she say earlier? That her father wants to convince everyone his world is the only one? She wants a different world, and I need to show her my world is the best place for her.

I wrench the boxers off her hips, and she moans expectantly. I move up, with greedy hands, to her breasts, and I pinch her nipple, relishing the little yelp it produces. "You belong to me, Adair. Not your father, not anyone else. And I belong to you."

She nuzzles her forehead against my chin, whispering in my ear, "I need you, Sterling. I need to feel something besides scared, and trapped, and—"

I spin her body away from me, dropping her gently on her feet and pushing her torso forward onto the bed. Leaning on top of her, I alternate kisses and sharp nips on the skin of her shoulders and back, enjoying the way they leave marks—proof she's mine. She squirms toward me, but I'm not going to give her what she wants until I know she'd die to have it.

I slide the tip of my cock against her clit. She tries to move again, urging me inside her, but I hold her hips in place, kneading the soft, supple skin of her ass in my hands.

"Fuck, your body is so beautiful. I love how it responds to me." I push into her briefly, and a low purr rumbles from her chest. I pull out, and her hips attempt to follow.

"Sterling," she pleads.

"Tell me you love me," I demand.

"I love you. You know, I love you." She almost sounds annoyed, and she wriggles in my grasp.

It's why I love her. She's so impatient for life. "And I love you."

I slam into her as hard as I can, and she strangles a cry. "*Yessss.*"

Our lovemaking is frantic, tinged with a sour edge that was never there before. I slow for a moment, considering if we should change positions, but Adair reaches back to grab at my hips, demanding that I go faster, harder, as if she needs this physical connection as much as I do.

I pump again and again, and each time Adair splays further onto the bed, her head nearly hitting the wall. If she's not careful, I'll end up fucking her straight through to my neighbors' room.

Her breathing quickens and I allow myself to match her. When we climax, it seems to last forever, and then she goes limp, sagging into a boneless heap beneath me. I pull back the covers and tuck her gently beneath them, noticing where the frame of the bed bit into her thighs, leaving long, purple indentations. I rub them gently as I slide in behind her, giving her a kiss.

"When you're in my bed, I know I can do anything," I say, tracing the curve of her chin with the tip of my nose.

She smiles vaguely, the corners of her mouth falling open as her eyes close, sleep beginning to take her.

"I love you," I say, but her only response is a faint snoring sound.

Sleep begins to take me, too, but not before I swear to myself that I won't quit until every last one of these condescending assholes either respects me or fears me. It's the only way I can keep their world from swallowing mine. It's the only way I keep what I've already won. It's the only way I keep her.

5

ADAIR

"The metal frame is cheaper, though," I say, hooking Poppy's elbow and guiding her away from the gorgeous ivory headboard she's latched onto in the more expensive section of the furniture store—the side she obviously prefers. "But it's a four-poster!" she argues. "It's on sale!" She pouts all the way back to the inexpensive metal headboard I'd picked out earlier.

Poppy insisted on coming with me to shop for stuff for her place—which just became our place. But she seems to be having trouble with my budget, which led to arguments and then offers to buy me the things I couldn't afford before I put my foot down.

The cost of freedom from my father might have started out reasonable—all it took was a large chunk of the inheritance Mom left me, and a visit to the campus housing office—but I'm struggling with how much things snowballed from there.

At Valmont, all freshmen are required to live on campus or at home. For the Valmont elites however, it works differ-

ently. Poppy and Ava managed to negotiate residence in one
of the on-campus duplexes reserved for students with families. This was technically a violation of University policy, but
since Poppy and Ava were guaranteed to renovate the apartment at no expense to the school, and since they agreed not to
host any parties, no one could come up with a reason why
they shouldn't be allowed. Also, I suspect some money passed
hands quietly between University officials and their parents.

I slept on their couch for a week after my brother's
wedding, never going home when my father and brother were
likely to be around, and never for more than a few minutes.
In the end, I realized I needed to make it official. If I want my
life to be my own, I have to get away from Windfall.

Poppy and Ava were excited when I asked if I could
move into the small room, most likely meant to be an office
they're actually using as a glorified walk-in closet. I'd only
had to agree to two things. Ava wanted me to guarantee that
if the shit hit the fan with my father, Sterling wouldn't end
up living with us, too. Poppy jumped in as soon as she said it,
letting me know it was still fine for him to come over. Her
only demand was that she be allowed to help me decorate. At
the time, I thought Poppy's half would be easier than navigating visits from Sterling.

Now, I'm not so sure.

When Poppy and I arrived at the home store, I had
plugged the absolute limit of my budget into the calculator
app on my phone. Without that precaution, Poppy would
have spent the entire sum in the first 60 seconds.

"There's not space for a four-poster in my room," I say,
"but you can get it if you like it."

"And then you can take the one I'm using now?" she says,
trying on the idea.

That is so not what I meant. "Poppy, that's sweet, but—"

"But what?" She lifts one end of the metal, full-size bed frame on display, and it creaks loudly. "This won't withstand a man like Sterling."

"It's not about that," I say, sighing. Why can't she understand what it is I want out of today?

"It's just that everyone in the complex is going to hear this every time you two...you know..."

"Have sex?" I offer.

She flushes. "Honestly, I know you don't want to take your dad's money, but I don't mind helping out. It's not a big deal."

"It is though," I say. "I'm at the point I'd rather have something crappy that's entirely my own."

Her expression says I'm speaking Greek. "If you say so. Can I at least get you some really nice bedding? Consider it a housewarming present!"

"Fine."

Some battles can't be won.

We make our way to the linens section, and Poppy actually licks her lips when she sees the store's main bedding display, an old Hollywood combination of lace, champagne satin, and silver chiffon. "This is freaking fantas—"

"Poppy, it's more than the four poster!" I stop her as soon as I see the price tag.

"Hush, you said I could get the bedding." She's already plopping sheets and throw pillows into a cart. Piled there in its romantic, neutral hues, it looks like the remnants of a bridal party.

"I want Sterling to feel comfortable. I'm not sure satin will help him forget what happened at the wedding." It's true. In the week since the wedding, Sterling has bounced back and forth between something like the pre-wedding version of himself and the sullen, angry guy I found trying to walk out of my life.

Poppy takes a step back to study it, sighs, and pulls the items out of the cart. "Maybe you're right."

I do my best to hide my shock and hurry her away from the display.

"How has that been going?" Poppy asks, moving to examine a much more neutral option. "You haven't really said much about where things stand with you two."

"He's angry, mostly. And obsessed with making our world *respect him*, whatever that means. I think he just needs more time. I can't stop thinking about his place in Queens, of how he grew up—and then to have my dad throw it in his face. I'm angry, too, but I want to move on."

"Have you wondered what you'll do if things don't work out between you two?" My brow furrows as I load an objection, but Poppy rushes on, "I like Sterling, you know I do—"

"Do you like him?" Lately, I'm not sure. Looking back, I'm not sure she's ever really liked him.

Poppy drops a set of pale blue, 800-thread-count sheets into the cart and fixes me with one of her deeply sympathetic looks. "I have nothing against Sterling personally—and I know your father just complicates everything—but what if you manage to keep him out of it...and it still doesn't work out? You two have a lot of differences, and you're only nineteen. Do you really want to cut out your whole family for a guy you've only known a few months?"

I bite back a saucy reply by telling myself she's just trying to look out for me. What can I say to convince her? Nothing I haven't tried telling myself, unfortunately. "I only have two people in my life who see me as something besides Angus

MacLaine's daughter. *Just two people* in all the world who will let me be something else. You're one of them, and he's the other. I don't know how else to explain it."

A flash of realization dawns on Poppy's face. "You have to see where it goes. Or you'll regret it later."

"Exactly. *Exactly.*"

Poppy's crimson lips finally crack into a smile. "I'm not trying to be pushy about it, love. I just want to make sure you're focused on what you need. Aside from these pillows. Holy shit, what are they even made of? Some kind of kitten fur? I've never felt anything so soft!"

"God, I hope not!" I say, feeling the pillows and laughing.

"Sorry, but these are for me. Sterling would never appreciate them," she says with a wink that says she's trying. Trying to like him. Trying to understand. I can't ask for more than that.

"Do you want me to wait here while you get your own cart?" I ask.

"I think I'm just going to come back later. I've been feeling the need for a refresh, and this place is giving me ideas."

It takes another hour to get everything we need for my new room, which leaves my bank account dangerously low. My inheritance from my mother wasn't much after taxes. Still, I'm glad I refused my father's offer to invest it for me. It means for now I have something to live on—but for how long? The feeling I get isn't exactly panic, more like a gnawing worry.

In the parking lot, it takes Poppy a couple minutes to figure out how to lay down the seats in her mother's BMW crossover, which she borrowed for this quest, so we can put the bed frame in. I end up doing most of the lifting, which is fine—it's my stuff, after all. But it leaves me panting and sweaty, and Poppy decides to cool me off with something from Starbucks. I don't want to spend any more money or run any later than we already are, but I don't quite know how to tell her. Sterling was supposed to meet us when we got back, to help move things in. But by the time we get there, we're running a half hour late, and a moving truck is parked on the curb in front of our building.

"Surprise!" Poppy says as we get out. "They're here to do all the lifting. And before you complain, they were going to be here whether they helped you or not. Ava and I needed to move some of our clothes back home."

I've known Poppy practically my entire life, but I don't think I'll ever get used to how much clothing she goes through. The door of the moving truck is rolled open, and well over half its space is filled with wood-frame wardrobes covered with zip-up canvas covers.

"As long as you're sure you won't have to do without something," I say, but Poppy completely misses the sarcasm.

"Of course not, silly. I get by my parents' a few times every week, anyway."

"Hey, Lucky," says Sterling, emerging from between the moving truck and the front door of our unit. His lips return to a scowling position as his eyes dart to the contents of the truck and not knowing quite how to process what he's seeing.

"That's my cue. Enjoy not having to get sweaty, Sterling," Poppy says, seamlessly transitioning to ordering the movers with the skill of a field marshal.

"I wish I'd known I wasn't needed," Sterling mutters, adding, "And you're late."

"I know, I'm sorry. It's Poppy—"

"She's out of control?" he guesses, but the words are biting, not joking.

"I should have called. I'm sorry—"

"Whatever," he says, dismissing me completely. "I have class across campus, and if I don't leave now, I won't make it." He turns his body slightly, as if to go, so I grab his arm and pull him towards me. "I can drive you. It has to be over a mile."

Why didn't that occur to me when he offered to come over and help?

"No thanks," he says, breaking free of me by taking a step away. He shoots me a forced smile, but there's nothing real in it.

And then he's gone, without even a backward glance.

ADJUSTING TO LIFE AFTER WINDFALL IS SURPRISINGLY easy. Poppy and Ava have a maid service that comes every day, so there's no need to clean or do dishes—skills none of us have ever had the opportunity to learn, and, with the possible exception of me, probably would never need. The street we live on is quiet, the other residents are mostly graduate students, who are friendly but preoccupied. This being the South, there are more than a few promises to get together for dinner, though. Of course, it probably will never happen.

Over the next couple of days, I see Sterling a few more times, always at his dorm. Every time I try to have him over to my place, he comes up with excuses about needing to study for midterms, which are nearly a month away. I tell myself it's because he doesn't want to accept rides from anyone at the moment, and my new place is extremely inconvenient for him.

But I don't really believe it.

There's no getting around the fact that things have changed, and definitely for the worse. It's almost like there's an invisible third person in our relationship. Every moment, every kiss, every touch is possessive like he's marking his territory.

I'm torn in two directions whenever we talk. I want him to relax and just be with me, free from all the crap in his head, but I can't relax myself, because I have to vet everything I say through a filter. No talk of my family or money or me moving out. We even got into a heated argument over a book.

It's exhausting.

The only reprieve seems to be an early spring, by Tennessee standards. By the first of March, it feels like May. I can't see it as anything other than a gift as the whole world longs for change as much as I do. The early warm front brings surprises with it. Magnolias are in full bloom, nearly two months early, in every garden, window box and flower bed at Valmont. The air, still cool and crisp in the mornings, seems to warm up just to carry their scent. It makes me think of Mom. It makes me wish she was here to help me make sense of Sterling and life and everything. If she were still around, would she have been able to keep my father from interfering in our relationship? Probably not. But, at least, she might have tempered it.

And every time I let myself wonder, I get angry. Because she isn't here. Because it's stupid to want what's gone. Because I have to make my days diamonds, whether anyone helps me do it or not.

I *have* managed to avoid my father, at least. We haven't had a single conversation since the wedding. But one day, as I come out of my Intro to Creative Writing class, I find his Maybach parked outside Stanton Hall.

One of our family's security staff is standing by the rear door, and when he sees me he calls loudly, "Miss MacLaine? Your father would like a word."

He opens the door to the Maybach, its rear seat nearly the size of a limo's, and there's my father, looking dead ahead, his jaw set with anger.

All the other students milling around stop in their tracks to look at me—some entitled bitch who's father calls her to business meetings. All I want is to run the opposite direction. Take every class on campus, then do all the homework, before reading every book in the library. Anything but get in the car.

And why shouldn't I?

Because he pays my tuition. There's been no way around it. No financial aid for someone claimed on her father's tax return. Someone who's father makes billions.

And I need that tuition money, because, if I ever want to be free of him, I have to finish school and make the kind of money that means I'll never need him again.

But mostly, because this moment was inevitable.

So, I get in.

It takes a second for my father to acknowledge me as he finishes something on his phone, and when he does, it's to let out a long sigh. "Adair, there's a matter we need to discuss."

"And now's the time?" I ask flatly. It's not like he's ever needed to talk to me before. "If this is about Sterling, there's nothing to talk about."

"You made that very clear the night of your brother's wedding. And I did my best to stay out of it—"

"Bullshit." He's probably just been too busy with things

that actually matter to him to bother tracking me down for round two.

"—since then," he continues, despite my outburst. "But something has arisen that requires that to change." He lifts the top of the armrest centered between us, and reaches inside, withdrawing a large manilla envelope.

"If you changed your mind, the least you could do is come out and say it," I snap, trying to ignore the appearance of the envelope, which fills me with cold dread. "You don't need to be dramatic."

"I received an email three days ago. The contents of that message are in the envelope," he says, handing it to me. "You should prepare yourself."

For what?

My fingers tremble as I unwind the figure-eight string closing the end of the envelope. Inside, there is a small tablet computer and a single, folded piece of paper. The message on the paper is a print-out of an email:

To: Angus MacLaine (owner@maclainemedia.com)

From: (anon@anonymous-remailer.biz)

Please view the attached video.

To avoid disclosure of its contents, send a check for $1,000,00,000 to the following address:

I stop reading as soon as I see *Queens, NY*. What am I reading? My head snaps toward my father, and the muscles near the corner of his jaw are as tight as cables. There's none of his usual perverse joy at my discomfort, if anything, he seems uncomfortable himself.

"The video has been muted," he says. "You should know that I did not watch it in its entirety, Adair."

He's beginning to scare me.

I tap the power button on the tablet, and the screen

blinks to life, a media player already loaded. An alarm somewhere in my brain tells me I'm suffocating, and I realize I haven't even been breathing. I take a second to steady myself before pressing play.

It's Sterling's dorm. He's standing near his closet, halfway out of the frame. Then I see myself coming in from the other side, wearing a pair of his boxers and one of his undershirts. When we both come together near the center of the frame, I realize it's a video from the night of the wedding. We had just come back from Little Love in the rain, and we're about to promise...

My eyes want something else to latch onto, and it feels like the car itself is spinning, my stomach doing flips that send wet, hot bile up my throat. I close my eyes to avoid throwing up, and when I open them again, we're having sex. He's biting my shoulders and back, and I'm...just letting him? Letting him touch me. Letting him claim me.

And, worst of all, letting *me trust him*.

Confusion gives way to revulsion. Then a sense of violation. It detonates inside me, rending my heart to pieces. But— worst of all—my brain keeps flashing images of then and now, which play like a hellish, repeating slideshow.

My father, sitting beside me but looking away, his hand shading his eyes against the sun streaming in through the car window.

My hands, as foreign as someone else's, holding a screen that shows my bottomless humiliation.

My love, not loving me.

Me, sitting in the car, somehow still whole. A lie.

Slowly, reality resolves as a soundtrack loops through my mind:

This is not okay.

This isn't happening.

I did not consent.

I did not want this.

And the one question at the center of all of them: *Why?*

The tablet is gone, the note, too, before I find myself fully in this moment. My father is stuffing them back into the envelope. He glances at me sidelong, one arched eyebrow betraying his indifference.

"What do..." I manage, but by the time I get it out I no longer remember what it was I meant to say.

"I've had some incredibly discreet individuals—none of whom saw the video—look into everything. I'm afraid there's no other conclusion but that it is exactly what it seems: blackmail." His dark eyes are soft, his voice gentle. It's the closest he has ever gotten to empathy.

The part of me that's desperately, all-consumingly in love with Sterling screams that it's not true, and those words somehow make their way out of my mouth.

Empathy turns to pity, and I look away as he speaks, "I intend to pay this demand. I know you think I don't care about you. I know you hate me. But I would pay a great deal more than he's asking to keep you from ever feeling like this."

"But you hate me, too." I don't understand what he's telling me. I always wanted him to say he loved me, or just give any hint he liked anything about me, however small. Until I realized he never would. "Malcolm is your perfect one. I'm..."

"My daughter. And a MacLaine." For once, he doesn't bother telling me I'm wrong. I want to accuse him, tell him he's lying. Scream at him. But there's no fight left, just a barren hole where my heart is supposed to be.

I can't help remembering what Sterling said at Little

Love that night, *he didn't even offer to buy me off.* "What *did* you say to Sterling at the wedding? I have to know."

"I told him I knew what he had done in the past, that he was unsuitable for you, and that he would never provide you with the kind of life I could."

"And that's all?" It doesn't make sense. Unless Sterling planned something like this all along. But I can't believe that. I would have known. I try telling myself that if Sterling did it, it was to support me—that it came out of him wanting to do something good.

But there's nothing good about this. Nothing justifies this.

"I asked him what his intentions were regarding you. This is not the answer I expected, Adair."

"You caused this," I say. I'm not thinking clearly, but I know at least that much is true. If my father hadn't come after Sterling, none of this would have happened.

"If it helps you to think so."

How do I even begin to respond to that?

But Angus MacLaine has another surprise, something completely beyond my ability to process, bombshell or not. He sniffs, a tick borne from having destroyed the blood vessels in his face and sinuses with booze, making them a leaky faucet. When he begins to speak, his voice is thick and strangled. "I'm sorry your mother isn't here to help you through this."

No.

It's all wrong. How dare he throw regret into this? How dare he take my worst, most vulnerable moment and use it to remind me of what I need and can never have? How dare he offer that non-apology?

My hand fumbles for the door handle, and when I find it I can only seem to get the door open by throwing my weight against it. It flies open and I fall out, landing me face-first on the pavement.

I hear the driver get out of the Maybach, trying to figure out what's going on. A gaggle of passing students laugh.

"Adair," my father's voice calls behind me, but I don't want to look at him. Now or ever.

I struggle to my feet, quickly, before anyone can try to help. Even though no one does.

One foot in front of the other, Adair. Just keep doing it.

It feels like every one of the hundred eyes on me has seen my sex tape.

I have a sex tape.

Ignoring is surviving.

I survive the last, soft plea of my father to get in the car.

I survive the laughter, the humiliation.

I even survive the path ahead of me, a dense blanket of fallen magnolia petals, paying the price for their early, reckless bloom, their lovely pink and white turning a rotting yellow on the pavement.

6

STERLING

"See you back at the dorm?" Cyrus says, checking his knobby Hublot watch, or as I like to think of it, a year's worth of tuition wasted on his wrist.

"I thought I'd walk over to Adair's," I reply. I've been avoiding going there ever since she accepted my offer to help her move—when she arrived late and didn't need me after all —and apparently it bugs her enough she's stopped returning my calls. It's time to do something about it. "If Poppy's free, you can come with."

"You haven't heard?" Cyrus says with a guilty, sidelong look. "She's back at Windfall."

"What?"

"I heard from Poppy. She came back from class yesterday and said she felt sick. So she went home. Poppy said she took half her stuff, though." Cyrus studies me carefully. "Poppy thought maybe you two..."

"She didn't tell me." I don't know what's going on, but if Adair was really sick she should have called me. I would have taken care of her. At least it explains why her phone has gone straight to voicemail for twenty-four hours.

Things haven't been good between us. It's true. After the wedding, she didn't seem like she wanted to talk about what happened. I didn't, either. But after a few days, I realized it was just avoidance. She wants to pretend nothing happened. Which just won't work. She won't talk about any of our problems. Not the wedding. Not money. Nothing.

If her father decides to stop paying her tuition—what would we do? I tried talking about how much it worries me, but it's like her brain can't comprehend what a lack of money could do to us. Honestly, it pisses me off.

She moved in with Poppy and Ava, and at first I thought it would be good for her. She would get away from Windfall and her family. But Poppy and Ava don't understand anything Adair and I are going through. And they see the world like the MacLaines do. Poppy is nice, sure, but her idea of hardship is breaking a nail when there isn't a nail salon open to fix it. And Ava coils herself in the corner whenever I'm around, like she might strike.

"I guess I am going back to the dorm, then. It's not like I can walk to Windfall."

"I have one more class, late afternoon. After that, why don't we go see her at Windfall? We can bring get-well presents." Cyrus has offered to lend me his car a few times since the wedding, but I'm done with handouts. "I was going to swing by my house, so it's no trouble."

I suspect he's accounting for my pride. But this time, I need to see Adair. "Yeah, okay. Thanks."

I'm trying to decide what kind of get-well present I can scrounge up when my phone rings, flashing *Valmont University* on the caller ID. "Hello?"

"Sterling Ford?"

"Speaking."

"This is Heather with the Dean of Students' office. The Dean would like to speak with you at once. Can you come now?" Her tone is all business, but there's more than a faint, Francie-like whiff of disapproval.

"Why?" My heart begins to race. I try telling myself it's some administrative chore, like correcting an enrollment form or something, but I'm not so sure that would need to be done immediately.

"All student affairs are confidential, so I couldn't say. I was just told to get you in here as soon as possible."

"I see." Whatever it is, it's serious enough to require confidentiality. Definitely not a simple form. Great. "I'll come right away."

"I'll let the Dean know. Goodbye."

I have to check the directory to find out where the Dean of Student Affairs is in the University's online directory. It's a few blocks away, and when I arrive I find an almost empty office divided by neat, sparkling-clean cubicles.

"Sterling Ford?" a woman asks from her perch near the entrance. She's about forty, but aiming for sixty judging by her bedazzled tunic and pearl necklace. She shoots a look at the only other person in the office, a young man, who immediately picks up a phone and begins dialing.

What's going on here?

"Yes," I say. "I was told the Dean needed to see me."

"Follow me, Mr. Ford." The woman rises from her desk and leads me through a rabbit warren of collegiate bureaucracy, depositing me in front of carved, French doors set with frosted glass. The name 'Dean Cheswyk' is etched in the glass. The secretary opens one door, saying, "Dean? I have Sterling Ford here."

I can't hear a reply, but the secretary pushes open the door and motions me inside. I step into a room that hasn't been contemporary since the 1930s. Green glass desk lamps, along with floor-to-ceiling picture windows, give the room its light, which is barely adequate. I find myself squinting to take in the man at the desk.

"Ah, Mr. Ford," he says, absentmindedly adjusting his tie as he rises to greet me. There's another man in the room, his face pinched and weasel-like, his neck somehow unable to fill the collar of his shirt. He's holding a brown briefcase in his lap, so he doesn't rise.

"I was told you needed to see me, sir." I say, taking the Dean's offered handshake, which is clammy and limp.

"That's right," he says, his plump, affable face at odds with his sad eyes. "Make yourself comfortable." He motions at the chair set in front of his desk, the one next to the weasel-face guy, then retakes his own seat.

Everyone exchanges nervous glances—mine because I don't know what this is about. The Dean looks guilty as if he's about to do something unpleasant. And weasel guy? He seems...excited?

"I'll come right out and say it," the Dean says. "You're here today because we have received a number of complaints about your behavior since you came to Valmont."

A number of... I stare at him. "What? From whom?"

"I'm not sure that matters," he says. "It's the nature of the complaints that's a concern."

"Professors?" I guess. "I had some trouble in the first semester, sir. Missed a lot of classes for a couple weeks. I was...depressed." I'm not sure which of my teachers would have complained about me, but I feel pretty confident I haven't done anything serious. I mean, Cyrus has only gone to about half his classes this year. "But I have hardly missed a class since then. My grades are good."

"I'm sure that's the case," he says, waving away my explanation. "The matters we need to discuss today are not academic in nature. They are questions of character."

I stop the *what the fuck* about to burst out of me and translate it to: "Excuse me?"

"Fighting. Underage drinking. Theft. Misrepresentation." The Dean lists each one nervously, like it's the first time he has had to talk about such unpleasantness.

"I got in a fight off campus, but—"

"Due to the seriousness of these complaints, the University has reviewed your initial application to attend Valmont. It seems you were less than truthful." The Dean turns to the other man, who opens the briefcase and hands him a sheaf of papers held together with a large butterfly clip. "It says here you indicated you had never been arrested for a crime."

Fuck.

"Juvenile records are sealed for a reason," I point out. I'm not sure what a lawyer would say, but it has to count for something. Except it doesn't. We all know it. But it's not like those records simply landed in the Dean's lap. Maybe he can be persuaded to overlook them if I convince him it's unethical.

"Which means such records cannot be used in a criminal court proceeding against you, which this is not," says the weasel-faced man.

The Dean gives him a look, and when nothing happens, he clears his throat meaningfully.

"Sorry. Peter Welles. University counsel." He hands me a business card.

A lawyer. Of course.

"Perhaps, if Mr. Ford could explain..." The Dean glances toward Welles.

He wants an excuse. I have one, but I hate using it. I measure out my words slowly, so the anger doesn't show. "I was abused as a child. My father was an alcoholic, and he beat my mother to death. Some of the foster homes I was in—they were almost as bad. I'm not saying I didn't get into trouble, but there were reasons."

Cheswyk seems taken aback. He hangs his head for a moment, and right about the time I think he's having a change of heart, he lifts it, his face as firm as stone. "All of which would have been taken under consideration had you been truthful in your initial application. As it is..."

"What?" I know where this is going, and I need to slow it down. "What are you telling me?"

"I know it must seem like your whole world is crashing down, son," he begins, his face the picture of sympathy—enough so that I believe he really means it, "but we are bound to determine your case according to the University Charter and its Code of Conduct."

This is it. I know it like the moment of impact before a collision. I can see it. I can't stop it. My hands grip the upholstered arms of my chair, and I feel the old wood creak in protest. I can't do anything but wait for him to tell me.

"After discussing the matter with counsel, a few of the other Deans, and some of the Alumni—"

I bark a laugh, imagining all these busy, important men lowering themselves to talk to me, and there's one person at the center of each group. "Like Angus MacLaine, perhaps?"

When I mention the name MacLaine, both the Dean and the lawyer share the briefest of looks. Then Cheswyk clears his throat, his shoulders squaring like a man walking out to face the firing squad.

"—the final decision rested with me," the Dean explains.

"And you didn't think you needed to speak with me *before* deciding?" Why am I fighting this? What's the point? Adair. She's the point. This is where Adair is, and this is how I find a way to give her the life she deserves. I can't give up.

"Mr. Ford," the lawyer begins, "your lack of truthfulness negated the need to speak with you. In other words, how can we believe the excuses you would no doubt provide us, when you have already shown yourself to be a liar?"

"That's enough," says the Dean, giving Welles a sharp look. "Very well, young man, what have you to say for yourself?"

"That depends on whether or not you really have decided everything," I say, and I immediately want to kick myself. My life is hanging by a thread and I can't keep from sawing at it?

"You have my word I will take anything you say under advisement," the Dean says, giving me a kind nod.

I wonder how many students have sat in this seat, having a similar version of this conversation. I wonder what Francie will say. I wonder whether I'm about to lose everything. I wonder what Adair will do when I tell her.

"I think this is Angus MacLaine's doing. He doesn't like that I'm seeing his daughter." I slow down for a second, noticing how agitated the lawyer becomes, but that the Dean is listening intently. "But we're both adults making our own decisions. He's the one who dug up my sealed records. He told me as much himself. And I didn't mention them in my application

because I was told the records were sealed for my protection—
so that the stuff that happened to me when I was a kid wouldn't
ruin the rest of my life. And, honestly, I feel stupid for believing
in a system that I know from experience fails all the time."

"I understand, son," Dean Cheswyk begins, and I can
already tell by his tone that he is unmoved. "But your speculation about how this all came to light doesn't matter. Do you
deny that both before and after you came to Valmont you got
into fights? That you broke the law by drinking while
underage?"

My silence answers his question.

"We spoke to your R.A. at your dorm," Dean Cheswyk
continues. "He likes you, so he refused to say he saw alcohol
in your room. Your roommate, too. But we found multiple
other students who did not feel a duty to cover for you. Still, I
respect that you didn't deny what I already know to be true."

"Lots of students here drink even though they are underage. Are you going to expel all of them, or just me?"

"Young man, I am not going to expel you from the
University, but there have to be consequences to your
actions. Along with your welfare, I have to consider the good
name of the University and what we want it to represent to
the world," the Dean says, the corners of his mouth pinched.
"Because you misrepresented yourself on your application,
and because of all the other behavior we have mentioned—
which you have wisely refused to deny—you will lose your
scholarship."

"What? You can't do that." I leap to my feet, and both the
Dean and Welles flinch in their seats.

"You'll find that I can."

"I can't afford to go to school here without the scholarship. You've been looking at my files, you know that." They might as well kick me out. Francie and I chose Valmont precisely because both of us together hadn't even been able to get pre-approval for the large student loans required for a school like this. The scholarship made the impossible possible. Without it...

The Dean turns to Welles, who hands him another sheaf of paper. Then the Dean hands it to me. "This is an application for financial aid. You can file it with my secretary, which you'll need to do soon. The second semester credit against your tuition, room and board, is rescinded."

"You're telling me I owe you for this entire semester??" It's not enough they've concocted a way to kick me out of school—they want me to pay them on my way out the door. "This is fucked up. I already know I can't get enough in loans. We tried."

"It's not too late to drop your courses, if you're concerned about the cost," Welles points out, revealing teeth slightly too bright and too big for his sharp face. "This early in the semester, tuition is still refundable."

"So, that's it?" I honestly can't believe what's happening —and yet, I can. I've been waiting for it since Angus MacLaine asked to speak with me at the wedding.

The Dean clears his throat, studying his hands. "Your scholarship was a privilege, not a right, young man."

There it is: the Dean's queasy expression, the weasel-faced Welles triumph. Taking my scholarship was all they had to do to get rid of me. They've taken out the trash.

"You've overcome a lot in your life," he continues. "And I'm sorry it sounds like you don't want your future to be at Valmont, for whatever it's worth."

"Jack shit, that's what." I glare at the two men in front of me, daring them to look me in the eye.

Of course, they don't.

The Dean mumbles something about luck and opportunities in strange places. Welles is already messaging someone on his phone. I can practically see the puppet strings dictating their every movement. There's no point to fighting them on this. Because there's only one person who needs to answer for what just happened: Angus MacLaine. His fingerprints are all over this. Apparently, I scared him more than I thought.

I throw open the Dean's office doors, surprised to find two members of the Valmont University Police standing there. They've been chatting with the secretary from before, and when they all see me, one of the officers steps between me and her, and the other reaches for the spot on his waist where his handcuffs rest.

"Officers," the Dean says, coming up behind me. "I don't think that's necessary after all, Daniel. Mr. Ford isn't going to do anything rash, is he?"

The officer with the cuffs gets a disappointed look, but backs off a couple steps. The other cop realizes he's blocking my departure, and ducks into one of the cubicles. I realize two things: first, these are probably the cops who investigated me on behalf of the Dean, and second, these people heard about what I did to the desk during my argument with Angus MacLaine. It's the only thing that explains their reactions. That's the thing about reputations. People never give you room to do anything but live up to them. Or, in my case, down to them.

"I'd better get going," I announce. "Since, I suspect you

all need to gather up the spare change falling out of Angus MacLaine's pockets."

No one replies, which is answer enough.

WOULD ADAIR MIND IF I KILLED HER FATHER? SINCE leaving the Dean's office, I've asked myself a dozen crazy questions. What is the waiting period like in Tennessee for purchasing a gun? How will I tell Francie? What would Angus MacLaine's neck feel like in my bare fucking hands? Is he at Windfall now? Am I about to find out?

"You alright, man?" Cyrus cuts into my thoughts, glancing nervously at me from behind the wheel of his car. We're headed to Windfall, and I honestly have no idea what I'm going to do when we get there. If I had told Cyrus what happened at the Dean's office, there's no way he'd be taking me to Windfall now. I'd feel guilty about it if he hadn't already betrayed me. If the Dean told the truth—and he had no reason to lie—then Cyrus was questioned by someone about my behavior. He never said anything to me about it, which gives me a pretty strong indication whose side of the fence he'll come down on in the end. He might not have given them anything to use against me, but when push comes to shove, he'll bend over backwards to let Angus MacLaine have his way, just like everyone else in this fucking town.

"Why wouldn't I be?" I say with a shrug.

"You're just...brooding a lot," he says. "More than usual, I mean."

So now I fucking brood?

"I think the situation with Adair is worse than I realized," I say.

That's the understatement of the year.

"Do you think her dad's putting pressure on her?" Cyrus wonders.

"You'd know better than me."

"Angus MacLaine doesn't ask. He demands. Once."

"And if he doesn't get his way?"

"Look, I shouldn't talk shit about anyone—"

"Just fucking tell me, already," I say, my temper slipping.

"Alright, shit," Cyrus says, turning off the satellite radio. "I've heard rumors, that's all. He's got an army of private investigators and a media empire. Everyone's got secrets to hide, you know? He scares the shit out of people."

"He doesn't scare me," I say truthfully. Angus has already done his worst, so what's the point fearing him?

"He *should* scare you. If a tenth of what I've heard is true..."

"Having second thoughts about taking me to Windfall?" I say as Cy pulls up to the security gate.

"Too late now," he says just before lowering his window to speak with the guard. "Cyrus Eaton. I should be on Adair MacLaine's list."

Of course, he's on her list. I wonder for a moment if I am —if it's even her list or if her dad gets final approval.

The guard flips through a couple of pages on his clipboard before replying, "I have you here, Mr. Eaton. Go ahead."

When we reach the front door Cyrus presses the buzzer, and the door opens immediately. Felix, the Windfall butler, has apparently been waiting for us.

"Please come in, gentleman," the old man says, but only out of obligation. It's clear he would rather I never come in these doors again.

I wonder what they told him about me. I wonder how

hard he'll make it for me to see Adair. I wonder if I'm the first person who ever cared what Felix the Butler thinks.

"May I ask the reason for your call today?" he says, scrupulously—but emptily—polite, as only people in the South can manage.

"We're here to see Adair," Cyrus says, shooting me a sideways glance that tells me something about the exchange seems off to him.

"I've been instructed not to admit any visitors for Miss MacLaine," Felix says. "She is not well."

"Look, I need to speak with her." I'm not above begging. She has to know what her father did, because she's my last hope to make this right. "It's urgent. I've tried calling her, but she doesn't answer."

"Perhaps she doesn't want to speak with you at present." He catches the look on my face, and a glimmer of sympathy seems to change his mind. "But I will ask her myself, since the matter is *urgent*."

Felix stalks off, leaving Cyrus and me in Windfall's foyer, a cavernous room ending in a grand staircase right out of *The Sound of Music*.

"I have a bad feeling about this, Sterling," Cyrus mutters.

Did I really think it would be easy once we got here? I wonder how long we have before security comes to eject us. "What should we do?"

"The butler said he had 'instructions.' That can only mean one thing."

I might not speak affluence, but I don't need him to translate. "Angus MacLaine told him not to let us in."

"Exactly." Cyrus sighs heavily. "The best I can do is tell them you went to the bathroom, try to buy you some time."

I hustle up the stairs , but just as I reach the doors leading to one of the building's two residential wings, they open. A man in a cheap, navy blue security uniform holds his hand up to me in the universal sign for *halt*.

From behind him, a silver-haired, botoxed, spray-tanned man I've never seen before emerges. "Mr. Ford. Miss MacLaine is not accepting visitors. I'm afraid I'm going to have to ask you to leave."

I hear movement behind me, and I turn to see a security guard appear at every exit leading from the foyer. An icy hand grabs my arm like a vise, and I realize I might never be able to see Adair again. But she hasn't chosen this. She wouldn't—not without at least talking to me first.

"Adair!" I yell. "Adair! Come and talk to me! Do you know what your rat-bastard father did?

"Mr. Ford," the silver-haired man says. "I'm counsel for the MacLaine family—"

"Great. Another lawyer."

"You've been asked to leave. If you don't walk out those doors in the next 60 seconds I guarantee you will be arrested for trespassing. Mr. Eaton as well."

My eyes flash to Cyrus, and he nods toward the door with a wild look in his eyes.

"Adair," I yell one last time, closing my eyes to concentrate, straining for some sound that she's nearby. Can I hear her coming? I just need the smallest hint I should wait and risk it. If I can talk to Adair, if I can tell her what her dad has done, I know she'll help me fight it.

But she doesn't come. And there's no way she didn't hear me. Her room is maybe 50 steps away. They could probably hear me at the main gate. If she's not coming, that can only mean one thing.

I feel a hand on my arm, and I react reflexively, slipping

the grasp and shoving with all my strength. The security guard stumbles backward, and I see a small spray canister appear in his hand. I square my shoulders, preparing to tackle him.

"Sterling!" Cyrus's voice cuts through the blood pumping in my skull. "This is only going to get worse. Let's go!"

The security guard aims whatever it is he has in his hand, and I force my feet to start moving toward the stairs.

"You are no longer welcome at Windfall," the lawyer says. "If you are found on premises again, we will have you arrested. I hope I've made everything clear?"

"Crystal fucking clear," I snap over my shoulder, throwing open the front door of the manor so hard it blows through its doorstop with a sharp, wooden crack.

My vision is a field of red and black, and suddenly a vivid daydream of Windfall burning—like Tara in *Gone With The Wind*—comes to mind. The thing that really scares me, though, is that it doesn't bother me in the least. I would burn this place to the ground just to watch the look on Angus MacLaine's face.

"I'm going to destroy everyone who fucked me today," I yell to whoever's listening.

Cyrus overtakes me, rushing to the safety of his car as though he's concerned about being arrested. It's not like he doesn't have bail money. "Look, man, I'm not saying it's right. But I've seen it before with other families. They're forcing her to choose between you and them."

I climb into his Mercedes, still lost to the fantasy of watching this place burn.

"Let's call Poppy. Maybe she knows what's going on." He starts the engine, and as soon as the controls unlock, he dials

Poppy over the car's speakers as he hauls ass down the driveway.

"Heya. How'd the trip to Windfall go?" she says, bright as ever. The girl could have a picnic in a hurricane.

Cyrus gives me an incredulous look before replying, "I'm in the car with Sterling now. We're leaving Windfall. They wouldn't let us see Adair. They threatened to arrest Sterling if he wouldn't leave. Me too."

"What the actual fuck?" Poppy says, and if she has cursed before, I can't seem to remember. If I wasn't ready to kill someone, it would probably be funny. As it is, her indignant response goes a really long way towards calming me down. If Poppy acted like everyone at Windfall, I'd know everything is lost. That means Adair hasn't told her anything. Adair isn't part of this. I hold the thought like a string of a balloon, knowing the second I relax, it will slip from my fingers.

"Poppy, what the fuck is up with Adair?" I want to come clean about having my scholarship pulled, but I can't bring myself to.

"No clue. She told me she felt crappy and was going home. I just thought she wanted Felix to cook for her. Ava and I are awful cooks, and—"

"I just want to talk to her," I cut off her nervous chatter. "Could you let her know?

"I'll try." She says it with the air of someone trying to turn back time.

"Poppy, doesn't this seem like...you know?" Cyrus says, casting a worried glance at me.

Poppy sighs, clearly understanding what he meant. "It does. Look, Sterling, you should probably prepare yourself. I know things have been rough, and I'm sure Adair tried, but we've seen this before. Somebody falls for someone on the wrong rung of the social ladder, and their parents go mental. Payoffs, boarding school, you name it, it's on the table."

"Adair wouldn't..." But I already know she would, because she just did. I just don't want to accept it.

"Wait until you can get in touch with Adair. She'll come around. You know what her father's like. Maybe she has to make it look like she's playing along."

"Yeah, that's probably it," Cyrus says, jumping on board. "Things will get back to normal, but only as long as you don't make the situation worse."

"Exactly," Poppy agrees.

"Sure, cool." I don't mean it. Have I been infected with the faux politeness of the South, too? Or am I too busy dwelling on what rung of the social ladder I'm on in their minds?

Or am I on it at all?

"Poppy, I'll be over in an hour or so, okay?" He ends the call. "Back to the dorm room?"

I slump in my seat. "Can you stop at a liquor store on the way?"

Why the fuck not? There's nothing left to lose.

"Are you sure that's a good idea?"

"You got a better one?"

He doesn't argue with me after that. Why would he? We both know the answer. There are no good options. No choices left to make. He can see that, even knowing half the information. I never stood a chance, which means that they're all right about me. So, why not enjoy the little time I have left?

7

ADAIR

"Adair, you have to get out of bed today."

Poppy's voice, muffled by the closed door, cuts through the musty air in my room, waking me up from a nightmare. Sterling and I were in New York. We'd been struggling to get by, I think. He wanted us to charge people money to watch us have sex. He kept saying it was the only way. I'm clutching the covers to my neck when I wake up, drenched in sweat, and bolt upright, my nerves as ragged as the moment I fell asleep.

It was just a dream. Just another nightmare.

How can anyone sleep as much as I have and still be so tired? What time is it, anyway? Day? Night? Dream? Nightmare? It's all blending into one endless black stretch.

I know my phone died a couple days ago. I forgot to bring a charger from my place on campus. I know I've been at Windfall for about five days, meaning it's been two since Sterling came by. So it's...Wednesday?

"Adair, can you hear me? I'm coming in."

"No!" I yelp, trying to leap up from the bed, but my body

is stiff and slow to respond. I've barely managed getting my feet on the ground when Poppy's golden silhouette appears in the door.

"Jesus, it's like a cave in here! How do you see?"

My eyes, acclimated to the dark, have no trouble seeing Poppy stalk across the room toward the blackout curtains blocking the outside world. "Don't!"

"Hush. It's for your own goo—" Her foot clips a stack of pizza boxes sitting on the floor, and she almost falls face first on them. The smell of mushrooms and cheese waft over to me, and my stomach grumbles so loudly Poppy can actually hear it.

She reaches the curtains and pulls them back a little, letting sunlight in the room. "There. That's better."

The light is headache-inducing, forcing me to squint. "What time is it?"

"Do you even know what day it is?" Poppy says, her brow creased in a way that reminds me of mom.

For a second, I let myself pretend she *is* Mom, that we're about to talk—that things are about to get better. But it only hurts more. "Wednesday, I think." I leave Poppy standing by the window and shuffle toward the ensuite to brush my teeth. I love a supreme pizza, but the onions are killer the next morning. So, is the heartburn.

"It's fucking Friday!"

I bite back a rare smile at the sound of fuck coming from her. There's always just a second of hesitation before she curses. "Alright, already. I'm up. What more do you want?"

"What's going on, Adair? Sterling and Cy tried to come by and see you, but Windfall security threatened to arrest them both. They were going to pepper spray them! You aren't returning anyone's calls. *People are worried.*"

I knew this moment would come. I can't keep avoiding people forever. But here, in my room full of all my things, with the doors closed, with the gates of Windfall manned by security—at least I feel safe. "One sec, let me brush my teeth."

When I come back into the bedroom, Poppy has fully opened the curtains, grabbed all the pizza and takeout boxes littered around the room, and plopped them in the hall outside my door. I nearly start to cry. Other than Felix, no one's bothered to check in on me. I feel more like a prisoner than a victim.

When Poppy sees me, her expression softens. She sits on my bed, patting the space next to her. "Whatever it is, I'm here for you, hon. No judgem—"

"I have a sex tape."

"Oh," she says, all color draining from her face. She opens her mouth to speak, but the words get lost in transit. Apparently, I found her mute button.

"Yeah. I found out from my father. He received a black-mail email."

"Oh."

"The message was sent anonymously, but it instructed him to send $1,000,00,000 to an address in Queens." I list each fact as emotionlessly as possible, because that's what these are: facts. I can't change them. Sleeping hasn't changed them. Ignoring them hasn't changed them. Time to start facing them. I watch Poppy's expression like a hawk. I've turned everything over so many times, I don't know what I think anymore. Because, although, these are the facts, I can't quite decide if I believe all the information behind them. Maybe Poppy's reaction will help me figure out what's real and what's a lie. God knows I haven't been able to figure it out on my own.

"Oh." Or maybe she's caught on repeat.

We sit in silence, and then, after a long pause, she says, "Isn't that where..."

"Yeah, it's Sterling's address."

"Oh." Poppy's face is inscrutable. I watch her wheels spin, but there's nothing there. Figures.

"Would you *please* stop saying that. It's not very helpful."

"That *bastard*," she says, but her eyes dart to me when she says it, like she needs me to signal how I feel about it before she can figure out how to be supportive. She's taking my side—just as soon as I show her what side that is. So far, this conversation is as illuminating as talking to a mirror.

"I don't know what to believe. I've seen the video. It was taken the night of my brother's wedding."

She pulls me into a hug, and for a moment I feel only skin-crawling violation. No one has actually touched me since I got the news. After a moment, though, the anxiety vanishes, and I find myself sobbing into my best friend's shoulder. By the time two large, wet spots have soaked through her jacket, I simply have no more tears inside me.

I'm a champion crier, I realize. I wonder if there's an Olympics event for it. I'd be a shoe-in. I'd get all the best sponsorships. Kleenex. The Grand Ole Opry. I can actually see this life, complete and rounded and real, inside my head. The last week has been like that. Every black thought conjures its own reality. The future I was headed to—the one with Sterling—is gone forever. Everything feels futile. Pointless even. And worse than that? I can't help thinking I'd always known we were doomed. I might as well acknowledge the cosmic joke in it.

"Do you think Sterling actually did it?" Her voice is tentative, but soothing.

"Who else would?" It's the same question I keep asking myself, hoping to find an answer. "You know what would be helpful?"

"What? Anything." She pounces on the opportunity to do something.

"What was your first thought when I told you? I mean at the exact moment you put all the pieces together." My judgement is obviously impaired. I want someone else to tell me what kind of man Sterling is. I'm not sure I know any more.

"Are you sure?"

"Yeah." I'm not, though. "Gut check time."

"I thought—*he wouldn't*," she says slowly, "but..."

"But who would ever expect anyone to do something like that?" I finish for her.

"Pretty much, yeah."

"And who else *would*?"

"Also that," she agrees.

"I don't know what to think, Poppy. It's hard even telling you. Like, I worry—will *you* ever see me the same way?"

Poppy's face bursts like a dam. It's a strange thing, to watch someone else's heart break for you. To watch them come apart, because your pain is just too much. "No, darling. No. No. Never. Nothing about this changes how I see you."

"I know you love me. I know you wouldn't abandon me. And I know you would never *want* it to change how you see me. It's just, I wonder, you know? When people find out, does my name change from 'Adair' to 'Adair with the sex tape?' It's just always there, this ugly feeling. Like an enormous monster. And to do anything—just get up and go to the bathroom—I have to pretend it's not there, just waiting to rewrite me into a person I don't want to be." The last words escape through a sob, but I don't want to feel sorry for myself. I just want her to understand.

"I will never, ever tell anyone." Of course, Poppy understands. Of course, she does. What would I do without her? Why didn't I share with her sooner? "And who else knows?"

"My father. My brother knows the video exists, I think, but he hasn't seen it. Which means Ginny knows about it." I feel queasy again.

"No one who will hurt you," she says with a relief I don't share, because I'm not certain she's right. "And Sterling?"

"I had a whole day where I decided he made the video, but that he never intended for anyone to actually see it— besides my father. Basically, I convinced myself he thought the writing was on the wall, and this was his way of getting us enough money to keep us free from my family."

"But it didn't make you feel any better," Poppy says knowingly.

"Worse, actually." It took me an embarrassingly long amount of time to realize how stupid this line of thinking was. "Because it would mean he made all the choices, used me without bothering to discuss it with me. It would mean that, whatever it is we have, it wasn't enough to make him see what it would do to me."

"Do you love him?" Poppy says, putting her arm around my shoulders.

It should be the biggest question of all after everything he's done—the one that I have to consider. But I don't. "Yeah. With all my heart. No question."

She sighs like she was hoping for another answer. "I thought so."

"But how do you tell if someone loves you back? I

thought I knew..." I trail off. It's too raw, and I'm too full of self-loathing. Another step in that direction and I feel like I'll fall through a hole I'll never claw free from.

"You always know, deep down," Poppy says, her voice suddenly small and sad. "My dad loves my mom. My mom doesn't love him, I think. And Cyrus doesn't—"

"Of course he does, he just—"

"No, it's fine. He doesn't love me *yet*." Poppy's face brightens, and I recognize the signs of someone taking my mom's advice and making diamonds. "You can grow to love someone. And Cyrus *is* the one for me. He just fell in love with himself first. He'll get there. He just needs to grow up some more."

"I'm sorry. I didn't mean to—"

"I *said* hush. You have nothing to be sorry for. But you should do what you had me do earlier. The first thought that jumps to mind when I ask 'does Sterling love you?' is..."

"He loves me." In the end, it's simple. I know Sterling loves me.

But he's like the ocean. Powerful and brooding and mysterious. What difference does it make if I know the tide will come in again—if that same tide washes me away? And that's what it's like with Sterling. Whatever I grasp is just a small part of a whole I can't see—and it's dangerous to make assumptions with a force as powerful and uncontrollable as that.

"Then you should at least talk to him," Poppy says. "If it helps, we can do it at our place with Ava and me there."

"Maybe." It's not the worst idea. I'll need closure, one way or the other, right? "But I don't know what I would say. Not yet."

"Then take your time. He's not going anywhere. And if he does, well, at least you'll have your answer."

I take a deep breath, and enjoy feeling like there is something fixed in my future. It already feels like a tether to reality. "Okay. That's the plan, then. But there is something I'd like you to do for me." I open the drawer of the nightstand next to my bed. "I wrote him a letter. Well, more of a note, really. Whenever we do end up talking, I think it will help if he reads it."

"I'll get it to him," Poppy says, giving me a kiss on my temple, which makes me fall to pieces. Dry sobs rack my whole body, and my friend keeps her arm around me. "We'll get through this. You don't have to do it alone."

I do, though.

8

STERLING

"Is something wrong?" Francie unspools the words without bothering to pause between them. I can't tell if she's worried or teasing. We haven't talked much on the phone since the holidays.

"What? Why would you think something's wrong?"

"Because you're calling me!" The edge to her voice is replaced with exasperation.

"Give me a break. I just wanted to talk," I say.

"Jesus, Sterling. Now I'm *really* worried. What happened?"

This was supposed to be *the* call. But it's already off the rails.

Over the last couple of days, I thought a lot about how to tell her. How to talk her down from wanting to fight the administration. How to tell her things are going to be alright. I never did figure that one out, actually. Not that it matters. Apparently, my carefully selected explanations flew out the window before I said a single word.

You're getting better at fucking up. You'll have a degree in it soon. Then you won't need this place.

I take a steadying breath, wondering if Francie can sense that, too. "It's just...trouble with Adair." It's not a lie, anyway.

"Ah, that explains it."

I can feel the outrush of Francie's tension through the cell phone's speaker. I could probably guess where she is in the house, what expression she's wearing.

"Well, is it advice you're calling for?" Francie continues when I don't.

"I'm not sure there's anything left to advise about."

"Oh, Sterling..." She fills the two little words with so much love and sympathy.

I feel better. And worse.

I really didn't think this through. What was I going to tell her, anyway? That I was losing my place at Valmont, at least in part because I lost my temper—again. Because it's definitely not the first time Francie watched me make that mistake. And somehow, every time I disappoint her, it gets harder to do it again. Maybe that would be a good thing if I were ten and she were my mother, helping me figure out how to grow up. But I'm nineteen now, and still making the same mistakes. What's left to say?

Isn't that the problem with letting other people get close to begin with? You give them power over you. Then, they mostly just use it to make themselves happier. That's how it's been for me with nearly everyone. And if by some miracle they keep loving you despite your repeatedly fucking up? You have to watch their heart break for you. You have to know you caused it. You can't escape.

I know I've already stuck the dagger in Francie. I just

can't bear the thought of watching her turn around to see me standing there holding the handle.

"Sterling, this is an uncomfortable pause, even for you." Francie's voice floats over me.

I'm not sure other people are built like me. I have a place I go to, far on the other side of Drunk Sterling. Somewhere there is no pain, no sadness, and no regret. When I go there, I make rules for my brain to follow—rules that keep the pain away. When I was little, it would be stuff like: *No food for Sterling until Sutton eats.* Or, later: *No lying to Francie.* It always works. I have no idea how, or why. It just does.

I make one now, in two parts: *I will ruin Angus MacLaine, and I will never burden Francie again.*

"Francie, I just needed to hear your voice," I admit to her. "You've always been there for me."

"You just wanted to feel home?" she offers.

"Yeah, I think that's it."

"I'm glad you called, Sterling. I like to give you your space. I know you need it, but it's still nice." From Francie, this is almost sappy. Neither of us is comfortable implying we need the other, let alone saying it.

Which is what makes this even harder.

"I don't think I ever properly thanked you," I begin.

"You've thanked me. And even if you hadn't—I always knew." Francie's voice is warm and light. Will she look back on this moment and remember it with darkness?

"It's just—I'm not easy to love sometimes."

There. She'll probably think I'm referring to problems with Adair. But if she looks back...

"Ha!"

"What's that supposed to mean?" I ask.

"You are *so* easy to love. Just...hard to understand."

"Right," I'm not sure how to answer, and it feels like we've done enough sentimentality, anyway. "Listen, I have class..."

"Alright. Scoot. Love you."

"I love you, too."

I end the call, considering what to do with my new rule. Ruining Angus MacLaine will take years, no delusions there. But what can I do to keep myself from being a burden on Francie?

For starters, no moving back to New York. No trying to figure out how to scrape together enough money for community college. No service or fast food jobs. They're a treadmill, not a road to where I want to go.

It hits me. There's one place I can go. One place that won't mind someone who likes to solve problems with brute force. One place that will pay for college. Assuming I live through it.

I hear Cyrus's keys jangling outside the door, and when he comes in, he takes a look at the empty bottles strewn around the room, my three-day stubble, and gives a disgusted sigh.

Am I really that repulsive?

"Sterling, I know things are shit right now, but would it kill you to spend five minutes every day cleaning up after yourself?"

"It's nice to see you, too."

It's not really his fault, but Cyrus is now my most frequent reminder of worthless, moneyed Valmont. And the one thing that made it important for us to get along—sharing a living arrangement—is going away. Not that Cyrus knows it yet.

"Fine. How are you? You look like shit."

"Not great. Did you hear anything from Poppy?" I can practically feel my interest in talking to Adair burn away. I can't imagine trying to carry out a long-distance relationship with a girl whose family represents the ongoing destruction of my life.

"Not what you want to hear, man. Adair isn't interested in meeting. Sorry."

That's one sign that's clear as day. Adair and I are over. Cy and Poppy keep saying to give it time, but what's going to change between now and whenever Adair decides she's up for seeing me? How long am I supposed to wait? Still, it will make half of my new rule that much easier. If Adair decided her life would be better with her family calling the shots, it'll make it that much sweeter when she sees how wrong she is someday.

"I do have stuff for you, though," Cyrus continues. He tosses a stack of envelopes, probably from our mail cubby in the dorm office, onto my desk.

Second from the top is a notice from the Valmont registrar's office, its cellophane window cutout displaying a garish pink packet of paper inside. I rip open the top of the envelope, getting a paper cut for my trouble. It reads:

Pursuant to the administrative action rescinding your scholarship for violations of Valmont University's Code of Student Conduct, your account balance is now ($29,872). If the balance is not paid in full within one week of the date indicated on this notice, your student status will be put on probation pending payment.. This change in status may endanger your housing and educational privileges...

I don't bother reading the rest. I check the date at the top of the letter, realizing it was marked two days ago. So I have 5 days before they kick me out of school. Less time than I thought.

"Nothing printed on that color of paper is good news. You ok?" Cyrus looks nervous, which just pisses me off more. I don't want his pity or sympathy. Even his nice gestures—letting Francie and I have the suite for Thanksgiving—ended up being shitty for me. I already feel lighter, just from unloading the burden of having to play at being friends.

"Nothing you need to worry about," I say, picking up the nearly empty bottles of whiskey and vodka scattered around my bed. I won't be needing them anymore.

"Whatever. Have a nice day." He's done with me, too. Cyrus turns to go, his eyes landing on the stack of mail on my desk. For a moment I'm sure he's going to say something stupid like: *It's not very much money for me. Let me give you $30k so my third Valmont residence is less depressing for me.* But he gives up trying, probably because, thick as he is, he knows I don't want to hear it.

I pull a couple of legal pads out of my desk and toss them in my bag. I need to head to the library to do research. The U.S. has 4 major armed forces, and I need to figure out which one offers the best terms for tuition payment, and which will give me the chance to gain the kind of skills that will be useful later. I ignore the tiny voice warning me this will break Francie's heart. I refuse to acknowledge the smug satisfaction this will give Angus MacLaine. But when I imagine Adair, sitting alone, full of regret, wondering how she got stuck here, I almost smile.

9

ADAIR

I get ready for class three days in a row.

On the first, I never make it out the front door of Windfall. On the second, I drive all the way to campus and circle the building for ten minutes straight, trying to see if Sterling is waiting for me to show up. But I get cold feet and go home where I find a small, wrapped package wedged between the seats of the car. Opening it, I discover a small clover charm. It takes me a moment to process how it got there. Sterling's birthday present, forgotten in the drama of that night. It's just been sitting there, waiting for me to find it. A ticking bomb. I cry for three hours straight. I consider throwing it away, but shove it in a drawer instead. For some reason, finding it makes me more determined to take back my life.

So finally, on the third day, I make myself park and go to class.

Branford Hall is four stories of red brick, tucked between a few massive oak trees and a small, one-way street that gets choked with students whenever classes let out. It takes me a few minutes to find a parking spot, and by the time I step through the doors of the building a cold lump has settled in my throat. People glance at me as I pass by, and I can't help wondering, each time, if it's a normal look—or if *they know*. The door to psychology is already closed, meaning class has started.

I have to fight the urge to turn around and run home. How can I survive every set of eyes in that room turning to look at me? How many times will I have to tell myself I'm okay?

I may not have been physically present in class for two weeks, but I had emailed my professor and kept up with the work. Which is probably why, when Professor Jones sees me sneak in, she smiles and hardly slows down her introduction to today's lecture.

Probably.

But what if she's trying to put me at ease? Does she somehow know?

The rational part of my brain is completely certain she doesn't. But the part of me that was afraid of what might come out of the crack in my closet door at night—gone since I was ten years old—is screaming with alarm.

It takes me a second to fight back my panic and focus on the lecture.

"Though Milgram's methods are still controversial today," Professor Jones says, her perfectly coiffed blonde bob acting like a frame for her sharp, aquiline features, "his work on obedience is nonetheless seminal."

A guy a few seats down shifts in his seat, and I flinch.

"Milgram believed there was a fundamental shift in social psychology starting at the industrial revolution and culminating in the twentieth century. He said, 'Often, it's not so much the kind of person a man is, as the kind of situation in which he finds himself that determines how he will act.'"

A wave of nausea rolls over me, and I do my best to keep hold of breakfast. One thing I'm learning about psych: it's hard not to apply every lesson to what's going on in your life. They actually warn you about it the first day of class. But what if your life reads like situations in a therapy manual?

Have I been stupid? Am I being unfair? If Sterling tried to blackmail my father, isn't he just trying to protect himself? Isn't that what humans do? Isn't that what he probably tried to come tell me?

I force myself to pay attention to the lecture, but every time I do, the first sentence seems relevant to my current situation. I try telling myself it won't always be this way, that eventually things will get back to normal—that what I need is time. But the minute hand of the watch on the wall keeps moving slower and slower, and I'm almost hyperventilating by the time there are five minutes left in class.

What if Sterling's been going to my classes and waiting until I show up? It sounds like something he would do. I need to leave. I shove my notebook and pens in my bag, and slide out the door, closing my eyes in a sort of prayer that when I open them, he won't be there.

He isn't.

I actually get the chromed handle of the Jag in my hand before my escape is ruined.

"Adair, where are you going?"

Ava is making a beeline for me, waving furiously as she dashes from Branford's main entrance. I see her other hand furiously texting on her phone as she makes her way to me, and for a second I wonder if Sterling has paid her to tell him where I am.

Which is just stupid, because Sterling has no money and Ava does nothing for free.

"Adair, I didn't know you were back in class. Are you alright?" She shoots me a furtive glance, but I'm not sure if that means something is up, or if Ava is just being Ava.

"It's the first time I've gone in awhile." I admit.

"I just texted Poppy," she says, turning to look back in the direction of Branford. "She's coming."

That's all it was. Why am I so paranoid?

"Were you two waiting for me?"

"What?" Ava looks indignant. "Full of yourself much? No. I was with Poppy literally 60 seconds ago. We were saying we should take you to lunch. And then I saw you. Don't be so paranoid."

"Sorry, it's been a bad couple weeks." The beauty of Ava —if there is one—is that you don't have to worry about her feelings. She has none. It's all surface, all the time. The ugliness is that she won't consider yours, at all. It's a trade-off.

"Poppy said something about trouble with Sterling," Ava says, already distracted by a couple of hot guys she noticed checking her out, "but she wouldn't spill the tea."

"You have no idea," I say. There's no way I'm telling her about the video. I've known her a long time, but sometimes I wonder if there's something broken in her. I can almost imagine her liking the idea of having a sex tape. And I can definitely imagine her gossiping about mine.

"Hey you two!" Poppy calls, driving by slowly but waving frantically. "Get in."

Ava hooks my elbow and starts dragging me towards Poppy's Audi. "Coming!"

A couple of the cars behind Poppy honk when she stops in the middle of the road so Ava and I can get in, and at that moment students begin pouring out of Branford, trapping all the cars like flies in amber.

"Noodles?" Poppy asks, flashing me a smile in the rearview mirror. It doesn't quite match the maternal concern in her eyes.

"Ugh. Carbs," Ava says reflexively.

"Works for me," I say. Carbs and I are old friends.

"Don't worry, Ava, I'm sure they have diet soda and salad," Poppy says like this is a viable meal option.

It takes another couple of minutes for us to break free of the campus bottlenecks, and Poppy finds the posh shopping center she's looking for not long after. I can't help noticing how many nervous looks she shoots me in the rearview mirror, though. There's something on Poppy's mind. She hands her keys to a valet, and we settle into sidewalk seating in front of the restaurant. A waiter comes over and asks for drink orders, and Ava disappears to use the restroom.

"Why am I here?" I ask Poppy, placing my hand on her menu and gently forcing her to lower it.

"What do you mean?" Poppy tries to sound casual, but it's too high pitched and she's lousy at hiding how she feels—at least from me.

"I know when I'm being kidnapped. You didn't tell Ava—"

"No! Adair, I would not tell Ava without clearing it with you. I just said I wanted us to go to lunch. That's all." She returns her attention to the menu with the focus of a doctor about to perform brain surgery.

I'm no longer hungry, no longer craving the sweet comfort of carbohydrates. If this isn't about the sex tape, it's about something else. "Tell me."

"What? There's—"

"You can't even look me in the eye, Poppy," I cut her off. "What are you not telling me?"

She finally drops her menu, and it's written all across her face. It's the same expression she wore at my mother's funeral: a sort of grim determination combined with nauseating anxiety.

"It's Sterling," she says. Her mouth starts to form five different words, none of which are actually said. Eventually, Poppy settles on the rip-off-the-bandage approach. "He's gone."

Gone.

The word echoes inside me, lodging in the center of my chest, and splintering through me. I crack open, and he spills out. Suddenly, I'm not at a cafe with my best friend, I'm in a hospital waiting room, waiting to hear about my mother but staring at Sterling's perfect, infuriating face. He's there holding out a bag with clown-size flip-flops I still have tucked in my closet. Then we're on a picnic blanket together. Then his hands are on me. Then he's sharing his secrets with me, telling me how he's too broken to ever be fixed. All of it relived in one second. And the last, worst moment is one I can only imagine: he hears me in the shower, calls in to me about clothes. His hands fiddle with his cell phone, setting it on the built-in shelf in his dorm room, with its angle perfectly aimed at the bed. He presses record, places a stack of books behind the phone screen, obscuring the light it emits so I won't notice he's recording us.

And when I come out? There's no love left in his eyes. I didn't see it then. But I see it now.

Tears roll down my cheeks, but they're not connected to how I feel, they're just some weird reflex. How can I cry when I'm already empty?

Poppy reaches into her purse and pulls out my copy of *Persuasion* along with *The Sun Also Rises*, the one I bought him for Christmas at The Strand along with the note I sent with her to give him, still unopened. "Cyrus came back to the dorm yesterday, and this is all that was left."

I take the book and letter and turn them over in my hands, feeling something shift. It's subtle at first, like the feeling you get when you misplace your keys—but I can feel it spreading like cracks in glass, breaking me without changing my shape.

"He did it," I admit. "There's no point fighting it any more."

I'm still the same person I was five minutes ago. Anyone passing by would say as much. But I can feel myself become different. Sadder. More jaded. Trapped all over again. And angry. *God, am I angry.* I could destroy whole worlds with it. I never let myself feel angry before. Confused? Sure. Upset? Of course. But angry? I couldn't. That could only exist in a world where Sterling used me like a dirty rag.

I never wanted to live in that world. But I have been living in it for weeks, pretending I was safe. Now I'm in some new afterlife. In just this one shopping area I see three places Sterling and I went together, like tombstones for graves I never want to visit:

Here lies Sterling and Adair. And here. And there.

Will campus be like that? Will Windfall?

"He's a total knob head. I'm so sorry, Adair." Poppy places her hand on my arm tenderly, like she's afraid I'll flinch. She knows me well.

I wipe the tears from the corners of my eyes, glad I didn't bother to put on makeup today. "I'm tired of seeing him everywhere I look."

"Seeing *who* everywhere you look?" Ava says, plopping into the seat next to me before figuring out the answer to her own question. "Oh. Right."

She glares at me like I've betrayed her. First, carbs, and now, feelings. How dare I?

"Sterling left Valmont," Poppy announces, probably trying to save me from having to talk about it.

"Without saying goodbye." I'm not sure why I feel the need to add this detail, but it feels pertinent.

"Seriously?" Ava says, and the corners of her eyes pinch with righteous fury. It's almost sweet. For her. "What a pig."

"We should go away somewhere. Spring Break's coming up." Poppy starts brainstorming possible getaways, joined eagerly by Ava.

I realize both of them are staring at me, waiting for my input. What were they saying? Something about Miami? "Getting away sounds nice."

It does, I think. I don't really know.

I've changed a lot in the past seven months. Sterling breathed life into me. But I wonder now if I just needed someone to fill the gaping hole left by my mom's death. I wanted Sterling to be everything I needed. But now I see that I was lying to myself almost as much as he was lying to me. Not that it excuses what he did. Nothing could. But it still shouldn't have ended like this. I'd give anything to make Sterling look me in the eye and tell me why he did it. Why did it take him leaving for me to realize what I really needed?

"No, Ava. You're not listening," Poppy says with a parent's long sigh. "I don't want to be the youngest person for five miles in every direction."

"Palm Beach is nice. Have you ever been there?" Ava

pouts. "And there is always a man ready to buy drinks for you."

"Just because you're comfortable dating retired men doesn't mean Adair and I have to watch. Back me up," Poppy says, looking at me.

I don't want anyone to look at me at the moment. I'm not exactly up for getting drunk at a beach while every man who comes by hits on one of us. It doesn't matter if it's in South Beach and the man is 25 or Palm Beach and he's 60. "What about the Keys?"

Ava snorts. "The Jimmy Buffett crowd? For fuck's sake!"

Poppy's nose crinkles and I can tell that she doesn't like my Keys idea, but it doesn't stop her from saying, "Adair should get to choose."

"Fine," Ava relents.

I want to get as far as possible, and I don't want a bunch of drunk college kids puking on my shoes. If I am going with two friends, there's a good chance my dad will agree to anything I suggest. I dare myself to think big, and as soon as I do the answer is there.

"I want to go to London."

Poppy squeals with glee. "It's *perfect*. The best shopping in the world. I mean, Paris and Milan are good, too, but—"

"Ugh, I hate jet lag," Ava says, but a smile has already crept onto the corners of her mouth. "I've never shagged a Brit, though. And it's on my list."

"Oh, and the Royal wedding is coming, so we can get all the commemorative merchandise and maybe we can even—"

"You are so British sometimes," Ava says, staring at her. "But, I guess that means I can still seduce Alexander before he's married."

"Good luck with that," Poppy says.

"I have high standards." The two dissolve into a debate about the Royal family that I quickly tune out. Weddings. Happiness. Love. Even sex. All of it makes me feel sick. But maybe the city being obsessed with a stupid wedding will mean the museums and book stores will be empty.

But all that really matters is that wherever Sterling went there's no way he's there. I need to put some distance between us. An ocean is a good place to start, and suddenly, I want to be gone already—away from Valmont and him and the minefield of memories he's left behind. "Can we leave tonight?"

10

ADAIR

God bless the British stiff upper lip.

Back in Valmont, if you say you're having a shitty day, people stop what they're doing and urge you to tell them about it—until it feels like you're living out every crappy thing all over again. But in London, I'm finding that people got used to living with pain about a dozen generations back. There's no wallowing allowed.

I don't know what I'd do without Poppy, but ever since Sterling left, whenever she sees me looking sad her eyes well with tears. It gets old.

We arrive at our hotel from Heathrow late, and my friends crash as soon as they see the beds. But I'm not ready to sleep. And the only place to get a meal is a late-night cafe across from our hotel, nearly empty in the half hour before closing. My waitress, a young British-Indian girl with dyed-purple pixie hair and a knowing smile, takes one look at me and diagnoses the problem. "You looked like you needed this," she says, pausing to drop off a slice of four-tiered chocolate cake along with the coffee and sandwich I ordered.

"Is it that obvious?" I say, my head swimming with the disorienting effects of jet lag.

"Yeah," she says, dropping the bill on the table. "Remember, love. Never let them see you bleed." Then she is off, disappearing to work on whatever it is waitresses do at closing time.

I decide to take her advice to heart. Wherever Sterling Ford is in the world, if he could somehow close his eyes and see me in London, I don't want him to see me pining for him or losing one glorious moment of this trip. I want him to see an Adair MacLaine who has moved on to a better life. I want to stay beyond his reach, and beyond my own regret. Which is so much easier to do here than in Valmont.

After coffee and cake, I leave an outrageous tip for the waitress and wander around London for an hour or so. I've travelled abroad before, of course, but that was with my family, who subscribe to the idea that people in other countries have nice things worth enjoying, sure—but it would be better if you didn't have to talk to any of them. I was never allowed to wander, never allowed to sate my curiosity for what was around the corner. It was almost more infuriating than not going at all.

London is the perfect mix of old and new. Our hotel is small but luxurious, located in the poshest area of Belgravia. I'm not sure it's exactly where I'd want to be for a long stay, but I already know I want to live here. Maybe not for my entire life, but I'm willing to be convinced.

By the time I can no longer fight off how tired I am, I take an Uber back to our hotel, and—for the first time in weeks—fall into a deep, dreamless sleep.

. . .

THE WORST THING THAT HAPPENS THE NEXT COUPLE OF days is that none of us can agree on what kind of fun to have. Ava prefers to sleep late and go clubbing. Poppy prefers to be up early, and can't stop talking about going to Saville Row to shop for clothes for Cyrus. I want to see some museums and libraries, but I quickly discover that going to either of those things with people who don't want to be there is worse than not going at all.

We hit the breaking point on the fourth of our five days in London. Poppy sets it off by trying to literally drag Ava out of bed, still drunk from the night before. I wasn't happy about getting up at 7am, either, but I've never quite figured out how to say *no* to my best friend.

It's not a problem for Ava, though, and within a minute all three of us are talking over each other and saying all the things we had so far managed to leave unsaid. It gets dark, but before anyone says anything friendship-ending, Ava actually comes up with the solution: today will be a "split up" day. Poppy doesn't like it, but I'm pretty sure it's just because she wants to keep an eye on me.

I already know everything I want to do, and it starts with a trip to Notting Hill, which is everything I saw in the Hugh Grant movie, and more.

London tends toward the posh and sophisticated. It's easy imagining every man in a suit going to a high-pressure City job. And I'm the least well-dressed woman on every block I walk down. Notting Hill is the opposite of all that. More than anything, it reminds me of the Nashville Farmer's Market. A mind-boggling amount of tents choke the city streets, selling everything from antique books to tie-dyed shirts and hemp beanies. Mouth-watering smells waft by from every direction, and at the exact moment I no longer smell delicious food, another cluster of street vendors making Afro-Caribbean chicken and rice appears, and I cave to temptation.

I'm not quite sure why I've kept Sterling's copy of *The Great Gatsby* in my backpack. I threw it in my bag at the last second of packing, I think because I wanted something to look at if I decided I still needed to understand where it all went wrong. And it's just stayed there ever since. I've had twenty chances to take it out, and every time I forget it's there I see it again and hear the waitress's advice about not letting them see you bleed.

I can't help myself, though. With my paper plate rapidly disintegrating from the effects of steaming hot rice and chicken jus, I pull out the dog-eared paperback and flip to a page at random. Sterling's clean, neat scrawl fills about half the margin on both pages, and it's almost as interesting to read his notes as it is to read Fitzgerald himself.

One passage reads: "It understood you just as you wanted to be understood, believed in you as you would like to believe in yourself, and assured you that it had precisely the impression of you that, at your best, you hoped to convey."

And in the margin beside it: "Never understood this. Probably b/c I don't care what impression I convey. Except maybe to Francie. Some of the looks I get from her are *almost* like this. But is that because I don't want her to suffer from worry about me—which amounts to doing her a kindness? Or because I've never had anyone whose opinion of me was better than my own (which is saying a lot, but also nothing at all)?"

Sterling's note is heart-breaking and infuriating all at once. On one hand, I wonder how he doesn't even seem to be aware of using the margins of *The Great Gatsby* like a journal. But how else would he process things? A poor, abused kid who lost his family, bounced around the foster system, and never had anyone to relate to? Sterling was a scared little kid when he wrote this, but it might have been less than a year ago for all I know. Sterling *never* seems vulnerable in person. But the boy who wrote in the margins of this book didn't go away because he grew into the body of a Greek god. I wonder if everything I knew of Sterling was just a facade built to protect the boy who wrote these notes. I wonder if it's so easy. I wonder if it's fair to judge from a note in a margin.

Suddenly, I get the feeling eyes are on me, and I shudder slightly. If Sterling could see me now he would definitely see me pining. Did he leave the book for me like an apology? Like, *Hey, Lucky. I know I did you wrong. But maybe if you read this and try to figure out what happened, you'll realize I'm not complete shit.*

Or is it something else entirely? Am I Daisy to his Tom? Would that make Sterling's blackmail of my father actually a test of me? If I'm Daisy, I'll pick heartbreak if it means privilege. Sterling wanted to know if I meant it when I said I didn't care about my family's money, and so he did what he did...?

I throw the book on the ground and a disgusted, frustrated scream escapes me. I hear people around me gasp—my floppy upper lip must offend them. I grab my bag and take two full steps away from the picnic table I've been sitting at. *The Great Gatsby* lies there on the ground, but it asks me a question as plainly as if it were speaking:

Do you want to leave it all behind? It's as easy as leaving me here in the dirt.

I think I do want to leave it—more than I've ever wanted anything, including Sterling himself—but it doesn't stop me from stooping to pick it up, shoving it roughly into the bottom of my bag.

I feel the tears streaming down my cheeks, and I look for a restroom—anywhere I could have a bit of privacy, really. But there is only a gilded box on the corner, trailed by a line of fifteen people waiting to pay for the privilege of peeing. Why is there never a restroom on this godforsaken continent?

I wipe the corners of my eyes with my sleeve and hold my head high. This immediately puts the people around me at ease—so much so that a few of the women nod to me in solidarity as I pass.

Never let them see you bleed.

TAKING AN UBER IS EASIER, BUT I DECIDE TO TRY A black cab—mostly so I can say I did. Poppy and Ava hunkered down in a pub talking to a few Scottish guys here on holiday, but I need to be alone with my thoughts. I tell the driver to take me to the British Museum, because somehow you're always alone in a museum even when it's full. We're stuck in London traffic almost immediately. I think it's worse due to the upcoming Royal wedding. My phone rings, and the screen tells me it's Malcolm. I don't want to answer—I don't particularly want to think about Valmont at all—but there's no telling what my brother or father might do if they felt like I was 2,000 miles away and unreachable.

As soon as I connect, I'm surprised to hear both Malcolm and Ginny on the line.

"We're pregnant!" they say in unison.

"Wha—I...oh my god!" I splutter, blinking rapidly. The cabbie turns, a bushy eyebrow raised, as if concerned I'm having some type of fit. I smile sweetly.

"I know," Ginny says. "The only thing more cliché than a Valentine wedding is a honeymoon baby."

"It's wonderful news, honestly. I just wasn't expecting it."

"Neither were we," Malcolm says followed by a slight grunt that suggests he's been elbowed in the ribs. "But we're very excited."

"I think your brother is a little shell shocked. We hadn't even discussed having a baby yet, but I guess life happens while you're too busy to notice," Ginny chirps. I can hear the look on her face: wide smile, starry eyes. She'd never talked much about kids before. It's not that I didn't expect them to have children. I just hadn't expected it to happen so soon. "We're due sometime in late October, early November, so don't get any ideas about staying in London. I expect Aunt Adair to be at all my showers."

"Got it," I promise, but I'm not sure I'll keep that promise.

"Okay, we need to call a few other people. Your dad is planning some big party."

"Already?"

"There's no reasoning with him. Apparently, he's thrilled to be a grandfather," Malcolm says. "Keeps talking about securing his bloodline. It's a bit ridiculous."

"He just wants you to change your mind about the job in D.C.," Ginny says.

"Not going to happen," Malcolm says. "That's why Adair needs to come home. Someone has to keep an eye on him."

"He has Felix," I remind them, not even sure they remember I'm still on the call.

"He needs family. You know that," he says it in a light tone, but I feel the dark current running through his words. Our father isn't happy unless one of us is around to order about. Now that Mom's gone, one of us has to take her place.

"Well, keep me updated," I say, suddenly feeling too tired to wander around a museum, "and congrats."

As soon as we reach Bloomsbury, a light spring rain starts. I get out, holding my palm against the mist as it blows in my face and join the groups of tourists streaming toward the museum. It's only open a few more hours, and I don't know if it's always this busy or people are escaping the rain. But, as expected, despite the crowds, I feel alone, maneuvering in and out aimlessly. I halt as a woman dashes in front of me, one hand on a stroller with a sleeping baby inside, the other stretching to catch an escaped toddler. The little boy laughs when her hands close on his arm and draw him back.

"Got you," she says, earning another giggle from him. She looks up, eyes apologetic. "I'm so sorry."

I smile, shake my head, and let them continue.

There's no father in sight. The poor woman is doing double duty while her husband is at work. I feel tired just watching her wheel the carriage around, so she can kneel to lecture the little boy in an unoccupied corner. With the number of priceless artifacts surrounding them, I can't blame her for being nervous. That's what Ginny is signing up for: trying to keep up with kids while Malcolm sits in meetings making important decisions with other important people.

I don't think I could do it. This is what I want. To explore and experience. To see the world and its history. And now that Sterling is gone, I can do that however I want to, whenever I want. No attachments. No responsibilities.

Entering a room full of objects from Ancient Greece, my newfound outlook on life is immediately tested by a couple pausing, hand in hand, to kiss in front of a collection of vases.

He tucks a strand of hair behind her ear. She gazes at him in adoration as he whispers something. I turn back the way I came, feeling like a voyeur stealing glimpses of their love story.

Sterling wasn't the man I thought he was. My father proved that. Even if I wanted to believe that Sterling would never make that video, it's not like I can ask him. He left without explanation. I wonder if one day the girl in the next room will wake up to find him gone without a goodbye, left to translate his actions. I stop to stare at one of the largest exhibits in this room: the Rosetta Stone. If only I could find Sterling's master key and unlock him, maybe then I could understand why he did it. Or didn't do it. Why he left. Why he didn't say goodbye. But maybe that's why I'm here, standing in a museum of objects lost to time. Each belonged to someone—someone with a story of their own, someone who loved and lived, someone who made mistakes and choices. It's comforting to know that it's all part of some grand, natural design that, in the end, we can't control. No matter what we think. In the end, we all die. Alone. Why not get used to that now?

The mother with the little boy and baby strolls by and smiles, but it falls from her face when our eyes meet. She points to the stone, "Read that, darling," she orders the little boy. He tilts his head and stares at it curiously, accepting the challenge. "Are you okay?"

It takes me a moment to realize, she's speaking to me—and that I'm crying. I swipe at the tears and force a smile. "Fine."

"It's a lot to take in, isn't it?" she says, wheeling the stroller over and lifting the baby into her arms. "To think that all this meant something once and now it's just here for us to press our noses to the glass and gawk at."

I can't help but laugh. "I guess you're right. I was just thinking about the inevitably of death."

"That's cheery," she says with a snort. "Going through a rough patch, love?"

"You could say that?" I can't help peeking at the baby in her arms. She's still sleeping, tiny fists curled up next to rosy cheeks that match her romper. "She's beautiful."

"She's my little rainbow after the storm," her mother agrees. "You know, that's the thing about life, you can look at the ruins and see everything that's lost or you can pick up the pieces and make something beautiful."

"What if there aren't any pieces left?" I whisper, staring at the baby.

"Our pasts always leave us something to hold onto. Sometimes we just have to dig to find it," she says, reaching over to squeeze my hand. "You'll find it. Just keep searching your heart."

She ruffles her son's hair, and he looks up at her with wide, moon-eyes. "I can't figure out what it says, Mummy."

"Well, maybe next time," she says to him seriously, winking at me. "Come along, darling."

I watch them walk away, until they disappear into the next room. Maybe she's right, and I've been thinking about this all wrong. I don't need to decipher Sterling. It's too late for that. But I need to understand what he left behind. I'm not the girl he met last August, and he's not responsible for that. Not entirely. So I can keep standing here in the ruins, looking at what's lost, or I can make something beautiful of what's left.

I'm tired of being stuck in the past—any past. Making my way through the Great Court, I leave it behind, stepping out of the museum and into bright, spring sunshine. The rain is gone, wet sidewalks the only evidence of the storm. I reach the street and begin to walk. I have no direction in mind. Maybe I'll choose to dig for those pieces Sterling left behind. Maybe I'll just wait for life to hand me new pieces. For now, I can go anywhere I choose, and the sheer freedom of that is exhilarating.

I hit a busy street a block or two away from the museum and the smell of fish and chips wafts toward me from a small restaurant. The effect is instant. My mouth waters but instead of my stomach rumbling, I clasp a hand over my mouth and nose as my stomach lurches at the greasy scent. A few people near me move away, widening the space between us. I keep my hand over my nose and cross the street quickly to get away from the terrible smell. When I finally look around, daring to uncover my face, I'm on a residential street, safe from the smell of greasy restaurants and too many people. But the only thing besides row houses is a blinking green pharmacy cross.

Life is handing me another sign. I pop inside and an older man in a white coat calls out a greeting.

I swallow, trying to calm my stomach, which is still churning a little.

"Can I help you?" he asks.

"Yeah. I was walking and I smelled fish and now I think I need..." I wonder what the equivalent to Pepto Bismol is in the UK.

He looks me up and down, no doubt taking in my pale face, and chuckles. "I've got it."

The man disappears behind the counter, and I wait at the register, pleased that the more time passes, the less queasy I feel. I'm digging out my wallet when he comes back and places a box on the counter.

I look at it and blink before laughing nervously. "Oh, I...no. I'm sorry I wanted something for my stomach."

"Read you wrong! My apologies." He pulls a bottle of chewable tablets out and replaces the box. "This should do it."

He tucks the pregnancy test under the counter as it hits me as suddenly and fiercely as the smell had a few minutes ago.

"Actually...I'll take that, too." I pay for both quickly, shoving them into my purse as I try to get my bearings and make it back to the hotel, praying Ava and Poppy are still out flirting with Scottish boys. Praying that I'm wrong. Praying that I didn't just find the piece of the past Sterling left behind.

11

STERLING

I never thought I'd come back here, but the devil must have a sense of humor because there's no time to make it to New York before I head to the next part of training. Summer's arrived in Valmont, and the campus is crowded with girls sunbathing on the quad and guys playing frisbee. The first summer session has started. It's hard to believe I should be here, trying to get ahead on my degree by taking a six-week session of Biology or some bullshit. Why did I ever think I belonged here? It looks like one of the glossy pictures in the brochure that Francie brought home my senior year. That brochure failed to mention that under the idyllic appearance, there's something rotten in Valmont. The money. The people. There's hardly a difference between the two.

I turn a few heads as I walk through campus in my freshly-pressed uniform, my hair's been cropped closely to my head. My face is cleanly shaven per expectation. I pass two girls who were in my lit class last fall and they smile at me, leaning to put their heads together. I can't help but smirk.

It seems a uniform is all it takes to have girls throwing them-selves at you. Not that I'm interested in another Valmont girl. I've learned my lesson there.

I'm not sure what to expect when I reach my old dormi-tory. I hadn't left much information about where I was going. Part of me expects to find the place empty. Maybe temporarily occupied by someone else, Cyrus long gone. I figure I might have to track down the residence hall staff to get the last of my belongings. But I guess, even rich kids need to get ahead on coursework, because Poppy leans against the wall, the door to the room cracked open. They're still here. My *friends*. Probably so they can get their corner office at daddy's firm and start their golf addictions. Seeing Poppy sends memories flooding through me. Not of her, but of eating hot chicken and birthday parties and the wedding. Memories of Adair.

"Hurry up! I'm starving," she yells.

"Found it," Cyrus calls, ducking out of the room with a book. He freezes, the door still half-open when he sees me. His eyes narrow, sweeping up and down me. "Sterling?"

I force myself forward. "I left a few books. I hope you don't mind if I..."

It occurs to me that Cy might not have kept the books. Hell, he might have a new roommate. Why hadn't I thought this through?

"Yeah, actually," he says. He casts an apologetic look at Poppy. "A few more minutes."

But she's not paying attention to him, she's too preoccu-pied murdering me with her eyes. I'm not surprised that she hates me. She's Adair's friend not mine, and she never seemed to particularly like me before I left.

"Hello, Poppy," I say casually. My uniform feels stifling

in the southern heat, but I'm glad I wore it, because her eyes flicker over it making mental notes.

Tell her where I am. Tell her I look good. Tell her I've moved on.

"I'm going to grab a bite," she tells Cyrus, pecking him on the cheek. "I'll see you in Finance." She tosses one last searing glare my way.

"Grab me a sandwich," he calls after her, but she's already gone. Cyrus sighs when she doesn't respond. "Sorry, man. It's a girl thing. Come on in."

I follow him inside the room and realize for the second time that I deluded myself coming here. Pick up some books? Tie up loose ends? That might be easier if every step I took in this city didn't remind me of her.

"It's weird seeing you in that uniform," Cyrus says. "It looks good on you."

Spoken like a true trust fund kid. Next he'll thank me for my service. I tug at my jacket, making sure there are no creases in it. "Thanks."

"I don't remember seeing any books. I think Poppy might have given them to Adair..." He moves a few piles of paper on the desk. It looks like he's actually spending time here. Maybe he always wanted to, but not with me around. It's not my room anymore. None of this is mine, so I just stand there awkwardly.

"And she probably burned them," I say dryly.

"You aren't exactly her favorite person."

I smirk, ignoring the weight his words drop on my chest. "The feeling's mutual."

After a few more minutes, he finds a stack, shoved under the bed. "Here they are."

It's only half of the ones I thought I'd find. Adair must still have some, unless she really did burn them. She returned my copy of *The Great Gatsby*—the only I really cared about getting back. For some reason, I almost wish she hadn't—like it would have meant shit for her to keep it. Her copy of *Persuasion* is gone along with the antique copy of *The Sun Also Rises* she gave me for Christmas. I shouldn't be surprised. I shouldn't be hurt. Those weren't my books anyway. These ones are mine, notes and all. It's not much reading material to take with me. Francie flat refuses to send me shit. She's still upset about what she calls my 'idiotic decision.'

"So, are you at bootcamp?" he asks.

"Finished. I have a few days before I head to Camp Lejeune for special ops assessment."

"Special ops?" Cyrus whistles, running a hand over his hair. I guess I finally impressed him. "Wow, just wow. And then?"

"More training, get stationed somewhere." I know the basics. I signed the paperwork. The details hardly matter though.

"Like Iraq or something?"

I suspect it's all the same to him. "Something like that. I don't really know."

"How long are you going to be in town?" he asks.

"Only until tomorrow," I say. "I figured I would tie a few things up. Say goodbye."

"To me?" Cyrus grins widely. "Thanks, man."

"I don't think anyone else will miss me." I have a fleeting fantasy of going to Windfall to bid Angus MacLaine farewell by pissing on the polished marble floor in the foyer. It might finally get Adair's attention. Nothing else has: not my calls or texts or emails.

"You really didn't come back to see Adair?" Cyrus presses.

"Would it matter if I did?" I shrug, ignoring how my heartbeat ratchets up at hearing her name. Sometimes, I think I dreamt her—that I dreamt all of this. But standing here now I know that's not true. All of it happened. *All of it.*

"You have a day," Cyrus says. "Look, I don't know exactly what went down between you two. She won't talk about it, even with Poppy. But I bet she wouldn't want you to wind up at war or something without saying goodbye."

"Doesn't matter. She's ignoring me. She has for months. She chose her family. You know that." He'd been the one to tell me exactly how it worked. He knows that it doesn't matter. She's made her choice—and it wasn't me.

"Write her a note," he suggests. "I'll make sure it gets to her. You've got twenty-four hours, right?"

"Yeah..." I hate the hope that surges through me at his suggestion. Cyrus might be the only way to reach her. Somewhere deep down I must have known that. I must have known that when I decided to come here rather than partying with the guys in Nashville on our last night in the states.

He grabs a notebook and a pencil for me. "I need to get to Finance and beg my girlfriend's forgiveness for fraternizing with the enemy. If you leave it here, I'll get it to her tonight. You're leaving tomorrow, right?"

"Are you sure?"

"At least, you'll know. Poppy told me something about girls wanting closure or some shit. I don't know, but it can't hurt." Cyrus claps me on the back. "Good luck, man. Stay safe. Lock the door behind you?"

"Will do," I say absently. I'm already thinking about the note—about what to say. The truth is that there's too much to say—too much we left unfinished. I can't put it all in a note, and it won't tell me what I need to know: why did she turn her back on me? Why did she choose her family over me? I know what Poppy and Cyrus said about social status and expectations. They said these things happen like I'd gotten a flat tire. I need to hear her say it before I'll believe it. In the end, I don't even try to write it all down. I settle for something simpler. A time and a place. The only way we're going to work through this is together, and if things are going to end, they should end face-to-face.

Maybe Cyrus is right and I was nothing more than a reckless fling to her, but he's wrong about one thing I realize as I fold up the note and write her name on it. This could hurt. A lot. I just have to hope it doesn't.

Hennie's is dead for a Tuesday night. My options were limited when it comes to places that mean something to her and I. There's no way I'm stepping one foot inside Windfall. Not after what her father did to me. I didn't feel comfortable asking her to my old dorm room, since I don't live there anymore. Plus, I don't want to give her the wrong idea. I only want to know why. Why she let her dad ruin me. Why she turned her back on me. Why she changed her mind about us.

I've got a few bucks in my pocket thanks to my last paycheck from the Marines, so I order a plate of hot chicken. Despite the fact that it may be the last time I ever eat the real deal, I can't find my appetite.

Henrietta herself is here, fussing in the back at the line cooks. I'd met Darcy's mother the first time I came here with my friends. If she remembers me, she doesn't say anything. Occasionally, she sweeps through the dining room and casts a look of disapproval at my full plate. But the more time that passes, the less interest I have in the food. I'd arrived early and taken up residence at a corner table. Between the location and the high-backed purple booth, the spot affords as much privacy as we're likely to get.

Not that it matters, because it's already twenty minutes past when I asked her to meet me. I can't bring myself to leave, though. Maybe she's running late.

"I know I don't have a lot of customers to scare off, but watching you sit here with a full plate for an hour isn't doing much for my self-confidence," a silky voice comments.

I look up into Henrietta's deep brown eyes. "Sorry, I'm waiting for someone."

"Is the food for her?" she asks. "Because you aren't going to impress a girl with cold chicken."

"No," I say. "It's for me—and how do you know I'm waiting for a girl?"

"I recognize when a boy is mooning after a girl," she says with a soft laugh. "When's she supposed to be here, honey?"

"Twenty-five minutes ago," I say after checking my watch.

She clucks. "That's not a good sign. You want a hot plate?"

I shake my head. I don't need her charity or her pity. "I guess I should get going."

"Stay a few minutes. Have you called her?" she suggests. "Maybe she got the time mixed up. I'm going to get you a hot plate of food."

She's off before I can stop her. There's a maternal quality

to her voice that reminds me of Francie. It's the tone she uses when she's trying to soften the blow of bad news. Francie usually tries to feed me during those times, too. But she actually might have solved my problem.

I've been assuming that Cyrus already got the note to Adair. It would be like him to forget or wait until the last minute. He's never had a striking sense of urgency. Why would he when the world usually comes to him? Pulling out my phone, I shoot him a text.

> Hey, did you give Adair the note?

Almost instantly I see the typing icon. I try to squash the swelling hope building in my chest. Even if he forgot, there's still time. I have until morning and Hennie's closes late. I can wait here until he gets it to her. I'll tell him to mention that I'm waiting.

> Dropped it off with Poppy. She gave it to her this afternoon, I think. Want me to ask if she read it?

His words prick the ballooning hope, and I deflate. Maybe she doesn't know how pressing it is to open it now, but it doesn't really matter. Poppy will have told her that I'm in town. If Adair can't even bother to open a note, then there's no way she's going to the trouble of coming all the way down here to talk.

> Don't worry about it. Thanks,
> man.

Standing up, I smooth out my uniform and drop a few dollars on the table. Not that I made much of a mess. The rest of my cohort are probably already screaming drunk somewhere on Broadway. If I hurry, I can join them and drink away the bitter taste of rejection. I'm halfway to the door when Henrietta catches up with me.

"Giving up?" she asks.

"She's not coming, and I've got a plane to catch." I force a tight-lipped smile. "Thanks, though, and sorry about the trouble."

Henrietta shakes her head and holds out a to-go bag. "You're not shipping out without a proper meal. I know they aren't going to feed you properly," she insists when I try to refuse. "And this girl? She's going to regret letting you leave."

"I doubt it."

"I don't," she says, wisdom twinkling in her smile. "Good luck."

Good luck? Nah. I'm done with luck. I'm done with her. Some things don't need to be said like goodbyes to ex-girlfriends, and some questions don't need answers like why you betrayed someone you loved. The answer to that is simple: you can't betray someone you love. You can only betray someone who means nothing to you. Maybe Adair thought she loved me. Maybe I was just some romantic idea to her—the bad boy she wanted to save. I don't know. I don't care. It's time to be done with her, with this town, with hoping my luck will change. From now on, I'm looking out for myself.

There's no one else to worry about. I decide my own fate from this day forward.

12

STERLING

THE PRESENT

I fold up the sheet, painfully aware of how the light paper feels heavy in my trembling hands, and tuck it back in the book. Then I place it back in the box—next to a pair of over-sized flip-flops I bought in another life. "I need to go."

"Sterling, I'm sorry. I..." Adair begins. She takes one step toward me, her green eyes wide with panic as a million scenarios play out on her face. Fear and hope and desperation and sadness.

And suddenly, I understand the woman standing before me now in a way that I never have before—in a way, I never realized she needed to be understood. And finally, I understand what's really at stake.

Turning away from her, I unknot the sash at my waist and shuck the robe from my shoulders. I hear every word she's not saying. They hang in the air between us—unspoken and unsatisfying. I don't trust myself to look at her. Not yet. I don't know if it takes me a minute or an hour to get dressed. I'm too absorbed in every motion, coaching myself through each button, each tuck, each knot. When I finally stand from lacing my shoes, I force my gaze up to where she stands like a statue next to a room service cart piled with cold food.

But statues don't cry, and there are tears in Adair's eyes. Part accusation and part heartbreak, looking at her rips a hole in my chest and exposes the missing piece of it I didn't know existed. I've carried a hole in my heart for years. I thought it was down to losing her. Now I know what I really lost when I left all those years ago.

And now I know why Adair's walls were so high when I came back, why she tried to stop me from scaling them, why she was scared to let me breach them. She couldn't let me back into the places she'd carved for me in her heart. That space no longer existed. I couldn't be the person she loved most in the world.

"I need to go," I repeat. Can't she see that? Can't she understand why?

Her head bows in defeat, a single tear falling freely through the air.

Sometimes, I forget that for a woman who was born with everything, there's one thing money has never bought her: forgiveness.

I cross to her, closing the distance between us in three long strides. Folding her in my arms, I pull her against my chest. Even this close, her body remains rigid. She's holding on to all of it: the truth, the secrets, the pain. I can't take that away from her. Not yet. I can only give her something else to cling to for now.

"I love you," I whisper into her hair. "Nothing changes that, but I have to go."

A choked sob escapes from her throat, and she sinks her fingernails into my forearms. "I can explain," Her voice cracks. "I should—"

"No," I stop her. I grip her chin and tilt her face to mine. Tears flow freely now—two currents pulling her into the past and threatening to take me with her. "There's nothing to explain."

"But—"

"I want to know," I reassure her, brushing away her tears with my thumb. "I want to know everything that you want to tell me. But you don't owe me shit, Lucky. Not an apology. Not an explanation."

"How can you say that?" She shakes her head, her copper waves slipping over her shoulders. "Why don't you hate me?"

"Isn't it obvious? I've never hated you. That's why." My palm rests on her cheek, hoping she understands what I finally do. "Love doesn't come with conditions. Not true love. Not our love."

"Don't leave."

I hear what she's really saying: don't abandon me. Don't walk out the door and disappear. *Don't leave again.*

I want to give Adair everything she deserves, but I can't stay. Not today. I gently pry her fingers off my arms and step away. I can't explain it to her. Not yet. An hour ago, Adair MacLaine was the most important person in the world to me.

She can't be anymore.

"I love you," I repeat as if saying it can numb the pain of what comes next for either of us. But I feel the anguish anyway, stretching taut between us with each step I take away from her—from the life I'd let myself imagine, from the life I'd decided to fight for, from the life that's no longer possible. I can only hope that whatever comes next doesn't break this thread that connects her to me. I have to believe that on the other side of this battle, there's something better waiting— for all three of us.

As soon as the door closes behind me, I remember that my car is blocks away. My hand pauses mid-knock. I can't go back yet. I can't risk facing her, even if it's only to ask for her car keys. Instead, I walk down the hall and pound on Luca's door.

"Be home, be home, be home," I mutter, continuing to bang on the suite.

Muffled cursing comes from the other side, but I don't stop knocking. The door flies open. "What in the actual fuck?" he growls. Instantly, his expression turns from annoyance to confusion. "What's up, brother? Christ, I thought housekeeping had gone feral. Come in."

I don't move, except to hold out my hand. "I need your car."

"You need...what?" Luca scratches his head. "Why? Where's yours?"

"It's a long story, and this is an emergency."

He knows I'm not asking. Luca steps to the side. "Let me grab my keys."

I step into the threshold, mentally counting each second it takes for him to cross the room. The keys are lying next to the disassembled pieces of a Glock and a cleaning cloth. That's when I remember I left my holster and 9mm in Adair's suite.

Luca grabs the keys and tosses them, they arc through the air and land in my palm. "Do you want me to call it around?"

I shake my head. I'm not waiting for a valet, even if my friend's VIP status probably jumps him to the head of the line. "I know where they park them."

"What about back-up?" Luca asks as I turn to go. "Two might be better than one in an emergency."

Not this emergency, I think to myself. I can't drag anyone

else into this. I shake my head and my eyes fall on the pieces of his gun. "I need to do this alone, but if you don't mind, I could use a piece."

Luca slides the pieces of his weapon together with a precision that can only come from being the bastard child of an elite military unit and a criminal fixer. He carries it to me and holds it out. "You know what you're doing?"

"Nope," I admit. Taking it, I tuck it securely in my waistband and loosen my shirt to cover it. "But I'll figure it out."

It's easier than it should be to get Luca's car out of the Eaton's valet parking lot. Getting out of Nashville at this hour less so. I can't unleash the BMW's twin-turbo V8 until I reach the interstate. Even then, I'm forced to weave through people heading to the suburbs at the end of day, making it impossible to floor it. I barely get the coupe over one-hundred miles per hour before I reach the Valmont exit.

"Name?" A new guard asks at the gate to Windfall.

This isn't going to end well. "Sterling Ford."

My hand slips from the steering wheel to the 9mm tucked into my waistband. Given the last time I visited the MacLaine estate I threatened to burn it down, I doubt I'm still on the approved list. That doesn't leave me many options.

The guard wanders back over to the window and leans down. There's a name badge pinned to his khaki shirt that says Ken. "I'm sorry. I'm not supposed to let you in," he says. "In fact, my information tells me to call the house if you swing by."

My fingertips graze the grip of my gun, the metal is warm from being against my body during the drive. Part of knowing how to handle a road block is not over-reacting. A knee jerk reaction will only result in disaster. Pulling a gun will only make Ken panic, and a panicked Ken will probably wind up a dead Ken. That's not why I came here today. In fact, it's counter-productive. The last thing I want is to leave Tennessee until this matter is settled.

"Typical," I say with a shake of the head, putting my hand back on the steering wheel. "Does Malcolm MacLaine treat all of his sister's boyfriends this way? He's such a dick."

"Honestly?" Ken scratches his ear and smiles. "I haven't been working here long enough to know, but, um, yeah. He's definitely a dick."

Never underestimate the power of finding common ground with someone. There's no easier path to making an ally than finding a common enemy. Or, at least, a pain in the ass. Now that I've got Ken on my side, I have to hope my next move doesn't blow up in my face. "Look, I know Adair and he had a fight. What's new? But she arranged for me to swing by and pick up some stuff."

"I wish I could..." He looks nervously over at the gate like he's really weighing his options. "Maybe if you came back with Miss MacLaine?"

"It's best we keep the two of them apart until they've both cooled off. Trust me. You don't want to stoke a MacLaine temper." Adair is the last person I want here. I don't know how she'll react when she finds out I came. I don't know if she'll try to intervene, but nothing is going to stand in my way. Not today. Still, I'd rather not have to kill Ken. "Can you call Felix? He knows all about this. Just tell him Sterling came by for Adair."

Ken chews on his lips before shrugging. "Why not? I mean, he practically owns the place."

He's trudging back to the guardhouse before I can ask him what that means. Felix practically owns the place? Since when? Adair told me that her father's will was surprising, but it can't have been that generous. I'm still contemplating the offhand remark when the gate opens.

"You're good," Ken calls, waving me through.

My foot stays on the brake pedal. "What did you mean about Felix owning the place?"

"I guess when the old man kicked it, he didn't leave the place to his kids," my new friend tells me.

"He left it to Felix?" That doesn't make sense.

"Nah. He's in charge of the trust or something until the grandkid is old enough. She gets it all. At least, that's what my buddy told me."

"Wow." I force myself to shrug this off like it's not a bombshell. "Good luck, man."

"You, too," he calls as I put the BMW into drive.

Driving toward Windfall feels different this time. I can't see it the same way, but I'm not sure what to do with all this new information. So, Angus MacLaine stuck it to his kids one final time? I'm not surprised about that. I don't doubt his intentions there at all. He didn't leave Windfall to his grand-daughter to take care of her or because he loved her. Maybe he told himself that's why he did it, but there wasn't a soft bone in that man's body for anyone, even his own daughter. If he left his estate to Ellie, he did it as one final show of disappointment in both his children. I don't know what Malcolm did to earn his disapproval. In my experience, it never took much to get on the patriarch's bad side.

But Angus MacLaine's motives dissolve from my mind as I pull around to the back of the house. I shut off the engine and draw out the gun. After staring at it for a moment, I reach over and shove it in the glove box on top of the fresh-from-the-dealership manual. I'm not here to start a war. Not yet.

My feet feel heavy as I walk toward the back door. It's as if my body isn't sure it wants me to take this any further. If only it could be that simple. Each step closer sends my heart pounding, blood pumping through my veins so hard that it pounds in my ears. Part of me wants to turn around and leave. Part of me knows that's what's best for her—for both of them. But I'm tired of being rootless. I'd made a decision about Adair and the future. I don't know what her secret means for that. I don't know what it means for me. But even as part of me feels tugged in the opposite direction, there's something stronger driving me forward. It doesn't care about my heavy feet or my racing heart or how I wound up here, it only cares about one thing.

The door swings open before I reach it and Felix studies me, wiping his hands on his apron before planting them on his hips. He's never been my biggest fan. In truth, he doesn't really know me. Despite everything Adair and I went through all those years ago, there's so much of her life she closed off to me. I used to think it was because she was ashamed of me. Now I know that it's her instinct: hide, protect, don't rock the boat. Felix knows that. It's why he let me through that gate.

"Adair's things are in storage. She already took everything earlier," he informs me, "but I suspect you know that."

"I do." Lying won't get me anywhere with him, and now, more than ever, I need him on my side. "I need to see her."

"See...her?" Felix tilts his head, a confused wrinkle deepening between his eyebrows. His mouth opens, and for a split second, I wonder if I'm wrong—if he doesn't know. But before he speaks, his jaw drops, and he stares at me. "You know?"

"I do now." A painful ache swells in my throat, and I swallow hard. The ache only builds until it's as powerful as the pounding in my chest.

He only stares, and it's in that moment that I realize there's a reason that Adair said the father was unknown on that document. No one knows—not for certain—except she and I.

I have to make him understand.

"I just need to see her." I take another step toward the door but he blocks it.

"I'm not certain that's a good idea," Felix says evenly. "Her parents..."

He trails away as I double over, shoulders beginning to shake. There's too much. Too much blood pounding in my body. Too strong a force dragging me forward. My heart is beating too fast, as though it's struggling to keep beating with the gaping hole at its core. "You don't understand." I force my eyes up, and for the first time in years, I don't hide my tears. "I have to see her. I didn't know."

"You..." Felix hesitates before moving aside to let me into the kitchen. "I'm afraid things are quite complicated."

It takes every ounce of strength I possess to straighten up and cross the threshold.

"What did Adair tell you?" he asks.

I shake my head. I don't know how to explain the truth—that she didn't tell me anything. That I'm the *unknown* in the box on a faded decree of legal guardianship.

"I just..." It's hard to speak. Until this moment the worst moment of my life was on a snowy night in New York, watching a kind woman lead my sister out of the room. I'd failed Sutton so many times, and I'd tricked myself into believing I'd made up for those mistakes—that I'd become a man.

But now I see I've been a boy playing the part, talking a big game, and missing the point. Any boy can get a girl pregnant.

But a man doesn't abandon his child. A man doesn't walk away from the woman he loves. A man stays. A man protects. And it takes a man to be a father.

"I didn't know." I repeat it like the words can absolve me of my sin. "If I had..."

I expect Felix to laugh at me. To mock me. To lecture me. I deserve it. I deserve much, much worse. Instead, he crosses to me and does the last thing I expect. He hugs me.

The last levee breaks and it floods out of me: the pain, the anger, the hatred. I've been holding it inside for years, letting it power me, but, more importantly, letting it hide the ugliness that can't be directed outward. The weakness. The inadequacy. The shame. I thought I could make myself a man by locking away the homeless boy, the scholarship kid, the dishonored soldier. But the only chance I ever had at becoming a man—a real man—has been right here all along.

And that's when I finally understand why I had to come —why it couldn't wait.

"I just need to know she's okay." I step back and square my shoulders.

Felix considers this. "And that's all you came here for?"

"Yes," I say, "for now."

"Is that a threat?" he asks, his face unreadable.

"No. It's a promise. There are things I don't know." I swallow, wondering how painful it will be to face the truth and knowing I have no choice. Not anymore. "I just need to know my daughter is safe."

"Of course she's safe."

I can't help feeling like a mouse trapped by a cat who wants to play with it for a while before deciding whether to eat it or not. Felix holds all the cards. He knows it. The whole family knows it. "I know you're taking care of her. I've seen you with her. That night here." For some reason the memory of sharing hot chocolate with Ellie tugs at my lips, but I refuse to smile. I can't risk allowing the memories to bombard me. "I won't say anything to her. I just need to see her. Please."

"I'm trusting your word on that. Ellie is fragile since her au...since Adair left. She needs stability, not more adults using her," he says. "Adair has always looked out for her—as best as she could. Her family hasn't made that easy for her."

"But Ellie doesn't know?" Is it so bad here that without Adair around, only Felix notices her?

"A child always knows," he says meaningfully. "So let me ask you one more time, is this all you came for?"

I don't know what answer Felix is looking for, but I know one thing. I promised Adair I was all in. I didn't know then how much more that promise would demand of me, but somehow I not only know that I'm all in, I know that I have no other choice. "For now."

"Wait here." Felix disappears from the kitchen, leaving me to my thoughts.

There's so much I don't know. I don't know why Adair did it. I don't know why she hid things from me—from the world. I don't know who else knows, but I suspect no one outside the MacLaine family. But despite all of that, I know her better than I ever have before.

I know why Adair MacLaine stayed in Valmont.

I know why she put up with her father and her brother.

I know why she gave up every dream she ever had.

I know why, after all these years, I came back to find her heart still broken.

Because she's had a walking reminder of what we lost when we gave up on each other—and I know now that Adair MacLaine never gave up on me. She never stopped loving me, and she sacrificed herself to protect the last unbroken piece of our love.

"Where are we going?" a small voice floats into the kitchen from the hall.

My knees threaten to buckle, but I remember what Felix said. She needs stability. I can give her that much for now. Maybe it will be enough.

He rounds the corner, and then she comes into view.

And she is her mother and she is me.

She is everything.

Her coppery hair is plaited into braids, and when she turns an appraising look up at me, I see my eyes staring back at me. "You again? Auntie Dair isn't here. Neither is my dad."

But I'm right here. I want to say it. I want to throw her over my shoulder and take her away from this place before it can hurt her like it did Adair. It takes every ounce of self-control I possess to stop myself from doing it. My eyes flicker to Felix. He's watching me carefully. Does he know what I'm thinking?

Would he stop me?

"Me again," I say, my mouth going dry. I clear my throat. "I actually popped by to check on you—for your aunt."

"Okay." This seems to satisfy her. She shifts to look at Felix. "Are there cookies?"

"What do you think?" he asks.

"We have a guest," she says seriously. "We should probably be *hospital*."

"Yes, we should be *hospitable*," Felix corrects her gently.

"Yes, *hospital*," she says stubbornly, and in that moment, I know that I'm not in love with the idea of her—of a family. I just love her. In a way, it's like she's always been there. No conditions. No fears. No walls. She has all of me.

"Shall we?" I flinch at how my voice cracks, but my little hostess doesn't notice.

She climbs onto a barstool and I join her. "Felix makes the best cookies."

"I've had them," I admit to her.

"Was your heart broken?" Her eyes are blue saucers and she reaches for my hand. "Felix says these cookies cure heartbreak and hang-somethings."

I fight a smile at the same time my whole body soaks up the feeling of her tiny soft hand on the back of mine. "Something like that."

"Felix made me these cookies because my heart is broken," she confides.

I resist the urge to carry her off again. "Who broke your heart?"

"Auntie Dair. She left," Ellie says sadly. "Dad made her. He called her a no-word."

"A no-word?"

"You can't say no-words or you get in trouble," she tells me. She peeks over to see if Felix is listening. "I don't think Auntie Dair is a no-word."

"Me either," I agree. I realize now that every reason I had before to hate Malcolm MacLaine was immature, at best, and shallow, at worst. I know because the hate I feel now is pure, molten. It comes from some primitive, previously untapped source. The same force fueling my desire to pick up Ellie and take her away from Windfall forever.

Felix places a plate of cookies in front of us followed by two glasses of milk.

"Thank you," Ellie chirps, instantly cheered up. She picks up a cookie as big as her tiny hand, but instead of eating it she holds it out to me. "For you."

"Thank you." I take it, unsure how I'll manage to swallow a single bite with the lump in my throat.

Felix takes off his apron and folds it up. "I need to check on some matters upstairs," he says, placing it on the counter. "There's more milk in the fridge. Ellie come and find me when you're finished with your snack. Mr. Ford, help yourself *to the cookies.*"

He waits until I nod. His message is clear: he's trusting me. I have no idea why. I don't owe the MacLaines anything, especially not my daughter.

I could walk out of here with her. How far could I get before they realize she's gone? Will he be the one to sound the alarm? Will he wait for one of her parents to look for her? I have a sinking suspicion that I could be out of Tennessee before anyone else notices. I look at the door. All I have to do is walk through it. Instinct will take me from there.

Next to me, Ellie's head swivels to follow mine. "Do you have to go?"

"Not yet." The longer I take to decide, the less time I have on the road.

"Are you going to Auntie Dair? Will you take me to see her?" she asks in a small voice.

My eyes shutter as all my plans evaporate. I can't leave.

Not like this. It isn't fair to either of them, and, in the end, it will only make what I need to do harder.

Felix understands that. It's why he left me with her. I don't have a choice but to leave her here and trust that everything will work out. It's what Adair's done for years. She's no fool. If she hasn't made a move, there's something blocking her from doing so.

"I wish I could," I say softly, reaching for another cookie —this time for my own heart's sake. "I bet we can find a way for you to see her soon."

"Really soon?" Ellie asks.

"It's my first priority," I say.

Ellie's pink lips purse, her blue eyes narrowing like her mothers do when she's tuning her bullshit meter. Finally, she sticks out her hand, pinky out. "Promise?"

I hook my own pinky through hers and shake. "I'm all in, kid. Promise."

"What is going on here?" a shrill voice cuts in, and Ellie shrinks back. My memories flash to the night I met her. She made herself small then, when her parents reprimanded her for speaking to me.

Without thinking, I turn my body to shield her from the intruder as Ginny MacLaine bounds into the room, a basket of fresh flowers hanging from her arm. She stops and her glare transforms from fury to horror.

"You aren't supposed to be here," she spits, brandishing a pair of gardening shears with her free hand. "You need to leave before I call the police."

I take a deep breath, willing myself to stay calm, if only for one reason. Shifting to look at Ellie, I give her another cookie. "Go find Felix, kid."

Her eyes—my eyes in her perfect face—dart between us

finally landing on her mother. "We were just having cookies and he said I could see Auntie Dair and—"

"He did?" Ginny's face matches her hair, and I know she's about to blow. "Well, Miss Ellie, you better believe—"

"I'll talk to your mom about it," I cut in. It makes me sick to call Ginny her mother, especially with how she's acting. "Better go find Felix."

Ellie's sense of self-preservation—one honed by years of living here, I have no doubt—kicks in and she swings her legs around. Before she can hop off, my hand shoots out to steady her.

"I'm much obliged," she says, reaching up to the counter to grab her cookie before she scuttles off.

When I turn back to Ginny, the red-hot rage has drained leaving her white as a sheet. "You need to leave," she says with a trembling voice. "I will call the police. The guard shouldn't have let you in. Malcolm made sure of that."

"Because of the last time I was here," I ask her coolly, "or because you don't want me near Ellie."

"Be-be-because," she stammers as she drops the basket on the kitchen island followed by the shears. "I don't need a reason. A grown man should not be alone with a child. It's inappropriate."

I slide off the stool, straightening until we're at eye level. "Not if the man's her father."

Ginny falters, her hands splaying to catch herself on the marble counter. "I don't know what you're talking about."

"Let's not play dumb. You've known the whole time. Malcolm might have been too focused on his career four years ago, but you..." I pace to the end of the island. "You remember me, don't you? That's your job. Remembering all those important details your husband forgets, like the name of the man who knocked up your sister-in-law—the man whose child you stole."

"We adopted Ellie," Ginny snaps. "Adair was in no position to—"

"Honestly," I interrupt, "I'm not interested in your side of the story."

"How dare you come here acting high and mighty when you vanished? We did you a favor."

"Is that what you see when you look at her? A favor? A responsibility?"

"Of course not. We've given her everything money can buy: the best nannies, toys. She's traveled. Look at the life we've given her and tell me how Adair could have done that alone without a penny to her name."

My blood freezes as the truth spills from her. I know she's being honest, because only someone as thoughtfully narcissistic as a MacLaine would brag about shaking someone down for her child so she could play house. But just as quickly, the molten rage is back, thawing my chilled veins. "Is that how you did it? Well, she's not penniless anymore."

"Is that what you think?" Ginny laughs, the sound high and piercing like nails on a chalkboard. "I thought you knew Angus left us all with practically nothing. So if that's your plan, to sweep her off her feet and take her family fortune—"

"Adair doesn't need money, she can take care of herself and our daughter."

Ginny winces at the reminder that Ellie isn't truly hers. "I doubt her little publishing company is going to pay for Kindergarten at Valmont Prep next year. It probably can't even pay for a birthday party. So stop calling her *your daughter*."

"She *is* my daughter." I'll keep saying it until it sinks in. "My flesh. My blood."

"And you left her," Ginny roars.

"I wouldn't have left if I'd known."

"Not Ellie. You left Adair. She did what she had to do to survive, because that's what people like us do. We don't fail. We find a way."

There was a time when her words might have struck. Not anymore. Because I no longer see the MacLaines or their family name or their money as marks of superiority. Every mistake, every sin, every crime, every choice—it's led me to this moment. "You have no idea who you're dealing with," I say, "but you will."

"You'll never win," she says as I walk toward the door. "We have better lawyers and resources. She belongs to us now."

My hand pauses on the knob and I resist the urge to yell at her. To tell her that Ellie isn't an object, something to possess or spend money on. She's a child. She's a family. She's Christmas mornings and scraped knees and chocolate chip cookie dates. And that's why it's easier to restrain myself than I would have thought, because now I know exactly why I will win—and why we'll win: because we have something worth fighting for.

13

ADAIR

He can't avoid me forever.

I look at the book sitting in the box. Next to it there's a tiny white cardboard box, smashed a bit from being shoved in with the books. I open it and stare at the silver charm inside. I've never worn it. By the time, I'd found it in the car—my long-lost birthday present— after Sterling had left, it had felt more like a bad omen than a good luck charm. Now, I take the silver four leaf clover charm out. It takes me a second of digging to find an old jewelry box. I string the charm onto a necklace I find inside and clasp it around my neck. It helps me feel closer to him, and let's face it, I can use all the luck I can get.

Because Sterling finally knows.

The thought is as comforting as it is nerve-wracking. Deep down I know where Sterling went, which is why, after I throw on a pair of jeans and a t-shirt, I get in my car and drive aimlessly through Nashville. I feel the tug on my heart, drawing me toward Valmont and Windfall and the truth. But the idea of facing them both is too much. When I find myself pulling into Poppy's building. I'm not sure what I plan to say to her. By the time, I reach her unit and knock, the whole twisted story is on my tongue ready to spill out of my mouth.

"Adair!" Cyrus's eyebrows raise when he finds me on his doorstep. His jacket is off, shirtsleeves rolled to his elbows and top button undone.

"Is Poppy here?" I ask hurriedly, peeking past him and praying to hear her soothing accent drift down the hall.

"She met her mom for a fundraising meeting. She'll be back in a few hours." He steps to the side. "You're welcome to hang out."

Cyrus takes a deep breath, moving into the doorframe. His hands slide up the metal threshold, and he leans closer. I catch a hint of whiskey on his breath. I bite my lip to keep back a sharp response and shake my head.

"I don't bite," he murmurs. "What's wrong with two old friends hanging out?"

"I just needed to talk to her," I say, bypassing his question. It's not that I don't trust him. It's more that I know how easily alcohol muddies up his brain. "Can you tell her I stopped by?"

"Sure." He straightens up, his mouth drooping at the corners. "I'm your loyal servant."

"Thanks." I hurry away before he can draw the conversation out any farther. I might have known him since we were kids but there's no way I'm going to talk to him about what just happened. For one thing, I don't exactly trust Cyrus Eaton. We might have grown up together, but being privy to his adolescence didn't instill a lot of confidence in me. For the other, I don't think he'd be much comfort to me. Poppy definitely would be. She'd promise me that everything would turn out fine. She'd tell me whatever it took to soothe the frenzy vibrating inside me.

But I can't deny that in the end, she's not the person I need to talk to about this. There's only one person that can help me make this right. There's only one person I need to explain myself to—only one person who needs to forgive me. And I know where to find him.

Percy is on duty when I arrive at Twelve and South. He greets me with a tip of his hat. "Miss MacLaine."

I smile warmly, doing my best to ignore the butterflies in my stomach.

"Lovely evening," he says as I step inside the elevator. "But I don't believe Mr. Ford is home."

"I'll wait," I say firmly, more for my benefit than his. I'm going to park myself in front of Sterling's door because I can't stand this secret burning inside me any longer. I've kept my mouth shut for years like I had to, but it's killing me.

"If you promise not to tell," Percy says in a whisper, "I'll let you in. I'm sure Mr. Ford won't mind."

I wish I shared that confidence, but it's not as though Sterling would just leave me standing in the hall. Whatever reckoning is coming between us, we'll do it in person this time. He says he still loves me. I don't know how he can. After he sees her—our daughter—that's going to change. He's going to realize that I fucked up. Big time.

"Are you feeling okay, Miss MacLaine?" Percy asks, the wrinkles on his forehead deepening under the brim of his hat.

"It's been a long day." It's the truth but not all of it. The truth is that it's been a long four years.

When we reach the top floor, Percy whistles as he takes out a master key and opens the door a crack. A second later, Zeus's nose shoves through the door.

"I think he's happy to see you," Percy says. "You know where to find me if you need me."

"Thank you." I wait until he's back inside the elevator to open the door the rest of the way, so Zeus won't bound down the hall after him. He's all over me as I step inside, jumping on his hind legs to give me kisses.

"He doesn't act that way when he sees me," a cutting voice remarks.

I look up sharply and find Sutton's blue eyes staring back at mine, her hands on her hips. She's wearing a worn tank-top and shorts, both articles of clothing short enough to show off as much of her pearly skin as possible.

"Sutton," I say in surprise. "I didn't know you'd be here."

"Sterling did," she says, nothing but her mouth moving. "I guess that means you haven't talked to him."

"I did, actually." I hesitate. If I had a hater club, Sterling's sister would be the president. We've barely spoken to each other, but it's clear she despises me.

She tosses her dark hair over her shoulder and saunters toward the living room. "And what? You lost him?"

It's a disturbingly accurate synopsis of my current predicament, but I keep this to myself. "He had to run an errand. I'm meeting him here."

"Nice of him to call," she grumbles as she plops onto the couch. Zeus jumps up and lays his massive head in her lap. She pats it absently while I take a chair across from her.

Traitor.

"So, how long are you in town?" I ask.

She gives me a look that clearly says *are we really doing this* and shrugs.

Okay, I search for a new topic. "Do you still live in New York?"

"Most of the time," she says.

"Are you in school?" I know she's younger than him, but that's about all I know about Sutton, except that she grew up with a different foster family.

"Not at the moment," she says with a smirk.

I'm reminded of the first time I met Sterling. He'd been an asshole from minute one. Apparently, the trait runs in the family. The trouble is, I know a thing or two about Fords. Most of the time, they're putting on an act. The smirking, arrogant disdain? It's just a survival mechanism. How long had it taken Sterling to warm up to me?

I don't have time for games like that now.

"So, you think I'm a bitch," I say, recalling the text conversation I'd accidentally read between her and Sterling.

"If it walks like a duck and it talks like a duck." She shrugs.

"You don't know me."

Her eyes roll so far back, they nearly stick there. "Let's see. Poor little rich girl. Dead mom. Dead dad. Depleted trust fund. Everything handed to you on a silver platter. Then again, that platter's a little picked over these days, isn't it? Daddy passed it around a bit too much?"

This time, I shrug. "Knowing someone's circumstances and knowing who they really are—those are different things."

"Spare me a dramatic story of how you've never fit in here," she says theatrically, pressing a hand to her forehead for affect, "and how you wish I could see we're not so different after all."

"Oh, we're different," I say, relishing the surprise that passes through her familiar eyes. "I might be rich..."

"*Were* rich," she corrects me. "I hear your little Scrooge McDuck money vault is a bit empty these days."

"I might have been rich," I say, not bothering to argue with her, "but I've lost people."

"You think I haven't lost people?" She jumps to her feet, dethroning Zeus who whines as her eyes flash.

"I know you have. You just got some of them back. And you got new people—a new family. Not all of us are that lucky," I say.

"Us?" she repeats. "What? You think that you have more in common with Sterling than I do? I'm his sister."

"A shared past doesn't mean you're the same," I say, patting my knee to call Zeus to me. "It just means you're connected."

"Oh my god! Is this little TED Talk over yet? I heard you were full of shit, but I had no idea it was going to be this bad." She stomps over to the kitchen and disappears. A second later there's an annoyed huff and she returns with a bottle of water. "Why can't he keep any booze here? How is anyone supposed to be around you sober?"

I stare at her. "Are you really asking that?"

"I know." Another eye roll before she continues in a singsong voice, "*Your father was an alcoholic. You should stay away from that stuff.* Look just because my dad drank doesn't mean that I'm a fuck-up, too."

"I'm not saying that."

"Please."

If she rolls her eyes one more time, I think I might actually slap her.

"Sterling doesn't drink," I say. "That's why he doesn't keep booze here."

"I know he doesn't drink, but that doesn't mean—"

"Have you ever been around him when he's been drinking?" I cut her off.

"No."

"Then, consider yourself fortunate," I murmur.

"Of course that's how you'd feel about it." Frost coats her voice, her eyes equally cold like the sky on a wintery morning. "Love has conditions, right?"

"No, it doesn't. But watching someone you love do that to themselves, it hurts you as much as it hurts them." I swallow, remembering the last time I'd seen Sterling with a bottle of whiskey before he left Valmont. Before everything went wrong.

"Sterling knows how to control himself," she spits back.

"No, I learned to stop looking for answers at the bottom of a bottle," he interrupts as the door clicks closed. "It turns out you never find any truth there."

I'm vaguely aware that Sutton turns toward him at the same time I do, but there's no room inside me for anything more than this overwhelming cocktail of giddiness and nerves and fear and hope I feel when I look at him. His hair is mussed either from our lovemaking or from him trying to pull it out of his head. It must be the latter, because it feels like a million years since he carried me to bed at the Eaton. A lifetime has passed since the last time I felt his lips on mine. Somehow the time apart feels longer than the years we spent separated before his return to Tennessee.

"She let herself in," Sutton says, tossing a contemptuous look my way. "I had no idea things were that serious between you two."

Sterling and I just keep staring at each other before he finally turns to her.

"It's that serious," he says.

"What? After everything? After her family just chewed

up everyone in their path and spit them out?" she shrieks. "After what her dad did to you?"

"Exactly," he says firmly. "Her dad did that."

"And she's completely innocent? Sorry, bro, I don't buy it. These people are rotten. Look at how they covered up her mother's death. That's fucked—"

"Enough," Sterling cuts her off.

"How does she know about my mom?" I ask in confusion, but as soon as the question is out of my mouth, pieces fall into place. "You sold the story to the news."

"Sell it?" Her eyebrows lift. "I did that shit for free. It was a public service."

"Goddammit, Sutton," Sterling mutters, pinches the bridge of his nose, peeking quickly at me. "That was a secret."

"It was," I remind him. He can't be mad at her for spilling it, since he's the one who told her.

"I don't understand how you came here hating her and now, well, look at you," she storms.

"Sometimes we get love and hate confused," he confesses. "Look, I promise I'll explain things, but right now, I need to talk to Adair."

"But—"

"Alone," he adds.

"I'm going to Jack's," she says furiously, grabbing a slouchy suede bag and throwing it over her shoulder. "At least he has booze."

"Sutton, don't do anything stupid," Sterling says.

Sutton levels a look of hatred so red-hot, I feel it burning on my skin. "Fine, but don't go easy on her."

The door slams shut behind her, and I close my eyes briefly, as I find myself alone with the man I love—the man I've been lying to for months.

14

STERLING

"Fine, but don't go easy on her," Sutton says, giving Adair a searing look of hatred on her way out.

The thunderous crash of the slamming door jolts Adair, who turns to look at me with the strangest expression I've ever seen. Regret and fear swirl across her beautiful face, and it's not clear if one or the other will win, or if both together will kill her where she stands. Her fire—which burns the color of her hair, which sheds light from every pore of her skin, and which I was sure could never be quenched—drowns under tears.

"Sterling, please," she says, her face contorting into a wicked funhouse mirror of itself. "I...I can..."

This life I've missed, the one we promised each other all those years ago, it was taken from me. Why doesn't matter—not yet. What I need is to take it back. Starting with her.

"Lucky—"

"Don't be mad, Sterling, I can explain. There's so much you don't know..." she trails off again when she sees me move towards her, shrinking inside herself with every step I take.

"You were mine. They took you from me. You *let* them take you from me. You *let* them take an entire life that *should have been mine!*" She turns away from me, but I snatch the point of her chin and force her to look at me. "Did you think I wouldn't claim what's mine?"

Her eyes, wide as the moon but dim as an eclipse, meet mine at last, but she says nothing. After all this time and everything we've been through, she still doesn't understand. She's been conditioned to expect the worst, especially when it comes to love.

"Answer!" I command.

"I thought you left," she says feebly. "You did leave."

"Wrong, Lucky. You're so fucking wrong. I never left."

A flicker of recognition dawns. "I didn't know. I thought—"

"I know *exactly* what you thought. You thought I was gone and wouldn't return. You thought they beat me. You believed *them*. But you belong *to me*." I watch realization dawn. A ragged sob escapes her lips, but it's not regret or fear that sends her tears streaming down her cheeks—it's relief.

"People lie to themselves their whole lives," I whisper. "They let others confuse or deceive them. I can't let that happen to us again."

I spin Adair away from me, drawing her backside against me and plunging my hand down the front of her jeans and capturing her mound with my hand. It swells, hot and wet, in my palm, and when my other hand tangles amid the hair at the base of her scalp, Adair melts against me. I twist the handful of her hair, bringing her lips to mine, claiming her with my mouth as my hands possess her body.

"You belong to me. It's inevitable. Indisputable. Don't even try to argue with me. Do you understand?"

Slick heat answers for her, her body comprehending instantly. I plunge my fingers inside her, releasing the moans of pleasure always there waiting for me.

"These lips are mine," I say, nipping the corner of her bottom lip, *hard*. A single drop of blood trails down her chin, dropping onto the mound of her breast. She barely registers the pain. She trembles, giving up the last remnants of her fear, as she's reborn in the safety of my possession.

Releasing her hair, I yank her shirt off with my free hand, my other continuing to massage away any remaining doubt. I throw the shirt across the room, watching her breasts sway in her bra. The sight of her body, even half-clothed, sends blood pumping into my cock.

"These breasts are mine," I say again, gripping one tenderly, then roughly.

"Sterling," she says, like she's calling to me from across a pitch black room. "I'm yours."

Two small words that mean everything.

She understands. Her words unlock my cage, unleashing me from all restraint. I spin her back towards me, and our mouths collide with desperate longing. I pop the button and zipper of her jeans, and wrench them down below her hips. She takes over the task eagerly, kicking off her shoes and wiggling out of the skin-tight fabric while I free my eager cock from my pants. Its head thumps against the soft fullness of her stomach, and my balls constrict painfully.

I coax her backwards, my hands on her shoulders, until she bumps into the wall of the kitchen. My fingers grip the elastic stretching over one hip, and she goes rigid, standing ready, willing, for whatever I want to do to her next. Locking eyes with her, I snap the elastic and a soft moan slips past her lips.

"You're so fucking perfect," I murmur, my hands moving to snap the other side. Her eyes roll back a little and she groans as I slide the ruined fabric across her drenched pussy and bring it to my face.

Her gaze flickers to the left, pink blooming on her cheeks, and I smirk. "What's wrong, Lucky?"

"I..." Her teeth sink into her lower lip, her eyes still carefully looking past me.

I redirect her chin, so that it's impossible for her to avoid my stare, then I inhale deeply. "All these years and you still smell like magnolias and vanilla, like new books and forever."

Her throat slides as I let the panties fall to the ground, and I lean to kiss her collarbone.

I bend and lift her, hooking her knees over my forearms and pinning her against the wall. Taking a moment, I appreciate the sight: her creamy thighs splayed wide, a soft thatch of coppery hair, and *her*, pink and wet and waiting. Her arms circle my neck and lock around it like she's holding on for the ride.

"I'm going to fuck you until you can't remember anything but my name," I growl, thrusting inside her, splitting her cleft and eliciting a sound so exquisite I could never in a million years tell if it is more full of pleasure or pain, more full of tension or relief.

"Tell me, does it feel good to belong to me? " I ask, claiming all of her with all of me.

"Yes," she admits, and if I have any doubt whether she truly understands what I'm telling her, it vanishes when she begs, "Take me, Sterling. Take what's yours."

I bury myself inside her, leaning back to accept the weight of her body so that I can push deeper, until I'm as far inside her as possible. She whimpers needily, her hips swiveling in a little circle to stroke her clit against me. It's a few short steps to reach the long, broad-armed couch beside the floor-to-ceiling window, and when we arrive I lift her from me, leaving her with an anxious, longing groan. I spin her around, draping her across the arm of the couch, presenting her swollen sex to me like a goddamn work of art.

"Tell me again. What do you need?" I ask, enjoying the listless way her body moves, unable to find release from the rapturous surge of longing.

"I need you to take me, Sterling," she says, the words thick and slow.

"Take what?"

"My body," she says, but I can tell she's unhappy with the answer. I brush the head of my shaft across her seam, providing a jolt of clarity. "Me. Take *me*. I'm yours."

I slide into her slowly, savoring her every response. The way her muscles loosen. The sound she makes, a thing without thought or intention, as varied and as natural as a storm. The near-hysterical, vibrating thrum she experiences the closer she gets to taking all of me. The utter, blank release of her completion.

I'm not sure how long we make love. Everything simply falls away. The things in our past. The distinction between her and me. Time itself. She is mine, and nothing will ever come between us again. We'll take back everything. And God help anyone who stands in our way.

I feel the hot explosion of my orgasm, feel the implosion of hers. I lift her limp form and lay her across the couch before settling next to her. She wraps herself around me instinctively, our bodies tangling together like vines.

She was mine once, five years ago, and she might have forgotten, but she's been mine every day since. She always will be. I won't allow her to forget again. I won't allow myself too, either. "I love you."

"Hmmmm," she sighs, the curve of her pink lips weaving a contented smile on her face. "I love you, too."

"And you won't forget?" I say, brushing the tip of my nose on the downy spot behind her ear.

She bites her lip, her green eyes flickering to meet mine. "I've never forgotten. I've always been yours. All of me. All of you."

I smile. "All in."

We linger there, knowing that the real world waits for us, cold and hard and unforgiving. Here and now, we shelter together, and nothing can touch us. We'd lost sight of that years ago. I won't make the same mistake twice. But learning from our mistakes, means we can't avoid the truth forever.

I nuzzle her neck, drinking in the intoxicating scent of her one more time. Then I finger her necklace. "You kept it."

"I figured a little extra luck wouldn't hurt," she says in a soft voice.

She's right. We could use more of that. But luck or not, we can't avoid the past forever. "We should talk."

Her languid body stiffens instantly.

"Don't panic," I coax. "I'm not going anywhere." I've imagined every terrible scenario. I might not know exactly what we're up against, but I can't fathom there being a possibility I haven't already considered. Not a single one can shake me. I'll continue to remind her of that, even knowing that only time will prove it to her.

"I don't even know where to start," she whispers. Her index finger trails my forearm, following along the lines of my tattoo.

"I'll start," I say, earning me a blink of surprise. "Ask me something."

"What is this?" she points to the ink. "Jack has one, too."

"So does Luca and Noah, but he regrets his," I say, my mind fading back to a different time and a different place.

Summer five years ago

Considering I'm supposed to spend the next three weeks proving that I'm at the pinnacle of physical fitness, it's a bit amusing to discover most of the dining options at Camp Lejeune consist of fast food. I settle for something they claim is barbecue and survey my situation. There are no empty tables. Quite a few families crowd around tables, moms and dads barking orders and cleaning up spills. It's a jarring sight after being at bootcamp. I'd come to think of my choice to enlist as a way to cut off the world. It had felt that way surrounded by a bunch of isolated recruits. Now I'm reminded that life—and the world—continues, even for a Marine. I finally spot two of the guys I saw in orientation this morning sitting at a table in the corner. I don't recognize either of them from Parris Island, so I assume they came from San Diego.

I walk over and set down my tray. I've learned that etiquette doesn't extend to necessity in the armed forces. If I need to sit to eat, I just sit down. Though it feels a lot more comfortable to do it with two men rather than a family with three kids fighting over chicken nuggets.

My appearance doesn't phase either of them. The blond continues devouring chicken fingers, but the black guy shoots me a warm smile.

"Jack Archer." He sticks out his hand, and I shake it firmly.

"Sterling Ford. I saw you two at orientation. You're here for assessment." It's a statement of fact, but one that opens the door to conversation. Whether they want to chat or not, I don't really care. But I'm not going to just sit here and pretend I'm alone.

"Yeah, we came from San Diego. Were you at Parris Island?" Jack asks.

I nod. "Just finished up last week."

"Why'd you sign up for more hell?"

I've been told that assessment is going to make bootcamp look like a tropical vacation. I guess I'm not the only one who's been warned.

"My instructor saw potential." I shrug and take a bite of my barbecue sandwich. It makes me miss Tennessee. Never thought I'd feel that way.

"Luca DeAngelo." The blond finally pauses long enough to introduce himself. His friend doesn't shake my hand. Instead, he bumps Jack's shoulder, his dark eyes lighting up like they're in on a joke. "Potential, huh? So, you've got a death wish?"

"I wouldn't say a death wish. I just don't really have much keeping me here." Is it possible to have disinterest in death? Honestly, I could go either way. Live. Die. It hardly matters to me. It doesn't matter to anyone else.

Jack's eyes narrow as if he's reading my thoughts. "Yeah, he's got a death wish. So, what's her name?"

"Her?" I repeat, digging into my fries and pretending I don't understand.

"Yep," Luca says. "There's definitely a her. Look I could give you some lecture about how it's not worth getting blown up over some pussy, but, honestly, there's no real reason to get blown up."

"Patriotism?" I offer.

Luca snorts. "Nah. That's not it. It's definitely running away from something—like your girl. That's how we all wind up here."

"What are you running from?" I lean forward.

"Who's the girl?" he counters.

"There's no girl." Not anymore.

"Not running from anything," Luca says, settling back in the plastic chair with a smug grin.

"Oh good, you're as stubborn as he is," Jack interjects. "I don't think it matters what we're running from, it matters where we're headed."

"I hear it's going to be hell," Luca says.

"I've got nowhere else to go. Might as well go to hell."

"That makes two of us," Jack agrees. "Just another bastard on his way home."

"Home?" Luca repeats. "Is your dad the devil?"

"Mine is," I say soberly. "You?"

"Wouldn't know," Luca admits.

"I think I'd like my dad more if he was the devil," Jack says.

"I guess all of hell's bastards are heading home then," I say.

Luca laughs and extends his hand finally. I take it. "It's a regular fucking family reunion."

"Nothi in infernum," Adair reads with a laugh. "Hell's bastards. I thought I needed to refresh my Latin the first time I saw it."

"Your Latin seems good to me," I say. "We got them done before everything went down—when we were in London."

She inhales sharply like she's been punched in the gut. A memory of her the night of the gala flashes to mind. London had come up then, but what happened there? I wait, hoping she'll finally start talking. I don't know how long I wait before I finally whisper, "You aren't going to scare me, Lucky."

She remains quiet, and I look down to find her sleeping in my arms. The truth can wait. For now.

15

ADAIR

I awake in a near-black room, and for a moment I can't
remember where I am or how I got here. My hands shoot
out in either direction, trying to find something to help me
make sense of the strange surroundings, then they move to
my stomach.

She's gone.

Panic threatens to overtake me, but then I feel Sterling
there beside me. Slowly, my eyes adjust, sketching the lines of
his bedroom in the faint glow from the lights on the street
below his building. The dread from my nightmare begins to
fade, loosening its grip on my chest. He must have carried me
in here. I roll closer to him, tucking myself between his arm
and chest, fighting back tears, and he stirs, sensing something
is wrong.

"You okay?" he says groggily, pulling me closer.

"Just a nightmare," I say, and even recalling it sends a
shudder down my spine. I try to swallow away the raw ache.
It's been a long time since I had *that* nightmare.

"You're safe, Lucky," he says, hugging me tightly. "I'm right here."

"I keep telling myself that," I admit. "But after yesterday, after everything you found out...it's like I can't believe you're still here. And then...You know what? It doesn't matter. It was just a dream."

I repeat it over and over in my head, tuning my focus to the beat of his heart. He's here. That should make me feel safer instead of more afraid.

"Do you want to talk about it?" he asks gently.

I start to say no, but as soon as my mouth opens so do the floodgates. "You're gone, and I'm all alone, somewhere strange, and I'm pregnant." I nearly choke on the word. We've danced around it. He knows. Somehow, it's still hard to say it—hard to remember it. "And then, I'm not pregnant, and I can hear Ellie crying and I keep looking for her, trying to reach her. I can hear her getting closer and closer, but every door opens to an empty room. I keep searching, but I can't find my way out and I can't find her. I'm all alone and trapped and she needs me and..."

I dissolve into frantic pants, and his arms tighten protectively.

"You're not alone anymore. I'm not going anywhere," he says, closing my eyelids gently with his thumbs before planting tender kisses there.

"I don't want to be alone again," I whisper. "Come find me."

His weight shifts, and he pulls my head toward him, my body responding to his implied command, my lips parting in anticipation. The scruff of his stubble scratches my cheek, and then his lips are on mine. There's a pang in my swollen lip, the place he nipped yesterday, and the spark of memory lights my body like kindling, pushing the anxiety and dread of my nightmare from me.

"I want you right here, next to me," he says, his tone languid and inviting as he continues to explore me with his hands and mouth. Each kiss, each brush of his skin on mine, erases more of the dream until finally it fades to a memory. "I want you to know that—no matter what—I won't let anyone hurt you."

For the hundredth time over the last few days, I wonder how I ever let myself believe he had abandoned me. My mind spins with flashes of our passionate sex yesterday, and of anger at myself for taking so long to trust him. But that too is driven from me when he rolls onto his back, pulling me on top of him.

I straddle him, aware of the hard promise of what's to come pinned between us. My eyes adjust again in the dark to reveal the lines of his body. But while the hewn curves of his muscles and his stacked abs are hard and brutally beautiful, he's relaxed. He looks like Sunday morning. Unhurried. Certain. He's liquid sex, and I want to melt into him, but he has other ideas.

His hands start at the tops of my hips, rubbing gently up my back and pressing my belly and breasts into the hollow under his chest, releasing a lifetime of tension there. He kisses my forehead and eyelids like he never plans to stop.

I burrow into him, drinking in the smoky notes of his cologne, which has long since faded into something that is only Sterling and always has been. I want to taste him, and I begin to kiss his chest, savoring the taut bands of his muscular pecs, then his collar, then his neck. I inch toward his lips, my hips moving with me and dragging my aching seam along his thick length. By the time my hair falls around us both, my mouth greedily sucking his lower lip, the promise wedged between us is nudging me open.

"Fuck, you're so gorgeous," he growls, the corners of a smile tugging against my mouth.

"You can't even see me," I tease, planting a kiss on his brow.

"I've got every inch of you memorized," he says, chuckling and kissing the hollow under my jaw, driving words from my lips. "I don't *need* to see."

His fingers knead my ass, and I slide my hips further up his torso, inviting more of him—but he tucks his arms against his sides and his hands grab my hips. He yanks my body up until his mouth is between my thighs.

He pauses and my body takes over, my hips bucking closer impatiently. His soft chuckle sends a soft stream of air brushing over me.

"Do you have somewhere to be?" he teases, lightly drawing his stubble across me. "Because I'm exactly where I want to be, and I plan to be here a while."

A whimper escapes me, and I lock my hips before they mutiny and take control. Finally, his mouth covers my cleft, the warm heat of his tongue licking across my seam. He urges my traitorous hips forward, adding just enough friction to make me light-headed.

I've never felt anything like it before. At first—in the brief flashes of coherent thought, anyway—it's almost better than normal sex, the sensation warmer and gentler. Within a few moments, it feels like he's connecting me to some deeper part of myself, and each time I exhale, it's not just air coming out of me, it's tension and stress and fear.

How does he always know what I need? Sometimes, when I look in the mirror, what I see looking back is something written in another language. But Sterling always knows how to read me, like he was born knowing my language.

My hands find his hair, tangling there in some desperate, subconscious attempt to tether myself to this man, who has so much power over my body and soul. Each second winds me around him, until there's only his skin against mine, the caress of his mouth, the scratch of his jawline. I coil and wrap but there's only one way to completely bind myself to him. "I need you inside me. Now."

Sterling doesn't object. He simply scoots my hips toward his, as his soft, warm sigh floats up to me like a summer breeze. What we did yesterday left me sore, but his attention so far has dulled that particular ache, and when he enters me, it feels like something I've only glimpsed and never known: the easy rightness of coming home.

"I love you so much, Adair," he says with wonder bordering on reverence.

We've made love with me on top before, but even then I always let him be in charge. But I take the reins now, riding him slowly as I work up and down, savoring every sensation as I guide us toward the edge. I watch his face, moving my pace to his, urging us on to the same path, and when he goes rigid, I let myself shatter, melt, dissolve.

I know he will catch me and put me back together —always.

And I won't forget.

"I'll be right back," he promises, slipping from the bed.

I watch covetously as he grabs a pair of sweatpants from the dresser and tugs them on. They hang loosely at his hips, and he disappears out of the bedroom.

Panic seizes me instantly, and I scramble out of the bed.

Picking up his abandoned shirt, I slip it over my shoulders and button it as I go to find him.

He glances over from the refrigerator, the light from the ice machine silhouetting his form. Sterling holds up a glass as I join him. "I was just getting you some water."

I fall in love with him all over again

"I wish you'd never left," I blurt out, feeling another crying jag coming on—all over a stupid glass of water.

But it's more than that. It's being taken care of by someone who loves me more than himself. It's loving him so much it physically hurts. It's feeling my breath hitch every time I see him again for the first time.

Sterling's eyes close and he places the glass on the counter, reaching out to take my hand. He kisses my knuckles, his eyelids still pressed into two firm lines. When he finally speaks, his words are thick on his tongue. "You have to believe that if I'd known, I wouldn't have left you."

"We can't change the past," I say, swallowing hard. We can relive it, however, and I can't avoid it any longer. He needs to know the truth. He needs to know what we're up against. "But you need to know."

"Are you sure?" he asks. When I nod, he leads me over to the couch, the glass of water forgotten on the counter. Zeus pads over, looks between us, and then flops to the floor at my feet like a guard dog.

"By the time I realized I was pregnant, you were gone," I begin.

Anguish clouds his eyes, and I force myself to look away. I know the pain of being separated from a child too well.

"I wish you'd tracked me down," he says fiercely and for the first time, there's a dangerous edge to his words. "I should have been told."

"I tried," I say flatly. "I called Francie. Did she tell you that?"

He shakes his head. "She didn't talk to me much when I was enlisted. Couldn't," he clarifies quickly. "There's not a lot of time for personal calls. She probably forgot to tell me."

"I doubt my frantic call to her slipped her mind. Look, she didn't want me to reach you, and I can't blame her."

"Francie would never—"

"I believe her exact words were that I'd done enough by ruining your life, and..."

"And?" he presses.

I take a deep breath, finally voicing the words that had haunted me for years, "She told me if you died out there, your blood would be on my hands."

They crack me open and spill out along with the tears I've been trying to keep contained. I can't hold back anymore. There's too much—too much he needs to know, too much I need to finally confront myself.

"But I'm right here," he says, his palm stroking my arm gently. "I'm sorry, Lucky. I'm not mad at you for not finding me. I'm just mad that I wasn't there for you."

"I wanted you there," I croak.

"Even after I left?" He shakes his head, that familiar self-loathing twisting his handsome face. "You're a better person than I am. I can't imagine what you went through. I can't imagine what your family did to you."

"That's why I went back to London." I shake my head, wishing I could slap my younger self for ever being so monumentally naive. "I thought I could hide it from them until I figured things out, but I was just fooling myself."

"You were...alone?" he asks in a strangled voice. "You didn't tell Poppy or...anyone?"

One side of my mouth curls into a sad smile. "I didn't want to disappoint everyone. I didn't want to hear their advice. I only cared about holding onto the last piece of you I had left, but I should have known better. You can't outrun your problems."

"God knows, I've tried," he says. "What happened in London, Lucky?"

"I made a terrible mistake," I whisper.

Summer five years ago

I've been pacing the length of the hall since Poppy texted that her flight landed at Heathrow. For the tenth time, I pause to check my reflection in the foyer's mirror, wondering if my flowy blouse is doing its job. It looks casual and summery for now. I won't be able to hide my swelling baby bump for much longer. I wouldn't have to if Poppy hadn't decided to come for a summer visit. Thankfully, she's not planning to stay at the flat I've taken in London since she's dragged Cyrus along for the trip.

The intercom buzzes and I answer with a quick, "Hello?"

"Miss MacLaine, I have two visitors for you," Bart, my building's front desk attendant says in a Scottish brogue so thick, I can hardly understand him. My father insisted I take a flat in a staffed building, but I'd chosen the neighborhood of Notting Hill for its low-key vibe.

"Send them up. Thank you."

My eleventh check in the mirror is accompanied by a nervous flutter and I instinctively press a palm to my belly. Even with my shirt pressed close to the bump, it just looks like I've been indulging in too much fish and chips. The truth is that until the last few weeks, I'd barely kept a meal down. Poppy's decision to stay in Valmont for the first summer session saved me from an earlier visit. It had been hard to hide my morning sickness once it hit. I'd resorted to coming up with an insane excuse about a sudden, once-in-a-lifetime study abroad opportunity landing in my lap to get out of Valmont before everyone figured out the truth. I'd left before the spring semester ended and planned to stay through the summer. For the last few weeks, I had been studying the toilet in my bathroom's flat. I could probably do a dissertation on porcelain, actually.

No one knows the real reason that I came here. No one knows that there's no study program. Well, there is. I found one to pitch to my father, knowing he would never let me go on my word alone. I even enrolled and let him pay the tuition, so there would be no doubt. I just haven't bothered to attend. I've been too busy gestating and trying to figure out what to do next. All I know is that if I stay in London as long as possible, I can have the baby before my family finds out and tries to stop me.

Because there's no way that Angus MacLaine would let his daughter have a bastard, especially once he realized who the baby's father is.

At first, I thought Poppy's visit would throw a wrench in my plans, but I'd never get by without seeing anyone from home until after the baby came. It will be easier to avoid everyone later, extend my study visa, and make excuses about staying for the holidays. It's not a perfect plan—in fact, it's hardly a plan at all, but it's all I have to work with.

A knock on the door startles me, and I feel another

flutter of panic like fragile butterfly wings in my belly. I pat my bump and whisper, "Showtime."

I take a second at the door, preparing myself to act like the same old Adair for the next few days. I don't know how I'll pull it off. Nothing about me feels the same. I'm not the person I was when I left Valmont. I don't think I'll ever be her again.

And then there's my secret. How am I going to keep this from my best friend?

"Because you have to," I remind myself. I'm all the baby has in the world. Taking a deep breath, I open the door.

Poppy shrieks, arms splaying in the air, as she rushes me. "I missed you!"

Guilt washes over me, making me feel sick and for one terrifying moment I worry that my morning sickness is back and that I'm going to throw up all over her. But Poppy's hug soothes me instantly. I don't usually like being hugged but this one feels good. Something hot leaks from the corner of my eye. That's when I realize that I'm crying.

Poppy pulls back, her hands on my arms. "Traffic was..." she trails off, staring at me. "What's wrong, darling?"

"Nothing!" I shrug free of her and dash my tears away quickly. Turning, I discover Cyrus standing on the threshold, laden down with bags. "You look like a pack mule."

"Good to see you, too," he says dryly.

"Oh, sorry, love." Poppy smiles sheepishly and helps him stack the baggage in the hall.

"Um." I stare at the bags suddenly worried that our signals are crossed.

"We came straight here," Poppy confesses as I lead them toward the kitchen where I put the kettle on for tea. "Our suite at the Westminster Royal isn't ready yet. I hope you don't mind?"

"No, of course not," I say, relieved. "You don't have to stay there, though. I have a guest bedroom."

It's my duty as a Southern woman to ask but I mentally cross my fingers, hoping they don't change their minds and decide to take me up on my offer.

"Oh no! We're all set. Cyrus scored the suite that Prince Alexander reportedly used to stay in when he was sneaking around with Clara Bishop," Poppy gushes while I take mugs from the cabinet. "That reminds me! There's paparazzi everywhere. I guess they're watching the house Alexander owns here, but I doubt they'd leave the palace for Notting Hill. Have you seen them?"

"Not really," I say, adding, "but maybe you will."

Cyrus rolls his eyes as she continues telling me every rumor she's heard about the couple since their tragic wedding. I'll gladly open the door for Poppy to gossip about the Royal family if it distracts her from asking me too many questions about what I've been up to for the last few weeks. Maybe she'll be so focused on getting a glimpse of them, she'll spend all her time Royal watching.

"I just want to see if there's a baby bump," she says.

I drop the mug I'm holding. It falls to the tiled floor and breaks into a dozen pieces. "What?"

"Darling, let me help you." Poppy circles to help me pick up the pieces. "I was just saying I wanted to see the royal baby bump myself. All the tabloids are speculating that she's pregnant and since her accident... It's the Brit in me. I can't help it."

"Sorry." I press a hand to my forehead. "I think I have a migraine starting."

"Why don't you sit down?" Cyrus suggests. "We can clean this up."

This earns him a blinding smile from Poppy. If she was smitten with him when I left Valmont, there's no doubt that she's head over heels for him now. I suspected as much when she called to say she was taking him to visit her London family.

"Thanks," I say, feeling dumb and hoping they buy my excuse.

"It's all this time in the city," Poppy says, continuing to make the tea. "That's why you're coming with us to the country this weekend."

"I'm what?" I stare at her.

"Don't even try to say no," Cyrus advises me. He stands up and looks around for the garbage can. "She hatched this plan during our flight, and I can promise you that she's not going to let you get out of it."

"I have class," I lie.

"Not on the weekend," she says. "We're just going down during the spring bank holiday. You won't have class then."

She's right. I wouldn't, and if I was attending classes, I would know about this bank holiday. But since I haven't been and since I'm not British I had no idea that I needed an excuse until now.

"You two should go. It will be more romantic," I say, grasping for one on the spot.

"We'll have plenty of time for that during our trip,"

Cyrus says, coiling his arms around her waist. Poppy tilts her head, black curls swinging around her shoulder, so she can kiss him.

I turn away, jealousy twisting inside me. I'm happy for my best friend but seeing them together only reminds me of how alone I am. My stomach flutters as I remember that I'm not alone. Not anymore.

Not ever again.

Poppy watches me, her eyes dark, and pulls gently away from Cyrus, shooting him a look.

"I promise we won't be all lovey-dovey the whole time."

"It's fine." I wave it off, hoping that I sound convincing.

"The truth is that he's right. I get him all the time," she says. "I want you. I can't believe you're going to stay here all summer. I have half a mind to stay here all summer with you."

"No!" It bursts out of me before I can swallow it back. "I mean, I'm so busy with this program. You'd never see me anyway. No need to waste your summer here."

"A summer in London is hardly a hardship," she says with a laugh, pushing a mug in my direction. "But Cyrus does want to go to the Mediterranean."

"You just have to decide if you want the French Riviera or the Italian Riviera," he says.

The two begin planning the rest of their romantic summer plans, and I blow steam off the top of my mug. The minty aroma of the tea leaves hits me, and my stomach clenches. I swallow, trying to keep down my breakfast.

Poppy pauses her itemized list of travel desires. "Are you okay, darling?"

"Headache," I lie through gritted teeth. "I'll be right back."

I don't dare try to say more. Opening my mouth feels particularly dangerous as my stomach roils. I walk as calmly as I can into the hall, but the moment I'm out of sight, I run for the bathroom. Throwing on the water tap, so they can't hear me, I only just make it to the toilet.

There's no way I'm going to pull this off. Not if morning sickness keeps hitting me out of the blue. I have no idea why they call it morning sickness anyway. It doesn't care what time of day it is as far as I can tell. If I'm conscious, it shows up whenever it feels like. Usually, my mint tea keeps it under wraps in the afternoon. Today, it set it off. Apparently, it's evolving—just what I need.

I take a few minutes to clean up. A quick glance in the mirror shows that I'm even paler than usual. That's saying something. I have no idea why people talk about a pregnancy glow. I look like a ghost. Other than that, there's not much difference. It's strange to keep this secret inside of me. I'm the only one who knows. Well, myself, and the nice ladies at the clinic down the street. There's no one to tell. No one I want to know. Not even my best friend, and I'm not certain why. Except that I know what she'll say. It's what my family would say.

I should get rid of it.

It's going to ruin my life.

I can't do this alone.

I don't need them to say it. I already know all those things. I think about it all day every day. But even though it's crazy, despite everything, this baby is the last piece I have of Sterling. That's the part I really don't want to explain. I shouldn't want even a piece of him. Not after what he did. Not after he left. The trouble is that I'm still in love with him. I think maybe I'll always be in love with him.

And that makes it impossible for me to not love this baby. I pat my belly, lowering my voice to a whisper, "Do you think you could take it easy on me for a few days?"

I rinse my mouth with some mouthwash I've stashed under the sink and decide I can't avoid my guests any longer.

When I return to the kitchen, Poppy's dark head is bowed close to Cyrus, and they're whispering. Panic surges through me. Had they guessed? Was it my herbal tea? Or did they hear me vomiting? Maybe it's just obvious. I don't think I have the so-called pregnancy glow, but maybe others can see it. But then she giggles. I don't think they'd be laughing over me being knocked up. When she lifts her head, a sheepish smile tugs at her lips.

"I was just going to come and check on you," she says, moving away from Cyrus to come fawn over me. "Do you want to lie down? You look pale."

"I'm fine," I say. The sooner I get this visit over with, the better. "I've just been staying up too late."

"It's summer." Poppy throws her hands in the air. "You aren't supposed to be studying or doing coursework. That's it. You're going with us to the country this weekend. You need a break."

"But—" I begin.

She holds up a slender finger. "If ifs and buts were candy and nuts—"

"Yeah, yeah," I cut her off. "Fine. When are we leaving?"

Her answering smile is so wide, I almost feel excited. "We'll drive down on Friday morning."

"Drive? Who's driving?" I repeat. There's no way my stomach can handle Poppy behind the wheel."

"I'll drive," Cyrus says firmly. "It's the safest option."

"You make me sound like a terrible driver." She pouts, moving to drop into his lap.

So much for them keeping the PDAs to a minimum. "You are a terrible driver."

"Enough about me. I want to hear about you. Are there any cute guys in your program?" Her eyes glint like a star twinkling in the night sky.

"I'm taking a break from dating." Forever, I add silently.

"Don't let him win," she advises me.

"I don't think he cares," I say flatly, wishing we could stay on the subject of my study abroad program, even if it's fake. I'd still rather make shit up than talk about Sterling.

"Then he's an idiot for letting you get away," Poppy says firmly. She elbows Cyrus.

"Agreed. He's a dick," he says. I wonder if she prepped him on what to say when the subject came up.

"He's history," I say, wondering if it sounds as hollow as it feels to say it. "Are you hungry?"

A change of subject is in order and now that my stomach has settled, I'm reminded of how empty it is.

"Famished." Cyrus winks behind Poppy's shoulder. "What sounds good? Let's go out."

"My body doesn't know if it's breakfast time or lunch or dinner," Poppy says.

"Lunch time," I decide for her, feeling a sudden urge for curry at the place around the corner. Suddenly, I'm starving. I dump my tea in the sink and grab my purse. "I know where to go."

Poppy studies me for a minute like I'm a stranger before she nods. "Lead the way."

I'm too hungry to wonder what she's looking for, but I can't help but worry that my best friend knows me too well to keep my secret for long. But I'm not ready to share my secret yet. For now, the baby's safe.

And hungry.

Landry Court stretches across two hundred acres of Hampshire. It's the sort of estate where Hollywood films period pieces. I'd seen pictures of it from Poppy's summers abroad for years. It's different to be here. The house is down a private lane. Overhead, centuries-old elm trees create a canopy of dappled green light, shading the drive up to the open, wrought-iron gates. When we're past them, I can't help feeling like we're driving into an Austen novel as the estate comes into full view. The house looms from a hill, its stately brick veneer belonging to another place and time. We pass manicured hedges as we wind our way to the front drive where an elegant woman with deep, amber skin and white hair waits. Despite the summer heat, she's wearing a long silk kaftan, which ripples around her as she moves gracefully toward the car.

Poppy meets her halfway and it's impossible to miss the resemblance. They have the same poise even as they embrace.

"Come meet my grandmum," Poppy calls to me when I climb out of the backseat.

Her grandmum inspects me for a moment, and I tug nervously at my loose, linen sundress. I probably look like a mess after being in the car for nearly two hours after getting stuck in London traffic on our way out of town.

"This is Adair," Poppy tells her.

"The friend you're always speaking of on your visits." Her accent is heavier than Poppy's and mixed with more than a tinge of Hindi. She wraps me in a warm hug. "It's lovely to meet you, Adair."

"It's wonderful to meet you, too, Mrs..."

"Aja," she corrects me. "Everyone calls me Aja."

"That's a beautiful name," I say sincerely.

"It means goat," she informs me, a familiar sparkle in her eyes. She really looks just like her granddaughter.

"Oh." I can't think of anything to say. "It's still pretty."

"It's fitting," she murmurs. "I'm very stubborn."

"Like you," Poppy says meaningfully, laughter in her voice.

"I think that's a compliment." I'm not entirely sure though.

"It is," Aja informs me. "A woman should be stubborn. I'm always telling my *priya* to be more obstinate." She wraps an arm around Poppy's slender shoulders.

"My parents really appreciated it when I was a child." Poppy leans against her and jealousy stabs me. Aja might be her grandmother, but it's clear they're close.

"But Poppy is a lovely lamb not a goat," Aja says.

"Yes, she is," I agree.

A man appears from a side door and bows slightly to us before turning to Cyrus who's circled around to the trunk. "Are your bags in the boot?"

"Yes," Poppy says, easily translating the British slang when Cyrus stares at him in confusion.

"Allow me," the man says, brushing past him.

Cyrus leaves him to the bags and joins us. He walks right up to Aja confidently.

"Aja, this is my boyfriend." Poppy steps away allowing him to move closer.

But Aja doesn't hug him, instead she extends her arm. He takes it, looking torn between shaking it and kissing it. In the end, he opts for a squeeze, looking uncomfortable. Aja continues to watch him, and I wonder if he's passing her inspection.

"The Eaton family?" she asks finally.

"Yes, Ma'am," he says, releasing her hand.

She doesn't correct him or tell him to call her Aja. Next to her Poppy bites her lip.

"They own the Eaton hotels," she volunteers as though this will warm her grandmother more, but Aja's demeanor remains chilly.

"Yes, of course. I knew it was familiar." She turns and beckons us to follow her into the grand foyer.

Inside the traditional English style gives way to an eclectic, but warm interior. The walls are papered with a lush floral print flocked with raised velvet in brilliant jewel-tones. Dozens of paintings hang in gilded frames along the corridor. The hall continues with a diamond patterned marble floor until it reaches a sweeping staircase. Everywhere I look there is something beautiful and expensive, but somehow despite the opulence, I feel completely welcome. It's the opposite of the mansions where we'd grown up in Valmont.

"I have you each set up in a guest cottage. I assumed you might want your privacy."

"Each of us?" Cyrus says. "That's—" he cuts off when Poppy shoots him a warning look. "Very gracious of you."

"I've had some refreshments laid out, but perhaps, you'd like a moment to rest after your trip?" Her keen eyes turn to me, and I wish I could shrink and disappear into the flocked wallpaper of the foyer.

"That would be lovely," Poppy says. "Then we can stay up late with you."

"Yes, us girls can visit," she says airily. "I'll have Max bring trays to your rooms."

"Thank you," Cyrus says, but Aja merely shrugs and goes to speak with a maid.

"I'm sorry. I should have warned you that she's very old-fashioned," Poppy says in a lowered voice. "I thought she might see me as an adult, but..."

"It's okay," he says, waving off her apology. "It's only a few days and then we'll be off on our own in Italy."

"About that? I've been reconsidering Cannes," she says.

"I think I will lie down," I say loudly before I get caught playing the third wheel again.

Aja appears next to me. "Let me show you your cottage. Poppy can take her boyfriend to his."

Cyrus looks relieved to get away from her dissecting gaze. Aja guides me through a dining room and out a pair of French doors.

"We've modernized," Aja tells me as we walk toward a small, white cottage past a hedgerow. "It took me forever to convince my husband and then it took forever to actually get anything done. The English are never in a hurry to change something. He passed away before it was finished."

"I'm sorry," I murmur, knowing exactly what it feels like to lose someone with business unfinished.

"Don't be. I miss him, but I finally have a modern kitchen," she says with a wink. She opens the cottage door and moves to the side, allowing me to enter. "After all these years, I feel certain I know you. I thought you would find this one the most comfortable."

The cottage, like the house itself, is a surprise. Most guest houses in Valmont are decorated to suit any one who might use the space. This one feels like it serves a distinct purpose. Built into each wall, bookshelves cluttered with hundreds of books greet me. Comfortable old chairs and beautiful Tiffany-glass lamps are shoved into every corner.

"My husband had a writer friend who would descend upon us to write his latest masterpiece every year or so. Some of the books are his, some my Thomas placed here for him. We started calling it The Bookery."

"It's amazing," I say honestly, unable to tear my eyes from the spines on the shelf.

"I knew you would approve," Aja says. "My *priya's* other friend maybe not so much."

"Cyrus?" I say absently.

"I think he's quite put out to stay in a separate bed from my granddaughter," she guesses.

"Oh, I don't know. We're very traditional in Tennessee, too."

"So I hear." Aja smiles, but her eyes skim over me and linger at my waistline for just long enough that I stop breathing. "But one can never be too careful with a boy like that. Unless I'm wrong about Mr. Eaton?"

She waits and I'm not sure what to say.

"I've known Cyrus since we were kids," I say lamely.

"I don't think you need to say any more." She pats my arm. "I'm sure he's fine, but there's something of the wolf in him. Not a good match for my lamb."

"A wolf?" I repeat. I can't pretend that I've always thought kindly of him, but calling him a wolf feels like an overestimation.

"In his eyes," she says, tilting her head. "You can't see it?"

"No," I admit, shaking my head. "I've never really thought of him as having a killer instinct."

"It's not the killer instinct, as you say. Some wolves are quite loyal, but only to their kind. He sees my Poppy as a lamb." Her hand flutters. "It doesn't matter. Perhaps, it's my name. I find myself seeing the animal in everyone."

"Poppy is right about me. I'm a goat," I say with a laugh.

"Yes," she says hesitantly. "There's something else, though."

"What?" I ask breathlessly, remembering how she studied me earlier.

"I'm not sure yet," she admits. "I suppose we'll have to spend more time together." She turns away. "All of the linens have been changed. You look like you could use a nap."

I try to smile brightly, hoping to counter whatever signs of exhaustion I'm showing. "Thank you again, Aja. I'll see you this evening."

"I'm looking forward to it."

The smile falls from my face as the door closes behind her. I like Aja. I love Landry Hall and the Bookery, but I can't shake the sense that Aja sees right through me to the secrets I'm keeping. *The question is can I keep the most important one hidden from her unsettling eyes?*

"Do you think she knew?" Sterling asks, breaking into the story.

"I don't know. Maybe I was paranoid. Poppy and Cyrus didn't seem to have a clue, but Aja?" I shake my head. "Yes, I think she did."

"What happened next?" he asks. "When did you tell Poppy?"

I take a deep breath, preparing to shock him. "That's just it. I didn't."

"We should go riding tomorrow," Poppy suggests after dinner. We've gathered in a large salon off the dining room. There's none of the uncomfortable period furniture I expected to find behind the Austenesque facade of Landry Hall. Instead, deep-cushioned sofas cluster around a stone hearth.

"You've had too much wine," I tell her. The rest of them are on their second bottle. I'm hoping no one notices that I'm only pretending to sip my first glass.

Poppy cocks an eyebrow. "You love riding, and this estate is beautiful."

"Cyrus doesn't ride," I point out, grasping for an excuse.

"I can ride," he says. "Unless you're going to show off."

"Adair can't help showing off on a horse," Poppy says with a giggle.

"What does that mean?" I ask with a frown.

"Only that you didn't even notice that time I got caught in the tree," she says.

"I'm not the one that didn't duck," I remind her, but I can't help laughing at the memory. I'd taken Poppy at her word that she was a seasoned rider. In fairness, she was— just not as much as I was. I'd left her behind, dangling from an oak tree.

"You only noticed I was missing when my horse rode by with an empty saddle." She pours herself more wine as we all laugh. She holds out the bottle, looking surprised when I hold up a full glass.

"I'm so tired. I'll fall asleep on you," I warn her. The excuse passes inspection, but when I glance over I find Aja watching me.

"Perhaps, riding should wait," she says after a moment, "for another visit."

My stomach flips over. I tell myself that she's only trying to decide what animal she sees in my eyes, but I can't lie to myself. Aja isn't just studying me, she's dissecting me. Whatever she sees is behind her suggestion and my disinterest is only fueling her speculation.

"You're right. We should go riding," I blurt out, eager to dispel whatever suspicion she has about me.

"As long as you go easy on me," Cyrus says.

"Of course," I say quickly, grateful that he's here suddenly. Poppy's been riding long enough to keep up with me. But if Cyrus is along, we'll have a reason to be more cautious. I'd asked the midwife about riding. She'd told me it was okay in the first trimester if I took extra care after I'd assured her that I knew what I was doing on a horse. I'm in my second trimester now, but barely showing. I haven't even felt the baby move yet. Going slowly, everything will be fine.

"I would join you, but my hip hasn't allowed me to ride for years," Aja says sadly.

"Oh, maybe we shouldn't..."

Aja shakes her head. "It's good for the horses. I can pack a picnic, if you'd like."

"I don't think we'll be gone that long," I say before the others can agree. "We have to break Cyrus in slowly."

The conversation devolves into each of us telling embarrassing stories from our youth. The kind of stories only old friends can have.

When we finally head to bed, I'm bone-tired and my friends are drunk. We reach the back of the house and Poppy frowns.

"Aja put me in that one." She points to a cottage on the opposite side of the property from where The Bookery is. "And Cyrus by you, so, I guess this is a good night to you both."

"How will she know?" Cyrus asks sloppily, grabbing her around the waist and trying to haul her toward the other side where him and I are staying.

"Oh, she'll know!" Despite the fact that her blood is probably more wine than water at this point, she sounds horrified.

"Good night!" I call, deciding to leave them to decide if they're going to break the rules.

This far from the city, the stars puncture the darkness —bright and unmistakable. I find myself looking for constellations as I amble back to the cottage, daring to gently rub my stomach as I imagine what it will be like to point into the night sky to show my child where each constellation shines overhead. Rocks crunch behind me and I drop my hand, breaking the spell. A moment later, Cyrus joins me, hands shoved in his pockets.

"You're alone," I say.

"Don't remind me." He shakes his head, tossing an annoyed glance behind him. "We should have stayed in a hotel."

"And miss this?" I murmur.

He glances up and shrugs. "We have stars in Valmont. We didn't need to come here to see that."

"I guess you're right," I say, thankful we've reached my cottage. "I'll see you in the morning."

"Why did you come here?" Cyrus asks as I reach for the knob.

"Here? You two dragged me."

"To London?" he clarifies. "You didn't even finish the semester."

"It was too good of a chance to pass up," I say smoothly, the lie having become second nature at this point.

"It had nothing to do with him?"

No one's questioned my decision to leave Valmont. After the video, my father seemed eager to put me on a plane and get me as far away from Sterling as possible. A bit too eager, honestly. The longer time passes the more I see it for what it was. He saw a chance to seal Sterling's fate, and he took it. I'd played into his hands. But coming to London was my move. I shake my head. "I have my reasons."

"Then you're over him?" Cyrus's words slur a bit, and he stumbles back a step.

"Go to bed," I tell him. "You don't need to worry about Sterling and me. It's over. I'm fine."

"You're lonely," he counters. "I can see it."

"I know what Poppy thinks, but—"

"It's what I think. I've known you a long time," he says. "I know when you're hurting."

"Okay, I will be fine. Eventually. But seriously, you don't have to worry about me," I say.

"But I do worry. Adair, I..." He trails away, turning his head to look toward the darkened house. "Do you want to talk?"

"You should stick to whiskey, Cy. Wine makes you a bit emotional," I advise him. I turn the knob and open the door a crack. "I just want to go to bed."

"Yeah, me, too." He takes his hands out of his pockets and steps toward me. I expect him to hug me, him being too drunk to remember how much I hate that, and I brace myself. Then his mouth is on mine.

My hands shove him back and he stumbles, nearly falling onto his ass.

"What the hell?" I step backward, feeling behind me for the door.

"Adair, I didn't—" He scrambles onto his feet and advances toward me. "Let me come in. Let me explain."

"Go the fuck to bed," I order him, backing inside my cottage the rest of the way and slamming the door shut.

Wiping the back of my hand furiously across my lips, I fight tears as I lock the door. He's drunk. It meant nothing to him or to me. But that doesn't change the fact that he kissed me.

Sterling was the last man that kissed me, and without thinking, Cyrus just erased that. He took that final kiss from me, and I hate him for it. Almost as much as I wish I could hate Sterling. I kick off my shoes and climb into the bed, pulling the sheets to my chin. This is why I came to London: to claim my life as my own. To get away from a world that constantly takes what it wants, not caring if there's anything left over for me. But as the first tears splatter on my pillowcase, I realize that I'll never escape that world.

It won't let me.

"He did what?" Sterling roars. He's on his feet, pacing the room in bare feet, looking like he wants to put his fist through the wall.

"He was drunk." The excuse falls out of my mouth.

"That sounds like a lie you're telling yourself." Sterling's anxious energy attracts Zeus, who comes to sit in the doorway, watching him with concern.

"It probably is. I just needed to tell myself something," I admit. "But I've never forgiven him really. Maybe it was a stupid mistake, but I hate that he did that to Poppy."

"The next time I see him..." Sterling massages his fist with the palm of his left hand.

"It was a long time ago, and after what happened next, it just never seemed to matter."

I find myself hoping for rain the following morning, so I have an excuse to avoid Poppy, and, more importantly, Cyrus. Instead, sunshine and blue skies greet me as soon as I look out the window. Trust the fickle English weather to give everyone a beautiful day when I need a storm. I dress slowly, wondering if anyone will say something about my riding attire. I hadn't brought riding clothes purposefully.

I doubt I could button my riding breeches. In the end, I opt for a pair of tight black leggings I planned to wear in the car on the ride home. They're stretchy enough to wear in the saddle and under a loose t-shirt, you can't see my tiny baby bump.

I skip breakfast and head to the stables. I want to get a feel for the horses and stake a claim on an older, gentler steed. Plus, I don't think I could keep down a bite after what happened. But when I reach the stables, I discover Aja heading out of a stall. She's dressed in a loose fitting one piece jumpsuit, her silver hair piled on top of her head. Despite the fact that I know she must be nearly seventy, she moves with a strength and capability I'd expect of someone thirty years younger.

"Good morning," she calls. "Finished with breakfast?"

"I wasn't hungry." I join her, patting the mane of a beautiful Arabian as she checks his water.

Aja's eyebrow ticks up, but she doesn't comment. Instead, she picks up a brush and begins caring for him. "This is Raina. I named him after the Hindi word meaning night."

"He's beautiful," I murmur.

"He's stubborn, but he'll heed a strong rider." She pauses and studies me for a moment. "He's a good match for you from what my granddaughter tells me."

"Oh," I search for something to say that doesn't sound like a lame excuse. "I thought we'd better take your calmest horses—for Cyrus's sake."

I hate even pretending to be concerned for him. After last night, I have half a mind to ask her which horse is likely to throw him. He deserves it.

"I'm not accustomed to keeping broken animals," she

says loftily. "Mr. Eaton shouldn't follow an easy path. Poppy fawns over him too much."

I bite back a smile. At least, she sees through him.

"You're friends with him," she says, misreading my silence. "I shouldn't speak poorly of a boy I hardly know."

"Sometimes I think we mistake the presence of someone in our life for friendship," I say softly. "I've known Cyrus a long time."

I can't help wondering if I know him that well, especially after he hit on me last night. Try as I might to blame it on the wine, I can see the move too clearly. I'd been tired but sober. It didn't feel as much like a drunken mistake as it did a compromised inhibition. With any luck it was a stupid man having too much to drink and losing control. Maybe then, he won't even remember it this morning and we don't ever have to talk about it again.

"He should ride Poppy's old horse. I've kept her for years out of sentimentality. She shouldn't give him any trouble," Aja says.

"Which one is that?" I ask.

"Stall three," she says, "and you will ride Raina. He will obey you. It will be a good, safe ride."

I flush, trying to decide if I'm reading into her comments. I can't help thinking that Aja knows what I'm hiding.

"I better check on the others. Get to know him," Aja says before leaving the stall.

I press my forehead to Raina's muzzle. "No funny business, okay?"

He huffs, stomping a back hoof like he doesn't appreciate being told what to do.

"I know," I whisper, "but it's not about me. Let's just

trust each other."

Raina blinks, his round black eyes staring eerily back at mine before his head bows. I would almost swear he understands the request. I spend the next half hour, saddling him and double checking the straps before wandering to stall three to prep Cyrus's ride. I snort when I see the name placard next to the door.

Princess.

Of course, Poppy named her horse princess. I can only imagine how Cyrus will feel about this development. Before I've finished saddling the mare, my friends appear, decked out in riding clothes.

"Oh, I should have told you to pack breeches," Poppy says when she sees my leggings. "I think I have a spare set."

"I'm fine," I say quickly.

"We missed you at breakfast," Cyrus says casually.

I search his face for guilt or anger or annoyance—any of the emotions I might expect to find after I rebuffed his advances last night, but all I find is the same old Cyrus Eaton. That's a relief. I don't want to be the one to break my best friend's heart, especially since I suspect Cyrus had no idea what he was doing last night.

"I wasn't hungry, so I came to check the stables."

"Going to ride this one?" he asks me.

"Oh, no," Poppy says. "Princess couldn't keep up with Adair." She looks quizzically at the saddle I'd buckled on her.

"Aja suggested she's a good fit for Cyrus."

There's a heavy pause followed by a burst of hysterical laughter from Poppy. I can't help but join her. Cyrus glares at us with a bemused smile.

"If you're done, maybe we could get a move on," he suggests.

"Sorry," Poppy says, brushing a bit of hay off his shoulder. "We didn't mean to laugh."

"Sure about that?" he asks.

I have to duck out of the stall to stop myself from falling apart again. There's something delicious about watching Cyrus knocked down a peg or two, even if he didn't know what he was doing last night. Maybe it's due to the fact that I've watched most of the men in my life strut around with puffed chests, bragging about their accomplishments and acting invincible. It's refreshing to see one of them being reminded that he's only human.

In the end, Cyrus accepts riding Princess with dignity, and Poppy chooses a handsome stallion named Gemini. We set off along the rolling hills of the Landry estate at an even pace that Cyrus can easily match.

Raina doesn't resist me, but I sense how much I'm holding him back. He's a powerful animal and I can only imagine what it would be like to ride him without restraint. I can't help hoping someday that I will.

The countryside is beautiful. Even half a world away, I feel at home on Raina's back. Thanks to Poppy and Cyrus the ride is smooth enough that I don't feel nauseous once.

When we pause at a poplar grove, Cyrus stops Princess and dismounts her awkwardly.

"I need to take a leak," he announces as he hands me the reins and disappears into the trees.

"Charming," I mutter.

"Next time, we'll go out alone," Poppy says with a laugh.

When will that be? Lately, I try not to look too far into the future. It feels wrong to hope for a time when life might be normal again. Even worse than that, sometimes I'm scared that it won't be. I'm scared my life will never be my own. I take a deep breath, reminding myself that I have this moment and the air in my lungs and a beautiful view. I have so much to be grateful for, and I just have to trust the rest will work itself out in its own time. My stomach rumbles as if reminding me that I can't avoid thinking about the future altogether, especially when it comes to my next meal.

"I almost wish we'd brought a picnic," I admit.

"We probably could have. He's doing better than we expected," Poppy says fondly.

I think of what Aja said about how she makes things too easy for him. That's always been Valmont's problem. It's an entire enclave devoted to the fine art of smoothing things over, and the women enable it. My mother did it, too. She always found an excuse for my father's drinking. It's what killed her. Ginny's already falling into line with the expectation, pretending nothing is wrong when anyone could see she's heartbroken.

Even me, I'm doing it right now by not telling Poppy about what Cyrus did last night. Maybe it was an innocent mistake, but she should know. He shouldn't just get to do whatever he wants with no consequences.

"Look, Poppy, last night, something happened," I begin just as Cyrus reappears from the trees. I clamp my mouth shut.

"Let's head back," he calls as he walks over and pats Princess.

"Okay. Adair is hungry anyway," she says brightly

before turning her attention back to me. "You were saying something happened last night."

"Never mind. We can talk about it later," I say, releasing Princess's reins back to Cyrus. Our eyes meet briefly, and he turns away.

"Just don't—" Poppy starts, but before she can finish her sentence, Cyrus attempts to mount Princess and fails. My head turns just in time to see the mare kick angrily at the failure, her back legs sweeping out. Underneath me, Raina startles at the sudden motion and rears. *My hands tighten on the reins too late and the last thing I feel is the air being sucked from my lungs as I hit the ground.*

"Fuck!" Sterling is on his feet, pacing across the living room again. I sit up, hugging my knees to my chest. "Keep going."

"I'm not sure I want to," I whisper, and he finally stops to drop in front of me.

"That was the accident," he says in a gentle voice. "The reason you don't ride horses anymore."

I manage a nod.

"Where did it hurt you?" he asks.

My hand presses to my chest and a sob wrenches free followed by another and another. Telling my story has worn away the numb oblivion I've clung to. I'd stopped thinking about it, because it hurt. I'd told myself that enough time has passed that I'd healed—at least, as much as I could ever expect to heal. Now I know that was all a lie. I never healed. I pretended. I never accepted. I surrendered.

"Oh God." I can't breathe. I look to him wildly. Can't he see it? I'm drowning in front of him. I'm dying.

"Inhale, Lucky," he says quickly, grabbing my hand and

breathing deeply as though to coach me. "Exhale. Okay, inhale. You've got this. Why don't we take a break?"

I shake my head. The only way out is through. Out of the dark. Out of the past. We can't stay here lost forever. We have to find our way out if we're going to survive this. We have to face this together.

He's here now. I can face anything. That's what was missing before.

Sterling smiles, his hand slipping down to rub my stomach. "Can you feel her kick?"

"I think so," I say. Sometimes when I focus I feel the soft flutter of butterfly wings, but I'm never quite sure if that's the baby. Maybe I just want it to be, so that I have some tangible connection with the life growing inside me.

"Let's name her." He knits his fingers through mine, lying down beside me in the clover field. "Buttercup?"

I jab him with an elbow.

"What? It was good enough for your horse." But he laughs. The sound of it moves like the warm tingle of a shot of whiskey inside me.

"Are you sure?" I ask. I feel like I've asked this before, but I never got an answer.

"Stop."

Something pricks at my brain. We've had this argument, but we haven't. I shake my head, but it remains foggy. "But how will we afford it?"

"I told you that she's all we need. Our own secret fortune," he says.

I smile even as a cloud moves overhead and blots out the sun. "I love you."

He doesn't reply. My fingers squeeze his hand but find

it's gone. I'm alone. A drop of rain hits my face and I startle, my eyes flying open to discover an unfamiliar face overhead.

"Oh, good morning," she says in a thick British accent. "Or good afternoon, I suppose. I was just changing your IV."

I gradually become aware of a cold trickle running up my arm. I glance down, confused, to discover a tube running up my forearm.

"I needed to flush your hep-lock. You probably felt that. Woke you up." She bustles along cheerily, and I blink trying to process her—and everything else.

I'm in a hospital. That seems obvious from the IV and the monitor beeping next to my bed. But I shouldn't be here. I was somewhere else—with him. I want to go back there. "Where am I?"

It's a struggle to speak. My tongue feels like I've been sucking on cotton balls. The beeping monitor pitches up, and I turn to stare at it, realizing it's measuring my heart rate. My hand flies toward my stomach, my body understanding before my brain can catch up, but I'm too tangled in lines and cords to reach it.

"The baby!" I croak. My throat goes raw but no tears come. Maybe I've dried out completely.

"Oh, no, lamb." She rushes over and pours me a glass of water. "The baby's quite alright. See look here!" She swivels another monitor, and I see a second rapid heartbeat.

My baby's heartbeat. Each little jump on the monitor soothes me. I stare at it until I feel calm again while she helps me take a few drinks from the cup.

"Here. Just be careful you don't bump the monitors."

She coaxes my arm out from the mess I've made of all the lines connecting me, and I'm finally able to settle my palm protectively over my stomach. "Is that better, mum?"

I nod, swallowing down the surge of emotion I feel at hearing that word. *Mum.* Mom. Mother. I can't quite identify with it yet. It still feels foreign like I'm trying my best to understand a word in another language but not quite grasping it.

"What happened?" I ask, but before she can answer. The door to my hospital room opens and Felix steps in, holding a cup. His eyes widen when he finds me awake, and he shuts the door quickly behind him.

"I'll let him tell you, and I'll send a doctor in. They'll want to talk with you."

"Give us a few moments alone before you do that?" Felix requests. His gentle nature radiates from him, and she agrees easily.

If Felix is here, then that means...

"Oh God," I blurt out. "They called you. They called..." *My family.* More importantly, my father. Of course, they would. That's what happens when you wind up in the hospital. I just wish I could remember why I'm in the hospital.

"Yes," he says soberly. "But please don't stress. It's not good for you—either of you."

"You know?" My voice is so small I'm not sure I even said it aloud until he gives me a grim nod. "And my father?"

"He's out at the moment, tending to some business. I expect he'll be back soon."

"Does he know?" I don't have to clarify about what. There's some minuscule piece of me clinging to the idea that my dad might be more concerned with seeing to business affairs than me. Maybe he sent Felix to handle it. Maybe he hasn't been here himself.

"He knows about the baby, if that's what you mean. Certain decisions needed to be made, and he is your next of kin. We flew out as soon as we heard. Your father has been staying at your apartment. Only one of us can be here overnight."

I stare blankly at him, trying to process what he's telling me. My father knows, but he's not here. Not for the moment. Naturally, it's Felix that stayed. I wonder if he even had to fight him on it. Dad doesn't like hospitals. He sees them as places of weakness, as though illness is a fault of character.

"He's going to kill me," I whisper.

Felix's mouth thins into a line. His lack of response tells me that my father is as angry as I expected.

"You are an adult now," Felix says. "You make your own decisions."

"That's a lovely lie," I murmur. "I wish I could believe it. What happened anyway?" Maybe it's whatever they're pumping through my IV, but I can't seem to recall more than bits and pieces.

"Your horse startled and you fell."

"But I've fallen a hundred times." I grasp for why this happened now. I'm a good rider. I'm better than good. I know how to take a fall. It's been drilled into me since I started riding as a child.

"You hit the back of your head on a tree. It knocked you out. Your friends got you to the hospital."

Poppy. Cyrus. I cover my mouth with my hand. Everyone will know now.

"They're quite worried about you," Felix continues, coming over to adjust my pillow. "They weren't allowed to see you at first, and as soon as we arrived, your father had you moved to a private hospital. He's not allowing visitors."

"Have they come by?" I ask.

"Yes, but they don't know everything," he says significantly, guessing the real question that I'm asking. "They are very discreet here."

My relief is short-lived because the door opens and a doctor steps into the room.

"Miss MacLaine, I'm Doctor Thompson. It's nice to see you're awake. You must be feeling rested."

I think she means it as a joke, but it falls so flat I swear I hear it thud against the tiled floor.

"Mr. MacLaine?" she asks Felix.

"No." He shakes his head. "I'm Felix, her..."

"Uncle," I butt in, afraid she'll make him leave.

"Well, then, Uncle Felix we're going to be doing some tests and..."

"I'll step into the hall," Felix offers, before he can be asked.

I want to stop him. I want to beg him not to leave me. But the word tests has me frozen in place. What kind of tests? How hard did I hit my head? I wiggle my toes, relieved to feel them.

"The baby is okay?" I press once I'm alone with Doctor Thompson.

"We're going to check on that." She flips through some paperwork, furrowing her brow as she reads notes, and then checks the monitors. As she does, a nurse wheels a cart into the room. "Let's have a look, shall we?"

I force myself to nod, reminding myself of the strong heartbeat on the other monitor. The doctor applies some blue gel to my stomach and fiddles with the machine, typing and adjusting.

"There we are," she says, turning the screen to face me. "Everything looks alright, but let's just take a closer look to be sure."

The last time I'd had an ultrasound the baby resembled a wiggling gummy bear. Now? There's no doubt that it's a baby. "Is it a..."

"Would you like to know?" she asks kindly.

I nod.

"A nice little break from all this troublesome business, I think. It's been a while since I did this," she warns me. "Let's see if I can do it. If not, we'll call someone down."

I wonder how much my father is paying for the first class treatment I'm clearly receiving. I peer at the screen, looking for any clues, but I have no idea what I'm looking at. Some things are obvious, a head and legs and arms, but as she zeros in, I find I can't make sense of anything.

"Well, that's clear as day."

"What is?" It looks like a mess to me.

She draws a line on the monitor, followed by two more. "Congratulations. It's a girl."

A girl. Tears leak from the corners of my eyes. Apparently, I'm not dried up, after all. I'm not sure why it matters. I don't suspect I'd have a different reaction if she'd told me I was carrying a boy. My dream flashes to mind. Sterling said *she* like he knew somehow. I have to remind myself that didn't happen. It wasn't real. Sterling doesn't know. He doesn't care. And yet...

"And she looks perfectly healthy," Dr. Thompson says

after measuring a few more things. I can't tear my eyes away as she continues her inspection, pointing out what she's looking at along the way. She falls silent, and I'm so preoccupied that I don't notice until I realize she's focusing on a large black spot on the screen.

"What is it?" I ask when the silence continues. I try to stretch my neck to see what she's looking at better.

She turns, offering me a reassuring smile. "There is a slight Subchorionic hematoma."

My heart stops beating for the longest second of my life. "What does that mean?"

"First, it is quite mild and not a definitive cause for concern. It appears the placenta has detached slightly from the uterus, just enough to allow some blood to gather there. It's a bit like a pocket. The good news is that it's very small."

"And the bad?" I can barely ask. How can she be perfectly healthy if this has happened?

"You might experience some bleeding, and we should keep an eye on it. You'll need to be very careful. Bedrest might be necessary at some point. We will monitor you and the baby very closely. I'm going to recommend you remain in London until you give birth, particularly given that injury to your tailbone."

"My tailbone?"

"You had quite a fall. You really shouldn't have been riding." The admonishment is gentle but stern.

"I've been riding my whole life," I say, feeling suddenly defensive. "I know how to take a fall."

"There's no good way to take a fall when you're expecting and hitting your head didn't help," she says, holding up a hand. "It's very likely there will be delivery complications. Your tailbone has fractured, which could prevent the baby from descending properly. It might be necessary to perform a cesarean-section. You can try for natural childbirth, which is ideal, but you will need to be closely monitored during labor."

I haven't even thought as far as that, about what happens when I actually have the baby. Isn't that the easy part? Painful, sure. But just something that happens. You get pregnant. You have the baby.

"I have to stay in London?" I cling to this one bit of good news. My father can't make me leave.

"I can't stop you from returning to the states, but I would caution against it. It's an unnecessary risk to travel that far. What's done is done, but you will need to be more careful if you continue the pregnancy."

"If..." I choke on the words. "How..."

"Your father seems to think you might not wish to continue it," she says. It's matter-of-fact as though she's just passing on information, but out of the corner of her eye, she watches me as she continues her assessment. "It's up *to you*, of course."

What had he told them? I realize with horror that while I'd been unconscious, he'd been making medical decisions on my behalf. "Did he..."

"He's not allowed to make that kind of a choice for you," she assures me, "unless you're ruled permanently incapacitated or the courts have granted him power of attorney."

"And then?" I ask.

"He makes the decision," she says, confirming what I already suspect. "Unless you appoint someone else."

"Can I do that?" I ask quickly.

"If you'd like. Would you like me to send someone in with the paperwork."

"Yes," I say, "as soon as possible."

Dr. Thompson smiles and I realize she's been feeding me breadcrumbs, trying to get me to follow her. Whatever my father tried to pull while I was unconscious must have alarmed her. I'm not surprised. Even if I could be, I doubt I'd have the energy for it.

When the doctor leaves, Felix comes back inside.

"Did you tell my father I was awake?" I ask.

"No, but I think I should call him."

I shake my head. "Not yet. There's something I need to do first."

I don't tell him what I'm up to, because I'm not sure he'll like it any better than my father will. When a hospital administrator comes in with the paperwork, I fill it out quickly and sign as Felix looks on.

"What was that about?" he asks.

I take a deep breath and prepare myself. "I gave you power of attorney. If something happens to me, I want you to make the decisions."

"Adair," he breathes. "I don't think..."

"I do," I say firmly. "In fact, I know. He won't respect what I tell him. If he has the chance, he'll terminate the pregnancy. The doctor admitted as much. I don't want that."

"Are you certain? You know how difficult this will be —how difficult he will make it for you."

"I know," I say in a small voice. "But I'm not going to get rid of her. I already decided that. It's why I came here."

Felix remains silent, studying me with his own quiet wisdom, before he gives me a tight smile. "Her?"

"It's a girl," I tell him.

"And the father?" he asks. "Does he know?"

Felix knows the truth. He's been watching. He will have pieced everything together. But that means, so will my father. That only leaves me one choice.

"I don't know who the father is," I lie. "I'd really rather not waste time trying to figure it out. It will be embarrassing—for all of us."

"Don't you think he should know? Whoever he is?" His challenge is mild, but I recognize it.

"No guy I know will want a baby," I say flatly. I squash the memory of the dream back into some dark, unvisited part of my mind. That's all it was: a dream. Sterling isn't here. If he hadn't left, he'd probably have disappeared after I told him. He didn't even bother to say goodbye. In the end, he gave up. He let Angus MacLaine scare him out of town. He let me stay angry instead of confronting me to explain his side of the story. He didn't even put up a fight.

"But you still want her?"

He sees what I'm hiding. The question is will he keep it a secret for me? "I love her. I don't need to understand why. I just do."

"Then, I will make certain your wishes are respected, but, Adair, you know there will be consequences."

"I know."

Outside the door there's a sudden fluster of activity and for a moment, I think there must be an emergency, until I hear a familiar booming voice shouting orders.

"Are you ready? I can tell him you're sleeping," Felix offers.

"It's okay." There's no sense putting this off. It won't change anything. My father won't have a sudden epiphany and grow a heart overnight. I was always going to have to face this day. At least, Felix is here. It's not quite as lonely as I feared. He squeezes my hand just as the door flies open. He storms inside, an annoyed Dr. Thompson at his heels. It's the first time I'd seen my father on his feet since he began physical therapy after his own accident. I'd heard he was walking, but I didn't know what to expect. Despite the physical presence he's always projected, there's a hitch in his step, a slight tremor shaking his body, and he leans heavily on a polished black cane with a silver wolf as its handle.

"Why wasn't I called?" he demands. "I told you to let me know if there was any change."

"This is quite extraordinary," Dr. Thompson says, rising rather than shrinking to his intimidation. "We were seeing to your daughter's medical care—a much higher priority than making a phone call. You would have been informed when time allowed."

"I imagine you'll find time to cash and spend my check," he growls, before turning and pointing his cane at Felix. "You were under strict instructions—"

"He just got here," I cry out. "He was just telling me that he was about to call you."

This successfully redirects my father's rage away from Felix, but not in the way I expect. He turns his dark, beady eyes on me and shakes his head, disgust curling his lip. "Why would I believe a thing you say to me? My lying, slut of a daughter!"

"Mr. MacLaine!" Dr. Thompson steps forward. "I don't care if you bought this hospital. No patient here will be treated like that by a visitor. Get a hold of yourself or you will be escorted off the premises."

"Why don't we ask your board if they'll support that stance?" he suggests. "I think you'll find I can speak to *my* daughter any way I damn well please."

"I think you'll find that I am always true to my word," she spits back, not showing any signs of being flustered. "Control yourself or leave. Those are your options. There are no more choices available for purchase or otherwise."

He considers for a moment before finally lowering his cane. "I'd like to speak with Adair alone."

"I don't think—"

"It's fine," I cut in before she can save me once more. I'd always expected his ugliness. I'd run from it before, but I can't run from it forever. I need to stand and face it. It's the first step in claiming what I want.

Felix casts a concerned look in my direction as they leave the room, and I manage to force a grin. He doesn't look any more reassured.

Dr. Thompson pauses at the door. "There is a call button on your bed. If you need a nurse for *any* reason, please don't hesitate."

When the door closes, neither of us speaks. Daddy clutches his cane. I wonder how much he hates needing it. He'd treated rehabilitation therapy like a hostile takeover. I'm not surprised he managed to prove the doctors wrong. MacLaines are stubborn like that.

"You're walking," I say to break the silence, hoping to direct the conversation in any other direction than me.

"You're pregnant," he says flatly.

Well, that didn't work the way I intended.

"I am." There's no point in trying to change the subject now.

He walks slowly toward my bedside, his cane landing with an ominous thud with each step. As he gets closer, I realize that he looks older than the last time I saw him. There's more gray at his temples. Lines fold his face into a weathered, weary profile. Even his black suit jacket fits him differently, pulling at the waist in a way it never has before. Maybe I looked past it when I saw him every day. Perhaps, he aged overnight. "What exactly was your plan?"

"Stay in London and figure things out," I admit.

A nostril flares as though he's holding down a snarl. It's there in his beady, hawk-like eyes: reproach, disappointment, disdain. "I don't know what's worse. That you're pregnant with some bastard or that you couldn't even come up with an intelligent plan to keep it quiet!"

"Sorry to disappoint." My arms wrap protectively around my waist. I don't know when babies can hear inside the womb, but I won't allow her life to be dictated by father's temper.

"Don't pretend as though you are the victim," he growls. "You put yourself in this situation. Who's the father? That piece of trash you were seeing?"

"I don't know."

"Tell me. It will make things easier."

"Easier how?" I ask suspiciously.

"You have three options, Adair." His lips curve into a rueful smile as he looks at my arms still cradling my baby bump.

"You don't tell me my options," I cut him off, wishing I'd asked Dr. Thompson to stay.

"Don't pretend that you're an independent woman. You are here on my dime. Do you know how much it cost to keep this quiet? To keep your friends away so they wouldn't know? To make certain no one ran a story about you?"

"Considering you own half the world's media, I suppose it shouldn't be too hard." Of course, that's what this is about. Appearances. Just like my parent's accident. Just like telling Ginny to remain silent about her miscarriage. Weakness won't be tolerated. Vulnerability could never be shown.

"Exactly! *Half*," he repeats. "The other half would love to publish a story about Angus MacLaine's whore of a daughter."

"I am not a whore." It seethes from me. I can't claim I meant to get pregnant. I didn't. But she was created by an act of love—at least, on my part. Every time he acts like it was just meaningless sex, he chips away at my resolve to see her existence that way.

"Is that so? Then who is the father?"

"I don't—"

"Know," he finishes for me. "Only a whore would say that. Don't argue otherwise. If you knew, that might suggest otherwise, but if you don't..."

That's what this is really about. He's baiting me, trying to prove what he suspects—that Sterling is the father. The problem is I don't know why he wants to know. He did everything in his power to get Sterling out of town. Now he's gone, and I doubt my father wants to drag him back.

"I don't see why the father is important." It takes effort

to get the words out without allowing my voice to break. It hurts to say it. Maybe because part of me knows it's true. Sterling isn't in the picture. Even Francie wouldn't help me reach him. I'd been cut out of his life like a tumor—and maybe that's what I was: something toxic he needed to root out before I ruined him, too.

"It's one of your options," he says, pulling a chair over to sit beside me. He doesn't try to take my hand. In fact, he stays as far as possible from me as though my failure is contagious. "Tell me who the father is and we'll arrange things."

My eyes narrow. I don't like the sound of that. "Arrange what?"

"The marriage, of course."

"You want me to marry the father?" I can't quite believe I'm saying it.

"For years, your social circle has included permissible choices. Say for instance that Cyrus Eaton or Montgomery West were the father. Either would be a suitable match, and their parents would certainly support it."

I open my mouth, but I can't think of a thing to say. It just hangs there. I feel like I'm being asked to play a child's game. I'll name candidates and my father will decide which are most like me, and which are not.

That's how my life was always going to turn out, I realize. It was never my own. It never will be. Not if he has anything to say about it.

"I'm not marrying anyone." He can't force me down the aisle.

"Then that leaves two other options. Terminate the pregnancy."

I swallow and level my eyes to meet his. They blaze back at me and I know that I'm not walking through this fire without getting burned. "No. I'm keeping her."

"I assumed you would say that." He sighs, the sound caught somewhere between a laugh and a groan. "Then, you're cut off."

I expect this. It's one of the reasons I left when I did. The longer I had before he found out, the more time I would have to get things in order. I'd planned to put some money aside, pay my rent in advance, do whatever I had to do to get by until I found a job. I thought I had more time. "I guess I am."

"How noble of you." His mouth twists, and I know exactly what he thinks of my decision. "Take the high road, will you?"

"If I had wanted an..." I can't bring myself to use the word. "I could have done that back home."

"Instead, you ran away like a child. Do you really think you have what it takes to be a mother? A single mother? A poor mother? No education. No means. You can't afford this place."

"There are other hospitals."

"Yes, there are other hospitals for citizens."

"I have a study visa," I say defiantly. "I paid the healthcare surcharge and—"

"You do not have a visa as you dropped out of the program," he interrupts me. "Did you think I wouldn't find out? You've been lying and stealing from me for months."

"Stealing?"

"The funds for your apartment, for your classes..."

"I paid for those things," I say, but even as I speak I

feel everything unraveling. No matter how hard I try to stop it, I can't get a hold on the situation.

"And how will you pay for them in the future? Will you stay in the country illegally?"

"Dr. Thompson wants me to stay. I'm sure she can help me."

"Likely," he admits to my shock. He never likes to admit that anyone else can be right. "You'll incur medical bills for your treatment here. They told me you would need monitoring following the accident. Those kinds of bills add up."

"I'll get a job."

"Even if you could, it won't pay for this hospital," he points out. "And I doubt they'll be willing to issue a work visa to someone who lied about her intentions for coming here."

"Plans change," I say flatly, but reality is wrapping itself around my heart and squeezing until I feel like I can't breathe.

"Obviously." He stands, giving me a nod, as he plants his cane on the tile. "I wish you luck with those plans. I will pay this bill and see that you have through the end of the month at your apartment. After that, you will need a better plan. Perhaps, one that doesn't *change*."

"You're just going..." He'd threatened me with this since I was old enough to drive. I'd always suspected it was a way to make sure that I came home.

"This is your choice," he says, starting toward the door. "I am not the villain of this story. I offered you my help. I offered you solutions. You chose to refuse that help. I'm just glad that your mother isn't alive to see this. It would kill her."

"No, it wouldn't. But I guess we'll never know since you killed her."

He turns sharply, nearly stumbling from the effort. "Keep your voice down. People will hear you.

"I hope they hear me in the hallway. I hope someone sells the story to the tabloids."

"Why not you?" he says in disgust. "Pay for your bastard."

"I would never disrespect my mother's memory that way." I can't believe he'd accuse me of selling out the family. Not after I'd covered up what he did. I'm just as complicit as he is. But, more than that, I can't stand the idea of my mother being remembered as the heart of a scandal instead of for the amazing person she was. "And you're wrong. Mom would say to turn this into a diamond. She'd be there for me. She'd find a way to help me. Because she knew how to love unlike you. I wish you'd been the one to die that night. I wish she was here now."

"Do you think I feel any differently?" he roars. "I can't change what happened."

"You could learn from it!" And that's the real issue. It's not that he made a mistake. It's that he can't admit it. "You call me a whore, but you're a murderer. What choices did you have? Go to jail? Lie? Pay people to turn a blind eye to what really happened? Who cut you off? Who took away all your power when you made a mistake? No one. No one ever takes anything from Angus MacLaine."

"Money is power, Adair. Money buys second chances."

I shake my head. "Don't you see? You can't buy a second chance. Second chances are given. And you'll never get one, because you killed the only person who would ever consider it."

He bangs his cane on the floor. "This is not about me."

Everything's about him.

"Is that what you want?" he continues. "A second chance? Why would I give you that?"

"Because you're my father, and you're the only parent I have left."

This finally stops him. He stands near the door, and for the first time in my life, my father looks small. Maybe I've finally bent him. Or maybe I see him differently now that I'm carrying my own child.

"I don't have to wait for her to be here," I say, placing my palm on my stomach, "to know that I will always put her first. If that means losing my inheritance, you can take it. You want the family name? I'll take mom's maiden name. I'll go to the public hospital. I'll sell whatever I own. I will protect her, because that's what a mother does. That's what Mom would do. She wouldn't make ultimatums. She wouldn't force me to do something I would regret for the rest of my life. She would give me a second chance. Actually, no she wouldn't. Mothers don't give second chances. Mothers just love you—the good, the bad. A mother's love is free. I don't have a mother to give me that anymore, but I can give that to my baby."

We regard each other with a silence that feels like it will never end. I can't help but think this will be how I remember him: quiet, rigid, small. I won't miss him. There's nothing to miss. All he's ever given to me was money and expectations. You can't miss those things.

His eyes shutter and then he finally speaks, "Adoption."

"What?" I ask, unsure I heard him.

"There is one more option. You can give the baby up. Stay in London, have the baby, and give it to someone capable of caring for it."

"I'm not giving *her* up to some stranger."

"Not a stranger," he says. "That would be too risky. If the wrong person found out you were her mother, there's no telling what they might try to do to our family."

"I don't think most people looking to adopt a baby are interested in blackmail."

"Ah, my sweet, stubborn, *stupid* child. You know everyone can be bought, but everyone is capable of betrayal. Learn that now before it's too late," he advises. "You are right about one thing, however. You won't give her to a stranger."

I'm too flummoxed to respond. I'm not sure my father has ever admitted I was right before. Still, I don't see how this is a real option, especially if we both agree that the baby can't be given up.

"The solution is simple." Angus MacLaine always has a trick hidden up his sleeve. He saves it for when he needs it most. I've watched him play it during billionaire-dollar mergers. He produced it during the investigation into the car accident. "She will stay in the family."

I press my hand harder against my stomach as I feel an undeniable kick, as though she understands what he's saying before I do.

"I will pay for the medical bills," he continues. "You will remain in London and give birth. After which, you will continue to have access to your trust fund and remain in the will. You can remain in London. Return to school. You will both be taken care of."

"And?" There's a catch. There always is with a MacLaine. "You'll just play granddad?"

"Yes," he says, catching me off guard, until he shows his final card. "Because you'll give the baby to Malcolm and Ginny to raise. No one will ever know the truth."

"I wish I hadn't waited until he was dead to return to Valmont," Sterling says darkly. "I wish I'd come back to kill him myself."

"He'd already won," I say wearily.

"So, they just took her from you?" He runs a hand through his dark hair. "Is that even legal? Did you sign documents?"

"Not exactly," I admit before plunging into the rest of the story. When I finish, he's pale. He moves onto the couch next to me and draws me into his arms, tucking my body against his, before kissing my forehead. I let myself cry, openly and freely, for the first time in years. It's ugly and painful, my sobs wrack my body until my lungs hurt. I've told myself not to dwell on the past, because I didn't think I could survive it. Now, standing on the other side of it, I'm left to wonder if I just gave up.

"Do you think...Did I give up too easily?"

His arms tighten around me, protective and strong, and I dread the first moment I have to spend without their comforting presence, knowing it's an inevitable fact of life.

"Lucky, you didn't give up. You never gave up." He tilts my tear-stained face up to meet his own red eyes. I didn't realize until this moment that he'd been crying, too. "I'm proud of you, but you don't have to fight alone anymore. I'm here now, and from this moment forward, we fight together."

"And you were in London the whole time?" I ask, dreading her answer. This came up once before when Luca had mentioned time we spent in London. I'd thought she was jealous, then. The more she tells me, the more angry I become.

She nods. "You mentioned being in London while you were serving."

Of course, she remembers that tiny detail Luca spilled at the gala. I'm not sure why he even brought it up. It was never a night I wanted to remember-—until now.

"I was there for a stopover on my way to final training in Afghanistan," I confess. "A lot of it's a blur. The night ended with whiskey and tattoos." I gesture to the brotherhood tattoo she asked about earlier.

"When was that?" Adair asks, and I can see her eyes flit back and forth like she's reviewing memories of her time there trying to figure out if one of them has me somewhere in the background. But she won't find it.

I'm the one who had a chance to fix things, not her. "December."

"Ellie was born in November," she murmurs. I feel like I've pulled a block out of her carefully constructed reality as realization after realization comes crashing down on her. She shakes her, forcing herself to smile through the obvious pain. "It's not like you knew we were there."

"That's just it," I say, feeling sick to my stomach. "I think I did."

Winter five years ago

For the first time in nearly a year, I'm finally out of the South. I'd expected my first trip from Camp Lejeune might be a trip to New York. After the way I left things with Francie, I owe her that, even if she's forgiven me. Instead, I've found myself on my way to the final phase of training before I'm giving a permanent assignment. I'd been told to prepare to leave the country when I enlisted, but I hadn't expected that to happen for a lot longer. I also hadn't expected to find myself in London.

"Wait, is this the first time you've been out of the country?" Luca asks, and I bristle. He shoots Jack an incredulous look, but he shrugs.

"Don't look at me, man. I haven't either." Jack's cool response stops me from overreacting.

"Really?" Luca repeats. "Never?"

"I grew up in foster care," I remind him.

"Single mom," Jack says. "We didn't exactly go on vacation."

In the last few months, we've gotten to know each other better, each of us skirting around whatever sad stories sent us signing up for the Marines. During the first three phases of special ops training, we'd stuck together. Unlike some of the other recruits neither Jack nor Luca joined to prove anything. We just didn't have a lot of options. It made it harder to relate to some of the more ride or die types training alongside us, many of whom had washed out and headed back to their Marine units. Luca liked to say that we were a sort of suicide squad and that made us stronger than some of the others. It's pretty damn easy to say you'll fight for someone else and then fail to live up to that promise, it turns out. But when all you've got is the fight, there's a certain glee to going balls to the wall. Plus, we'd discovered that we all had our own particular set of skills.

I'd always been good at numbers with an interest in literature, which meant I'd taken to code cracking and a few of the foreign languages we'd been introduced to. Jack's talent lay in his steady hands, trained from years of teaching himself instruments. He ranked at the top of every marksmanship test. He could even slow down his heart enough to get a shot off at a record-breaking distance, a feat which meant he'd been flagged for extra training as a sniper. It was something we were all expected to do to some extent, but Jack? He's the one they'll call in when they want to take out a high-level target from a helicopter. Luca's particular skills don't fall into a training category. He's just fucking insane. If an ounce of him fears death, he's never shown it. He walks into every training scenario with a sort of jubilant nihilism. I can never decide if he's going to be the one that saves the entire unit or gets us all killed.

"Look, we need to celebrate," Luca says. "We've got

one night in London before they send us to the ninth circle of hell. We should make it count."

"You're going to get us discharged before we even get assigned to active duty," Jack says.

"What? No! I know London. I have family here," he says as we brush past a few other trainees in the hall on our way to the stairs.

Jack lifts his eyebrow behind Luca's back. We've pieced together enough about Luca's family from things he's said to know he's not talking about a typical family. I'd guessed but Jack was the one to look it up and discover that the DeAngelos were a well-established, far-reaching criminal organization. Of the three of us, Luca's been the most tight-lipped about why he joined up. I can't help thinking his chaos in a bottle routine is hiding something darker. I just can't figure out if he's running from his past, his family, or himself.

"Are we going to their house for family dinner?" Jack says dryly.

"Believe me, you don't want to hang out with my family. Not when you have a city like this at your disposal." He snaps his fingers and whips around, continuing to walk backwards. Somehow he manages to not knock into anyone, but, probably, because everyone moves out of his way. "I've got it. I know what we're doing tonight."

I brace myself. I can only imagine the trouble he could get us in a city this size.

"Does it involve a felony?" Jack asks.

"Stealing ah a horse isn't a felony—"

"It actually is in North Carolina," Jack says.

"—if you're only borrowing it," Luca continues. "I was

never going to keep the horse, so it would have only been a misdemeanor. No big deal."

"I still don't understand why you took the fucking horse." He shoots me a look, and I correct myself with a sigh. "I mean, why you *borrowed* the horse."

The only time we'd left base at Camp Lejeune for a night out had involved said borrowed horse, a police chase, and some serious sweet talking. Thankfully, the officer had a soft spot for Italians, and Luca had flirted our way out of trouble before it got back to any of our commanding officers. Jack and I hadn't agreed to a night out since.

"Hey, where are you heading?" A deep voice calls when we reach the lobby. We pause to find the last member of our usual group standing with a few ranking officers. Noah Porter tips his head toward the men he's talking to before making his way to us.

"I'm taking them out for the night. Want to come?"

"Is that a good idea?" Noah asks, but his question isn't directed at Luca but at us.

I grimace, not sure how to answer. Noah is the exception to our inner circle. To be honest, I'm not quite clear on how or why he wants to hang out with us. Because Noah is everything we aren't. If the Midwest had an official mascot, it would be Noah Porter. The corn-fed, farm boy came from a family with six kids, all of which have joined the military in some fashion or another. But Noah, he's the shining star. The Marine. Soon-to-be special operative. The town probably throws a parade every time he comes home. We should hate him. I should hate him.

The trouble is that he is one of the nicest human beings on the planet. Sometimes it's hard to see how the gentle giant wound up here, learning how to track, spy, and kill. But I've seen him in training exercises. He's ride or die, and he means it. I can't help but worry that he's going to be the first one of us to spend Christmas as a folded flag on his family's fireplace mantle.

I think this is why Luca enjoys baiting him so much. Whereas Jack and I genuinely like Noah, Luca's affection is as hot and cold as a broken faucet. I think he sees him more as a toy to play with than a living, breathing friend.

"Look, if you want to sit around and drink tea and fawn over photos of the royal baby, be my guest," Luca drawls, "but I want a decent meal before we spend the next few weeks picking sand out of our dinner."

""That's not a bad idea," Noah says. No doubt he expected something a little more exotic. Honestly, we all did.

"And then we're getting tattoos and getting laid," Luca adds.

That sounds more like what I expect of him.

"You're just going to go out and sleep with some random woman?" Noah says in disbelief.

"It's cute how shocking you find that," Luca says. "But yeah, that's exactly what I'm going to do. I haven't fucked anyone since officer—"

"Maybe you should sit this one out," Jack cuts in gently.

"Nah." Noah shakes his head. "I'm not going to stop you guys from having fun. I'd rather not hang out here all night, but I'm not getting a tattoo."

"About that," I begin.

"Everyone's getting a tattoo," Luca orders, leaving no room for argument.

Noah opens his mouth to protest, but I shake my head. There's no point debating it. We stand a better chance if we get him drunk enough to forget about it.

"Where to first?" I ask.

"Well, there's this little restaurant in Notting Hill that makes real meatballs."

Noah nods his head. Large portions of meat seems to be the one real connection the two have made.

"And a tattoo parlor just down the street," Luca adds, flashing a wicked grin.

It's going to be one hell of a night.

"I'm not inking the word hell on my arm." Noah and Luca have been having the same argument for the last hour. It had continued over dinner, and no pressure Luca exerted could sway him.

Luca had spent the entire night performing persuasive gymnastics, with Olympic-level focus, while a never ending stream of food arrived at our table courtesy of the house. I guess they knew they had a DeAngelo sitting in their dining room. He'd acted in stark contrast to the behavior I'd seen from the wealthy elite of Valmont. He didn't demand or condescend. He walked in, gave his name to the maître d' and the rest took care of itself. I rather appreciated the casual style with which he handled it, but I didn't quite want to think about why I got my meal for free.

"He's not going to drop this," Jack mutters to me as we leave the warm restaurant to stumble into the chilly darkness.

"At least, he's not making us get Santa on our ass," I say, nodding to the holiday decorations that were strung over every street lamp, shop front and home as far as we could see. Over dinner, we'd even been served a pizza shaped like a reindeer. Apparently, the British took the holidays very seriously.

I shoved my hands in my jacket against the biting wind. Given that we were headed to Afghanistan for the final phase of our training to run real-world drills, I hadn't brought along a lot of civilian clothes. I'd be in uniform most of the time. I hadn't counted on spending time outside the hotel before our early flight out.

"Not much for Christmas, huh?" Jack asks, hanging back with me while the others continue to fight.

"It's complicated." Last year this time I was with Adair, making love to her in a tiny, squeaky dorm room bed before spending the holidays with her in New York. It isn't that I miss her. I've come to terms with the fact that I'd just been another shiny new object that lost its luster for the rich bitch. I will, however, miss Francie, who I still haven't seen since I enlisted. We'd spoken on Thanksgiving and she'd been sending care packages to North Carolina, but I have no idea if I'll get a chance to talk to her on Christmas. There are a lot of Marines with real families back home to call, guys like Jack.

"Isn't it always?" Jack drops it. He's good like that, always knowing when I don't want to talk anymore.

A troop of carolers pass us, beginning a chorus of *Gloria in Excelsis-Deo* as they do. They smile cheerfully, and I have to resist the urge to heckle them. Maybe the holidays are a peaceful time of year for some people, but I can count on one hand how many happy Christmases I've had. A memory of the holiday party at Windfall taps at my brain, but I slam the door on it.

But the song must have given Jack an idea, because he calls up to Luca. "Hey, what about Latin?"

"Latin what?" he asks.

"For the tattoo. Instead of Hell's Bastards, we do the Latin translation."

It's Luca's idea that we need to permanently cement our brotherhood with inked forearms.

"Great," Luca agrees. "Who knows Latin?"

"I do."

We all turn to Jack in surprise.

"What?" he asks with a wide grin. "I'm not just a pretty face."

"Still blasphemous," Noah says.

"Why don't you sit this one out? Or get something else?" Jack suggests, not unkindly.

Noah turns to me obviously looking for support, and that's when I spot the fear behind his eyes. "You really going to do this?"

I'm about to ask him if he's afraid of needles when a Bentley pulls by, parking just across the street. I can't help admiring its classic, elegant lines. There's something so British about it. A driver pops out, opens an umbrella against the falling snow, and hurries around to open the door for the back passenger. A long black cane appears first and catches my attention, and I stop. I have no idea why until the man emerges, standing with bitter resolve. He pushes away the umbrella like it's offensive to him, and as he does, I catch a glimpse of his face under the streetlamp. I'm a thousand miles away from Valmont, but somehow it's caught up with me.

I don't notice that the others have continued until Luca's voice slices through the night. "Ford!"

It happens in an instant. Angus MacLaine's dark head turns toward the sound, his gaze sweeping across the street and landing on me. He pauses as our eyes lock.

I take one step off the sidewalk, my hand curling into a fist, before my brain has caught up with me. Before I take another, a strong hand closes over my shoulder.

"You coming?" Noah asks in a low voice.

We've been training for moments like this. I've spent the last few months studying how to react when caught off-guard and what to do when you face the threat of a deadly enemy. MacLaine's driver turns, surveilling me in a way that tells me he's here to provide more than car service. But he's old, and I doubt he's got as little as I do to lose. It would be so easy to cross that street and take them both down. I could probably count on Luca to join me. He doesn't need a reason to start a fight.

And then Angus MacLaine makes the decision for me. He places one hand on his bodyguard's arm and turns away, walking with a limp toward the gated building behind him without so much as one final glance.

"Come on," Noah urges.

I shake it off, or I try to, but adrenaline hums through me from the encounter. We catch up with Luca and Jack, who'd stopped fifty paces away. Luca's eyes glint with whatever wicked thoughts are currently dominating his brain, but Jack's are furrowed with concern.

"What was that about?" he asks.

I may as well be honest, because I finally know what I need to do—and I'm going to need them to help me figure out how to do it. *That's the man who ruined my life,* I tell them, *"and someday I'm going to destroy him."*

"That's when you came up with your plan," she says softly as the memory fades.

"I was so consumed with hating him, I never stopped to consider..."

"If I was in the building..." trails Adair.

Realizing how close we came to finding each other—on a different continent and without knowing we were in the same city—just makes it more painful for her.

For both of us.

"I could have done something. I could have checked. Before you had to go through everything you did. But all I could see was revenge." I realize my hands are still fisted and force myself to relax them. "But looking back—it was like I could feel you were there somehow. Like I knew Angus MacLaine would get out of the Bentley. My body stopped to wait before my eyes understood what I was seeing. Probably sounds crazy."

"If you didn't know I was there, what could you have done?" Adair says, apparently determined not to pass the buck of self-loathing.

"I don't want to keep dragging us back into the past. I want us to move on, but I have to know why," I say.

"Why?" she repeats.

I choose my words carefully. After everything she went through without me, I won't pile on another accusation, but why did she choose to go through it alone? "You didn't have to do this alone. I wouldn't have left you. Why..." A horrible realization dawns on me, and I bury my head in my hands. "The drinking. The fighting. I'm sitting here acting like I was some prize catch instead of a damaged sperm donor."

"Don't," she says in a wounded voice. "Ellie's amazing *because* you're her father."

"Why didn't you tell me?" The question explodes out of me.

"I didn't know where you were!" she fires back. "You just took off without a word."

"I came back. I looked for you." *You didn't come.* I manage to swallow the last bit before it gets out.

"My friends thought it was better not to tell me," she mumbles. "Poppy only got the guts up to say something a few weeks ago."

"I sent you a note."

"I didn't get it," she says in a small voice. "Did you get mine?"

"You sent me one, too?" I ask, shocked.

"Before you left. I think. Honestly, I'm not sure how long it took them to come clean that you'd gone. I wasn't coping well after the video."

"Video?" I echo the word, trying to make sense of it.

She takes a deep breath, her face as pale as the glowing moon outside, and I brace myself for whatever she's about to tell me.

"The video of us having sex," she says in a rush.

"The *what?*" I'm back on my feet, needing to dissipate the surge of adrenaline her words sent shooting through me.

"You didn't know." Her eyes close and she sighs in relief.

"That there's a video of us having sex? No, and I have a few questions now."

"I don't have any answers," she says with a shake of her head. "It had to have been my dad. He had private investigators looking into you."

"I remember," I say in disgust. I'd never forget having my sins dredged up by Angus MacLaine. I'd also never forgive him for it.

"He told me there was a blackmail note and he gave me an address in Queens and—"

"You thought I would do that to you?" I ask in a quiet voice.

"No," she says honestly. "At first, I was too shocked to think. I just hid like I could make it disappear. I wouldn't talk to anyone. By the time, I was ready to face it..."

"I was gone." Anger vibrates through me, but as I turn to pace the opposite direction, I catch sight of her face and I realize that this didn't just happen to me. It happened to us. For years, I've suffered under the delusion, I got the raw end of the deal. Now I know she went through things I couldn't imagine. "You know, Shakespeare could make a great play out of this."

Her answering laugh is hollow like a fading bell. "That's the truth. Can you forgive me for thinking the worst of you?"

"There's nothing to forgive, Lucky. I might be angry— furious, even—but it's only because I wasn't there to protect you from being hurt." I'm angry at her father and her friends, and, mostly, myself.

"You're here now," she says.

"And I'm all in," I promise her. "We're going to make this right. *All* of this right."

"I'm not sure we can. They're never going to let her go," she says. "I don't know if I'll ever..."

"We're going to get her back, Lucky." I say it like an oath, because it is.

She turns tired eyes on me and gives me a numb smile. "It's not going to be easy. They made sure of that."

"Did they actually adopt her? Because that paper was a decree of guardianship." My mind is already turning things over, making a list of people to call and favors I'm owed.

"There's more to it," she says. "It's complicated."

"Isn't it always complicated with us?" I ask, leaning to brush my thumb across her lip. "But this? This isn't complicated. I've seen them with her. It was everything I could do not to carry her out of that nightmare when I went to see her."

"You went?" she asks in a strained voice.

"I assumed you knew."

"I guessed, but...it doesn't matter." She sighs deeply. "Did anyone see you?"

"Felix. He brought her down to talk to me," I say and hesitate before adding, "and Ginny."

"Shit. That's not good."

But there's something I can't ignore any longer. "No one knew I was her father? Malcolm? Ginny?"

I don't know why it stings. She owes me nothing. Not after I left her to carry this weight alone. Maybe that's not what bothers me, though. I'd counted on Adair's family being surprised at my change in circumstances when I returned. I'd even used her brother's narcissism-fueled obliviousness to my advantage.

"Felix and Ginny both suspected. Ginny's been acting crazier than usual since you showed up in town. Felix never bought my lie that I didn't know who the father was," she says.

"And your father?"

"He never bought it either, but Angus MacLaine could always be counted on to avoid difficult conversations if he had an out."

"Why?" I ask. It's the one question I need an answer to for my own sanity. "Why not tell anyone? If people had known, word might have reached me."

"And let my father continue to wreck your life? I thought you left, and, even if you weren't the one who made that video, I was so hurt and alone and *scared*."

She'd acted on instinct. I can't fault her for that. I can only spend the rest of my life making this up to her.

"And I stayed," she continues, "even after...I stayed and I loved her when they didn't. I stayed, and I protected her from all of them. I stayed and filled the cracks they left in her with all of my love, because they made certain I was powerless to do more. I stayed and watched them play house with her, because getting to be near her was better than losing her altogether."

Kneeling in front of her, I take her hand. "I swear to you, no one is going to hurt our daughter anymore. I won't allow it."

"They have lawyers and money and contracts on their side," she says, "and they made sure that I had no way to fight them when I realized the mistake I made. We can't just walk in there and take her back."

"I know." It's what stopped me from doing it earlier. "You needed resources. They kept them from you. I know some people who can handle things like this. I'm going to get a meeting with them as soon as possible."

"Sterling, this whole town belongs to my family," she reminds me in a brittle voice.

When I'd come back to Valmont, I'd found a different woman waiting for me in the place of the girl I left behind. I'd caught glimpses over the last few weeks here. The more we spent together, the more I saw her and that fiery personality I'd fallen for years ago. Now I understand what happened. Now I know why she stayed while they slowly chipped away at her. She's come to life again slowly the more time we spent together, and now I see the mysterious piece of the story that explains everything. And I know what I need to do.

"It doesn't belong to them anymore." Truth burns in my words, because nothing will stop me. Not anymore. "This is our town now."

"But—"

"There are things you need to know," I stop her. It's time I come clean, too. "Things that are going to scare you."

She knits her fingers through mine more tightly. "No, it won't."

For once, I hope she's as stubborn as she sounds. I plunge into my other problems, realizing how insignificant they feel now. Judging from Adair's pale face when I finish telling her about the Bratva, she doesn't share that sentiment.

"I don't just have problems," I finish, "I have rivals. I have enemies."

"No." She shakes her head, but her hand doesn't leave mine. "*We* have rivals. *We* have enemies."

"Adair, I'm not sure you know what you're getting in to," I start.

"I'm starting then I look," she says dryly, squeezing my hand. "And I'm all in."

THE LAW OFFICES OF LAIRD & WHARTON ARE understated and serious, but also vaguely tense. The young, ambitious lawyers here would shove their mothers out of the way to get ahead, and you can feel it in the air, like a warning.

"Sterling Ford, here for a meeting with Ms. Laird and Mr. Welles," I tell the receptionist, a thirty-something woman wearing an oversized, hand-knit poncho with garish makeup, as if Betty Page got up one day and dressed like Martha Stewart.

She smiles brightly but says nothing, instead pushing a button on her phone and speaking into her headset. "Ms. Laird," the woman says, "I have a Sterling Ford here."

She listens a moment, then rises to her feet. "This way, Mr. Ford. Ms. Laird and Mr. Welles will join you in our conference room."

I go over the conversation I want to have in my head. Cameron Laird is the attorney who helped me anonymously purchase—and then sell on—my shares in MacLaine Media. She's young, ambitious, and very talented. And somehow, *despite* being a lawyer, she seems like a good person. We'd spoken on the phone earlier about Ellie, as well as another matter.

I requested one other lawyer be here as well, one I've met before, but who probably won't remember me. I'd warned Cameron as to why. In the past five years I've had a lot of time to consider lawyers, especially Mr. Welles. Since he's still practicing, I assume he's on good terms with the State Bar Association, a feat that can only be explained by assuming Welles kept his fingers crossed when he vowed to uphold the law and avoid conflicts of interest.

The timing of my scholarship getting pulled five years ago simply can't be a coincidence. Someone was paid to take a stack of thin evidence—provided by Angus MacLaine—and make it amount to something that would get me banished from Valmont. Who better than a lawyer who was supposed to be representing the interests of the University, maybe one who worked for and had sway over the Dean of Students? And after what I learned today, the crime I want Welles to answer for has gotten a lot bigger in scope. His actions contributed to my daughter living a nightmare—a nightmare Welles will be living soon.

"God, you're unbelievable, Welles. Every time I think you've hit rock bottom, you dig a little deeper," a woman says, upset enough that her voice leaks into the hallway.

"You're just fucking jealous I'm going to make partner when they announce it next month, even though you came to work for your older brother," a man replies, his thin, nervous voice at odds with the message he's trying to convey. "Look at this fucking meeting, you know? You helped this Ford guy, who's *stupid fucking rich*, with whatever-it-was, and when he comes back needing more help he asks for me. Says something, don't you think? I know your brother will agree with me. "

I guess my hunch that the professional Ms. Laird and the gutter-snake Mr. Welles wouldn't see eye to eye was correct.

The receptionist shoots me an apologetic look, looking slightly confused to see me grinning like a kid at Christmas, and raps quickly on the door sending the two lawyers to rigid attention.

Cameron recovers first, springing up to offer me a handshake, "Mr. Ford, how wonderful to see you again."

"Hello, Mr. Ford. I'm Peter Welles." He doesn't bother coming to shake my hand, instead sitting at one end of the conference table, his neck struggling to fill the small collar of his shirt and giving the unmistakable impression of a gopher popping its head out of its hole. My hands flex instinctively, as if even they are smart enough to know this guy's neck needs wringing. It's functionally no work to imagine Peter Welles looking into the mirror as a boy of 12, and, seeing the weasel-face staring back at him, determine his future profession: scummy lawyer.

He also doesn't recognize me. *At all.*

It takes a lot of self control not to rip his head right off his bony shoulders.

Cameron closes the door, and I take stock of the room we're in. Dark, with just a couple windows along the exterior wall. Contrary to television and movies, most law offices don't actually have floor-to-ceiling glass walls and permanently open blinds. Legal stuff is nasty shit better kept to closely-guarded cloisters. The real rule of thumb for law offices seems to be: the thicker the walls are, the better your secrets keep. And these walls are thick. A brass band could march by outside, and I bet we'd hardly notice.

"Mr. Ford, we spoke briefly on the phone, so I have some idea why we're here, but why don't you fill my colleague in on your situation?" Cameron says, taking a seat at the other end of the table, opposite Welles, and leaving me between them, like a bone for two dogs to fight over.

She and I didn't discuss this in much detail, but I approve of the choice.

"I've recently discovered I have a daughter—one I didn't know about." It takes me five minutes to discuss enough of the details to get the advice I need, but without going into so many details that Welles gets distracted by how batshit crazy this story actually is.

"I'm so glad you came to us," Welles says, seizing the floor as soon as he can. Dollar signs shine in his eyes. Not only am I *stupid fucking rich*, according to his own words, the MacLaines are practically American royalty. He's not just getting a payday but a scandal.

Good. Impress me, you little, little man.

"This is a life-altering event for you," he continues, "and

you're clearly the wronged party here. What kind of resolu-
tion were you hoping for?"

"I want the restoration of my parental rights—as soon as
possible."

"That will take a court petition, getting on the docket,
then the inevitable motions and the MacLaines will definitely file for continuances as long as they can," Cameron
says using her sorry-for-the-bad-news-voice. "It could take
months just to get the petition heard."

"Dammit," I say, feigning disappointment. I knew that
already thanks to the legal offices of Google, so I had time to
get over it. Welles doesn't need to know that, however. "Isn't
there some way to speed things up?"

"With what you've told us, I don't see how—" she begins.

"*Of course* there's a way. Where there's a will, there's a
way, eh Mr. Ford?" Welles shoots me a sly wink.

She frowns at her colleague, shooting him a warning
glance, which he completely ignores. "Short of a child
welfare issue reported to the county by Family Services,
there's nothing in court procedure that will require a quick
hearing."

"Exactly," says Welles smoothly.

"I'm confused," I say slowly before sliding fresh bait onto
my hook. "Is there a way or isn't there?"

The two stare at each other across the conference table,
locked in a battle of wills. She says "no" at the exact moment
he says "yes."

They both start to speak at the same time, and when it
becomes clear neither will cede the floor to the other, they
ratchet up in volume and intensity until they are both on
their feet.

"You're talking about fabricating information, Welles."

"That's *your* characterization, not mine."

When I hold my hand up to silence them, they can't stop before offering one final parting shot each.

"You *do not* fuck with family court!" she barks.

"You just have to be willing to go the extra mile for your clients," he says, turning to look at me with a silent question.

Which one of them is going to do that?

"Ms. Laird?" I say, turning to look at her. "Would you excuse us?"

If being a lawyer doesn't work out for her, Cameron should consider acting. None of this is news to her, but she played it all perfectly. It takes my words a second to settle in, then she gives Welles a look of such perfect malice I almost believe she's mad to see me get sucked in by her colleague.

"That'll be all, Cam," Welles says, a nakedly smug look of victory on his weasel-face.

She storms out without even a glance in my direction, leaving me alone with Welles.

"There was a lot happening all at once," I say conspiratorially to him. "I take it that someone needs to report an incident to Family Services?"

"Yes, it's really just as simple as that. The law allows for semi-anonymous reporting in child welfare matters. Teachers and other people who work with kids, they're *mandatory* reporters. If they see kids being mistreated, they have to file a report. But what happens if a plumber or a subordinate employee sees their employer hitting their kids? The law protects them if they want to come forward. They can claim they are effectively 'in a compromised situation,' and their report will be investigated despite being anonymous. It's hardly ever used."

Welles looks proud of himself, and in spite of myself, I'm

tempted to use what he just told me. I already discussed what direction I'd take with Cameron on the phone when I set this up, but it doesn't hurt to know there's a way to use the system if a real emergency with Ellie presented itself. I'm not in a position to draw unwanted scrutiny on my past or current business.

"But wouldn't the MacLaines know someone who works at Windfall reported them? They could get...punitive...with staff," I suggest. It's important I give Welles an out. One last chance to prove he's not scraping the bottom of the legal barrel for whatever scum he can use in his practice.

"Why would I worry about them? *You* are my client. The only thing is, the report needs details and plausibility. I'll write it myself. I've been to Windfall a few times," he says, puffing out his skinny chest. It's the detail he thinks will close the deal but he's opened a door he can't close.

"Wait, do you represent the MacLaines in other matters?" I stand up from the table and button my suit jacket. "How can I trust you to represent my interests? This meeting is ov—"

"No, no, Mr. Ford. Nothing like that." He shows me his palms, held at shoulder height. He's beginning to realize his mistake, which makes him desperate to prevent my walking out the door. "I've never *officially* represented the MacLaines. They had a problem with their daughter a few years back. Gold-digging boyfriend. I had just started work as counsel for Dean Cheswyk at Valmont U. We did a deal. Furnish evidence that would make their problem go away."

"And you found that evidence?" I repeat like I'm turning this over in my head. The truth is I want to hear him say it. I want him to admit what he did.

"Yeah. You know, get the kid kicked out of school *for stuff he actually did* without dragging the daughter into it too much." His eyes search my face without a trace of recognition, but his apprehension has already made his palms sweaty, because he rubs them absentmindedly on his trousers, leaving a dark blot. "Look, you need me. The MacLaines? They're going to fight, and they're going to fight dirty. This is going to be huge. We'll get the media on our side. You do a few interviews. We get that report made. Their own company will do the rest. I mean, have you seen the stories about them covering up MacLaine's wife's death? They can't handle more bad press, and we'll pile it on. They probably even have some old staff who'd be happy to burn them. You know what they say about revenge."

"Yeah, I do," I say quietly. "I know a lot about revenge."

He pauses, momentarily confused. "We can get started right away."

"I'm sorry, Mr. Welles. You misunderstand why I can't work with you," I say, watching his face melt into a sort of sad mess. This man doesn't hear 'no' enough. "I'm not the type of man who gets off when the shit circus comes to town. I just want my kid back. Preferably without traumatizing her for life. Nothing else matters. Good day."

He splutters a final, feeble attempt to salvage his new client. "I'm sorry to hear that. If you want to pursue the matter we discussed, give me a call. You'll have a couple months to consider it. Family court moves slowly!"

I stomp out of the office in a huff, and Welles, reluctant to be seen as the cause of this, or to apologize in front of his colleagues, disappears into a restroom.

I'm not surprised when Cameron slides into the elevator just as the doors are starting to close.

"How badly did he fuck himself?" she asks, unable to keep a smile off her face.

"Pretty badly." I pull the tape recorder out of the breast pocket of my suit. And click it off. "He explicitly advised me to fabricate evidence. Then he offered to do it for me. And *then* he admitted to taking money under the table in a scheme involving Angus MacLaine and one of the deans at the University."

"He'll end up disbarred," she says, her eyes closing as a deep, warm smile spreads on her face. "Serves him right."

"I'm just glad I was able to do it right," I say, and when I see the quizzical look on her face I elaborate. "I didn't make him do any of that. He was just...dying to show me he could. How much did you tell him I was worth?"

"Billions," she laughs, and it rings with the bright melodious sound of a person who just shed a heavy weight.

"You have a good day, Sterling. And don't think I've forgotten what really matters. Your daughter. Despite what I said up there, there is more we can do, and I'm on it."

"Thanks, Cameron," I say, getting off the elevator as she stays on. "We'll speak soon."

Cameron's laughter is still ringing in my ears when I step into the lobby, and, despite the pressure of my current situation, I feel lighter, too. I've been focused on revenge for five long years. I wanted pain. I wanted fear. But now I'm starting to understand that revenge doesn't just hurt the victim. Revenge is poison. It warps you. It changes you. It makes you into the monsters you think you're fighting. I never wanted revenge. I wanted to see bad people pay. I wanted to believe being a good person mattered. I wasn't out for revenge. I was looking for justice.

Justice restores. I can't change what Welles did to me.

Maybe he deserves worse than losing his job, but he won't abuse his power as a lawyer again, and, damn, knowing that feels pretty good.

Before I can settle into this brighter outlook on life, my phone rings. I check the caller ID and brace myself for a lecture. Sutton and I need to have a long talk, so I can explain how and why things have changed. "Hey, kid. Sorry, I kicked you out last night."

"You should be more careful with your family, Ford," Nikolai's voice says evenly, and realization grips me in a cold panic.

"What have you done?"

"Nothing. I'm just having a friendly chat with Sutton. She's very entertaining. I see stubbornness runs in the family."

"If you touch her," I begin my warning.

"I won't. You have my word. Unless, of course, we can't find a way to deal with our mutual problem," he says. "My brothers are getting impatient, shall we say? I would hate to have to send a stronger message."

"I don't know what you want me to do about this. If I knew who the witness was, he'd be a dead man." Maybe I haven't changed as much as I thought, but a man has a right to protect his family, doesn't he?

"But you have a friend who does know," he points out. "I have to say it doesn't look good to be seen talking to the FBI, Ford. People might make assumptions. I told my brothers you would never crack, but now we find out about Agent Porter, and well, I don't like being proven wrong."

"I'll deal with it," I snap. I don't know how, but it's not like I have a choice.

"It's always a pleasure doing business with you." I can

hear the feline smile in his voice. "And, Ford? The clock has started. Tick. Tock."

He hangs up, but his threat lingers in the air. Nikolai Koltsov has a short fuse, and it's been lit.

Tick-tock.

I am the worst boss in history. Not that I'm the boss, exactly, and I never will be if I can't get my head on straight. My thoughts keep wandering between flashes of last night and the wicked skills Sterling demonstrated in bed and worry over what's to come.

Because he knows. He finally knows.

I swore I would never tell him—never tell anyone. But burying my head in the sand isn't going to work any more. It feels as though every moment between the day he left and the day he walked back into my life has been leading to this. And there's so much more to wrap my head around: the FBI, the Bratva, the man he's become, the man he wants to be. I can't stop asking myself if he wants to be that man for me or for himself. I can't decide if it's an important differentiation. It feels like it is.

My phone rings. Sterling's ear must be burning. Of course, I'm always thinking of him, so maybe not. I answer it expecting news from his meeting with Cameron Laird. "How did it go?"

"Exactly what I expected," he says in a clipped tone that tells me his mind is elsewhere. "Look, something's come up. You're at your office, right?"

"Yes," I say slowly.

"Thank God." His relief is palpable. "Stay there."

The demand moves my emotional barometer from introspective to paranoid in an instant. "What's going on?"

"I've got everything under control," he says.

That's a pretty clear indication that things are out of his control.

"Sterling, tell me now."

"Nikolai decided to make a little statement," he says, continuing in a rush when I gasp. "He's got Sutton, but I have a plan. If you can't reach me this afternoon, don't worry."

"Oh, sure," I hiss into the phone, hoping none of my colleagues can hear me. "I'll just hang out here while you play cat and mouse with the Russian mafia. Are you ever not in trouble?"

"I guess not," he says dryly. "I promise everything is fine. I know exactly who to talk to, and I'm going to get to the bottom of this. Don't—"

"Worry," I finish for him, pinching the bridge of my nose. "I know. I'll just read a book."

"Good idea," he says, missing my sarcasm. "Love you."

He hangs up before I can respond, and I'm left staring at my desk. I shove my phone back into my bag, feeling a little numb. There's no way I can concentrate on edits for my first acquisition. I need to lose myself in a book, the way I only can on a first read. I rifle through a stack of possibilities someone's plopped on my desk looking for one that will sweep me away from this mess, even for a few hours.

Stay there.

We're going to have a serious talk about ordering me around later. For now, I'm forced to comply. The last thing he needs is for Nikolai to grab me, too. I get the impression he can compartmentalize and handle this like he claims. I'm not so sure he'd be able to do that if I'm involved. Or maybe I'm reading too much into his need to repeatedly tell me I belong to him when we're in bed. Either way, I'm stuck in the office for the day while my heart and my head are somewhere else. None of the manuscripts in my slush pile grab me, and then it hits me. In all the chaos, I'd nearly forgotten about the secret I found in a locked drawer at the Eaton.

I pull my mother's manuscript out of my black Louis Vuitton Neverfull tote, Poppy's congratulations-on-the-new-job gift. Trust her to know how to make me look like a professional, even when I show up to work in a loose, linen sundress without make-up. I need all the help I can get. I'd barely had time to swing by the Eaton, change, and grab the bag by the time I pried myself away from Sterling's bed. So much has happened in the last two days, I haven't even looked at it since I found it in the drawer. I can't believe it's only been two days. Maybe it's spending so much time reliving the past with Sterling as we piece together our time apart, but it feels like years since I pried open the locked drawer at the Eaton and found her book. I trail my fingers over the title page, wishing I could unlock more than just the drawer.

My mother wrote a book. I still can't quite process it. It feels as though I should have known she was a writer. I keep searching my memories for one of her writing or even talking about it. But there's nothing. No clue. No hint. The most evidence I can scrounge together of her literary leanings is how strongly she encouraged me towards books my whole life.

"What's that?" Trish interrupts my day dreams, holding a coffee mug emblazoned with the words *Bless your heart. You just flipped my bitch switch.*

"Sorry," I say quickly, shoving it to the side. I have a different manuscript I'm supposed to be working on. "It's personal. I should get back to work."

"Already cheating on your first book. Don't worry, I won't tell," she teases, tilting her head to read the title page. "Mac-Laine? Did you write that?"

"My mother," I say.

"I didn't know your mother was a writer."

"Neither did I," I confess. "I found it."

"Have you read it?" she asks.

"Not yet." I stare at it. "Should I?"

Trish sips her coffee thoughtfully. "I would," she finally answers, "but I'm nosey."

"So am I," I say with a laugh. "But I promised you those edits and—"

"Adair, you have weeks to get those edits in," she stops me, "and if I'm honest, you've seemed a bit distracted today. Maybe you should just read it and get it over with."

"I don't know that it's just the book distracting me." I chew on my lower lip as a mental list of all my current preoccupations starts scrolling through my brain.

"Tell me that your other distraction is six feet of smoldering manhood," she says in a lowered voice. "I've been meaning to ask if he has a brother."

"A sister," I say apologetically.

"Is she as hot as he is?" Trish asks.

"She's gorgeous," I confirm, "but a bit of a..." I search for a kinder term than bitch that still gets the point across.

"I have not outgrown my bad phase." Trish grins. "Bad boy. Bad girl. I'm a sucker for them."

"Let me see what I can do," I offer. I doubt Sutton will be interested in anyone I try to set her up with, but maybe it will give us something else to talk about. Like it or not, and she definitely doesn't, I'm going to be a part of Sterling's life moving forward. A big part. I need to start smoothing over that relationship as soon as possible.

"In the meantime, read the book," Trish says firmly, taking her mug and wandering over to the front desk to accept a delivery.

I pick up the title page and turn it over, making a new stack. What if I hate it? What if she wrote about us? I'm pleased to discover chapter one written at the top. It still takes effort to read the first line. *Summer always brought a fresh wave of tourists, making every foot of the small island loud. There was no escaping the noise, so like most, she avoided all the places she usually loved.*

By lunchtime, I'm halfway through. I'm so absorbed that Trish has to tap me on the shoulder.

"Want anything from the place around the corner? You look like you're going to skip lunch," she says.

"I'm good." I flash her a quick smile, tapping my pencil on my desk.

"You are an editor," she says with a laugh. "I can't pry you away from a story."

She disappears along with most of the staff, leaving only those of us with our noses buried in books behind. Today, I'm not stuck in Nashville. I'm on a small island off the coast of Washington state, puzzling over the toxic romance developing between two such vividly painted characters that I feel like I know them.

My mom wasn't just a writer. She was a great writer. The discovery leaves me equal parts excited and sad. It's bittersweet to find this piece of her that she never showed to anyone. I tumble back down the rabbit hole of her story until a shadow falls across my desk.

"I'm really not going to starve," I tell Trish past the pencil I'm biting between my teeth.

"You can't keep avoiding my calls," a cold voice replies, and I look up to discover my brother glaring at me.

"I'm at work," I say, shuffling mom's book to the side so he can't get a glimpse of it. I doubt Malcolm would approve of me reading it or making notes in it or flirting with the idea of publishing it.

"We need to talk," he ignores my reminder entirely and takes the chair opposite me. My stomach flips over.

About what? There's so many things we need to say to each other—few of them pleasant—but Sterling was clear that I should avoid my family until we settle things.

"Malcolm, I'm busy."

"Reading books?" he says with a sneer. Of course, he wouldn't find any value in that.

"Editing books," I correct him.

"Perhaps," he hisses in a low voice, leaning forward, "you could go to work on a different story. The press is having a field day digging up dirt about Mom's death. It makes us look bad."

"It makes Dad look bad," I say flatly.

"It makes all of us look bad." He grips the edge of my desk until his knuckles are white. "You can't just ignore this. We need to find out who leaked that story and get it under control."

I already know who leaked the story. Sterling told Sutton

and, well, Sutton doesn't like me very much. I'm not about to tell Malcolm any of this. "We didn't do anything wrong. Our father did, and he's dead, so he can't even pay for it."

"You would have liked that, wouldn't you?" Malcolm releases the desk and settles into his chair with a grim smirk. "What kind of daughter wishes her father had gone to prison?"

"Do you really want me to answer that?" I think of Trish's mug. My bitch switch has definitely been flipped.

"I want you to give a damn about what's happening to this family!" he roars. The other editor who skipped lunch looks up from her book with a frown before returning her attention to it. She clearly cares more about being interrupted than what we're fighting about.

"Why should I?" I ask slowly and carefully. I want him to answer. I want to hear his shitty, self-serving logic from his own lips. It will make all of this easier.

"You aren't the only one who stands to lose out if more damage is done. Ellie's inheritance is at stake. Not that I expect you to—"

"Do not presume anything where she's concerned," I cut him off. "It's not your place."

"It's not?" he repeats. "You can't rewrite history, Adair." He pushes to his feet, an accusing finger flying my direction. "*You* fucked up. *You* paid the price."

"Is that how you sleep at night? Telling yourself that I deserved it? I've always wondered." I'm on my feet now. My fingers twisting around Sterling's clover charm like a talisman.

"We did you a favor," he spits back, "and I've been paying for it ever since."

"A favor?" I repeat. "Fuck you, Malcolm."

I want to scream at him to get out. I want to threaten him. I want to tell him that she's mine, and I'm taking her back. But I don't want to see her dragged into the middle of this. I want to protect her from the worst of it. I always have.

"We all saw what you couldn't," Malcolm says in a furious whisper. "You were never cut out to be a mother. No matter what you thought. Where would you be now if we hadn't dealt with your problem?"

His words aren't the slap in the face he expects, even if they hurt. They are what I need to hear, however. Any doubt I had about fighting this—fighting them—dissolves into rock-solid certainty that I'm doing the right thing. I'm almost glad he came. Almost.

"Get out," I say in a soft voice. There's no point to yelling or screaming. I've spent most of my life kicking up a fuss trying to be heard. I'm done with that now.

I'm done with covering up my father's lies. I'm done with pretending Malcolm isn't turning into him. I'm done with ignoring the cracks in his marriage—the cracks in his wife. No more playing house, pretending to be the American success story. I don't want any of it. I only want what's mine.

"I guess I have to clean up this mess all by myself." He shakes his head. "You're a disgrace to the MacLaine name."

"I think that's the nicest thing anyone's ever said to me."

"Don't forget that your daughter bears that name," he says.

Not for long. Sterling and I haven't discussed it, but I know he'll agree with me. Ellie isn't a MacLaine, she's a Ford —and she's going to escape all of this.

"Ginny said you wouldn't help, but I didn't believe her. I didn't think you would stoop so low as to abandon your family. Well, consider it done. You don't want to be a

MacLaine, you're out. But don't you dare show up on our door. We're done with you, too. *All* of us, including Ellie."

I close my eyes and take a deep breath before the boiling rage inside me bubbles out of my lips. It's what he wants: to bait me. He's done it for years. Dangling Ellie over my head is the number one move in the MacLaine playbook. It's how they've kept me quiet.

For one moment, I'm tempted to lunge at the bait, afraid that he'll make good on this threat. I grasp the clover charm tighter and remember every promise Sterling made that we'll protect Ellie no matter what. I mash my lips into a thin line to keep myself from screaming, knowing he'll just use it against me.

"You really hate us that much?" he asks after a prolonged silence.

Winter five years ago

Six weeks. That's how long it's been since I've gotten more than three hours of unbroken sleep. Probably longer, given that I'd woken up every hour to use the bathroom starting at eight months. My eyes droop and I lean back in the recliner, a curved pillow propped carefully with two other cushions on my lap and a sleeping newborn on it. Ellie fell asleep nursing, but her lips continue to form tiny O-s in her sleep. I'm afraid to shut my eyes, worried she'll fall or roll. Putting her on my chest would be a better solution, but I'm even more afraid she'll wake up. Her eyelids flutter in her dreams and a sleepy smile flashes across her face.

And then I'm afraid if I close my eyes, I'll miss

moments like this—precious, perfect moments that are slipping away too fast.

"You should get some rest. I can take her," Felix offers.

But I shake my head, determined to power through. "I want to watch her sleep. She smiles. See."

Felix leans over and catches another grin. This one looks not unlike she's had too much to drink and passed out. Milk drunk.

"She's flirting with the angels," he whispers.

"What?" I say with a soft laugh.

"That's what my mother used to say when a baby smiled in its sleep." He straightens and turns an appraising eye on me. "You need more rest, Adair. You're still recovering."

"I'm fine," I lie. The truth is that I'm so tired that it feels like an anchor's dropped inside my skull and it's trying to drag my eyelids down. It takes work to keep them open.

"You lost a lot of blood," he reminds me, bending to carefully take Ellie from my lap. She stirs, arching her body, her neck straining, before settling sleepily onto his shoulder to continue her nap.

The day after my twentieth birthday, Elodie Anne MacLaine arrived in the world with only two settings: sleeping angel and diva. She'd been set to diva upon entrance, getting stuck on her way out as if to make it clear she was going to live life on her own terms starting from day one. Since then, she's displayed enough MacLaine stubbornness to further cement her status in the family. Although, I suspect she gets a fair amount from her father as well. The incident unfortunately resulted in a hemorrhage that required a blood transfusion and a longer than typical hospital stay. Felix has been hovering over me ever since.

"I can rest later," I say, even though the idea of crawling into bed is gloriously tempting.

"Rest now," he orders, rocking back and forth on his feet.

I grip the arms of the chair, but I can't bring myself to stand up.

"She'll still be here when you wake up," he promises. "I'll make sure of it."

"I know." But my lip quivers. She might be here in a few hours, but the truth is that I don't know how much longer I have with her. I drag myself to the bedroom, climbing into bed around the baby cot attached to its side, and curl into a ball. Closing my heavy eyes, exhaustion overcomes me but I can't sleep. Every ounce of me aches for it even as my brain switches to overdrive.

I'd had the finest medical care money could buy, Felix stayed with me the entire time, and everyone agreed that it was best for the baby to nurse for the first few weeks while Ginny and Malcolm prepared to take her home to Windfall. Moving into the family home had been one of my father's conditions. I suppose he half expects one of them to slip up and reveal the truth—that the baby isn't really theirs. Or maybe he just needs a woman around to keep under his thumb. Because my condition had been that I would not return home. I'd made him promise to let me go, to finally allow me to have a life of my own. It was all I'd ever wanted.

Before.

I don't know what happened or why I allowed myself to believe that I'd be able to make peace with the adoption.

Maybe my father's repeated reminders that my brother and Ginny were far more prepared to be parents influenced me. Maybe I believed what he said about me. The truth is that I'm a coward. I'm too scared to strike out on my own. I have no way to pay the astronomical cost of her private birth and care. No money to put a roof over our heads. And I doubt a single twenty something with a newborn is a hot commodity on the job market, even if I could score a work visa.

"Go to sleep!" I scream into the pillow, wishing my brain had an on-off switch.

This is becoming my favorite game, remembering all the mistakes I've made and then running through all the rationalizations I've been forced to adopt. Every time I play it—which is pretty much any time I try to go to sleep —I lose. I always find myself here with a hollow pit inside me filling with tears. Because I can remember and I can rationalize, but I have no idea how to let her go.

I'm running out of time to figure that bit out.

Eventually my body always triggers some survival mechanism, and I fall asleep only to be woken by Ellie's mewling, newborn cries. I'm still tired every time. Today's no different.

"She probably needs to nurse," I call to Felix. I'm not sure why. I doubt he can hear me over her crying. Throwing off the covers, I pad into the living room to take her and stop dead in my tracks.

Ellie isn't crying because she's hungry, she's crying because my father is holding her out at arm's length inspecting her. If her fussing bothers him, he shows no signs. Instead, his face remains detached. Felix watches from a short distance, looking exactly the opposite. He vibrates with the same manic energy I feel now like he's being pulled toward her.

"She has your hair," he says in a business-like tone.

Unlike Felix, I can't smother the instinct to rescue her from him. I rush over and snatch her from him, cradling her body close to my chest. "Shhhh. Mama's here."

My father clears his throat loudly as if to signal his disapproval of that term.

I ignore him and return to my chair, moving to situate the pillows around me as Ellie continues to scream.

"And your temper, it seems," he adds.

"You shouldn't have woken her," I say. Unhooking my bra, I work to calm her enough to feed her.

"What are you doing?" he asks in a strained voice, turning his back to me.

"Feeding my baby."

"Must you do it *here*?"

"Where would you like me to do it? Buckingham Palace?" I snap, frustration getting the better of me. I don't have the time or interest to assuage his fragile masculinity —not until I finally get her to latch on.

He peeks over his shoulder but quickly returns to his studious observation of the opposite wall. "Perhaps, you could cover up?"

"I'm fine. Thank you." There's no way that I'm going to let him make me feel guilty about *this*. I might have made some mistakes, but taking care of her isn't one of them. I continue to nurse her.

"Would you like some tea?" Felix asks carefully.

"Surely you have something stronger than tea," my father responds.

"We don't have anything," I tell him.

"What?" He finally turns around like he needs to see the words coming from my own lips.

"I just had a baby," I say. "I haven't been stocking the bar."

"But you knew you would have company. It's the proper thing to do. Your mother would never have been so thoughtless."

This is the new weapon in my father's arsenal: reminding me of how much I pale in comparison to her. He'd utilized it a few times in Valmont, but he's taken the comparisons to a new level since he found out about my pregnancy.

It takes every ounce of energy in me to dredge up the sugary sweet southern attitude he expects—the one that will keep this encounter from going sour. "I'm sorry, that I was thoughtless. I guess you'll have to go buy some. There's a store on the corner."

He stiffens at the suggestion, and I remember that he's not a man who buys things for himself.

"Felix," he barks. "Go buy some bourbon."

That's when I realize that he's completely helpless. Money might buy power. It might open doors. It can even close them. But money doesn't make the man, not if there was no man to start out.

Felix disappears with a furtive glance in my direction, returning a moment later with his wool overcoat and hat. "Adair, would you like anything? Should I pick up dinner?"

"I'm not hungry," I mutter. Anxiety churns in my stomach like bubbling acid making the thought of eating a bite while my father is here unthinkable.

"A little something," Felix coaxes. "Remember, you're still eating for both of you."

"If she's not hungry, drop it," Daddy orders. "She needs to take off the pregnancy weight before she returns to public life."

I wince, casting my eyes down to Ellie, who's fallen asleep again, and cradle her closer, taking care not to wake her.

But Felix doesn't back down. "She has plenty of time for that, but now she needs to look after her health as well as the baby's."

My father turns slowly, pivoting his body around the tip of his cane like a compass. His upper lip curls, and I brace for impact. It's not like Felix to challenge him. I didn't expect to ever see it. But if Felix is intimidated he doesn't show it. I've seen my father argue before with business associates. Those times it was like watching two goats lock heads, the more determined won by refusing to give out regardless of cost or time or reason. That's not what this is. There are no horns for my father to meet, and, for the first time, I see him not as the willfully stubborn creature I'd always believed him to be, but as a snake, rising from its coiled position, deciding whether or not to strike.

But Felix's response is not what I expect. He doesn't submit like a cornered mouse or freeze like a deer, he doesn't move at all. But somehow, he grows larger than I've ever seen him until his presence looms over us like that of a challenged bear.

"It doesn't matter as she won't need to feed the baby much longer," my father says with a shrug. The snake could strike but why risk getting crushed. "Do it if you like. She can waste the food or eat it. What do I care?"

"What do you mean?" I ask slowly.

He locks in on me instead. "Perhaps, Felix would like to get the bourbon I requested."

"Felix," I say softly, knowing I can't fight with Ellie in my arms, "could you please run down to the store? I'll take some cookies."

"I'll be back shortly." It's a promise and a warning rolled into one.

"What did you mean about me not feeding the baby?" I ask as soon as he's gone.

"Your brother and Ginny arrived with me this evening. They're getting their hotel suite ready to take the baby, and we'll fly back in a few days. Ginny wants to do some Christmas shopping first."

"They're here?" I can't process this. "Why didn't you tell me?"

"Does it matter?" he asks. "This was the arrangement."

"She's a person, not a piece of property. I can't just ship her over to their hotel in a few days. I need to get her things together. I need to get her used to a bottle. I need..."

I need to say goodbye. I need to memorize every bit of her— the way her fingers curl around mine when she's falling asleep, her soft adorable snore, the copper hair as fine as down that curls at the nape of her neck. I need to figure out how to put her in someone else's arms and walk away. The list is too long, and I realize that I could spend the rest of my life trying to finish it.

Because a mother isn't supposed to say goodbye. She's supposed to stay.

"A few days?" he repeats, not noticing that I've fallen silent. "I imagine they'll want to come tonight. Perhaps, tomorrow morning. Ginny is excited to meet her daughter and take her Christmas shopping. I'm sure they've thought of everything she needs. You can pack up anything you want to send along. It's not as though you'll want baby crap cluttering up your apartment." He laughs as though we're in on some joke. When I don't join, he finally pauses. "You are staying in London like we discussed?"

Instead of answering, I sit in stunned silence. I tell my body to nod my head, but it doesn't comply. A dozen responses jam in my throat as my brain tries to decide which one to send to my lips. I can't even think, so I watch Ellie sleep and hope this mess will untangle itself.

"I bought the flat," he continues, "as per our agreement. You are staying here?"

That was laid out in the document I'd signed. They didn't trust me to sign the adoption paperwork after the baby was born. So a contract was drafted, promising that I would allow Malcolm and Ginny to adopt the baby. They insisted I sign it. In exchange, all medical bills would be paid for both of us. I'd keep the flat in London. And Ellie would be a MacLaine. We all agreed to anonymity. Only a few people know about it. My family. Judd Harding, my father's lawyer. Felix. It's their insurance policy, and the plan I agreed to, knowing it's best for both of us.

I am staying in London. I just have to say it, accept it, and move on. But then, tiny fingers close around mine, Ellie smiles at me in her sleep, and the whole world shifts on its axis.

"No." For a moment, I think my brain got the signals

crossed and jolted the wrong answer out of me. I can't believe I said it.

"You're not staying in London?" His brow furrows, confused. It's not a predicament he's accustomed to so he paces across the room towards us.

There's nowhere for me to go, but I don't shrink as he approaches. I puff up, arms locking around my daughter. Something wild takes a hold of me. Something I don't know if I should trust, but which leaves me no choice not to. "Don't come any closer."

He stops in his tracks, and I think it might be the first time he's ever followed a woman's direction. It's certainly the first time, he's ever done anything I asked of him.

"Adair." His tone is rich with warning. "Everything is arranged. *You* agreed to it. It's for the best."

"No," I repeat.

There is no other answer crowding my thoughts now. I know exactly what my choice is: I will not give up my daughter.

"You are not in a position to say no to me," he roars. Instantly, Ellie's eyes snap open and her startled cry shatters the air. The pure panic in it shocks him enough to shut him up.

"You can't force me to give her up." I shift her onto my shoulder, shushing her gently as I try to soothe her. "Don't worry. I'm here."

"You'll ruin her life," he murmurs.

I look up sharply, expecting to find the malevolent snake poking its clever head out of the grass. Instead, there's just a man. There's nothing powerful or intimidating or impressive about him. He's stopped, propping himself with his cane, and I don't know if he's tired physically or mentally, but he looks wrung out, sapped of whatever vital force usually propels him.

"Like her father's parents ruined his," he says.

I've told the lie so many times it's become automatic. Soon, I'll believe it, too. "I don't know—"

"We're MacLaines," he stops me. "We always know a lie when we hear it."

Do we? I've always thought I could see through people, but I hadn't been able to see through Sterling. I'd glimpsed him. It wasn't until he opened up, peeled off his armor piece by piece that I finally saw who he really was. And then, I'd turned out to be completely wrong.

My father seems to be thinking the same thing. "He was poor. He grew up with nothing. No money. No security. No family. A mother who couldn't protect him, and look what he became. A liar. A con man. He used you without a second thought. What happens if he comes looking for you? What if he tries to shake you down again?"

"He won't," I say. Somehow I know this is true. He got what he wanted. My father sent the check. He left town. Except he didn't just leave town. Francie told me he'd joined the Marines. She told me he lost his scholarship. She blamed me.

And I'd been so blinded by my broken heart, I didn't see what was right in front of me. A MacLaine always knows a lie when we hear it.

"I told him I knew what he had done in the past, that he was unsuitable for you, and that he would never provide you with the kind of life I could."

I'd believed my father because he wasn't lying. Not about the tape. The tape existed.

"Is it true?" I ask. "Did you have his scholarship yanked?"

He wags his finger at me. "He deserved worse. Don't feel sorry for him!"

"Did you send the money?"

"What money?" he repeats.

"The blackmail money. Did you send it?"

"Of course," he snarls. "I won't chance that filth leaking out to the press."

And there it is. He didn't do it to protect me. He did it to protect himself, his reputation, his name.

I don't really care why he did it. What I do care about is all the pieces that don't add up. If Sterling's plan was to take the money why did he join the military? He didn't give the money to Francie. She'd made that clear.

"He didn't have any other options. So if he dies out there, his blood is on your hands."

"And the money?"

"What about it?" he snaps.

"It's spent, deposited...?"

He hesitates before finally saying, "No."

Why would Sterling Ford ruin his life with my father's uncashed check in his pocket?

"It was a game, Adair," he tells me. "A broken boy played a game with your heart, and when a bigger player came to the board, he attacked. He sent me that tape for one reason."

I'm tired of half answers and insinuation. "What was that?"

His eyes flicker over me before skittering to the wall again. "So, that I'd never be able to look at you the same way."

A piece of me I didn't know could be broken shatters. I don't know if he's right about Sterling. Maybe I'm a fool, and I never really knew him. Maybe there's some day I will understand. But regardless of whether he's right about why he did it or I'm right that he didn't do it, I'm still responsible like Francie said. I stood back and watched while he was stripped of his pride. That's why he didn't track me down or say goodbye. I didn't deserve it. Not then. Not now. I never will. "Then, I guess he's not going to come back."

The front door opens, and I stand, ready to run to Felix.

"Finally," my father says. "I need a drink."

"When don't you?"

"The moral highroad doesn't suit a sinner. You're not a martyr. You're just a stupid girl who's read too many books to have any common sense. You want to keep your baby?" he asks. "And give her what? You don't own the clothes on your back. You can't feed her. You only have one way to protect her. Me. This family. You can't do this on your own."

"Keep the baby?" A shrill voice repeats.

I look up in time to see a vase of flowers slip from Ginny's fingers followed by the sound of breaking glass. Malcolm glares beside her. Felix bustles past with a bottle of bourbon, looking determined to stay out of the matter.

"What are you talking about?" Malcolm demands.

"We don't need to discuss this right now," I say.

But my father is already talking. "Your sister has had a change of heart. It seems she's chosen the bastard over her family name."

"Noooo," Ginny moans.

"We have a contract." Malcolm storms into the room, heading straight for the baby like he's going to tear her out of my arms. I recoil, clutching Ellie to my chest. "We've seen to everything. The paperwork is drawn up. The name change is ready to be filed. Ginny just finished the nursery plans. She's been dreaming about this for weeks!"

But I'm not looking at him. I'm looking at his wife. Ginny hasn't moved an inch, but all the blood has washed from her face. She takes one wobbly step but can't seem to go any farther.

"I wish I could give you what you need, but you have to understand, she's my baby."

"That I paid for," Malcolm grumbles.

"She's not something you can buy and sell." I hold her closer, wondering how they can't see this.

"And yet you had no problem taking my money and running out of the country to have a child out of wedlock," my father piles on.

I look to Felix. He stands in the corner, watching all of us, and I wish he would step in and calm everyone down. He's the one who can handle my father and soothe Ginny and distract Malcolm. Why isn't he? *Help!* I send the S.O.S. silently, but instead of answering he turns away. Why would he do that now when I need him the most.

Malcolm and Daddy continue to level threats, but I tune them out, rocking from side to side to keep them from waking the baby. There's no point in arguing with them. Not right now. Once a MacLaine has lost their temper, there's nothing you can do but wait for them to cool down again. And then there's Ginny. I can't bring myself to look at her.

We had never really addressed what happened at

the wedding. She'd gone off on her honeymoon, returning to their place in D.C. after so Malcolm could continue his position. I'd only heard from her when she called to tell me she was pregnant. She hadn't even been the one to tell me when they lost the baby. I'd gotten the bad news from my father by text. Most of the arrangements regarding the planned adoption had come through my father during his visits. This is the first time I've actually been in the same room with her since her wedding.

Like most brides, she'd dieted obsessively leading up to the big day. That day, she'd glowed like someone had turned on a lightbulb inside her. She's as thin today as she was then, maybe even skinnier. But there's no rosy cheeks or happiness radiating from her. Instead, there are dark circles under her eyes and her high cheekbones don't look sharp and elegant, they look sunken and gaunt. It's like all the bits under her skin that make her up are deteriorating. She's tried to cover it up with make-up: thick, camouflaging concealer and bright, pink lipstick. Is all this from losing her own baby? What is losing the chance to adopt Ellie going to do to her?

"Ginny, I'm sorry," I begin.

"No, you aren't," Malcolm snaps.

But Ginny takes a deep breath. "Can I hold her?"

"Is that a good idea?" Malcolm asks, his eyes darting between us. He reaches for her arm as if to stop her if she decides to anyway. "I don't want you to get attached."

"I'm already attached." She yanks her arm free. "And, regardless, Elodie is family."

"Yes," I speak up before the guilt eats me alive. Even agreeing to it, each step she takes toward me increases my sense of dread. When she reaches for my daughter, I hesitate.

"I'm not going to steal her," she says gently. Our eyes meet and I see something I thought we'd lost there: understanding.

"Watch her head," I advise, passing the baby to her, my hand hovering protectively under her. "She's still floppy."

"Floppy?" Ginny repeats with a smile. "Is that a technical term?"

"I can't think of a better way to describe it."

The rest of the room is quiet until my brother clears his throat. "We'll give you a moment."

I breathe a sigh of relief when the men leave, and it's just me and her and the baby. Ginny studies Ellie's sleeping face, then she inspects her fingers and toes. It's not like earlier when Malcolm was upset over me changing my mind. She's not checking out a potential acquisition. She's trying on the role of mother. I know because it's the first thing I did when they handed Ellie to me in the hospital.

"She's perfect," she says softly.

Ginny wants to be a mother. I know that. It's why she's looking at her that way. The oddest wave of jealousy roles over me. She's everything I won't ever be now. A college graduate. A wife. Wealthy. But somehow I still have the one thing she wants.

"I'm sorry," I say again. "I can't explain why. I just know I can't live without her."

"She's your baby. You love her." She looks up and gives me a brittle smile. "I just wish I hadn't fallen in love with the idea."

"You and Malcolm will get another chance. You two just got married. I know losing the pregnancy was rough. I'm so sorry you went through that. I can't imagine how much that hurts, but you can't give up." I want to reach out and take Ellie back, but I can't bring myself to take her away from Ginny.

Ginny swallows, returning to stare at Ellie who's smiling in her sleep again. "I can actually. Or, rather, I should. We had some tests done. I can't have children."

"But..." I don't know what to say to this.

"I can get pregnant, but I'll probably never carry to term," she continues. "Cruel, isn't it? But you're right, there will be other babies. We can adopt. It will take time."

"I didn't know." Why hadn't my father told me? Would it have changed my mind? Not about keeping Ellie. Nothing could do that. But I might have thought about things more before I agreed to this plan.

"They're going to cut you off," she murmurs. "What are you going to do? Where will you go?"

"I have friends," I say. Now I really want to grab Ellie from her arms, even though she's not being harsh. She's being as gentle as possible. It's the truth that hurts. Still, I know Poppy will help me get on my feet once I tell her the truth. She'll be furious. I can't blame her for that, but I know she'll understand once I explain.

"Are you going to stay here?" she asks.

"I don't know." I wish she would stop asking questions.

"London is expensive. Maybe you should return home."

"I'm not sure that's a good idea." More than anything I

want to be free of Valmont and my family moving forward. Right now, though, I want to hold Ellie and remind myself that I'm making the right decision. I'm sure that Ginny means well by asking me about my plans, but she has to know I haven't had time to think about this. If I had, I would have come to this conclusion earlier and she wouldn't be standing here with me.

"So, you're going to stay here alone with a baby?"

"We'll be okay."

"If you came back, I could help you. Eventually, they'll see reason," she says.

"Will they?" Not for the first time I wonder if Ginny and I are living on the same planet. I don't understand how she can write off all the ugliness she's seen.

Another reason that I can't trust her to raise my baby.

"I'll make them," she says fiercely. "You don't have to do this alone, Adair. Bring the baby. I'll get you an apartment. I have my own checking account. Malcolm doesn't have to know. It will be our secret."

"I just wait for them to change their minds?" I shake my head. I can't see how that's going to work.

"Look. You think you can do this, but you shouldn't have to. You aren't alone in the world. Plus, surely, the baby's father is in Valmont. Was it that jerk from the wedding?" she asks.

I shrug. "Not sure. I didn't feel like handing out a bunch of paternity test requests."

They all think I'm a slut. I might as well lean into it.

Ginny doesn't seem phased by this proclamation. She only nods. "If you figure it out, you can make the dad take care of you. Both of you. But only if you're in the States."

I start to tell her that Ellie's father isn't there either.

That he won't be around to help me or take care of his daughter, even if he wanted to be. But it doesn't matter. What's done is done.

"Just think about it," Ginny says, passing Ellie to me finally. I press her comforting weight to my chest and kiss her forehead.

"I will." I won't though, and we both know it. Ginny will go home, and I'll stay here with Ellie. We'll all be okay —somehow.

"Adair, there's something you should know. Something they aren't telling you." She bites her lip as though she's having second thoughts about telling me herself. "I really shouldn't. Malcolm made me promise not to say anything. He said it might change your mind, but that hardly matters now."

The pit in my stomach opens up again. "What is it?"

"It's your father," she says in a soft voice. *"He's dying."*

I open my eyes as the memory fades and stare at my brother.

"You really hate us that much?" he repeats.

The answer comes easily after remembering every reason behind it. "Yes."

"Noah, it's Sterling," I say as soon as the line connects. There's no time to waste with pleasantries. Each second lost could cost me. "We need to talk."

"Is that so? How's the life of crime?" Noah doesn't sound like an FBI agent. He never sounded like a military man, either. Instead, he's always reminded me of an exasperated parent. Maybe that's why he annoyed me during training. That annoyance shifted to hatred after what happened in Afghanistan.

"Cute. Listen, we have a mutual problem. Let's solve it together." Right now, he holds the key I desperately need to unlock the answers hidden from me. If I want to keep Sutton alive, I need to know who's been talking to the FBI. I'm in a parking garage in downtown Nashville, somewhere even I didn't know I'd be—until about five minutes ago. It's probably just paranoia, I know. But that's the thing about paranoia—it exists because it can be useful. Noah is probably somewhere in a FBI surveillance van, waiting for someone to incriminate themselves.

"It's more your problem than mine, actually."

"You have no idea," I mutter. "Look Nikolai Koltsov just called me. They have Sutton."

There's a sharp intake of breath. Sutton herself told me Noah had tracked her down, that he liked her. I can't blame him. It's hard not to love someone as blatantly and unapologetically abrasive as Sutton. She just makes you want to. "I told you they were serious."

"I believed you. I didn't expect them to move so quickly, but apparently, they realized the FBI is in town." I have to bite back a few choice things to say about this. Noah might have warned me, but he's also endangered everyone I love by sticking around to stir the pot. "Your source. The one who's informing on me and them. I need you to tell me who it is."

"That's a pretty big fucking ask, Ford." Noah tries to sound pissed off, but he's a lot less dismissive than I expected. Something about it bothers him, too.

"Yeah, yeah. Ongoing investigation. Leverage. I get all that—"

"I really don't think you do," Noah says. He's as effortlessly condescending as a parent, that's for sure. "I gave you a heads up as a courtesy. And my offer still stands. You tell me what you've been up to with the Koltsovs, and I can keep you alive. I can get a team down here to extract Sutton—"

"Let's put our cards on the table," I stop him. I just need to convince Noah my method will get him better results. In other words, I need to find something more compelling than persecuting me—not easy, but not impossible. "I know you don't have shit, okay? If you did, you would arrest me, then use whatever you had to try to make me flip."

"That's a lot of assumptions—"

"Maybe, but I know you're a decent person. You don't

like the idea of leveraging my safety just so you can do your job. And you like Sutton, you don't want to see her get hurt." He's quiet on the other end. "This is simple math, Porter. The Koltsovs. My people. Your people. Three different groups, all caught up in something that feels off, right?" No one just gets the Russian mafia handed to them on a silver platter. Or me, for that matter. Not only am I good, I'm careful. Something doesn't add up.

"I know the fucking players, alright?" There's a long pause on the other end of the line, and I can hear Noah changing location. A beefy metal door slams shut, and then I register the unmistakable sound of wind blowing over his phone mic. Either he really did get out of a surveillance van, or he went out on a rooftop. "Alright, our conversation is private now."

Something about the direction I'm taking the conversation has spooked him—enough that he couldn't let us be overheard. Interesting.

"There's someone we're not accounting for," I say.

There's a long pause on the other end of the line, but eventually he answers, "I know."

"Someone says they have evidence that incriminates me," I have to be careful how I discuss this. For all I know, Noah is recording everything I say. "But why give that information to you, Noah?"

"...when it would be much more valuable in extorting you. I know. I was wondering how long it would take you."

"You're being played. Whoever this is can't be trusted with any of this, so are you really going to risk Sutton's life on a wild card?"

"I wish I could believe you were a team player, Sterling,"

Noah chides. "That's the whole problem. If I give you this information, you aren't going to turn around and use it to help the FBI. You're going to undermine the little progress we've made on the Koltsovs."

"And if you were able to do something with the information, you would already have done it. Look, you trusted the wrong person before and I know you see blood on your hands. Do you really want to have Sutton's blood on them, too?" There's another bout of silence, and I hear what sounds like a soft sigh of resignation. I've almost got him. "Whoever promised you evidence to use against me, they are in danger of fucking the Bratva. And anyone thinking of doing that can't afford to let anyone find out. You're never getting more. Whoever is doing this just wanted to scare me away. But that's not happening, ever. So tell me. I'll keep her safe. I'll keep everyone safe. That's all."

"I can't believe I'm fucking telling you." Noah pauses, then drops his voice again. "It was an email sent to me through an anonymous remailer based in eastern Europe. The sender said they have video of you, Jack, and Luca doing business with the Koltsovs. A meeting at the Westminster Royal. Almost two years ago."

I remember the meeting. I also remember the protocol for the meeting, which is spy-speak for all the stuff that's done to keep away unwanted eavesdroppers. The protocols for Bratva meetings are extreme to say the least. Either Luca or Jack betrayed me, or there's a traitor within the Bratva, or it's a bluff and there is no video recording. There's no other angle I can see. And then it hits me—so easy and simple I can't believe I didn't see it sooner. It's not about someone. It's all down to some *place*.

"Thanks, Noah. I owe you one."

"Sterling?"

"Yeah?"

"I *will* collect. And not just for this one." That's the thing about Noah. He can only be manipulated so far. And he never forgets.

THE BARRELHOUSE ISN'T OPEN YET, SO I MAKE MY WAY to the alley entrance, which goes down a half flight of stairs to a basement space Jack is in the process of turning into a recording studio. Kai is there, struggling with bundles of fat, heavily rubberized cords.

"Fuck," he barks, dropping his bundle of cords and shaking his hand. Then he sees me and gets an embarrassed look. "I bent a fingernail backwards."

"I hate that," I say, mostly because I'm not sure what else to say. I've never bothered to feign interest in small talk. It's not that I don't like Kai. Quite the opposite. He's just been playing for Adair's team, which placed us in the rivals category. That's probably going to change. But today, I'm not here to talk to him.

"Jack?" I bark loudly, hoping he'll emerge from one of the dimly lit hallways disappearing into the cavernous space beneath the Barrelhouse.

Kai takes his throbbing finger out of his mouth so he can speak. "He's upstairs. We were trying to figure out the wiring plan for the studio."

"This can't wait."

Kai takes a look around at the mess of cords, naked wiring, amps, mics and guitar stands, and heaves a heavy sigh.

"Well, it wasn't getting done in one day, anyway. I'll just tell Jack I'm going to lunch on my way out."

"Thanks."

Kai disappears up the interior stairwell, into the Barrelhouse proper, and less than a minute later Jack's feet appear on the stairs, followed by someone else.

"You need to talk about something?" Jack says, and by the time I see the pair of thousand dollar Italian leather shoes appear behind him, I know Luca has arrived, too. I called him on my way here. Apparently he was closer.

"I know who has been talking to Noah."

"What? How the fuck did you figure that out?" Jack says.

"About time, actually." Luca says, and when Jack gives him a disgusted look he adds, "What? I was getting bored."

"It hit me when I called Noah—"

"You called Noah?" Luca says in disbelief. "Were you going to run that shit by us?"

"I didn't really have a choice." I fill them in on the situation with Sutton. By the time, I finish, Luca's trigger finger is twitching. "So, yeah, I called Noah."

"Why are we wasting time with him?" Luca asks. "I can have a location on Nikolai within the hour. He won't see us coming."

"Because I prefer my sister without bullet holes in her," I say flatly, "and because taking out one Koltsov will only attract the attention of his brothers. I'd rather deal with the source of our problem. Finding out who's informing means we can make the whole problem go away."

"Sutton can take care of herself," Luca argues.

"Not everyone I care about can," I explode.

"Well, we can, so I assume you're talking about Adair," he

says. "Keep a close eye on her. It's not like she can just opt out of your life. You've got enemies. You're both going to have to face that."

His advice might mean more if that's all there was to it. "It's more complicated than that."

"It always is," Jack says, not without sympathy.

"Look, I'm just saying we have options that don't involve—"

"I have a daughter," I interrupt softly.

"Like a...kid?" Luca blinks rapidly. It's rare to catch him completely off guard. In this instance, I know how he feels.

"Adair was pregnant when I left," I confess, feeling some of the weight of this mistake lessen by telling my friends. They listen as I run them through more details. When I finally get through what happened to Adair after she found out, they're silent.

"Wow, I can't..." Jack sucks in a breath. Then he does something I don't expect. He claps me on my shoulder. "Congrats, man."

The show of affection knocks Luca out of his stupor, and he grins foolishly. "I really thought I'd be the first one to discover I had a love child."

"We all thought that," I mutter, managing a small grin myself.

"Look, Jack's right. Congrats. I know what family means to you."

"So, I guess this means you're sticking around here?" Jack guesses.

I nod. "But it also means I have to deal with the Koltsovs once and for all. Nikolai said something I didn't understand before. I think he knows she's my kid. So, that really only leaves me one option: remove the threat by any means necessary."

"But if we can't find the source..." Luca says.

"Any means necessary," I repeat. "If it comes down to satisfying the Koltsovs concern that I'll talk, there's a pretty easy way to do that."

"You wouldn't," Luca says.

"Yeah, he would." Jack shakes his head, but there's understanding in his brown eyes. He's always understood sacrifice better than Luca.

"We won't let you," Luca says like this is a done deal.

I glance at Jack and he nods almost imperceptibly. If it comes to it, I can count on him to take care of it. If I have any say, I'll put the bullet through my own brain before I force him to, but I'll do it to keep Ellie safe.

"So, that's why I went to Noah. Call it my Hail Mary."

"And you actually got him to talk?" Jack sounds impressed, which is rare.

"Yeah, but he doesn't have any clue what's going on. He thought it was a Bratva rival or a foreign government, I think —he was stuck on the wrong detail."

Luca and Jack look at me uncomprehendingly, and I realize I'm going about everything the wrong way. It's harder to keep my head clear with my sister involved. She isn't some faceless hostage. She's Sutton and she likes crappy cereal and bad music and snow. "Noah received an anonymous email—"

"Email can't be truly anonymous. Data has to be physically present somewhere," Luca interrupts.

"That's not the important part. The email said the sender had a video recording of our meeting with the Bratva at the Westminster Royal."

"Bullshit," Jack says, "No one could have compromised that meeting."

"They checked me so thoroughly for weapons and bugs, I needed a cigarette after," Luca agrees. "They don't fuck around with that stuff."

"For fuck's sake, you two. Can I just finish?"

"Sorry," Jack mumbles.

"So sensitive," trails Luca under his breath, but his sarcasm is lacking its usual sparkle. We're all worried about Sutton.

"It's all connected. I didn't see it before, because I've been working with half the information. Adair and I were talking and she made it sound like she tried to reach me after I left. Called Francie, even. But I gave a note for her to my roommate, explaining things. She didn't get it."

"Okay," Jack says, "but what does that have to do with any of this?"

"Everything, and if I'm right, this isn't going to just be about getting the Bratva off my back. It's going to nail the bastard responsible for all of this to the wall. My old roommate? His name is Cyrus...Eaton."

Jack and Luca get there at exactly the same moment, and when they realize how simple the answer is they turn to look at each other in disbelief.

"Eaton hotels. Our meeting with the Bratva was at the Westminster Royal—"

"An Eaton Hotel," Luca says, humming the jingle used at the end of all the company's television advertising.

"We didn't see it because we *never* thought what happened five years ago—before we even met—could be connected to our trouble with Noah."

"And why would we?" Jack says, whistling. "Your old roommate is in a lot of trouble."

"It'll be done by tomorrow morning," Luca says, and Jack and I turn to find him screwing a silencer onto the pistol he keeps tucked into his shoulder holster.

"Woah, Luca. Pump the brakes," says Jack.

"Why? Has anyone ever needed killing more than this guy?" Luca responds like we just told him two plus two is five. "Does he even know how dangerous it is to spy on the Koltsovs? What they'd do to him? It'll be a mercy."

"You're not thinking big enough," I tell Luca. "I didn't at first, either. But the recording was made about two years ago, right?"

"So?"

"So it was sent to Noah last month."

"Which means this Cyrus fucker sat on it for nearly two years—until you showed up in his life again." Luca's brow furrows.

"Yeah," Jack gives me a glance that says *I'll take it from here* before continuing, "Which means Eaton Hotels have been gathering information about their guests *for years*."

"You got a guest room?" Luca asks me. "I think I'm giving up my Platinum Elite privileges with the Eaton hotel chain."

"It's just sitting somewhere, waiting to become useful. Can you imagine how valuable that information is?" Jack asks neither of us in particular.

"It's not as valuable as it is dangerous." Six months ago, I would have thought about the dollar value, too. But that's what I'm figuring out about having things you can't afford to lose: it changes the math.

"It's pretty powerful leverage. Enough to get Sutton back, and maybe enough to get the Bratva off our backs," Jack says.

"We're going to steal it, aren't we?" Luca says, the devil's own grin lighting his dark features, adding quickly, "And get your sister back."

"No. *You're* going to steal it," I correct him. "I'm going to make sure Cyrus can never hurt anyone I love again."

"Fine," growls Luca, beginning to unscrew his silencer. "But shoot him once from me, okay?"

19

ADAIR

S taying put is no longer an option, no matter what I
promised Sterling. He has his enemies to deal with, and
I have mine.

I keep replaying the moment Ginny told me my father
was dying in my head after Malcolm leaves, no longer able to
concentrate on my mother's manuscript. It worked because
Ginny wasn't lying. Not then. Felix even confirmed it later
that night. Cancer had taken root, rotting him from the inside
out, despite all the money and all the doctors. And then the
cancer spread until it was untreatable, spreading past the
confines of his body to infect his business, his household, and,
of course, his family. By the time, I realized it had reached
me, it was too late.

I wouldn't make that mistake again.

Shoving my mother's manuscript into a desk drawer, I
toss my phone into my bag and scrawl a hastily written note
to Trish. I'm out the door a few minutes later. On my way to
my car, I flip through my mental calendar. I promised Sterling I would let him handle things. We'd both agreed to go

about this through the right channels, so we'd never risk losing Ellie again. I'm going to keep that promise, but I'm not going to let my brother rewrite history. Not anymore. I've let them control the situation far too long.

Ginny's idea of mothering involves a small army of nannies and over-scheduling. I think she's convinced herself that if she drives Ellie to dance classes and gymnastics and preschool and then dumps her on someone else, she's done her part. She's so obsessed that I've never even been allowed to pick Ellie up from a single lesson. Now I'm beginning to realize, it's not just about the role she's hiding behind, it's about keeping me in my place.

Shame. Regret. Helplessness. I'd been so weighed down by them for years that I'd started to believe they were right—that I wasn't enough and I never would be. I'd boxed up the memories of what happened years ago and tucked them somewhere dark and deep—a place I wouldn't go looking for too often. Telling Sterling, forced me to return there. Confronting Malcolm, opened the box, and now that it's open, I can't keep myself from what's inside.

Winter five years ago

Traveling with an infant is a nightmare. Traveling with an infant this close to Christmas is worse.

The flight from London to Nashville was considerably less comfortable than any other I'd taken in my life. Angus MacLaine made good on his promise to cut me off entirely, even after I announced I'd be bringing the baby to live in Tennessee. Thankfully, Ginny kept her promise as well, helping me get a ticket to fly back. She'd convinced me to take her help rather than ask Poppy. I guess for the first time someone in my family is looking out for me, and now I can come clean to Poppy in person. I can't imagine telling my best friend that I ran away to London to have a baby over the phone. Some things need to be said in person.

"Adair!" Ginny waves me over as soon as I'm through customs and past the security doors. She hurries over, grabbing my bags. "Here, let me help."

"Thanks," I say, wondering if I sound as exhausted as I feel. Ellie is the only one of us who got any sleep on the flight, but that's not saying much. Now she's curled into a baby carrier, napping soundly on my chest.

"How did she do?" Ginny asks as we make our way to the valet parking station in Terminal Garage One.

"She is not a fan of flying," I admit.

She gives me a sympathetic smile. "And how did you do?"

"I walked the aisles for nine hours trying to keep her quiet."

"That bad?"

"I think everyone in economy was plotting to throw us out of the airlock." There'd been a few who managed to sleep through Ellie's nine-hour-long protest, but not many.

Her Mercedes is waiting for us when we reach the valet station. She tips the man extra. "Thanks for keeping it out."

"No problem," he says, staring at the bills like he's already spending them.

"I got a car seat," she says. "I mean, I already had one before..."

"Thanks," I say, feeling uncomfortable suddenly. She's been understanding about everything—too understanding. It only makes me feel worse about changing my mind.

I climb into the back and try to maneuver Ellie into the car seat. The movement jars her awake and the protest begins again. Ginny gets in on the other side. "I think we need to adjust this." She wiggles and tucks until the straps are expertly secured around my daughter.

"Thanks. I'm not very good at that yet. She didn't ride in the car much in London," I admit sheepishly.

"You'll get it figured out." She gets out and slides into the driver's seat. "Are you going to ride with her?"

"I think I better." I can't imagine she'll ever calm down if she's back here all alone.

Ginny spends the entire ride to the hotel catching me up on all the gossip I missed while I was gone. I drift in and out, too tired to keep up with who's getting divorced, been cheated on, or gotten remarried. It will all change next week anyway.

I'm surprised when we pull up in front of a run-down motel on the outskirts of Nashville. Two floors are stacked into a block of rooms. A long exterior corridor lines the top. From the looks of it the metal railing was once painted red, but it faded along with a welcome sign that points to the front office. Next to the office's door, there's a vending machine with cracked glass and an ice machine labeled out of order in black marker. There are a fair few vehicles here even mid-day, or I might have thought the place abandoned. It's not exactly up to MacLaine standards.

Ginny glances over her shoulder, chewing on her lower lip. "It's the best I could do to keep you close but give you some privacy. I figured you'd want to keep a low profile until..."

Until I find the courage to tell my friends that I have a baby now? Until I face my father? Until I have a plan? I swallow, my tongue feeling thick in my throat, and nod. "You're probably right. It's not that bad."

Maybe it is, but it could also be worse. When Ginny told me she arranged a hotel room for me to stay in until I figured out my next move, I'd naturally assumed she meant at the Eaton. But she's two steps ahead of me. Of course, I don't want to show my face there. Not yet. Not until things are settled one way or another.

"It's only for a few days, right?" she says as if she can read my thoughts. "That gives you time to talk to your friends. Maybe even go to see your father."

"Yeah," I agree half-heartedly as I unbuckle Ellie. She wakes up with an ear-splitting scream and I hurriedly press her close, shushing her gently until the crying diminishes to a whimpering mewl.

"I'll get the bags." She holds out a key. "You're already checked in."

I turn the plastic keyring over in my palm and read 113. At least we're on the ground floor.

The inside of the motel isn't much better than the outside. I ignore a dark stain on the purple carpet by the door and carry Ellie to the bed. One look at the worn coverlet sends me searching in my diaper bag for a blanket. I spread it over the bed with one hand as best I can and lay her down to change her. Ginny drags my suitcases in and looks around. Even after the door closes behind her, I can hear the roar of the highway. The loud whoosh of a truck rattles the room's cheap windows.

Our gazes lock like we're playing chicken, before Ginny finally asks, "Where do you want these?"

At the Eaton. I bite back that response and tip my head toward a table shoved into the corner. Getting them away from the disturbing stain near the door is my first order of business. I carry the dirty diaper to the bathroom trash and discover a roach crawling across the bathtub. The skittering movement of its legs raises the hair on the back of my neck, and I rush back in to pick Ellie up from the bed terrified I'll find something crawling on her.

I'd told myself up until now that I'd take a few days, get over my jet lag, get Ellie settled, and then reach out to Poppy. I can already see that timeline shortening to a few hours. There's no way I can stay here with Ellie and feel safe. But Ginny's already done enough. It's not like she can afford to do more without making Malcolm suspicious about what's draining her account.

"Do you want to grab some dinner?" she asks once she's plopped both bags down on the table.

"I think I'm going to call Poppy."

"Are you ready?"

I am now. I can't explain to her that I don't have a lot of choice in the matter. I'm avoiding my friends to protect my pride. But I can't do that at the cost of endangering Ellie. "I'm not sure I'll ever be ready, but I can't put it off—for Ellie's sake."

"I'm sorry. I should have checked this place out better. I found it on the internet and it's so close to Nashville and Valmont." She shakes her head. "We need to find you both some place better."

I'm sure that Ginny didn't know there were hotels in the world where there were no mints on your pillowcase or turndown service. "You've done so much for us already," I say, voicing my earlier thoughts. "After everything I put you through, you didn't have to help me —help us."

"Of course, I do. We're family. Family looks out for each other."

"Is that how it's supposed to work?" I ask dryly. Someone should tell my father. "I thought family cleaned up messes and kept secrets and made threats."

"Some MacLaines operate that way, but I'm not a MacLaine by birth. I guess where some see messes, I see opportunities." She forces a smile, but it fizzles quickly like she's only got so much more energy to give to righting all the wrongs committed by my bloodline. "Are you tired? You could lay down. I'll keep an eye on Ellie."

"Actually, I'm not. I just want to call Poppy." If there's one person in the world who will make me feel like everything might turn out okay, it's her. The truth is I know she won't be disappointed or judgmental. I think that's the reason I've avoided telling her for so long. Part of me feels like I should be punished. I might love Ellie, but there's no way around it: getting pregnant with her was a mistake. It's going to be a lot harder to stay mad at myself when someone forgives me.

"You call her. I'll hold the baby," Ginny urges me.

I hand her Ellie gratefully and step out the door for a little privacy. Poppy answers on the second ring.

"It's the prodigal daughter!" she cries on the other end. "You've been avoiding me."

"I've been busy." There's no lie there.

"So busy you couldn't do more than respond to a text once a week? Did you meet someone?" she asks.

"I wouldn't say I met someone exactly. There's definitely someone new in my life, though."

"Spill. I want all the details," she gushes.

"I was thinking we could meet actually." I take a deep breath. "I'm home for a bit."

"Wait? What? You're here? In Valmont?"

"I just got in." But a giddy scream drowns out my response.

Poppy seems torn between elation and accusation. "I can't believe you just showed up...I'm supposed to go out with Cyrus to Christmas shop but I can skip it. I can't believe you're here! I wasn't sure you'd ever come back from London."

"Neither was I."

"I can meet you somewhere. Are you at home?"

"No," I say quickly. I glance at a tall weed growing through a crack in the sidewalk. "Let's meet somewhere for dinner. I'll text you."

"I can't wait to see you!" she squeals before hanging up.

I return to the room to find Ginny swaying with Ellie in her arms.

"How did that go?" she asks.

"We're going to meet for dinner," I say, scrolling through my phone. "I have to think of somewhere low-key that is baby-friendly." And not packed for the holidays.

"Why don't I just stay with Ellie?"

"Oh, I don't know if..." I haven't been away from her since she was born.

"It's going to be crazy everywhere this close to Christmas," Ginny points out meaningfully.

Not only will it be hard to get in most family-friendly places but it's a lot more likely I'll be seen with a baby this time of year. I might be ready to come clean to Poppy, but

I don't want to star as the gossip at every Christmas party in Valmont, especially my family's. Still, it's not that simple. "She doesn't take a bottle very well, and I can't exactly pump."

"How often does she eat?" Ginny asks.

"Every two hours, or whenever she starts screaming," I admit sheepishly.

"Then feed her, head out, and be back here in two hours," she says with a shrug. "You can take my car."

I shake my head. "There's no way I'm stranding you here. I'll call an Uber."

"Even better."

Without the baby, there are more options and I text Poppy to meet me at a nearby Hennie's before I show Ginny everything I think she might need to know. "If she's wet, there will be a blue line on the diaper," I say, holding up a clean one. "Now the tabs go in the back and—"

"I know how to change a diaper, Adair," she cuts me off with an amused snort.

"Oh. Of course." I don't add that I didn't know until a nurse showed me how. Despite the fact that she obviously has a step up on me where babies are concerned, she listens patiently to the rest of my advice, which includes everything from Ellie's favorite ways to be comforted to when to dial 911. When I finish, she's staring at me with a puzzled expression. "What? Ok, I know. I'm going over-the-top."

"It's not that." She shakes her head. "I didn't expect you to be so...prepared. No offense."

"It's been trial by fire," I confess, kissing Ellie's forehead, "but she's worth it."

"I can see that," Ginny says softly. "Adair, I—" An

incoming alert buzzes on my phone, and she stops. "I think your ride's here. You better hurry. See you soon."

Maybe it's the fact that I've never left Ellie to go out before or maybe it's where I'm leaving her, but it feels like my feet are encased in concrete, each step away harder to take than the last. Ginny waves me off when I reach the Uber sitting in the parking spot next to her car. After the door closes, I pause and listen for the slide of the lock. Getting into the car and closing the door turns out to be nearly as hard as walking away. The driver stares at me like I've grown a second head.

"You're going to Hennie's?" he says impatiently as I buckle up.

"Yeah. The one off 155," I add quickly, afraid he'll take me to a different location farther away.

He bobs his head and takes off while I swivel in my seat and watch the motel, my heart aching, until it becomes a spec on the road behind me. When I can't see it anymore, the aching becomes so intense that I nearly tell him to turn around. It takes every ounce of restraint I possess to stop myself, but I can't help feeling like I left my heart behind in room 113 of the Half-point Motel.

By the time I spot the familiar Hennie's sign, glowing in purple and red neon, I think I might vomit. Poppy's car is in the parking lot, which only makes me feel worse. Dragging myself out of the car, I thank my driver who doesn't bother to reply and prepare to face Poppy.

"You're wasting time," I say as I stare at the swinging door, half hoping it will open and Poppy will spill out and carry me inside. But she's already in there, waiting, and I can't avoid this any longer.

As soon as I'm inside, I glance around the familiar

interior. It's a bit different than the Hennie's I grew up with in Valmont. Not as clean, for one thing, but that's hardly a surprise since the owner spends most of her time at the original location. But the menu hanging above the counter is the same as well as the purple, high-back booths, and black and white tiled floor. For the first time, since I landed in Nashville, it feels like I've come home. Movement catches my eye, and I turn to see Poppy flagging me with a grin, her long arm waving me toward a booth in the corner.

She looks exactly the same as the last time I saw her. She's traded summer sun dresses for jeans and a sweater more fitting the cooler December temperatures, but it's the same smile, the same hair, the same warm, friendly eyes. It should be comforting. Instead, I feel a million miles away from her.

"You look wonderful," she says, bouncing up to give me a hug.

The truth is that I'm still holding on to at least forty pounds of baby weight. That's probably a generous underestimate for my own sanity. It hasn't occurred to me until now that she'll notice. Will she wonder why? I run a hand over my less-than-flat stomach, smoothing my shirt, self-consciously before I sit across from her.

"I already ordered enough to feed an army! So I hope you're hungry."

"Great," I lie. There's no way I'll be able to eat a bite, even after I tell her the truth.

"Couldn't stay away for Christmas?" she guesses, filling in the awkward silence between us.

"I guess not," I force myself to say.

"I can't blame you," she says, continuing to do the

heavy lifting of small talk. "I'd want to come meet my new niece, too."

"New niece..." I repeat with a slight shake of the head like a wire's crossed inside my brain.

"I've heard their back with the baby," Poppy says as though this is obvious. "I mean everyone is talking about the cancelled Christmas party. No one can blame them. Having a baby and half of Valmont in the same house— even Windfall—is a bit much. Ginny is probably exhausted."

The room constricts with each word she speaks until I feel like I'm about to implode. The heart I thought I'd left behind beats so rapidly that I can't bring myself to stop her —to correct her—before my brain begins frantically piecing together what she's saying.

"Where did you hear they were back with a baby?" I finally manage to ask, hoping news is traveling slowly, hoping that this is all a misunderstanding, hoping that the dread I feel is unwarranted.

"Everyone's talking about. Probably since no one's seen them since they arrived," she says. "Is Ginny a really paranoid mom? Or are you two still on bad terms?"

I'm on my feet before she finishes the last question.

"I have to go," I blurt out. Only then remembering that I don't have a car. I whip out my phone and request a ride, trying to swallow against the bile threatening to spill out of me all over the scuffed tile floor.

"What's wrong?" Poppy says, her eyes wide as if my obvious panic is wearing off on her.

But there's no time. No time to explain. "I have to go. Why are there no Ubers?"

"I can drive you." She grabs her purse.

"No, I should..."

A confused employee in a black apron appears with two trays full of food, stepping back before I nearly knock him over in my attempt to run out the door. Poppy yells a thanks and follows after me.

I don't think I just start heading toward the street, planning to run in the direction I came from, hoping I can remember my way.

"Adair!" Poppy's frantic cry slices through the air, and I stop instinctively. "What are you doing? Let me drive you."

I turn to look at her, my teeth sinking into my lower lip and realize she's my best option. She doesn't ask any questions until we're both inside her car.

"Where am I going?" It's simple. It's to the point.

"The Half-point Motel. It's about ten minutes away," I say, punching it into my phone to get directions. I wait for the questions that I'm sure will follow this information, but she starts driving, even though her brow furrows.

"I'm sorry," I say, between panicked pants. "I should have told you. We just have to get to her. Maybe it's all a mistake."

"Darling, you aren't making sense," Poppy says soothingly. "You can explain later. Just try to breathe. We'll be there soon."

Poppy's driving is anxiety-inducing on the best days. Today, she barely stays on the road, leaving me to clutch the door handle as we swing recklessly between lanes, but I don't say anything because we are flying and right now, I can only think of reaching Ellie.

It's all a misunderstanding, I tell myself. But I'm a MacLaine. I always know a lie when I hear it. The trouble is that I haven't been listening. I was so desperate for a solution that I didn't see what's right in front of me. The skeevy motel. Ginny's overly helpful attitude. Her willingness to help me get home and sort through this.

"Please be wrong," I mutter under my breath over and over. Poppy casts a worried look in my direction before jerking the wheel hard to pass a slower vehicle at breakneck speed.

"There it..." I start to point out the faded, old motel as it comes into view but my words die from my lips when I spot the flashing red and blue lights. Two police cars and an ambulance occupy the spots in front of my room. Poppy slams on the brakes and we skid to a halt in the parking lot. I'm out of the car instantly, running toward the police officers and the open hotel door. I'm nearly there when one steps in front of me, holding out his palm.

"Miss, I'm going to need you to—"

"My baby!" I yell, trying to push past him. "Is something wrong? Is she okay?"

"Your infant was inside?" he asks.

"Yes, I don't understand." I look around and realize Ginny's car is gone. "Did she kidnap her?

But the officer is talking into his radio, no longer paying attention to me. "The mother's here. Yeah, I'll take care of it."

"Where's my baby?" I demand.

"Your baby is fine," he says, but there's no softness in his face. Instead, he looks disgusted. "A concerned guest called when they heard the crying, and the management let us into the room."

"Wait? What? She was crying, but where was..."

"She's been taken into protective services. You can't

leave a baby alone around here. Do you have any idea what could have happened? You're lucky someone even called. This area isn't full of a lot of concerned citizens."

"I didn't leave her alone." How could he think that? "She was with..."

"You should be more careful about who you trust, because we found her locked in that room wearing nothing but a dirty diaper on the bed. And I know the weather isn't that cold, but a baby that little can't regulate their body temperature."

Now I understand the disgust, because I feel it myself. It coils around me and squeezes until I'm sure I'm going to throw up. My knees weaken and I sway on the spot. Ellie was alone. Scared. Cold. And it's all my fault.

"Please. This is all a misunderstanding." I can't believe anything else, even though I know, deep down, this was planned. "My name is Adair MacLaine. I left her with my sister-in-law. She rented the room. There must be a record. If we can just talk to her or the manager."

"I know who you are, Miss MacLaine. Your name is on the registration."

"I didn't rent the room," I start to explain.

"Your credit card is on file. It says you arrived here earlier today."

"Yes, I flew in from London." I can't believe this is happening. I can't believe I was stupid enough to trust them.

"And you have family nearby?"

I know he recognizes the name, but he's not interested in doing me any favors. "If I could just call my father."

"He's been notified," the officer says. "Protective services prefer to reach out to family in these cases.

Sometimes the child can bypass foster care when there's an appropriate guardian available."

"No, you can't do that!" I say wildly.

"You really haven't left us a choice," he says coldly. "If you won't care for your baby..."

"I love her. I would never do anything to hurt h—"

"You already have," he cuts me off, and the rebuke knocks the wind out of me.

He's right. Not in the way he thinks. I didn't abandon Ellie, but I put my trust in the wrong person and she paid the price. She's become a bargaining chip—another possession for the family to fight over. I never should have brought her back to Valmont. I never should have taken that risk.

"Is everything okay?" Poppy steps by my side.

I didn't see her leave the car. How can I explain this to her? But then I realize, she might be my only hope. She knows me. Her family is powerful. Maybe—just maybe— all isn't lost. I cling to the idea like a life raft.

"Miss, this is official police business," the officer says dismissively, making additional notes on his pad.

"Perhaps, I should ring Captain Larkin," she says sweetly, but her dark eyes narrow into slits. She might not know what's going on, but she has my back. "I need to speak to him about the police officer's ball my family is hosting. I'm certain he can clear things up."

The officer pauses and finally looks at her. He sighs, dropping his head a little. "I have no idea what is going on here," he says. "I only know the facts. Captain Larkin's already abreast of the situation."

"How?" I butt in. All of this is happening so fast. Too fast.

Planned. Planned. Planned. The word skips around my brain to an irritating tune like my own mind is upset with me. Because I knew before I ever landed in Nashville or stepped foot on the plane, even before Daddy arrived in London with the adoption paperwork, that I was outmatched. Three against one with no allies of my own.

"Believe it or not, he doesn't tell me these things," he says in a clipped tone. "But he's been quite clear on the situation. We're to work directly with your family. You should thank him really, he's put a gag on talking to the media. Anyone talks and he's firing everyone who touches this case." He stalks off to talk to another officer.

"What is going on, Adair?" Poppy sounds genuinely scared. She has to have pieced together a bit of what's going on. She knows I'm hiding something.

None of that matters. I dart closer to the room, trying to get to the door. I just need to see her. I just need to know she's okay. The officer looks up from his conversation and places one warning hand on his holster.

I nod as if to say I understand and that I'm not going to try anything.

Poppy joins me, watching but not speaking, and we creep to the open door. There's another officer in the room, taking photographs, and a pair of medics blocking the view of the bed. My heart beats like a an animal caught in a trap, desperately trying to break free but knowing the effort is futile. There's a balled up diaper on the floor. My bags are gone from the table. The room is bare and sterile until a shrill cry shatters the somber scene. I'm vaguely aware of Poppy's startled jump, but I don't think. I just go.

"I'm going to need you to back up," the officer says.

"Please," I sob, my own tears matching Ellie's panicked cries. "She needs me. I didn't leave her. I won't take her. Just let me calm her down."

The officer looks over, her eyes meeting that of the female medic's. Some silent conversation passes between them, before the medic nods.

"Just get her calm," the female officer says, "but don't go anywhere. Don't make this any worse."

I rush to the bed, snatching Ellie up and trying to ignore the medical instruments strewn around her. They had to check her out after they found her like this.

"Is she okay?" I ask the medic, cuddling her close. Ellie's face turns into me, quieting for a moment before she begins to root.

"Cold," she says warily. "But otherwise in *excellent* health." I hear it there: doubt.

Can she see how this doesn't make sense?

"I didn't leave her," I say numbly, lifting her tiny hands to kiss her fingers. "I will never leave her."

Another look is exchanged, but neither speaks. They've been given their orders.

Poppy steps into the room, hesitating near the door. She's smart enough to understand what's going on. I owe her an explanation. We both know it, but now isn't the time, because I don't know how much time I have left.

"Should I call Captain Larkin?" she asks, but the question rings hollow. We both know that he's already been called by someone with more power and money and influence, by a man you don't say no to if you want to keep your public service job.

I shake my head. I just want to be here while I can. I push aside anxious images of what comes next: fighting and threats and loss. Because even as I try to focus on this moment—on the feeling of my daughter in my arms—scenarios play out in my mind, and they all end the same way no matter what path I take.

Two weeks ago, I'd sat in London trying to figure out how to say goodbye and knowing it was impossible. It still is. But sometimes goodbyes are a luxury the world doesn't give you. Sometimes life just takes and leaves you with more scars than memories. If you ever heal at all.

I don't have enough memories. I never will.

"Miss MacLaine, we need to take her now," the officer says gently. She doesn't try to pry Ellie out of my arms. She's giving me time, precious little of it, but still time.

"Please, don't." But I know no one is coming to save us. There's only one person who might have once, and he doesn't even know we need him. He never will. Because of me. This is all because of me.

"What is going on?" The officer from earlier stomps into the room, and I can't bear to look at him. I hear everything I need to know in his tone. He's not going to let this ruin his career. He's got his orders. Whatever crisis of conscience won me a little leniency from the others doesn't afflict him.

I bury my face against Ellie's soft head and breathe in her scent, feel her downy hair tickle my nose, pray that the world stops spinning and we stay in this one moment forever.

And then it's ripped away.

She's ripped away, torn from my arms, along with my heart, torn from my chest. I lunge and reach and stretch to reach her until a metal cuff clamps around my wrist. A small voice reads me my rights, but all I hear are my own screams and her cries. I fight and fight and fight.

And lose.

I WAIT OUTSIDE THE DANCE STUDIO, SUNGLASSES HIDING my swollen eyes. The tears have finally stopped, but in their place is a hole that hollows me to the core. When Ginny's white Lexus pulls into a handicapped spot close to the entrance, I scramble out of the Jag before she can beat me inside.

"Hurry up, Ellie," Ginny snaps as Ellie chats animatedly, unbuckling herself with the distracted air of someone mid-story.

"But I was just getting to the part where Felix told me—" Ellie protests.

"You are five minutes late."

I'd planned to wait until Ellie was inside and then confront my sister-in-law, but something inside me breaks when Ginny yanks her out of the seat and begins dragging her toward the door. I step into her path, arms crossed.

"Drop her arm," I say quietly.

"Auntie Dair!" Ellie squeaks, trying to run toward me.

Ginny's grip tightens and Ellie yelps. I take a step closer, and she finally lets her go. Still glaring at Ginny, I bend down and Ellie throws her arms around me. I ignore the horrified look on Ginny's face and soak up as much of the hug as possible.

"I missed you. It's been two days!" She strains against my arms, so she can look me in the eye. "Are you really not coming home?"

I wrap her back in a hug. "I live somewhere else now."

"With Mr. Ford?" she asks.

"No." I shake my head. "Not right now."

"But you love him, right?" Ellie presses. "Mommy told Felix that you were blinded by love and that's why you left. Is that why you're wearing sunglasses?"

I can't quite hold back a tell-tale sniffle, so I take them off. "No. I see just fine."

"Promise?" she holds out her pinky finger.

I hook mine around hers. "I promise."

"But if you aren't blinded by love, you can come home," she says.

She's turning into quite the little lawyer.

"Ellie, you're late," Ginny reminds her in a strained voice.

"I have to go to dance class." She sticks her tongue out like she's being punished. "Will you wait?"

I glance at Ginny, who pauses mid-text to wait for my answer. "Not tonight," I say, "but I'm glad I got to see you."

"I miss you!" Ellie buries her face against my shoulder. "They took all your stuff out of your room. I looked and looked and there's nothing and Felix says it's okay because I got *mammaries*."

"Memories," I correct gently. Reaching to my neck, I unclasp the silver clover. "Do you know what this is?" I place it around her neck.

Ellie takes the charm in her fingertips and studies it with awe, before shaking her head.

"It's a good luck charm," I tell her, leaning back on my heels. "A four leaf clover. When you wear it, I'll be with you the whole time."

"Promise?" This time she doesn't hold out her pinkie. She just stares into my eyes. I see Sterling there, looking back at me. Hopeful and a little angry and trusting and innocent. He doesn't see himself that way. He never has but it's so much clearer to see those parts of him in the eyes of his daughter.

"I promise." And I mean it with every fiber of my being. Standing up, I give her a quick kiss on the forehead and shoo her inside. She studies the charm the whole way.

"I should call the police," Ginny says when the door closes behind her.

"And tell them what?" I ask. "What lie will you spin this time?"

"You know that we were given guardianship over her. You can't just show up and put ideas in her head and—"

"Guardianship," I cut her off. "I'm still her mother in every way. You two are not her parents."

"Are you threatening me? Maybe I should call the police. I should have when you broke your promise and he came to the house. How could you do that? How could you tell him after what he's done to this family? He's only going to hurt you and her."

"He would never do that."

"Then why didn't you put his name on the birth certificate?" she demands.

"I don't have to explain myself to you. Not anymore." I take a step towards her and she flinches, but this time there's no Malcolm there to step in and save her. It's been a long time since he cared enough to concern himself. "It's time to fight your own battle—face-to-face—this time."

"I always fight my own battles," she seethes.

"No, you don't. Did you know I felt sorry for you once? I thought you were in over your head with my family, but now I know you're just like my brother and my father—even my mother. There's always an excuse for their behavior. There's always an angle to be manipulated. But you can't change basic facts. I'm her mother. You aren't."

"You don't stand a chance against us." Her hands ball into fists as her face goes pale. "Nothing's changed. We still have all the lawyers, all the money, the police report, the witnesses."

I shake my head and despite everything, I can't help but laugh. I look over to the studio window. Class has begun, and in the center of the students, Ellie is turned the wrong direction, dancing to a completely different beat than everyone else. She's mine. My little girl. *Our* little girl. I fought and lost before. I won't lose her again.

"Everything's changed," I tell her, "especially me."

"Cyrus is supposed to arrive fifteen minutes from now. Is that enough time?" I'm alone in Adair's suite at the Eaton, talking to Luca and Jack over an encrypted communication hub running out of Jack's G-Wagen. We've run this setup before, dozens of times on damn near every continent, but never with our own skin in the game.

It adds spice, to say the least.

It also means we can pull it together in a pinch, and we're running out of time. The most difficult element was getting Adair to agree to follow my instructions without an explanation in advance. I just promised her I wouldn't order her around again after this. I wouldn't risk it.

Luca is meeting with the hotel manager, Mr. Randolph, who's been trying to get a private meeting with him for a couple of weeks. Randolph's name has been on my list since before we returned to Nashville—ever since he embarrassed me at Thanksgiving five years ago, in fact. Today, the entire Eaton dynasty gets what it deserves, right down to the asshole manager.

"We knew we'd be threading the eye of the needle with this. You getting cold feet, Ford?" Jack has the easy job—he always does.

"You're just mad you *still* have to stay in the car," Luca chuckles.

We have an impressive array of tech at our disposal, earpieces and mics so small no one will see them by accident, wireless cameras, and a fiber-optic splicer that costs more than a modest house. Someone has to manage all of it, and who better than Jack, since he made most of it? I hadn't been surprised when he'd led us into a hidden room in the back of the Barrelhouse and a stash of equipment. Jack might want to be out, but old habits die hard. I'm not certain he'll ever relax into the life he claims to want entirely.

Normally I take point, Luca covers me discreetly, and Jack provides operational support from nearby, usually somewhere unglamorous like a utility closet or a shitty van. But today Luca and I are both working at the same time, which gives us almost no ability to improvise and absolutely no room for mistakes.

We all know the score: once I start my discussion with Cyrus, there's no going back. He'll figure out what I know and how I know it. He'll move to protect his data trove, which we know now is in a safe next to Randolph's office downstairs.

It was surprisingly easy to discover where Cyrus keeps the data cache from his family's vast holdings. The Eaton is wired into a standard cable company fiber optic network, and it only sends and receives encrypted data. Contrary to movies and television, encryption is nearly impossible to break. It's one of the reasons the U.S. government spends so much time pressuring tech companies to put hidden backdoors in its products. But finding where someone's keeping that shit isn't difficult at all.

All Jack had to do was splice into the network hub for the block the Eaton hotel sits on to confirm our theory that the company's flagship hotel is more than just that—it's where they're storing their dirty laundry. Massive amounts of data are being routed there from IP addresses all over the world.

If I wasn't so close to this, I might be impressed. The complexity of the operation is worthy of a foreign intelligence agency. The potential for blackmail is staggering.

What happens when Eaton Hotels wants to open at a prime piece of real estate next to Red Square? Well, it definitely helps to have dirt on a number of government officials. It also explains the Eatons knack for cutting through red tape. How else could they manage to own hotels in the heart of Moscow?

"It's a quarter to one," Luca says through the headset. "Are we go?"

"Go," Jack says.

"We're go," I agree, checking my watch. Cyrus is meeting me in fifteen minutes, but he might arrive early. If he follows his usual daily routine—stopping in the main office as soon as he enters the building—everything will be fine.

Powerful people have a tendency to be paranoid bordering on superstitious. Accessing sensitive information comes with its own routine. The simple fact they've never been compromised before tells them their routine is working, so they almost never change it. That's the flaw in his system. It tells us more than he could ever imagine. Like the fact that the name he's made for himself in the stock market is probably built on the information he gathers from the illegal surveillance. Why else would he keep an office at the hotel when he's hardly involved in its management at this point?

First, he goes to his office as soon as he sets foot on property. Then he reemerges ten minutes later, sometimes stopping to talk to the manager, Mr. Randolph. The amount of data being sent is too vast to decrypt for the ten minutes he's on site—it would take hours or even days—which means the computer in his safe must be storing the data in its decrypted form.

Get in the safe, and the data cache is ours. Sutton will be safe, and so will my family.

Through my comms, I hear a knock on the door. Luca's appointment has arrived.

"Ah, Mr. De Angelo, right on time," says Randolph.

They exchange pleasantries, and then I hear a door close.

"Why did you want to see me again, Mr. Randolph?" Luca's smooth tone is designed to comfort prospective clients, help them talk about difficult things. People are lulled by his effortless, almost bored bastardry.

"Trouble at home, I'm afraid," says Randolph, his quavering voice betraying his nervousness.

"The wife?"

"You always get married with good intentions," Randolph says, "but yes..."

"I'm sorry to hear it's not working out," Luca says, sounding anything but. "I've always found that an ending is also a new beginning..."

"I'm hoping," says Randolph.

It must be hard to solicit the execution of your wife. Even for someone like Randolph. He just can't bring himself to be more explicit. But we need him to say it—if I don't start scratching Noah's back, he might end up being my second shadow for the rest of my life. A money launderer hiring a hitman is just a big enough fish to satisfy him for a bit.

"I might be able to help you. We're talking because you recognize my family name, no?"

That's good, Luca, keep him on the hook.

"I—I've heard of the De Angelos, yes. And you indicated you help all kinds of people with all kinds of problems..." Mr. Randolph trails off, hoping Luca will say it for him.

"You seem like quite a successful man," Luca offers.

"I like to think so."

"What's your take home? Two hundred thousand?"

"I—um, I'm not sure what you mean."

"Just doing the math, Mr. Randolph. You're nearly fifty. Been making good money for awhile now. Probably have a house, stock portfolio. Am I warm?"

A long pause follows, but eventually Randolph answers, "Uncomfortably warm."

"Don't push him too fast," I warn through our comms.

"And you've been together more than ten years?" Luca asks. He's alluding to the length of time a standard prenup lasts. After ten years, a divorced wife gets half of everything.

"Yes."

"I can help you with your problem. The price is one year of salary. Two hundred thousand dollars."

"*What?*" Mr. Randolph says. Clearly, he was expecting a lower fee.

Jack's voice pipes through the comms, "Oh shit, guys, we have a problem. Cyrus is here. He just pulled into the garage. We have to call it off."

"Luca?" I ask. Sometimes, all you need is a history. My one-word question says everything it needs to. Only Luca knows if he can get us where we need to be.

"Time?" Luca asks.

The question is for Jack, but Randolph doesn't know that, so he answers. "Sometime in the next month, I should think. But I can't do two hundred thousand. I just...can't."

"You've got sixty seconds, Luca. No more. It can't be done. If Cyrus thinks anything is off, we'll *never* get that data," Jack reminds him.

"You never know unless you try," Luca says, putting a hint of sheepish guilt in his voice, so it sounds like he's still talking to Randolph. "What can I say? I'll give you my Platinum Elite discount. Fifty thousand. In bearer bonds. The money can't be traceable."

A few agonizing seconds crawl by, but eventually Randolph answers, "You can make it look like an accident? It would be better if there's no investigation."

"Naturally," Luca agrees.

"Then we have an agreement," Randolph says.

I hear a chair creak slightly, followed by footsteps.

"What do you think you're—*urrrkh*."

Faint sounds of struggle spread into the dead silence of our comms. After another few seconds, we hear the sound of a body dropping onto the floor.

"Jesus Christ, Luca. What are you doing?" Jack yells.

"Relax. Randolph's taking a nap," Luca says.

"How does that help us?" Jack snaps.

"No time to explain," Luca says. "Trust my genius, okay?"

Ominous sounding thumps filter through his mic, and I realize he's hiding the body somewhere. I hear a doorknob turn, and then another.

"Are you in Cyrus's office?" I guess.

"Yes. Shut up."

I tear out of Adair's apartment, and, skipping the elevator in favor of the stairs, run down them as fast as I can. This is why I'm always the point person. Jack is too risk averse, and Luca hasn't met a kind of trouble he doesn't want to be in. He just conspired to commit murder, then committed assault, and now he's throwing in trespassing. If things go any further sideways, we'll be lucky if we can find a way to stay on American soil, let alone in Nashville.

"You better know what you're fucking doing, Luca," I say, a little out of breath. I exit the stairwell near the bank of elevators in the lobby, but see no sign of Cyrus. Either he hasn't made his way up from the garage yet, or he already headed into the business offices.

"It's a keypad," Luca says, relief flooding his usual coolness.

He means he's found the safe, and that it's unlocked by keypad, not by using biometrics. It's the first good news of the day.

"Planting the camera now," Luca says.

"Ok, your feed is live," Jack says, monitoring the signal from Luca's camera. "Now get out."

There's a pause of about ten seconds, then Luca hisses almost inaudibly, "I can't."

I look around the busy lobby frantically, just in time to see the back of Cyrus's head disappearing into the hallway behind the reception desk.

"Cyrus, yo!" I bellow.

He stops and spins on his heels, trying to figure out who called him.

I wave energetically and call his name again. He finds me immediately, his brow furrowing. "Sterling" he calls across the lobby, checking his watch. "What's up? Visiting Adair?"

I freeze up for a moment, unable to reply. I don't have an excuse ready—because I didn't plan on being here.

Jack rescues me, though.

"You're getting drinks from the bar," says his disembodied voice in my earpiece.

"I thought I'd grab a drink from the bar. We should catch up. What's your poison?" I ask, crossing the last few paces to the reception desk.

"You off the wagon again?" Cyrus says, turning toward me fully, but not leaving the door to the hallway.

"Now's as good a time as any," I say pointedly, leaving Cyrus completely baffled, but giving Luca the signal he needs. "To get off the wagon, I mean."

Luca emerges into the hallway behind Cyrus, then ducks into Randolph's office.

"Yeah, why not? For old times' sake, right?" Cyrus says, his easy grin coming out. "Whiskey neat. What else?"

"Right," I say, "I never paid attention to what other people were drinking."

"I've got something I need to do real quick," Cyrus says, "See you upstairs?"

"Sure thing," I say.

"That was too fucking close," Jack says. "You okay, Luca?"

"Yes," Luca says under his breath. "He's going into his office now."

My heart feels like it's beating in my throat, but I force myself to go over to the bar.

"I see his hands. He's punching in the access code," Jack shares.

The bartender finishes making a drink and turns to me,

rubbing the antique, polished zinc bar absentmindedly with a rag. "What can I get for you, sir?"

"Can I order room service here?"

"Of course, Mr. Ford," the bartender says without missing a beat. I have to hand it to the Eaton family. The service really is excellent. I don't even have to tell him where to send the drinks.

"Whiskey neat. And a club soda with lime."

"I'll send it right up, sir."

I wait until I'm in the elevator, alone, before I ask, "Do we have it?"

"I'm slowing down the replay and bumping up the contrast to deal with low light," Jack says patiently. "You're much better at planting cameras, Ford."

"Oh, *fuck you*," Luca coos. "I'm killing it today."

"I have the code," Jack says, ignoring him. "Two three four seven."

"I guess I'm going to go have a drink with my old room-mate without strangling him," I say through gritted teeth, flexing my fingers. All I have to do now is keep Cyrus busy while Luca lifts the data. I can feel my fight-or-flight reflex let off, feel my eyelids get heavy. There's no feeling quite like an adrenaline hangover. Maybe I should have ordered coffee at the bar.

I'm waiting in the kitchen when Cyrus knocks on the door a few minutes later. Room service dropped the drinks off almost as fast as if I'd waited for them at the bar.

"Jack, are we live?" I ask.

"Yes."

I hand Cyrus his drink as soon as I open the door, trying to give the impression I've already had a couple. "How the fuck have you been, Cyrus?" I ask, playing the part of old college buddies finally catching up.

"Not bad. I'm not gonna lie, Sterling. We kept saying we'd get together, but I didn't think you really meant it."

"Why not? We're both busy is all. Hard to find the time."

"Right," he says, before his head bobs with a question. "Where's Adair, anyway?"

"With Poppy. They went shopping or something. Didn't you know?"

"I don't fucking keep track of that stuff. I've got enough to worry about, you know?" he says, looking around the suite. "I'm glad Adair's finally moving in here. I can keep an eye on her."

I resist the nearly primal urge to beat him into oblivion. Something tells me that there's cameras in her suite, and Cyrus is looking forward to the footage. "Probably."

Cyrus drops into a chair in the living room, surveying the boxes Adair left strewn, half unpacked everywhere. "You planning on staying in Nashville? Last time we spoke, you weren't sure."

It's a perfectly innocuous question for him to ask, but I already know he wants me to leave town. At first I thought he wanted me out of the way to make another play for Adair. But that's probably not it. He has to know she's never going to screw Poppy like that. He tried once. No, he wants me gone before one of us figures out he was behind that video five years ago. He's scared of me. People with lots of secrets have lots to lose— and Cyrus has more secrets than he knows what to do with.

"I've gone back and forth. Actually, I wanted to ask you about something Adair mentioned," I say, taking a seat across from him on the couch. I take a sip of my club soda.

"Oh?" He takes a sip of his whiskey.

"Adair gave Poppy a note before I took off. Did you ever see it?" I give Cyrus a hard look. I'd chalked up our mislaid communications as tragic bad luck when we both mentioned trying to reach the other. Once I realized what Cyrus has been up to with the Eaton surveillance, I began to wonder if there's more to it than that.

"Yeah, maybe." He shrugs like he's searching for the memory, but I can see it there in his eyes. "I remember dropping off some mail."

It's a smooth lie, and a plausible one. He sips his whiskey, looking at me over the rim of the glass like he doesn't have a thing in the world to feel guilty about. If I didn't want to reach down his throat and rip his heart out, I'd probably be impressed.

"That's what I said." I flip my palms from down-facing to up, the universal body language for *who knows*.

"Still a vodka man, huh?" Cyrus deflects as soon as he can.

"Yeah." I lift my own glass. I'd learned a long time ago that people will see what they want. My club soda looks an awful lot like a vodka soda to Cyrus, because he wants to believe I'm still the drunk asshole he manipulated so easily all those years ago. "Anyway, we've just been trying to sort through it all. Put the pieces together. We were stupid kids. Don't want to make the same mistakes, you know?"

Cyrus's eyes narrow at the corners, but he pins a smile to his face. His eyes flit to the door, but I pretend not to notice, taking another large drink. "Yeah, you two were really hot and cold. I couldn't keep up with it. I don't blame you for taking off. Adair is drama. No offense."

Well, if I don't get to kill him, Adair probably will when she hears this bit.

"She didn't get my note either. Probably, because she was in London." *Try to wriggle off that hook, you fucking worm.*

"I know," he sounds completely wretched, but only in the showy way rich pricks use to get away with being assholes. "Poppy made me promise not to tell you. She said Adair wanted to move on."

I let the conversation lapse a moment when I hear voices in my earpiece.

"I'm in the safe," says Luca. "It's pretty standard. Liquid cooled so if someone tries to drill the safe it will ruin everything. The drives are all set in with screws and not prongs, though."

"What happened to the multitool I gave you last Christmas?" Jack says peevishly.

"I don't have it," Luca says evenly.

"Check the desk," Jack says, "Otherwise, I'll brush you one in the lobby."

I realize Cyrus is looking at me expectantly, and do my best to tune out Jack and Luca. "Women, huh? I guess I'm going to have to really work on getting Poppy to like me."

"Might be a lost cause," Cyrus says. "Poppy doesn't hate many people, but..."

"I wonder why she hates me," I say. "I bet you know."

"What are you talking about?" he asks, shifting his weight to the edge of his chair like he's considering storming out.

"You know a lot of things you shouldn't, don't you? I bet you know about the sex tape and the blackmail." I lean forward, directly across from him, until I can smell the liquor on his breath. He can try to bolt for the door, but he won't be able to before I grab him.

"I don't know what the fuck you're talking about." He puts his glass on the coffee table and stands up. "It was good to catch up. I hope you and Adair figure all this out, but—"

"No, you don't. You wouldn't want us to figure this out," I cut him off.

Cyrus glances at the desk, his eyes landing on the screwdriver Adair left there after jimmying open the locked drawer.

"Don't get any stupid fucking ideas," I say. He doesn't know it, but I could let him reach for it without forming a single bead of sweat. There's a Glock in the box nearest me. The kiddie pool has closed. Cyrus might think he's ready for the deep end, but I'm the deepest, darkest ocean. He has no idea.

"You haven't changed, Sterling," he says, suddenly relaxing. "You can take the kid out of the ghetto, but you can't—well, I shouldn't have to say the rest."

He pauses for a moment, regarding me with an amused smile, before unbuttoning his jacket and sitting back down. "Of course I set you up. Actually, I ought to *thank* you for that. I don't know why I thought Adair would screw over Poppy. Stupid kid myself, I guess. It would have been a good match. Her family's empire and mine. But Adair was never a team player," he continues wistfully. "Poppy is, though. Not my first choice, but her family's net worth has doubled. Imagine what I can do with that money. And you? You taught me how easy it is to manipulate people. Honestly, I think I learned more from you than all four years at Valmont."

"I'm glad to be of service," I say flatly. "I'm not so easy to manipulate anymore."

Cyrus Eaton actually laughs. Tilts his head back, opens his throat nice and wide, and roars with laughter. "You don't get it," he says. "I own your secrets. You think you have power over me now? It's *exactly* the opposite. I could bury you with what I have on you. You think I'm talking about five years ago? I'm not. And you don't even know!"

I rise to my feet, my pulse thundering in my ears.

"Sterling, don't," Luca's voice says quietly over the comms, startling me. It's incredible how easily a human being forgets the illusion of privacy. Even me. Even here. But Luca is my friend, and that means he knows I'm about five seconds from snapping Cyrus's neck. He knows it'll take everything I've got to fight it.

"It's not worth it," Jack says.

What the fuck are they talking about? This is exactly what they signed up for. We've never been afraid to get our hands dirty.

"If you want him dead, I'll do it," Luca says in an even tone. "You've got people to lose now, remember?"

When I woke up today, I knew everything I wanted from life. Maybe for the very first time. I came in here with a plan and all it took was Cyrus Eaton laughing at me, and I was ready to throw it all away.

And for what?

I think of Jay Gatsby floating dead in his pool, never learning his lesson. I see that scrap of paper Adair left me on the pillow. Those words. I've been fighting the past's current for so long, desperate to prove I'm stronger than the ocean of mistakes behind me.

But all I need to do is get out of the water.

"Cyrus," I say calmly, waiting for his laughing to fully stop.

"Yeah? What do you need, Sterling? Need to borrow my car? I've got five now. I'll *give* you one," he chuckles, admonishing me by waving his index finger. "But you have to ask nicely."

"Sterling, we have all the drives," Jack says quickly. "Luca's out. I'm plugging one in now. Standby."

His laughter rushes toward me, stopping short like the tide shifting. It can't reach me anymore. I'm too far on land for it to touch me.

"You offered me to the FBI, didn't you?" I say, giving Cyrus something to chew on, biding my time until I know I've won once and for all.

"You *are* smart, I'll give you that. But the company you keep... *Organized crime*, Sterling? What would Frankie say?"

"It's Francie, actually."

"Like I care."

"Sterling," Jack's voice sounds on the comms. "We've got everything. Looks like three years or more. It's even labeled neatly in the file tree."

"Do you not understand what you've done?" I ask Cyrus.

"The sex tape? Relax. Only 3 people ever saw it, and one of them is dead now."

"You violated Adair," I say. "You set me up."

"And you got a million bucks for it," Cyrus says, "Too bad you didn't find out until you were in the military."

"I never got that money."

"Seriously?" Cyrus looks like I just handed him a Christmas present. "Angus really was a tightwad. I kinda thought that's where you got all this." He points to my watch and my shoes, evidence that I'd come into money somehow.

If he only knew, he probably wouldn't be laughing now.

Jack's voice comes over the comm again. "Sterling, everything's in position."

I drop my voice so much he has to strain to hear me.

"Your whole world is about to come crashing down. If you *ever* come near me, my friends, *my family* again, if you so much as think of doing something, you're a dead man. The Bratva don't take kindly to people spying on them."

Cyrus's confident mask slips. His Adam's apple bob once, twice, and finally, when he gathers enough saliva, he replies, "Leave town now. Or I share everything with the FBI."

I allow myself a smile. "But, Cyrus, you don't have anything to share with the FBI."

The pleasure of watching him figure this out is almost orgasmic. His eyes flit back and forth, accessing the bits of information he needs. When he does, he explodes upward and runs to the door, furiously dialing on his phone at the same time. He throws open the door and crashes into someone.

"Poppy," he says, "What the f...I was just having a drink with Sterling." He leans and kisses her on the cheek.

She doesn't move. Adair is right behind her, looking furious. Neither smile. In fact, Poppy's cheeks are flushed so red they're almost purple. Cyrus can only watch in horror as she reaches her hand to her ear and pulls out a wireless earpiece.

"P-p-p-poppy," he splutters, backing away from her with his palms held up and out, like he needs them ready to deflect the blows that are coming.

Adair meets my eyes, and the momentary sweetness of victory sours. I knew it would be short-lived. Adair never wanted to break her best friend's heart, but Poppy deserves to know. I grew up watching a toxic relationship. I saw this for what it was, and she doesn't deserve that. The only way to be sure he couldn't twist things around and keep her in his pocket was for her to hear it from his own mouth. No matter how much it hurts. She'll probably hate me for it—

hell, I hate me for it—but she's never liked me much anyway.

"You unbelievable wanker." Poppy starts hitting, first with her open hand, just slapping Cyrus over and over again as he sinks to his knees and covers his face with his arm. Eventually she closes her fist, and then she starts swinging from the hip. I think I can hear one of the bones in her hand break, which is what happens when you punch a human skull, but she doesn't stop. "I can't believe I wasted all of this on your tiny dick. Seriously, you know you're practically dickless, right? Oh, and you're wrong, by the way. About my family's net worth. It's quadrupled. We're looking to invest. Maybe I'll buy some fucking hotels!"

Cyrus spins away from her, and, brushing Adair aside, strides toward the elevator, pretending not to hear her as she continues to scream.

When he reaches it, the doors slide open to reveal Jack and Luca wearing smug grins.

"Hey, it's dickless," Jack says.

"I've heard that about him," chimes in Luca, pushing a stunned Cyrus out of his path.

Cyrus darts into the elevator, tapping the button for the ground floor like it will somehow make the doors close faster. When we lose sight of him at last, he's raking his hand through his hair, queuing up to yell into his phone. But it's not like he's going to find someone who can help. There's no way to buy himself out of this mess.

Luca and Jack argue as they walk down the hallway, debating Luca's improvisations. But I'm hardly paying attention. Poppy's anger is draining into sadness. Adair grabs her and holds her tightly.

I hesitate, wondering if I should apologize. Adair shoots me a warning look that tells me now's not the time.

"We should leave," Adair murmurs, wrapping an arm around Poppy's shoulder. "Find somewhere private."

"I can't go back to our place," Poppy sobs.

"Go back to mine," I tell Adair. "I have some unfinished business, still."

It's time to settle this once and for all.

STERLING

The Cafe de Flore is a lot like its namesake in Paris. Located at the corner of a bustling intersection, the main attraction is a 50-foot swath of sidewalk cafe seating. The people watching is excellent, and the espresso goes great with a newspaper or book. The blue-collar French fare is serviceable.

That's what the reviews on my phone said, anyway.

I'm attracted to this location for an entirely different set of reasons. Whenever I'm hoping to avoid being murdered by a business partner, like the Semsynovey Bratva, I know meeting in a very public place might not guarantee I'll live, but it sure does make killing me inconvenient. I also need a place that's guaranteed to be busy enough to prevent surveillance. Nikolai knows the FBI is watching me. He'll appreciate the location. But the Cafe de Flore's real clincher is the hospital around the corner. I learned the hard way that when someone might consider killing you, it's best to have medical care accounted for in advance.

Our meeting is set for 7 o'clock, and it's almost time.

The Bratva is—first, last, and always—a business. And Russian business etiquette frowns on being late to meetings, especially ones with foreigners. Part of the reason I was so unsettled by Nikolai's last visit was that it was unannounced. Spontaneity is generally reserved for assassinations.

Typically, if the Semsynovey Bratva wants to meet with someone, it doesn't really occur to them that the person will decline. And—if for some stupid reason that person did—the Bratva would just throw their hands up and sigh. It just means more work for them. Now they have to eliminate someone. It's incredibly unnerving, knowing how banal killing is for them.

And that's why I need to be careful. I was asked to leave Nashville. But I didn't go. I was told to deliver the informant. But I let Cyrus go free. So really, the question is, would Nikolai Koltsov kill me in front of fifty witnesses on a busy street in Nashville, knowing he would likely spend twenty years in prison?

The answer is: definitely. *That's* why people are scared of him.

Nikolai is on time. He spots me immediately, ignoring the seating host, and heading directly to my table. I stand, knowing a polite gesture won't go unnoticed.

"Hello," he says brusquely, glancing to the tables on either side of us, one with a girl reading a book while sipping a cafe au lait, the other with a couple of women giddily gossiping over a bottle of rosé. His eyes snap to me. "Sitting between ladies? That's not very gallant of you."

"Neither is taking a man's sister," I point out.

"I would not call your sister a lady."

He makes a fair point.

"Still, you'll find she has no cause to complain," he says.

"We just had a little chat this afternoon. Got to know one another. She's very fiery."

"Yes, she is," I agree. "But where is she?"

"Close. Where is my little bird that sings too much?" he asks carefully as a waitress appears.

"Can I get you something to drink?" she asks.

"I have discovered something," Nikolai says. "Your whiskey is delicious."

He expects me to order it for him. Of course. "One West Reserve, please."

"Coming up," the waitress says brightly, already heading toward the cafe interior. I gave her a $50 bill as soon as I sat down a half hour ago. She's supposed to keep an eye out and come by right away if I raise my hand. Shit like that impresses Nikolai.

"This is a nice place for a chat," I say. What I'm really saying is: I vouch for the security of our location.

"Should we wait for our friend from Washington?" He means the FBI, and specifically Noah.

"He's got other plans."

"Good. What is it you have to say?"

"Your brothers wish to avoid any risk I might pose to them. I appreciate this. I also want to see this risk removed."

Nikolai nods his head, almost imperceptibly.

We pause for a moment to let the waitress drop off the whiskey. Nikolai slips her a hundred dollar bill, and kisses her hand as he passes it to her. Her eyes rake up his arm, over his extensive tattoos, expensive designer suit, and flashy Breitling, and she actually bites her lip. He could have her across the table in five seconds. He knows it. He wants me to know it, too.

After the waitress leaves, he finally answers. "Yes, the

same way we know of your name being mentioned in a sealed indictment. It...worries...some of my brothers. Some think, maybe this might be used as leverage over you."

"I've recovered the sole copy of the materials in question, along with other videos that might interest you." I point my index finger to the breast pocket of my jacket to signal I'm reaching for that and not a gun. I slowly remove a burner cell phone. This morning, Jack loaded it with all the surveillance Cyrus had on the Koltsovs, then queued up a video with helpful subtitles about the meetings that were compromised. I hand it to Nikolai, and he taps play.

He watches for about a minute, then mashes pause, lets out a deep growl, and drops the phone into his pocket. "And the source?"

Luca and Jack were split on what to tell Nikolai about the data. Luca said we should just tell the truth by naming Cyrus. Jack pointed out that this was the same as killing Cyrus. In the end, I decided to use a detail that seemed unappealing to investigate further, and that was vaguely close to what really happened, just in case. "He's in a cage."

"Your cage or my cage?" Nikolai asks.

"Consider it our cage."

"And these were all the videos?"

"There were more, all stolen from hotel feeds. We destroyed everything, except what I just gave you," I lie. "Too many enemies. Too many problems."

He goes still and closes his eyes. Whatever's happening inside his head, I know he's trying to figure out if he believes me. What if I kept more videos than I gave him, just as insurance or leverage in a future disagreement? What if I made copies of the data? He has to believe everything I tell him, or nothing I tell him. Anything else doesn't really help clarify his decisions.

"You should have given the rest of the files to us," he says.

"Nikolai, last time we spoke, you said your brothers owed me one—"

"Yes, and some would say letting you live after we asked you to leave would more than repay any debt." He senses value. Like any businessman, he doesn't want to let go of it.

"I've done you another favor." His eyebrows arch, probably at my presumption. "I took care of your bird and made sure no one hears any of his songs."

He purses his lips, and by the time I've finished, they've vanished to a thin line. I have no idea what it means.

"I suppose you could see it that way, but what do you want from me?"

At last, I understand what he's getting at. The way he looks at the world, resources aren't wasted. People don't destroy things of value to make their lives easier. For him, there has to be something else. Or I just don't make sense. And not making sense to a man like him is dangerous—to say the least.

"It's better that a friend should find your secrets than an enemy keep them, don't you think? Better that Washington loses leverage over that friend. I don't want to deal or bargain. I want to settle in Nashville. That's it."

Nikolai Koltsov weighs up everything I've told him. He doesn't need to consider whether the information I gave him is legitimate. If it's not, it's just more work for him. He can just find me again. He doesn't *have to* do anything at the moment. "I watched you. It's been a couple weeks now. You love that girl. You want to stay," he says, an almost romantic glint in his eye. "But—can I be honest with you for a moment? Man to man?"

"Of course," I say slowly. This is taking an unexpected turn.

"You fight in public. Always screaming. Angry. This is not how a gentleman treats a lady, Sterling."

Did I just get fucking relationship advice from the Bratva?

"I think that's behind us," I say. "We had a lot of..."

"History?" Nikolai says, flashing a knowing smile.

"Exactly."

My cell phone, which is on the table, begins vibrating. A message flashes on the screen:

He's headed in your direction.
Five minutes.

"Nikolai—"

"Yes, I read it. Time to go. " He downs the last half of his whiskey, standing at the same time. "Yes, very good. West's, was it?"

"That's it."

He nods in my direction, ducking out from beneath the umbrella above us and raising his hand. Another man stands, revealing Sutton sitting behind him. She glares at me. Standing, she saunters over. There's not a hair out of place, but she's not happy.

"Exactly, why did I just spend the day with an overly polite, flirtatious Russian man?" she demands.

"It's a long story," I say as another text comes through.

Don't know how he located
you, but he's almost there.

"I'm listening," she says.

"Look, this isn't a good time." I'd rather she not be here when Noah shows up.

"Are you serious?"

I stand up and kiss her on the forehead. "I'm really glad you're okay, and I'm really sorry I put you through that. Maybe it's time for you to head back to New York?"

"Are you kidding? That was the most interesting thing that's happened to me since the FBI showed up at my dorm room." She crosses her arms, tilting her head defiantly. "I'm going to transfer to Valmont."

"That is..." I trail away as a large, black SUV stops catty-corner from Cafe de Flore. Noah jumps out of it, scanning all sides of the intersection for signs of me. I wave, and when he sees me, his expression turns feral.

"You look busy," Sutton says as he marches toward us. "I'll catch you at home."

"Adair's there," I call after her. "Try to be nice."

She gives me a far too enthusiastic thumbs up to be genuine. Skirting past Noah, she blows him a kiss.

"I got my sister back," I say as he approaches.

"I have eyes," he says as he draws up next to me. "You met with Koltsov."

"You knew I would," I say, gesturing to the seat Nikolai just vacated. "Coffee?"

"You think I'm playing games, Sterling? You're the subject of a federal investigation, and you're blatantly meeting with Bratva on a street corner."

"I wasn't going to meet a Koltsov in a dark alley." I drop my voice. "You knew I'd have to do this."

"Yeah," he matches my volume, "but that doesn't mean you get to walk away without consequences."

I guess our alliance is over. It's possibly the shortest-lived one in history. I'm not surprised. Noah sees everything in black and white. He always will. I can't expect him to understand gray.

"I'd like to report a crime," I say, dipping a hand into my other jacket pocket and drawing out a neatly-folded manilla envelope. I slide it across the table to Noah, who makes an annoyed grimace while opening it. He removes a small, digital audio recorder.

"What's this?"

"It seems one of the local businessmen got the wrong idea about our friend Luca. Can you believe he asked Luca to kill his wife?"

Noah looks like he can believe it. Probably since he's privy to Luca's FBI dossier. Still, he has to listen in order to figure out where to take the conversation. But he hates having to catch up, and he despises me watching him do it.

He clicks the play/pause button, and an audio recording of this evening's comms starts playing. Noah glowers as he listens to our banter until the moment Randolph agrees to a price of $50,000.

"What am I supposed to do with this?" he says, tossing the recorder down on the table in disgust.

"You're always looking for bad guys. I got you one gift-wrapped," I say, leaning back comfortably in my chair. "Consider it a thank you present for helping me get Sutton back."

"That's all this is? You don't expect me to just take this and walk away, do you?"

"Not really. But you probably should."

His whole body flexes, his massive, linebacker frame straining against the seams of his suit. I probably shouldn't bait him so much—but I can't help myself when he makes it so easy.

"You haven't changed. You'd rather step in shit than back away," he says, pocketing the recorder.

"Someone has to do the dirty work," I say, savoring the look of outrage this produces. "We can't all sit around polishing our idealistic attitudes."

"You really don't think you're in the wrong, do you? You never have. Not then. Not now."

"What would you know about hard choices? You almost got Luca, Jack and I killed. You were dead fucking wrong about what was going on in Afghanistan, and a lot of people died."

"I didn't kill them. I didn't steal guns. *Someone* has to draw the line in the sand—"

"And you expect to draw that line for everyone else?" I ask.

"You're a piece of shit, Sterling. You were a piece of shit when I met you, and you're a piece of shit now. All the people in your life—they'll end up paying for your mistakes," he says, jabbing at me with his index finger. "You know it's true."

I stand, forcing myself to button my suit jacket, telling myself to walk away, even as my hand curls into a fist.

"I know you want to take a swing at me, Ford," Noah says, reading me like a book. "Go ahead and *try*."

"So you can arrest me? I'm not that stupid."

"You think I care about that?" He gets up, edging closer to me until we're chest to chest, and makes a show of pulling his FBI badge out of the interior of his suit pocket before tossing it on the table. "I need to make sure you understand me perfectly. When I nail you—and *I will*—it won't be for picking a fight. That's too cheap for you. I'm going to crucify you. I'm going to make you regret every bad decision you ever made. One day soon, you're going to look up from the smoking crater that is your life, and you'll see me standing there, wearing this same smug grin."

I can't help myself. I shift my weight backwards as if I'm going to throw an overhand right, but tuck my forearm in at the last minute, slipping inside his guard and striking the side of his head with my elbow.

The blow does almost nothing—aside from piss him off. He just shakes his head sharply, like a bear trying to figure out who dared to throw something at him.

Noah takes two choppy steps forward, his arms raised like a boxer's, but instead of throwing a punch, he feints. I step backward, bringing my own guard up, but Noah's faster. He hooks a leg just behind my foot, and charges his shoulder into my chest as hard as he can. I fly backwards, crashing into the table next to us.

Every conversation around us stops, and most of the people there gasp in surprise. People stand and begin to back away, some of them even straddling the low barrier used to mark the footprint of the cafe seating, trying to get away from the melee.

"C'mon, Ford," Noah gloats. "This is too easy!"

I flip onto my feet straight from the flat of my back, grabbing one of the wooden bistro chairs next to me and swinging it at Noah. He can't escape—our space is too confined to get out of the way. He does the next best thing, though, which is to distribute the blow across the broad frame of his back. Still, the force of it drops him to one knee, and he has to use both hands to avoid smashing into the pavement.

"Had enough, Porter?" That blow had to hurt—but he's a tough son of a bitch. I know he's not done. He answers with a vicious uppercut, a move I see so late I unbalance myself trying to avoid it. He launches forward like a sprinter exploding from the blocks, planting his shoulder in my stomach and bearing me to the ground.

I'm not a small man by any measure, but I'm not as big as Noah. He has the advantage when his weight's on top of me. He rains down blows, most of which I deflect with my forearms. He catches me cleanly twice, though, once over my right eye, and once on the left cheekbone. The telltale sting of blood hitting cold air tells me I'm bleeding, but thankfully it's not affecting my vision.

Twisting my body to the right, I roll from flat on my back to my side, allowing me to cover my head with just one arm. My free hand finds a wine bottle, and Noah doesn't see the blow coming. The bottle smashes into his temple, and his weight slumps on top of me, almost knocking the wind out of me. I lever him off of me, noticing the groggy look in his eyes, the trickle of blood pouring out from his hairline. One good shot to the button—the spot under the ear where the jaw meets the neck—and he'll be out cold.

I place one hand flat on his chest, holding him down, and cock my other arm.

Even through his haze of pain, Noah looks at me with perfect hatred. He's never entertained the idea what he did in Afghanistan was wrong. He probably never will. I start to throw my punch, but someone grabs my forearm.

I look up and find Luca grinning at me. "You know I hate missing a play date."

"What in God's name is going on here?" a man's voice calls from the cafe entrance. He's short and fat, wearing an impeccable silver suit, complete with a burgundy neckerchief. He waddles over, his feet somehow never leaving contact with the ground.

"I'm very sorry," I say, "Mister...?"

I need to smooth this over quickly. Noah wouldn't break his word—he won't arrest me for hitting him. The Nashville police won't care one way or the other.

"George Laurent," the man says, taking stock of my appearance: expensive, tailored suit, Breitling watch, thousand dollar loafers—all of which are either torn, scuffed, or slightly bloody. "I own this cafe."

Noah sits up, shaking off the last cobwebs from being hit in the head with the bottle. He probably needs to get out of here before anyone realizes he's an FBI agent.

"My friend and I had a little disagreement," I say. "Fighting over which one of us is picking up the check."

Laurent's mouth presses into a grim, humorless line. "I'm calling the police."

"That won't be necessary," I insist. "I'd like to take care of the bill for all of your guests, and of course I'll pay for any damages."

The few remaining diners around us perk up at this offer, quickly changing from scowling at me to looking expectantly at Laurent.

Noah smolders, his face roiling with disgust at hearing me try to buy my way out of trouble. He doesn't think money should change anything about life. I bet part of him even wants to be punished for fighting. But it's not as big as the part that burns for payback, or the part that wants to be the best at everything he does. He needs me to do this—because he's unwilling to. Same old story.

"I don't know," Laurent says, a faint trace of dropped consonants pointing to English being his second language. The cafe name, his style. "It's a lot of damage."

It's really not. I count one table, two chairs, and an umbrella. Replacing it should cost less than a thousand dollars. I don't care. Getting out of this cleanly is worth a lot more to me.

I switch to French, mostly so the people around us are less likely to object to my buying him off, but also because a French man prefers being spoken to in his native language. I hand him a business card. "Envoyez-moi le chèque."

He takes the business card without hesitation, giving me one more careful look. "Et leurs dîners?"

He wants proof he'll come out ahead before he'll let me leave.

I slide an Amex Black out of my wallet and hand it to him. "Oui."

"Très bien," Laurent says, tucking the card into his pocket and shuffling back towards the interior of the cafe.

"I'm glad your French is better than mine," Luca mutters. He offers his hand to Noah, but he refuses the help.

Standing Noah, dusts himself off. Then, he puts his hand on my chest and leans in close, knowing every person around us will be straining to hear every juicy detail. "Your luck will run out. I'll be there when it does."

"I doubt it." Lately, my luck's been turning around.

2 2

ADAIR

"**A** re you *ever* going to stop pacing?" Poppy asks.

"What am I supposed to do? He's been gone for almost two hours. What if something went wrong?" I actually wish I could calm down—but it's no good. The second I try to sit down I find myself back on my feet trying to outpace the weight bearing down on my chest.

We're at Sterling's apartment, just Poppy and me. I don't feel safe at the Eaton anymore, for obvious reasons.

"You're upsetting Zeus," she says, rubbing behind his ears.

Actually, he hasn't left her side since we arrived. I pause to consider this and realize I'm being a selfish bitch. "Oh my god. I'm sorry. I'm stuck in my own head, and after what happened earlier..."

"That's not your fault," she says. "I'm the stupid girl who convinced myself he loved me back."

"Loving someone is never stupid." I lower onto the couch beside her, pushing Zeus to the ground, so I can hold her.

"It feels stupid," she says with a sob, "in hindsight."

I'm not sure what to say to her. I know from experience that empty platitudes like *there's plenty of fish in the sea* and *everything happens for a reason* is like pouring rubbing alcohol on a gaping wound. It hurts and it's unlikely to help.

"Look Cyrus is a dick, I should have told you that sooner," I admit.

"He hit on you, didn't he?" she asks.

"He was drunk. It didn't mean anything," I say.

"Don't make excuses for him," she says, wiping her eyes. "Everyone makes excuses for him, even me. No more."

"Something tells me, he's not going to get off so easily this time," I say.

"I just...he made that sex tape of you. I keep thinking I'm going to throw up." She reaches up and locks her hand over mine.

That's a sentiment we share, and I'm more than a little put out that Sterling didn't warn me about what he'd discovered.

"He deserves whatever he gets," she says fiercely.

"They usually do," Sutton says, coming through the front door and tossing keys on the counter.

"Sutton!" I jump up. "Are you okay? Did—"

She cuts me off with a withering glare. "Don't pretend to care."

I start to tell her that I do care, but I don't have the energy. Instead, I shrug.

"So, what did he do?" Sutton drops onto the floor, crossing her legs under her.

"You don't want to know," I say when Poppy's lower lip trembles.

"You were way too hot for him anyway," Sutton says matter-of-factly.

This actually manages to perk her up. "Thank you." Poppy gathers herself a little, sitting up straight like she's determined to be sociable. "You're going to school in New York, right? What are you studying?"

"I haven't decided." Sutton flashes me a blinding grin. "But I'm looking into transferring to Valmont in August."

"Oh, I can help you with that! I know everyone in admissions." Poppy begins peppering her with questions, momentarily distracted by a mission to help someone.

I'm trying to see this as a positive and not obsess over how much she hates me when the door flies open to reveal Luca and Jack, laughing and joking, holding Sterling up.

"See? They're fine," Poppy says from the living room.

"You call this *fine*?"

I back up enough for Luca and Jack to help an unsteady Sterling through the door. His face is a mess. The cut over his eyebrow is slowly leaking blood into the corner of his eye, forcing him to keep it squeezed shut. Another cut on his cheek has fully clotted, but it's still a nasty gash.

Sterling shuffles into the room, brushing off Luca and Jack—it's obvious he wants to look like he's in better shape than he is. He flashes me a wolfish grin. "I'm fine, Lucky. Never better."

"Did Nikolai do this?"

"Nope," Luca says, fighting to get the words out between laughs.

"This is courtesy of Uncle Sam, actually," Jack clarifies unhelpfully, enjoying the look of horror on my face for a moment before continuing. "Only Ford could get in a fight with an FBI agent and *not* get arrested."

"I've never understood why my reputation is worse than

his," Luca says. "Sterling gets into at least as much trouble as I do."

What the fuck am I hearing?

"You fought with Noah?" I guess, not finding this nearly as funny as everyone else.

"He made it clear he wasn't being an FBI agent at the moment I hit him. Noah and I have history, remember?" Sterling slumps into one of the stools facing the kitchen, a strange, satisfied grin spreading on his face. "It was a long time coming."

I try to calm myself down by remembering that thirty seconds ago I was worried he would die. "As far as I remember, your plans didn't involve meeting Noah..."

"He figured out where I was somehow. That's why Luca was following him. He was never a danger to me, though," Sterling adds quickly.

"Says the man in need of a hospital. Where's your first aid kit?"

"Maybe Jack should do it," Sterling suggests.

"Jack needs a drink, and this place is a desert," Jack says. "Let her do it. She's going to need to learn how."

"Where is it?" I say, using my best don't-fuck-with-me voice.

"In the cabinet next to the trash can," Sterling relents.

I open the cabinet door, surprised to find there's nothing else inside, just an olive green rucksack full of tiny compartments. I heave it free of the cabinet, surprised at the weight. "This has to weigh thirty pounds."

"More like forty," Sterling says, grimacing as he flexes his back.

"I need a drink, too," Luca declares. "You in, Sutton?"

"She's under-aged," Sterling barks.

"I don't think you get to pick and choose which rules to follow," I tell him.

"For once, I'm with her," Sutton says.

Poppy pauses, twisting her fingers together. "Maybe, I should stay..."

"Oh, I almost forgot," Jack says. "I picked up a lock change kit. We should deal with that first."

"A lock change kit?" I repeat.

"For Poppy's place," he says, "so that jackass can't get in."

"But his things are there," she says miserably.

"We can take care of that while Jack does the locks." Luca nudges Sutton, who nods. "We'll get rid of it."

"Like put it on the curb?" she asks.

"Sure," Luca says with a shrug.

"Not set it on fire, right?" Sterling butts in.

Luca does an admirable job of looking hurt. "I wouldn't."

"Say it," Sterling demands.

"We won't set it on fire."

I'm not sure if Sutton or Luca looks more disappointed about this.

"We'll leave you kids alone," Jack says, flashing a wide grin.

"How mad are you, exactly?" Sterling says, his grin slipping, as they leave. He shakes his head a little, like his thoughts are fuzzy.

"I think I'll forgive you." Honestly, I'm just glad he's here in mostly one piece.

"Good, good," he says, pulling me close to him and brushing a kiss on my lips.

It feels good. I try to kiss him back, but his head snaps back as he lets out a yelp. "Sorry, did I do something?"

"My cheek, it's a little tender," he says, leaning forward

gingerly and pressing his lips to the curve of my neck, making me forget what I'm supposed to be doing.

"Hey, cut that out. Let's get you cleaned up first."

"Yes, ma'am," he says, feigning his best southern accent.

I start digging through the first aid kit, looking for bandages and disinfectant, but I can't find anything remotely like that. "What are these?" I ask, holding up what looks like a badly bent pair of scissors.

"Clamps," he says simply.

"What are they even for?" I ask. The closest looking thing I've seen are eyelash curlers.

"Stopping arterial bleeding," he says, letting out a chuckle that causes him to wince.

"Seriously? Where's all the normal shit?"

"There are some butterfly sutures in the pocket next to the strap," Sterling says, pointing.

It takes me a few minutes, but eventually I find antibiotic ointment, cotton swabs, and sutures. Sterling instructs me patiently, but I can't help getting the feeling he's drowsy. "You sure you're okay?"

"Me?" he asks. "I'm fine. It's just an adrenaline crash."

I clean the cut over his eye with an alcohol swab, expecting him to wince in pain. But he looks stoic as I rub burning hot alcohol into his wound, then dab ointment into it with a swab. "What's an adrenaline crash?"

"After your adrenaline spikes—I mean really spikes—"

"Such as when fighting an FBI agent in a downtown Nashville cafe?" I try to sound stern, but, honestly, I'm too relieved to have this behind us to stay angry at him for getting in a fight. He's been building toward it all day.

"Yeah, after that, your body goes back to its normal equilibrium. It's like going from Superman to just Clark Kent."

"So you're only a mere mortal now," I say.

"Clark Kent is always Superman. Sometimes he just hides it."

"So you're saying, you still have superhuman stamina?"

"Only one way to find out." He pulls me close, not mistaking what I meant. His lips are on mine, and without thinking I bring my hand to his face—right on top of the gash on his cheek I haven't cleaned yet. He flinches hard, almost jumping out of his skin.

"Sorry," I plead. I don't think it's totally my fault, but he probably doesn't see it that way.

"Never be sorry, Lucky," he says as I take care of his cheek just like I did his brow. His hands fiddle with the straps of my dress. "How was your day?"

I fill him in on the highlights, glossing over the worst of it. He's got enough to worry about.

"You okay?" he asks when I finish.

"Fine." I tell myself it's the truth, because while we might have dealt with some problems today, there's still a lot left for us to conquer.

"Liar," he whispers. "It's going to be okay."

"Done," I say, leaning down to his perch on the stool and kissing the side of his brow that's not cut up. I pull him to me, planting both my hands as far away from his face as I can, on his back—I don't trust them anymore.

He winces in pain anyway, and I jump back. "What now?"

"Sorry. Kidney."

"Well, what can you do?" I say, my hand flashing to my mouth as soon as the words are out.

"What can I do?" he says, repeating the phrase again with maximum incredulity, a hungry look coming over him. He stands and lifts me over his shoulder in one fluid movement, and just like that he's carrying me to the bedroom.

He almost tosses me on the bed when we arrive, and has to flex his back to loosen it up before crawling on top of me. I feel his cock beneath his suit pants, rubbing against the thin fabric of my skirt, and instantly, I'm ready.

He leans down and kisses my collarbone, his hand cupping my ass and drawing my hips against his. "I didn't know fighting was a turn on for you."

"Neither did I," I admit.

He shoves my skirt up and my legs open in invitation.

"We need a condom. I missed my pill," I warn him.

"In the drawer of the nightstand," he says.

I roll over slightly, my hand searching the interior of the draw, but it's bare. "Nothing there."

"In a box under the bathroom sink," he mumbles, letting me slip from underneath him, and propping himself on his side as I disappear to the bathroom.

"Which sink?" I call in to him.

"Left, I think," he says distantly.

It's not the left sink, or the right. There's another cabinet mounted about the toilet, though, and—thank God—the box of condoms is in there.

"Found one!" I declare triumphantly, returning to the bedroom. Sterling's still propped on his side, his back turned to me. I climb on top of him, kissing behind his ear and taking care to avoid his sensitive spots—or, at least the ones I know about.

He lets out a strange grunt, almost like he's clearing his throat.

"Sterling?"

Avoiding the large, swollen, purple welt on his side, I shake him firmly.

He responds by letting out a long, deeply satisfied snore. I finish tugging off his pants, which takes some effort since he's out like a rock. Tossing them on the ground, I pull off my dress.

"Damn. You owe me one, Ford," I whisper, slipping into the space beside him and listening gratefully to the sound of him breathing.

I ROLL OVER, SLEEPILY RUNNING A HAND ACROSS Sterling's chest. Moonlight streams through the large windows, casting him in shadows. Overhead, blue light shines as my ringtone slowly seeps into my consciousness. Who is calling me in the middle of the night? Sterling stirs, and I shift to grab my phone off the nightstand before it wakes him. As I go to silence it, the screen flashes *Malcolm*. My eyes skip to the time, and I hesitate a moment before answering. I can't think of many reasons for my brother to call me at this hour, but I've learned the hard way what happens when you don't take important calls.

"It's one in the morning," I tell him in a whisper. Sterling shifts behind me, rolling to his side.

"Where is she?" Malcolm demands.

"What? Who?" I'm still half-asleep, but the moment the questions leave my mouth, I know why he's calling with deep, nauseating certainty. I'm already swinging my legs over the side of the bed when he responds.

"Ellie. You took her!" He's shouting now, and I'm on my feet.

"I don't have her." But he's too busy ranting to hear me. "Malcolm! How long has she been missing?"

"You tell me," he yells. "I came home late from the office and ducked my head in after Ginny told me what you did this afternoon. She's not in her bed. There's nothing on the cameras. You know where—"

I'm wide awake now. Despite that, I don't hear Sterling until he lifts the phone from my hand. "Malcolm," he barks, "shut the fuck up and tell me when the last time anyone saw her was."

For a second, I'm frozen, unsure what to do. He glances at me, his face reflecting in the phone's light. There's a sort of cool composure to his features, his jaw set and determined, his attention on the call, but there's panic in his eyes that mirrors my own. I scramble for my dress, throwing it on as quickly as I can.

"We're on our way," Sterling says, hanging up on my brother.

"Sterling..."

He holds up a finger as he tosses my phone onto the bed and strides over to his pants. He takes his own phone out of their pocket and dials someone. Shoving it between his shoulder and his ear, he pulls his pants on roughly. "Nikolai, I thought we had an arrangement."

"What's going on?" I ask as I finish tugging on my shoes. I've run out of simple tasks to distract me, so I begin pacing the room waiting for him.

But Sterling is right behind me, listening intently, as he digs his keys out of his pocket and tilts his head in the direction of the door. "I'm asking where my daughter is," he says in response to the man on the other end. "You're the one who threatened her! I thought we were good."

"Oh my god." I think I'm going to throw up. I'd known about most of the Bratva's threats, but he hadn't told me that they'd found out about Ellie.

"You swear on your fucking life?" Sterling roars. "If you touched her...Fine." He pauses to put on his shoes, and I wait.

"What is going on?" I repeat my earlier question.

"I don't know. Nikolai gave me his word." He heads toward the door, and I'm beside him, unsure how my legs are even moving. Zeus is sitting next to it like he plans to come along, and Sterling shoos him away.

"And that's it? You believe him?" I ask.

Sterling turns to me as he holds open the penthouse door, his blue eyes dark and unsettled like the sky on the verge of a storm. "I do. Believe me, he wouldn't give it lightly."

"But who would take Ellie?"

We share a look that says it all. If we weren't here together, we might suspect each other. There's no accusation on either of our parts. It would be a stupid move, but one we were each likely to understand. It really only leaves us in the dark.

"Are there others like the Bratva?" I ask, somewhat hesitantly, as we get in the elevator.

"I guess," he admits, his head hanging. "None that are actively pissed at me, as far as I know."

How could I have thought it would be this easy? Sterling's been clear with me about his past. I know he's involved with dangerous men. Why did I think crossing one enemy off the list made us safe?

He calls Luca on our way to the car, giving them instructions and listing off names to track down as he screeches out of the parking garage. Nashville is sleeping, its neon signs calling to empty streets. We barely pass any other cars, but

Sterling whips around all of them, reaching the highway with record speed. He doesn't slow as he merges off the ramp, he just goes faster, still rattling off names to his friend.

"Who are those people?" I ask when he finally hangs up.

His hands grip the steering wheel, his gaze staying on the road ahead, but I catch the slight slide of his throat. "Potential enemies."

"There are that many?" I ask flatly.

"I tend to leave an impression," he says. "Some of them are friends."

I shake free the cobwebs in my head. "They can't be both."

"I promise they can. Rivals are as often friends as enemies," he says darkly, and I know he's thinking about Cyrus.

Who else can't we trust?

I don't ask any more questions as we speed toward Windfall. Instead, I find myself praying to whoever might be listening as I count the green mile markers dotting the highway, each getting me closer to her. I have to believe that. I don't think I'm capable of considering any other scenario. Dread consumes me when I spot the exit for Valmont, threatening to turn me inside out.

It's the fastest drive of my life.

It's the longest one, too.

Maybe Sterling is right about friends and enemies. Maybe sometimes the truth exists in paradox.

E very light at Windfall greets us as we pull to the open gate.

"Where the fuck is the security guard?" I ask.

Sterling studies the gatehouse for a moment, a muscle ticking in his jaw, before he floors the gas and shoots forward down the drive. "All of this feels wrong."

"What does that mean?"

"Just keep your eyes open," he says as we pull into the front circle, "especially on your brother and sister."

He bounds up the stairs two at a time, reaching the front door before I've reached the stone steps. Windfall looms over me like a spectral ghost peeking its head from my childhood closet. When I reach the entry, I walk into a full-blown confrontation. Sterling has Malcolm by the shirt collar, lifted off the ground.

"Do not fuck with me!" he shouts.

"Why would I do something with her? She's ours," Malcolm splutters, his face reddening from Sterling's grip.

Felix hovers nearby, seemingly with no intention of intervening.

"Stop," I demand. Instantly, Sterling lowers Malcolm to his feet, dropping his hold without warning and leaving my brother to stumble forward. Ginny darts toward me, her eyes skittering wildly in her head, as she tugs her silk dressing gown together.

"What did you do with her?" she asks, jabbing a finger in my chest.

"For the last fucking time," Sterling roars, but I hold up a hand.

"We are here to help you find her. Sterling can do that if you answer his questions."

"How?" Ginny turns a scathing look on him.

"I don't have time to explain it to you, but let's say I'm trained," he bites out. He looks past her, his eyes meeting mine. "In fact, I don't know why we're wasting time arguing with them at all." He stalks off towards the stairs. "Which way is her room?"

"East wing," I call, maneuvering around Ginny to follow him up the main staircase.

"Where are you going?" Malcolm says. "You think we haven't looked there? The police are on their way."

"Believe me, you haven't looked like I will," Sterling mutters, clearly not concerned over whether or not my brother hears him.

Behind us, Ginny is whispering frantically to her husband, but he's busy glaring up at us. I look away, choosing to mimic Sterling. My foot catches on the thick carpeting and I lurch forward, Sterling catches me and helps me upright. "I know it's hard, Lucky, but you have to give your brain enough blood to think. Focus everything on your surroundings," he coaxes me. "Stop paying attention to that pit in your stomach or how hard your heart is beating. That's not important. We need to think. We need to see. Do you understand?"

I bob my head, doing my best to take his advice. I lead him to her bedroom, and it takes every ounce of me not to crumple to the floor when I see her shoes by the bed.

"Is there anything off?" he asks as he paces around the room, stopping to check the windows.

I scan the room, looking for the obvious: mud on the carpet or a ransom note or signs of a struggle, I guess. "Everything looks normal."

"We're not looking for abnormality, really. Just anything that doesn't quite add up."

I look again, trying to ignore the way each item in the room twangs the strings of my heart. Her dolls. Her jacket hanging on a hook in her closet. Drawings and crayons on the table under the picture window. Her covers turned down. An imprint on her pillow from her head. It's all there, but it's so quiet and abandoned that the only thing I know is missing is her. Then something catches my eye.

"Her Buddy Bear is gone," I say, pointing to the bed.

"Her what?" Sterling asks.

"It's a stuffed bear that I gave her as a baby. She sleeps with it. Every night. She can't sleep without it." I clap a hand over my mouth. The bear's gone. She's gone.

My baby is gone.

Again.

My knees buckle, and before I can stop it, I vomit on the floor.

Sterling is by my side, a hand on my back. "The police are on their way," he says, "and they will help us find her. The bear missing is actually a good thing."

I turn watering eyes on him. How can any of this be a good thing? How can he stand there and calmly expect the police to find her?

"If the bear's gone, she grabbed it," he says, answering my unspoken question. "If someone snatched her, she probably wouldn't have been awake or had time. Either whoever has her knows she'd want the bear or Ellie took it with her. Maybe she's hiding? This is a big house."

I force myself to consider this. Malcolm and Ginny may have looked, but judging from the state of the house, they hadn't been tearing things apart. Her room is still neat and organized. There were no signs of struggle downstairs. The only evidence that she's missing is an empty bed and panicked parents.

"We're going to keep looking," Sterling says firmly, like we're just tackling a to-do list.

"And if we find her? They'll take her again," I shout, finally losing it. "They'll point the finger, and they'll drag up dirt. They'll say we had something to do with it."

"Exactly," Sterling says in a lowered voice as if he suspects the walls are listening. "It's all a bit convenient, especially after what happened to you this afternoon."

"I just want to find her," I say desperately. "I don't even care if I never get to see her again. If she's safe..."

Sterling kisses my forehead, before tilting my chin so our eyes meet. "I swear on my life that nothing will happen to her. I won't allow it." He steps away. "Where would you go if you were hiding?"

"She can't be hiding." I shake my head. "It doesn't make sense. It's the middle of the night."

"Don't think rationally. Think like a four year-old. Where would you have hidden?"

I hate dredging up memories of my childhood—too often, I discover landmines after I've stepped on one. In the end, the answer is easy. "I usually left the house."

Sterling looks like he wants to ask why, but stops himself.

"It was scary inside the house. Daddy was on a rampage, drunk," I add, the chill of unpleasant memories slithering up my spine. "I always felt safer outside. But if they checked the cameras, they should have seen her."

Sterling's eyes narrow, but he doesn't speak. "Do you remember your birthday party? All those years ago?"

"It was pretty unforgettable," I say flatly. Even thoughts of how miserable that night turned out can't distract me from my purpose here tonight, though. "What does that have to do with Ellie?"

"You knew where all the cameras were," he says. "You knew how to avoid them. A well-honed survival instinct."

"Ellie wouldn't know that. She's only—" I protest.

"I agree, but everyone else in this house knows where the cameras are, right?"

"What are you saying?" I ask, unable to process what he's alluding to. I can see it, but it's just far enough away that the details are too blurry to make out.

"Keep an eye on all of them. *All* of them," he says.

We wind our way back downstairs quickly to find Ginny and Malcolm talking in hushed voices.

"Where was the security guard?" Sterling asks, and they startle apart.

"What are you talking about?" Malcolm asks, storming to the base of the stairs.

"There's no one at the gate. It's wide open."

Malcolm's eyes pop at this information.

Sterling's head shifts ever so slightly, confusion clouding

his eyes before shifting back to business. "We're going to search the grounds," he says. "I think you should help."

"We're waiting for the police," Ginny says. "They'll look."

I take a step toward her as though getting closer will enable me to understand why she's acting like this. "You'll look. Now."

"Yes," Malcolm agrees, to my surprise. "If the gate was open...Well, we should do as much as we can to determine if she's on the grounds. It could take the police hours to search. We should start."

"Someone has to wait for the police," Ginny says.

"If you want to sit around while she's out there alone, go right ahead." I don't bother to wait for her to stammer out another selfish response. But it works. Ginny follows us to the door.

"Felix, can you update the officers?" Sterling asks before we step outside. He nods grimly.

"But perhaps I should go with you," he suggests.

"Someone does need to be here. In case she comes back," Sterling says. Ginny glares at him, her mouth twisting like she wants to spit venom. He ignores her. "We should split up. Malcolm and I will work our way to the gates. You two start toward the back."

"Who put you in charge—" Ginny starts.

"For fuck's sake, Virginia, just listen to him," Malcolm cuts her off before I can. She falls silent instantly.

I don't wait for more instructions. Pulling my phone out, I turn on its flashlight and start around the conservatory wing.

"This is all ridiculous. We aren't going to find her in the dark," Ginny says. "Someone took her. That's why he's distracting us, so they can get away."

I whirl on her. "Neither of us would do anything to harm our daughter. She is everything to us!"

"Everything? He's known about her for what? Five minutes?" she scoffs. "I can't believe Malcolm is listening to either of you—"

My palm cracks across her face so hard that her head flies to the side. I've been holding in that slap for years. Her own hand flies to her face protectively as she glares at me, rubbing at the imprint of my palm on her cheek.

"You vicious bitch," she shrieks. "I don't—"

I don't wait for her to finish the thought. "I'm going this way. We need to split up, remember?"

I stalk off towards the pool house, redirecting all my energy to finding Ellie. As I get closer to the pool, my breathing becomes shallow before it catches altogether. A dark shadow floats on its surface, lit from below by the underwater lights. I force myself to move closer, as my feet fight me the entire way. I'm a few steps from the edge when I realize someone's left a pool lounger floating in the water. I exhale with relief. Shining my flashlight around the area I catch a glimpse of movement.

It's Ginny, heading toward the stables. It's a strange choice, given that we got rid of the horses years ago when I stopped riding, but I guess if Ellie is hiding, it's a good spot. At least Ginny is finally doing something productive. Sterling's words bounce around my head, and I find myself following her, flashlight off, keeping enough of a distance that she doesn't spot me. I'm certain he's doing the same with Malcolm. She pauses at the stable door, glancing around her, and I duck behind a tree trunk. Once she's inside, I creep toward the door, peeking through it to find her unbolting the door to a stall. She steps through.

"Ellie!" she calls and I move out of sight again as her voice rises with more panic. "Ellie!"

She tears out of the stable so quickly that she doesn't see me lurking in the shadows. Ginny rushes toward the house, and I duck into the stables, going to the stall she opened. There's a blanket and pillow, along with a granola bar wrapper and a juice box. Lying next to it is Buddy Bear and an overnight bag.

I stare for a long time at the scene, replaying how Ginny came here instantly—to this stall, to unlock this door. It's not a coincidence. I just don't understand it, and I don't have time to figure it out. It's clear Ginny expected to find Ellie here. Another wave of nausea hits me at the thought, and I battle memories of the night at the cheap motel. Ginny's never had an issue endangering Ellie to get what she wants.

How could I have left my daughter with her, even for a moment?

How did I let them drive me from this house?

As long as I was here, I could keep her safe, even if only in the most basic way possible. Even if it only meant making certain she had clothes and food and warmth and love. Guilt threatens to consume me. Leaving Ellie with Ginny at the motel was a naive mistake. Leaving her with Ginny every time after was a leap of faith. I'd believed that after the courts granted her guardianship, she'd won—at least, in her mind. But she'd known who Sterling was when he showed up at Windfall. She'd seen all of this coming. None of that explains this move.

I pick up Buddy Bear and look around, clutching him to my heart. "Where are you, baby?"

Turning toward the door, I nearly trip on the bag in the dark. I turn my flashlight on it, wondering how long Ginny planned to hide her away in here. I grab it and unzip it, expecting to find more granola bars and snacks. Instead, it's full of clothes. Not the pastel, flowery dresses Ginny sticks poor Ellie in day in and day out. Adult clothes. I pull out a shirt and stare at it. Then a pair of pants. It's my clothes. *My clothes.*

Ellie, hidden away in the stables that held my horses with a bag of my clothes waiting with her.

"Ellie!" I scream, dropping the bad and jogging through the stable. "Ellie, are you in here! It's...me. Come out."

Come out. Come out. Come out. I chant it over and over in my head like I'm casting a spell. She's not here. It's clear from Ginny's reaction that she was supposed to be. I try not to think of the acres of land that stretch in all directions. Of the number of ponds and lakes dotting the property. Of what kind of animals might prowl my father's kingdom. I try to think of her.

Where would you hide? Sterling asked me.

I stop and close my eyes. Where would I feel safe? Where would I go? And suddenly, I'm pressed safely in a dark corner, cloaked in soft cashmere as the smell of my mother's perfume blossoms around me. Daddy never went there when he was angry. It was her place. It was safe. It was always safe.

I run towards the house, stumbling in the dark but never falling. Throwing open the door to the kitchen, I hear yelling upstairs. Ginny's voice cuts through the air. She's yelling at someone. Felix? I don't stop long enough to know for sure. Instead, I seize my chance to get upstairs, past her, past her devious plan. Taking the servant's stairs, I wind my way up to the second floor. My mother's room is now Ginny's. She pretends to sleep in Malcolm's room, but she took over the space as soon as my father died, boxing up my mother's scarves and dresses, taking down her curated collection of art in the corridor. But despite her changes, my mother's presence lingers in the space. Ginny's make-up sits on her vanity. The bedding has changed. All of these small changes might not add up too much, but they feel wrong, like the room itself is slowly rejecting each one like a heart transplant that doesn't take.

My mother's clothes are gone from the closet, replaced by Ginny's, and the comforting sensation I once felt stepping foot inside has vanished. Even when the clothes and shoes shoved inside, it feels sterile and empty. I force apart the hangers, hoping to find Ellie hidden amongst the clothes, drawn to the safety I once found here. But she's not here. I slump against the wall.

Through the years, it's been harder and harder to hide how much my daughter takes after me and her father. Fragile like a bomb, passionate, strong-willed. They've tried to stamp it out of her, chipping away at her like a piece of granite, determined to make her into their vision of the perfect child to fit their perfect life. She's resisted it at every turn, becoming something more beautiful, more fitting of the raw material she was born with—something that looked dangerously like me.

Me.

She's like *me*.

I'm in the corridor, passing the main stairs, ignoring Ginny's voice calling after me as I rush by to the opposite wing of the house. My wing. My room. *My* daughter.

There's nothing left inside my quarters now, even the few boxes I'd left behind that day have been moved. The room sits hollowed from the inside with no sign of life.

"Please," I murmur, running to the closet. Malcolm emptied it already. There's not a single bit of me in the large space my own mother so carefully planned in anticipation of her little girl. But as soon as I flip on the light, a small bundle stirs on the floor. Sitting up, Ellie rubs her eyes, blinking from the sudden brightness.

"Did I win?" she asks sleepily.

"Ellie, oh my God." I lift her into my arms, pressing her tiny body closely to mine, burying my face in her hair and breathing in her soft, perfect scent. She still smells like my baby, even after all these years. "What are you doing in here?"

"Mommy told me we should play hide-n-seek with you," she says, her voice smothered slightly by how tightly I'm holding her. I loosen my grip only a little, so I can see her face.

"You were playing a game?" I ask.

"Yes, but it wasn't any fun. It was dark," she says, her lower lip beginning to tremble, "and she told me you would come and take me for a sleepover, and I tried to wait...does this mean I don't get to stay with you?"

"You aren't in trouble," I kiss each of her cheeks. "I'm sorry it took me so long to find you."

"I didn't like where mommy told me to hide," she says in the hushed tone of a child confessing to a crime, "so, I came here. I always feel safe here."

"You're safe," I whisper to her, "but we need to go tell everyone that, okay?"

I take my time walking out of the room. When I reach the corridor I see the faint flashing of blue and red lights, and it feels as if a hook pierces me through the chest, trying to drag me back in time. It's different this time. I have to believe that.

It's the only reason I can keep putting one foot in front of the other. I block out the shouts of people below and focus on Ellie and how her thin arms twine around my neck.

"Oh thank God!" Felix's voice is the first to break through the protective bubble I've cast around us.

The next is less comforting. "Give her to me!"

Ginny blocks me on the stairs, snatching at her, but Ellie cries out, refusing to let me go. There's a cluster of police officers in the foyer along with Sterling and my brother. Everyone is frozen for a moment, each processing the scene before them. Then, all hell breaks loose. Ginny uses this to her advantage, reaching for Ellie again.

"Don't touch her," I say in a lethal whisper.

"We found your bag," Ginny says, holding up the black canvas duffel from before along with Ellie's bear. "You were going to kidnap her!"

I'd been so focused on finding her that I'd forgotten about the planted evidence.

"What is she talking about, Adair?" Malcolm demands, moving toward the base of the stairs.

I force my way past Ginny, edging away from Malcolm at the stairs to move in the direction of where Sterling stands with the police.

"You need to start explaining what happened now," Malcolm continues. "I never thought you would stoop as low as taking her in the night."

Sterling tenses next to me, moving to stand between me and my brother but I step forward, choosing my words carefully. Thanks to Ginny's game, Ellie is scared enough. I don't need to add to her confusion. "Do you really believe that?" I ask him quietly. "Have I ever done anything to put her in jeopardy?"

"The courts thought so," he says, but he sounds uncomfortable. He knows the truth. He's watched. Maybe Malcolm once believed all the lies Ginny and my father spun to get custody of Ellie, but that's the thing about spinning deceit, one wrong move and everything begins to unravel.

"They did. How couldn't they with all that glaring evidence?" I point out sarcastically. "I suppose I didn't learn my lesson. A bag of my clothes—what was I thinking?"

"Arrest her!" Ginny screams. "You heard her admit to it."

I turn to the police officers, ignoring the panicked look on Sterling's face. "Why would I come back with her?"

"Because we caught you! You couldn't get away, so you're going to try to make it look like it's a misunderstanding." Ginny stomps towards us, and Ellie shrinks in my arms as if to make herself invisible.

A female officer's eyes narrow, noticing this. She turns her studious gaze on me. It takes me a second to realize I know her, but I place her immediately.

"History's been known to repeat itself," she says so quietly that only I can hear her.

"Maybe history repeats itself to give us a second chance to do the right thing," I say.

"It doesn't add up," the officer says loudly. Her colleague rolls his eyes, hitching his thumbs on his belt.

"Jami," he says, his tone ripe with condescension, "this is Malcolm MacLaine. You know who he is."

"Oh, I know. So does the chief and everyone else." Her lips purse as she shakes her head.

"So, we should probably let them sort this out. It seems to be a family matter," he says carefully.

"No!" The word spills from both me and Ginny at once.

"You know who we are," Ginny continues, pointing her

nose in the air. "I'm pressing charges. She doesn't even live here anymore. She came to my daughter's dance studio today and threatened me. I'm not safe." With each word, she trembles more like she's working herself up.

"I think they're right," Malcolm says gently. "We don't want this to get ugly."

By ugly he means that he doesn't want this leaking to the press, affecting his campaign prospects, doing more damage to our floundering family fortunes.

"It's going to get ugly, MacLaine," Sterling says, finally speaking. "You know that."

"I'm sure something can be arranged," he says with a dismissive wave.

"No, some things in life can't be bought and sold. You'd know that if you were a—"

"And you're an expert?" Malcolm interrupts with a sneer that carves his face like a jack-o-lantern.

"No one cares that she was just going to make off with our child in the middle of the night?" Ginny stomps a foot. "There is nothing to work out as a family. She might as well be dead to us. Now give me back..."

"No!" Ellie shrieks, clawing at my shoulders as Ginny tries to take her away from me.

"Stop," I beg Ginny as she tugs relentlessly. I finally release Ellie, scared she'll be hurt.

"I don't want to go with you!" Ellie yells. "You said if I was good and I stayed put, I could go with Auntie Dair when she found me. I want to go with her."

"You don't know what you're talking about, darling," Ginny says quickly. "You were waiting for Aunt Adair, right? She said she was going to come and get you."

"You said it." Ellie shakes her head, her jaw jutting out.

"You said when Auntie Dair found me, I would go with her, and to give her the bag, but I could only go if I kept it a secret and stayed quiet as a mouse."

"You unbelievable bitch," Sterling says under his breath. Ellie's eyes widen at the use of no-words, but before she can correct him, Jami holds out her arms.

"I think I should have a little talk with Ellie." She looks at me. "If that's okay with you?"

I nod, swallowing at the raw lump that forms when she asks me. Not Ginny. Not Malcolm. Me. Maybe it won't change anything. But it means everything in this moment.

"I do not consent," Ginny starts.

"Virginia," Malcolm cuts her off through gritted teeth. "Do as the officer requests."

"I'm going with her," she says defiantly. The officer looks to me for permission again. I nod.

"Can I go to bed?" Ellie asks the officer. "I'm so sleepy."

"How about I tuck you in?" Jami says.

"Can Auntie come, too?"

Ginny stiffens, but I smile reassuringly. "I'll come up in a few minutes. I need to talk to Sterling."

"How rude of me," Ellie says, yawning widely, while fluttering her hand at him. "It's nice to see you, Mr. Ford."

Sterling's hand reaches for mine, and I hear the slight break in his voice as he responds, "Sleep well, Ellie."

Ellie will be safe, and Ginny's come too unglued to realize that everything out of her mouth only incriminates her more. Still, watching the officer carry her up the stairs feels like an out of body experience.

"I think you need to answer a few questions, too," the remaining officer says. "How did you know where the little girl was? This is a very big house. Mrs. MacLaine seems to think that's a big coincidence, and so do I."

I hope that having one of the officers believe me cancels out his determination to bootlick my brother and his wife. I'm too tired tonight to fight it. Although, I know I'll never sleep. I'm not sure I'll rest again while Ellie remains under this roof.

"A hunch," I murmur. "She hid where I hid as a little girl."

"Where was that?" He jots down a note.

Sterling's hand tightens on mine. "Maybe we should call our lawyer."

"Guilty people call their lawyers," Malcolm says, joining us.

"You aren't leaving us much of a choice," Sterling growls.

"My mother's closet," I interject, answering the officer's question.

"She was in your mother's closet?" he asks in confusion, no doubt scrolling through memories to remind himself that she's dead.

"No, it's where I hid. She hid the same place," I explain.

"So you found her in Ginny's closet?" Malcolm asks. "We searched all our rooms—"

"I found her in *my* closet," I correct him. "Ellie was hiding in her mother's closet."

"I'm sorry, are you saying—" the officer starts.

"I think it is best to let us handle this," Malcolm cuts him off. "As you said, it's family business."

"I'm her mother," I tell the officer. "He's her father. When she was a baby, Virginia MacLaine tricked me and got legal guardianship of her."

"I...well..." His pen hovers over his notepad like he can think of neither what to say nor what to write.

"Adair," Malcolm says in a warning tone. "Think of what you're doing. Consider the consequences."

But I'm done living a lie. I squeeze Sterling's hand, knowing we have a long fight ahead of us. "I know exactly what I'm doing. I should have done it years ago."

"This can't be taken back," he hisses. "You'll have nothing."

"She'll have the largest share possible of MacLaine Media," Sterling cuts in, finally moving between me and my brother. This time I let him. I can fight my own battles, but love means not fighting those battles alone.

"That's not possible," Malcolm says, shaking his head. "You wouldn't..."

"I already did." For the first time since we arrived, Sterling smiles. "The company should stay in the family. *Our* family."

"You think you can just show up, flashing your bank account, and take whatever you want?" he asks. "I have news for you: I'm a MacLaine. I don't just have money. I have power. People know who I am. They listen to me. They do whatever I tell them."

"God, you sound like our father," I say, wondering when my big brother became so little. "He'd be proud."

"And you!" He turns on me next. "He'd be disappointed in you. This isn't over. I will keep you two in the courts until she's eighteen if I have to."

"We're not giving up," Sterling starts.

"No," I stop him. "No, we won't. We aren't going to do that to her. We'll figure something out, but we have to make the right choice for Ellie."

"Adair, she's our daughter," Sterling says, searching my face for clues to my change of heart.

Behind him, Felix is watching all of us, his face carved into solemn relief. Our eyes meet for just a moment, and then he tilts his head so slightly no one else would notice. It's a message. I'm doing the right thing. I'm doing the hard thing. I never had to look for someone to love after Sterling left. I had her. But loving someone means always doing what's best for them, even when it breaks your heart.

"I know," I say sadly. "I've thought for years that I didn't fight them more because they kept me under foot. They made me sign agreements. They threatened to ruin me financially, socially. I never really cared about all of that, but I couldn't risk not seeing her. I couldn't risk losing her. Or that's what I thought. Don't you see?" I wait for him to nod, but he just stares at me in confusion. "They'll tear her apart limb by limb until they break her, too. I don't want that. I love her too much. If...if..."

I know what I have to do now. I know I have to let go.

"We'll do it the right way," Sterling says, speaking only to me now like we're the only people in the room.

I force a smile, reaching up to stroke his cheek. "Mac-Laines don't fight fair. They don't care who they hurt. If they won't protect her, I will. That's my job. I'm her mother. I have to keep her safe." I whip around to Malcolm. "But you have to do something about your wife. You can't trust her. She's—"

The wail of a fire alarm cuts me off mid-sentence before I can say *crazy*.

24

STERLING

Adair runs toward the stairs as soon as the alarm sounds, but I throw an arm around her waist. It takes effort to haul her outside, but as soon as I see smoke plumes wafting across the staircase, I know I have to. She screams and kicks, yelling Ellie's name. I'm vaguely aware of the police officer calling for back-up, of Malcolm MacLaine dialing his security detail like they'll know how to handle this, of Felix grimly joining me.

"Ellie!" Adair sobs.

"Jami, can you hear me? Are you on your way out?" The officer radios his partner, but no response comes.

Thirty seconds has passed. That's too long.

"Stay here," I order Adair, whose mouth drops open to argue. I cut her off. "Don't argue with me, Lucky. I've been through worse. I will get her out."

"I'm coming with you," Malcolm says. The surprising display of masculinity stops me in my tracks.

"I don't need more people in there to get out. Let me handle this. Trust me." I don't wait to argue more with any of them, but before I reach the front door, Adair lets out a blood-curdling scream that vibrates in my bones.

I swivel to find her pointing at the roof in horror while she screams Ellie's name. Felix wraps his arms around her.

"They're up there," he yells, his words nearly drowned out by Adair but clear on his lips.

I run inside, knowing exactly where to go. Smoke is billowing through the entry now. Windfall is going up like a tinderbox. It's burning impossibly fast, the flames already reaching the plants in the atrium as I race inside and look for a swinging door I never expected to walk through again. It feels like a thousand lifetimes have passed. The stairs leading up to the roof feel even more narrow than I remember. The walls seem to slant in on me, the air thickening until it's hard to breathe. The door at the top is shut and when I try the knob, it's jammed. I shove at it until it gives way.

Ginny's standing near the small half-wall that runs along the roof's perimeter, Ellie squirming in her arms. She turns at the sound of the door opening, her eyes catching the light from the dancing flames in the stained glass dome that rises in the center of the landing.

"We're not going anywhere," she says, sounding oddly calm. "This is our home. No one can make us leave."

"You can stay, but I need to take Ellie with me." I approach her slowly, calculating how much time I have based on how quickly the fire is moving.

"She was supposed to be mine," Ginny explains, her hands gripping my little girl so fiercely that she cries out in pain. "He promised me. Angus. Malcolm never kept his promises, but Angus did. He promised me a baby when I couldn't have one. I just had to pretend. No one could know she wasn't a MacLaine."

"She is a MacLaine," I say, taking another step toward her. I can feel heat radiating off the glass dome. That's not a good sign.

"No, she's not, but Adair didn't know that. No one did, but Angus." Her voice is distant—far away and lost in memories. "And Anne, of course. Anne told me. Her greatest shame. She'd written it all down somewhere. Angus could never find it. Never prove it, but he knew. It's so hard pretending a bastard is yours. He did it well. Adair never deserved his kindness. If Adair had only been like her mother... Her mother was a survivor. Not like Adair. Not like me."

I don't like the sound of that. I move closer, but my quick movements startle her and she steps back, her heel brushing the edge of the wall and causing her to lose her balance for a second. Ellie shrieks and clutches Ginny's leg like she can stop them both from falling. I freeze.

"Come down with me and explain. Be a survivor, Ginny," I urge her.

"You know better than that," she says. "I saw the file the private investigator dug up on you. People die. Don't they, Sterling? Especially around you. Especially at war—and that's what this is, isn't it? War?"

"It doesn't have to be." I need to keep her talking while I assess the surroundings better. My memory of the night I was here with Adair years ago is clouded with heady memories of first love. I know the landing must look out over the front drive because Adair had pointed to it. She'd seen Ginny. I don't allow myself to linger on Adair. She's safe and Ellie is depending on me.

"You know better than that." Ginny laughs. "It's all a competition. Who has the most money and power and clout?

You should have come back and gone toe-to-toe with Angus. Malcolm was never a match for you."

"It's over now. I have no interest in hurting your family." I'm surprised to discover I mean it.

"After everything they did? He ruined your life. He just took it from you. That's what they do. They take. Malcolm? He takes. He has a mistress, you know. She's pregnant. I'm not even sure why he goes to all the trouble of pretending. Love only turns to poison in this house. Love can't survive these walls. That's why it has to burn to the ground. They deserve it. Can't you see that? They deserve to watch all of this go up in flames."

There's no use in continuing this charade any longer. I'd made the mistake of seeing Ginny as a fragile, kept mouse, too weak to make it on her and thus grateful for her box. I was wrong. So wrong. She'd been beating her head against the walls, slowly slipping away into madness and despair while everyone around her assumed she was simply *not a MacLaine*. Not up to the task of social appearances and party planning. Not even up to being a trophy wife.

"Ginny, let her go." I'm no longer asking or pleading. The glass dome radiates so much heat my skin is beginning to burn. We're out of time.

"No." Her head turns to look over her shoulder, a wicked smile curving over her lips as she bends to lift Ellie.

"Noo!" I yell at the same moment the glass dome shatters and flames rise from its wooden beams. Ginny's arm flies up to cover her face, her body providing an unintentional shield for Ellie. I'm dimly aware of the slicing burn of shards of glass, but I finally see my opportunity. I lunge the last few feet and swipe Ellie from her.

"You're bleeding," Ellie says, and I look down to see her own face is scratched up.

"I'm fine." I'm still talking, so that's a good sign. Now I need to get us out of here.

"You can't take her!" Ginny throws her body towards me, reaching for my feet with bloody hands.

"We need to leave now," I tell her, easily moving out of her grasp. She rolls to the side, her eyes landing on the flames and widening as though she's just realized what's happening. I can't get them both out. I can only hope she follows when she realizes how this is going to end.

The door knob is white hot and I startle before pushing past the pain and clasping it.

It's locked.

The door locks from the inside.

How could I forget that?

I step back and aim a well-placed kick, praying it gives. But this isn't an operation in the middle east. This is a mansion in Valmont, Tennessee with steel reinforced security on every door. It's not going to budge, which means I have to find another way out.

Ginny is still on the ground, curling into a ball and weeping. I move to the edge of the roof, looking down to find Adair staring up. When she sees me, she tries to dart towards the house, but Malcolm grabs her arm before she can run in after us. I look down as the sound of sirens mixes with the crackling snap of wood and plaster giving way to flame. Fire trucks. They're too far away. They aren't going to reach us. The landing isn't on the second floor. We might have stood a chance if it were. I might have trusted Malcolm to catch her, at least. But the landing is in its own special spot, no doubt some maintenance place to care for the atrium. It's not meant to be an escape. Windfall has never been meant for that.

It's a prison. It always, and it would have been if not for the fire devouring it from the inside out like a parasite. My eyes meet Adair's one last time, and I realize there are so many moments we'll never have. I'll never see her in a wedding dress. I'll never wake up in our house. I'll never rush her to the hospital to have our baby. They're all gone, and I can't take back a single one.

And she's not here with me now. Ellie is and I guess if this is the last moment we have, I don't want to spend it fighting to survive. I want to spend it in love.

I kneel to the ground, placing my daughter gently on her feet, my back to the flames roaring behind us.

"Is someone coming to save us?" she asks, trying to strain to look over my shoulder.

"Yes," I lie. "We're just going to wait for them a minute."

"I knew someone would come because I'm wearing this." She points to a silver clover necklace. "Auntie gave it to me. It's a good luck charm."

I swallow at the sight of that stupid birthday present I'd left forgotten in Adair's car, now hanging on our child's neck. "Smart thinking. Do you trust me?"

She considers my question for a second. "Yes, because she trusts you, but also..."

"Yes?"

"I'm not sure. I just do." She holds up her stuffed bear. "Buddy Bear likes you. He thinks you're brave."

"I think you're brave." I clasp her upper arm. "This isn't going to make sense to you," I say in a thick voice, "but I love you, Ellie, and I've loved you your whole life."

"It's good to love people," she says seriously. "Felix told

me. He says love is what makes the world round. I love you, too, Mr. Ford."

I wrap my arms around her, because she is every moment I ever wanted, all the love I ever craved, and in the end, that's enough.

"It's getting hot," she whispers. "I hope they come soon."

"I'm just glad I'm here with you," I tell her, because I wouldn't have this any other way. I'd still race into that burning house. I'd still walk through that locked door. The flames are so close that I can feel my skin starting to blister from the heat, and I spread myself as much as I can between the fire and her. It's not much, but if it's all I have to give, I'll give it to her.

When my shirt catches fire, I release her and she screams just as the landing door bursts open and a gray-haired head emerges from the smoke.

Felix.

He rushes toward us, nearly tripping on Ginny who claws at him as he passes, and throws his jacket over me to smother the flame. "You forgot the door locks!"

But he always knows where his charges are.

"Get her out of here," he says, pointing to Ellie. "I'll get Ginny."

I grab Ellie, my body running on pure adrenaline, and sprint down the stairs. Fire and smoke is everywhere. I pause long enough to yank Felix's jacket over her, then I round my body into a protective shell and take a leap of faith. Sometimes, the only way out is through.

25

ADAIR

The atrium collapses and so does my heart, sucking the screams from my lungs. Malcolm won't let me go. Even after we saw them on the roof. Even after Felix ran inside after them. His hold on me is firm and unrelenting. I don't know why he cares. I'm not the one he chose to save. I never will be.

Fire licks up the sides of Windfall, blackening its white walls, dragging it into ash and ruin. Hell is reclaiming it. Soon there will be nothing left.

Nothing left but the diseased bones it leaves behind.

I was never going to escape it. How could I? That's the price it demanded. My love. My freedom. My soul. Its appetite will never be satiated. It is as greedy as my father. But all things fade, especially powerful men and their fortunes.

Years ago, I swore to never tell a soul the truth. I swore on everything I had—and now the devil's come to collect. Angus MacLaine might be gone, but I can't help thinking he's orchestrated all of this from whatever circle of hell he burns in. Nobody breaks a contract with him.

My knees give out first, and I crumple to the ground as another bit of the East Wing collapses. There's no way to stop it. Nothing to do. Some days were diamonds but never again.

A shout goes up from a team of firefighters, and a moment later, one hustles out of the door carrying a small bundle. They rush it to the back of an ambulance and a spluttering, coughing Ellie emerges covered in black smudges from a jacket.

I push up on my palms and run to her, unable to stop myself from grabbing hold of her even as the medic presses an oxygen mask to her nose. The medic doesn't stop me, she just works around me as I pepper her with kisses, grabbing her hands to inspect them, looking for signs of damage.

"I love you," I whisper again and again while she clings to me.

It's not everything. But it's not nothing. I glance up to see Malcolm watching us with a strange expression before he turns sharply to the sound of more firefighters.

"Gurney!" one yells, and I can't bring myself to look. I can't bring myself to hope. It costs too much.

"Take this," the medic instructs, gesturing to the mask, "and make sure she keeps it on."

I cuddle Ellie against me and for a moment, it doesn't matter that Windfall is burning or that people I love are inside or that nothing will ever be the same after tonight. He promised he would protect her. He kept that promise.

A gurney rushes toward the ambulance next to us, and I realize he's kept more than promise. He promised he wouldn't leave me again.

"We have to take them to the hospital," the medic says, joining us. "You want to ride with her?"

"Yes, but can I..."

"Hurry," she advises.

I cross to Sterling in time to see his eyes flicker. Taking his hand, I can't find the right words to say to tell him how much I love him and what he means to me.

"Hey, Lucky." He tries to turn to me but groans. "You can't get rid of me. Told you I was all in."

"Miss," a medic pushes past me and covers his face with oxygen just as his body begins to shake. "We need to get him to the hospital now."

"Is he going to be okay?" I call.

The medic grins as he reaches to shut the ambulance door. "I'd call it a miracle, but I think he's just lucky."

EPILOGUE

Nine months later

Adair

He came back to me in the spring, so we chose late April when the magnolias are in full bloom for our wedding day. The air is warm enough to release their perfume across the yard as caterers and florists and photographers bustle in and out of our new home, a large, white farmhouse with a porch that wraps entirely around it, perfect for three of us and one large dog. Magnolia trees line the drive, their snowy blossoms draping over it like a bridal veil. The land behind the house is in the process of being transformed into something out of a fairytale. Even I don't know exactly what to expect.

"The tent is up," Poppy announces, sashaying into my bedroom wearing a blush, silk robe, embroidered with her initials—her gift for being my maid of honor. "Champagne tower is still standing. Cross your fingers the dog doesn't knock the table."

Of all the requests I made for the wedding, which she insisted on planning, having Zeus as the ring bearer is the one she disapproves of most. She's been a good sport about it, because she's Poppy.

"He will," I promise her. She continues to run down a list of who is doing what, how far behind this or that is, before she pauses. "Those are beautiful."

She reaches to inspect my earrings. Delicate flower blossoms hang like bells, an opal dripping from their centers, from a thin, golden hook.

"My mom gave them to me." I haven't worn them often. Every time I'd tried it felt wrong. After Sterling proposed, I realized I was meant to wear them on my wedding day. "It makes me feel like she's here with me."

"Oh, darling, she is." Poppy hugs me tightly before dashing off to oversee more business.

A loud pop startles me and I turn to find Trish with a guilty smile and an open bottle of champagne, wearing a matching silk robe. "I think we need to toast."

"We could just get drunk," Sutton says from her spot on the floor. She's not wearing the matching robe, but I consider it a victory that she's here and in a fairly decent mood. I haven't figured out yet if she's putting up with me for Sterling's sake or Ellie's.

Poppy joins us, grabbing a glass of champagne. Even Sutton takes one.

"To proof that true love does exist outside stories," Trish says, raising her flute. "And to Adair, editor extraordinaire, whose book got its third starred review this week."

I flush, shaking my head, as I tap my glass to the others.

Sutton swigs hers and plops back down with Ellie who is coloring a picture on the ground, her copper hair twisted into a pretty bun, but still in her pajamas.

"My mom's book," I remind Trish quietly.

She sighs, the sound a mixture of happiness and resignation. "There's as much of you in that book as her. Be proud. She would be."

I hope she's right.

Looking to Ellie, who's guarding her picture like a dragon, while Sutton pretends to sneak peeks, I know Trish is right. Motherhood is unconditional love. Not just love you give or receive but love that permeates every ounce of your being, changes you, makes you someone better. Feeling that for Ellie gave me the gift of my own mother back. I know how she felt. Someday, I hope Ellie has a daughter of her own. I hope she never makes the mistakes that I did.

After the fire, the first few weeks were the worst. It was confusing for all of us. Ginny's death made it difficult to know how to proceed, and Ellie struggled to understand not only the loss of the woman she thought of as her mother but Felix as well. The only saving grace was Malcolm's decision to leave Valmont and move to Oregon, a bittersweet choice since he relinquished guardianship without hesitation. We'd been to doctors and psychologists. We'd done everything we could to ease her transition, and we'd finally revealed part of the truth with the encouragement of her therapist. I'd been sick for an entire week leading up to telling her that I was her mother, wondering if she'd be angry or hurt that I'd lied. Instead, she'd asked a lot of questions, all leading back to one central concern: did that mean she would get to stay with me?

She just wanted to be loved. She wanted to give her love. And she wanted to feel safe doing it. We've continued to take it slow, letting her help us choose her new house, answering her questions about Ginny as delicately as we can while still being truthful. I don't know what the future will bring. We can only take it one day at a time.

At first, she'd been more reserved with Sterling, especially when he first got out of the hospital. The scars on his hands scared her, but as they healed, the gap between them grew smaller and smaller each day. He never minded. His only concern was making her feel safe. It had taken two months to get her to call him Sterling instead of Mr. Ford. Neither of us are sure when the right time is to tell her that he's her father.

"Everyone needs to get dressed!" Poppy announces, swiping the bottle of champagne before Trish and Sutton get too tipsy to walk down the aisle. Sutton gets up to change with a frown.

Ellie jumps to her feet, her eyes bright with excitement. Then, her lips fall into a thoughtful frown. She touches the sterling silver clover hanging from her neck. "I can wear my good luck charm, right?"

"Of course." I bend and lift her onto my hip. She's had a growth spurt since her fifth birthday and her legs dangle too far for my tender mother's heart. I'm not ready for her to grow up, but I can't stop her. I glance down, finally able to see her drawing. There are three stick figures, two tall and one a bit smaller along with a black lump with ears. "Who did you draw?"

"You and me and Sterling and Zeus," she chirps. Her eyes widen and she wriggles in my arms. "I forgot something!"

I place her on her feet and she adds something to the

paper. She picks it up, cradling it to her chest, and then folds it in half.

"What did you forget?" I ask.

Her eyes twinkle like her father's, and it takes my breath away. "It's a secret. I drew it for Sterling." She bites her lips before wagging a finger at me, beckoning me closer. "Mommy, I have a question."

I will never get tired of hearing her call me that. I kneel beside her and nod seriously.

"Is Sterling..." she trails away before getting a burst of courage "...my daddy like you're my mommy?"

I'm momentarily stunned into silence. We'd been warned that she might figure it out or ask, even that she might overhear one of us say something carelessly. I hadn't expected it to happen so soon. "Well..." I search for the delicate, but truthful answer and realize there's only one. "Yes. He is your daddy, but it's okay to have big feelings about that."

Ellie nods, clutching her picture for him close. "Do you think he would let me call him Daddy like I call you Mommy?"

I nod, unable to form words past the lump in my throat. "I think he would love that."

"Can you give this to him?" she asks, adding quickly, "But don't peek at it!"

"It's bad luck for a bride and groom to see each other before the wedding. Can I give it to him after?"

She looks seriously unimpressed by this idea, and I see another flash of Sterling.

"I'll take it to him," Sutton offers, already in her dress, and I startle. I had no idea she'd been listening. "Anything you want me to tell him, pipsqueak?"

Ellie starts to shake her head and stops. "Yes, please tell him to save me a dance."

It's such a formal declaration that Sutton and I can't help sharing a smile.

"Will do," she promises before heading to the study where Sterling and the boys are waiting before the ceremony. She looks relieved to get away, and I can't blame her. She's more comfortable around her brother and his friends.

The door to the bedroom opens and Poppy comes in, her arms laden with a blue garment bag. She's buzzing with excitement as she lays it across the King-sized bed. Everyone in the room stops, even the stylist curling Trish's hair, as she unzips it and carefully removes my wedding dress from the bag. Poppy spreads it over the bed with reverence before turning shining eyes on me.

"You're getting married," she whispers.

"I know!" I burst out in tears and she gives me a fierce hug, pulling back to check my make-up in a panic. I blink, my lashes wet from crying. "Don't worry. It's waterproof."

The girls help me into the dress, buttoning, zipping, and adjusting, and when Poppy smiles, I turn to look in the mirror. I'd chosen the gown because my first thought when I saw it was that it looked like something out of *The Great Gatsby*. Its ivory silk bodice is beaded with elegant pearls that continue to the skirt which hugs my hips ever so slightly, enough to showcase my curves but still allow me to move freely—another of my demands. I have no desire to spend tonight feeling uncomfortable. I'm going to dance under the stars in the arms of my forever.

Loose lace sleeves flutter from its straps to my elbows. The lace that continues across the back is secured with four covered buttons that allow glimpses of my skin to peek through before it gathers at my tailbone and flows into a delicate train that puddles behind me. I feel like I've stepped into a dream.

"Are you sure about the veil?" Poppy asks as she helps me clip a diamond barrette in my hair. She'd made me buy one just in case I changed my mind.

But I haven't. My hair is curled and pinned loosely at the nape of my neck, with a few soft tendrils brushing my shoulders. "I want to be able to see him clearly."

Enough things have come between us in the past. Today, nothing, not even a veil is going to do that.

"So, you're sure about this?" Poppy teases as we stare at the mirror.

"I'm all in."

Sterling

"AN EXCESSIVE AMOUNT OF FLOWERS WERE JUST delivered, according to Poppy," Kai informs me as he joins us in the study. He hands me a card as Jack pours him a drink.

"For me?" I look at the ivory envelope curiously. It's not the first gift to show up directed at me. A number of business associates had sent well wishes and extravagant gifts leading up to today, likely suffering under the impression that I'm planning to return to *my job* after the wedding and the long rehabilitation period leading up to it. Third degree burns turned out to cause more than a little nerve damage.

"Still haven't told anyone?" Luca asks, eyeing the card.

"Have you?" I ask. I'm not the only one planning to

silently slip into retirement. At least, retirement from our less-than-legal pursuits.

"I've made it clear I'm being a bit more picky when it comes to clients," he says with a grin, swigging from his whiskey glass. "Now, we just have to get that one to come on board."

"Nope," Jack calls, overhearing us. "I'm out. I'm a small business owner. I don't have time for your shenanigans."

"Shenaningans?" Luca repeats, clutching his chest. "You wound me, Archer."

"Don't act like you have a heart," Jack says dryly. "You two will get into plenty of trouble on your own."

They've been at it like hens since I'd first pitched my idea to them. Why wipe the slate entirely clean? There were plenty of people who could use our help and our skills. People who actually need us. Kids like me with shitty parents. Women being preyed on by assholes like Cyrus. The people that the law doesn't know how to protect without breaking its own rules—a problem that none of us have.

Except Jack, apparently.

I ignore Jack and Luca's debate and open the envelope. "You said this came with flowers?"

"Lots of flowers," Kai says. "It looks like a florist exploded. It's actually really romantic."

"Romantic, huh?" Jack teases.

"I know what's romantic. I make my living singing love songs."

I slip the card out and read it, unable to hide my surprise when I see Nikolai's name signed at the bottom. I'm not sure if it's a gift or a threat, but I suspect the former after his relationship advice.

There's a knock at the door and Sutton's dark head pokes inside. "Everyone decent?"

"Unfortunately," Luca says.

"Terribly disappointing." She joins him, passing me a folded piece of paper. "From your daughter."

My daughter. I'm not sure I'll ever get used to that. I love those words. I love hearing them. I love thinking them. Still, it's surreal like someone turned a mirror on my life. Everything is there, but somehow it's all changed, too. Upside down. Inside out. It should make me uncomfortable, but it doesn't. It just feels...right.

I unfold it and smile. Judging by the looks of it, she's drawn me along with her and Adair. Zeus, a near constant in all her pictures, is at our feet. The new house in the background.

"What's that?" Luca asks, looking over my shoulder at a round blob in the air next to Ellie's stick figure.

"No clue," I admit.

"Your kid's a shitty artist," he says, taking a sip of whiskey.

"She's five."

"I'm just saying that her talents lie elsewhere. Maybe she'll take after you." He elbows me in the ribs.

"I hope not," Jack says. His smile falters when he sees my face, and he changes the subject. "So, we're losing the first of us. I think that means we need to open another bottle."

"Go ahead." I do my best to let go of the joke. Jack wasn't being serious, but I do worry about it. I want Ellie to be safe no matter what. I might be willing to straddle the line between law and crime, but I'd prefer she stay safely on one side. Sutton's laugh rises in the room and I watch her, dark head bowed sharing a joke with Luca, and wonder if I need to worry about her, too. Nothing could convince her to go back to New York.

"Stop corrupting my kid sister," I call to Luca.

"As if he could corrupt me," she says with a pout.

There's another knock, and since everyone's in here, I brace myself for the hurricane that Poppy's become over the last few weeks. She's already been here five times to make sure we're on schedule. No amount of evidence seems to prove to her that we're self-sufficient enough to put on tuxedos and wait in a room.

I open the door, ready to reassure her, only to discover Francie there, holding Zeus's leash. "It's nearly time. I thought we'd better get him ready."

"That's our cue," Jack says. He walks to me, extending his hand. I take it, and he pulls me into a hug. "You ready for this?"

"Because we've had to extract you from tighter spots before," Luca adds, joining us. His dark eyes dance.

"No doubt in my mind," I promise them.

Luca grins, whistling as he heads out the back door to wait for the ceremony. Jack smiles again before releasing my hand.

"I'm happy for you," he tells me before joining Kai to go wait with Luca.

"Me, too," Sutton adds, managing to sound sincere.

"You two will be friends someday," I promise her, wrapping my arms around her in a tight hug. She looks so grown up in her gold, lightly beaded dress, but her round, blue eyes take me back to when she was a little kid, looking to me for guidance. I'm determined to be there for her. "I want us to be a family. I don't want to lose any more time."

When they're gone, Francie comes over and fiddles with

my bowtie, not bothering to hide the tears pooling in her eyes. She's dressed in a simple navy dress that Adair and her picked out when she arrived last week. The two bonded over how little they cared about clothes, much to Poppy's horror.

"You look beautiful," I tell her. She does. Her warm brown skin glows as brightly as her million watt smile.

"I look old," she says with a sniff, brushing invisible lint from my shoulders.

I shake my head. A few strands of gray have made themselves into her tightly woven braids. "You look the same as the day we met."

"You remember that day?" she asks. "I thought you were too busy ignoring me."

"I was intimidated," I admit. "You weren't like the other foster homes they sent me, too. You were...scary."

She laughs, and I can't help but join her. "I had to scare you."

"Was I that bad?" I ask, already knowing the answer.

"Nope, you were just worth saving," she says quietly. There's no mistaking the look in her eyes or the emotion in her voice. She's also guarded herself around me, like she's approaching a wild animal. I can't blame her.

"I'm sorry I was trouble," I murmur. "Thank you for not giving up on me. Thanks for always being there."

"I always will be," she promises me.

"I know...Mom." I've never said it before. I've thought it. I've felt it. But something always held me back. For a long time, it was guilt. Because I had a mom, even though she was gone. Then, it was fear. I didn't want to make her into something she didn't want to be. But I don't see the world the same way I did then, not even the same way I did a year ago.

Francie didn't have to love me. She did it anyway. She

didn't have to stick by me when I fucked up—and I fucked up a lot. She never budged. I didn't understand—couldn't understand it. Now, I do. She's always been my mom, patiently waiting for me to see it, too.

She hugs me with all her strength, which is considerably more than her slight frame suggests. "About damn time."

When we finally let go, she brushes away tears. "We need to get you married!"

I pull a box out of my pocket and open it to reveal the rings.

"Adair is a lucky woman," she says with a wink as she helps me tie it to Zeus's collar.

Zeus, who seems to understand the gravitas of the situation, sits like a statue as we thread Adair's ring through the ribbon. Adair's worn a simple diamond engagement ring since I proposed. Mostly, because I'd been too impatient to ask her to wait for the custom ring I'm giving her today.

I'd taken the engagement ring and had it made into a necklace for Ellie, wanting her to feel as much a part of today as possible. Adair's actual wedding ring features four half carat pear-shaped diamonds set in a cluster. At first glance, it just looks like a huge rock, which wasn't really my attention, but closer inspection, shows the narrow points of the diamonds meeting in the middle to form a delicate clover. Pavé diamonds halo the larger stones, and two eternity bands of diamonds are joined to serve as the official wedding band. She's going to fuss over its size, but I don't care. If it was up to her, she'd be happy with a rubber band. I want everyone to know she's mine.

We finish getting Zeus ready and Francie hands me the lead of his blue leash.

"Does she know?" she asks.

"Not yet," I say with a grin.

"You're up to something," Francie guesses.

"I've had some time to think about this," I admit. I fell in love with her years ago, but today she's going to be mine at last.

Adair

AVA STEPS IN SO THAT POPPY CAN PERFORM HER MAID OF honor duties when it's time for the ceremony. She lines us up with a grim determination that feels more like she's sending me out to a firing squad than to get married. I wait to the side as Sutton exits the back door followed by Trish. Poppy gives me one last squeeze, smiling from ear-to-ear, that I'm about to see all her hard work finally achieved.

"Okay, it's your turn," Ava orders Ellie, who's clutching her flower girl basket tightly in her tiny fists. She looks up to me with wide, terrified eyes.

"I want to go with you," she whispers.

"The flower girl goes before the bride," Ava tells her, but I step closer as her hand closes over the door knob.

"It's fine. She can walk with me."

Ava gives me a look that says I can explain this to Poppy later, but, honestly, it's better this way. Today, I'm not just marrying Sterling, we're becoming a family. It's more than I ever dreamed of and I want her by my side. Outside the music shifts from Canon in D to the Wedding March, and I smile at Ellie.

"You ready, baby?" I hold out my hand.

"One more second," she says, holding up her index finger, all her nerves suddenly gone.

"I think we better..." I trail away as Sterling comes into the room, Zeus on a leash at his side. The man can wear a suit, but he owns a tuxedo. It fits his body perfectly, showing off all the assets I'm getting in this merger. His dark hair is combed to the side, his face clean shaven for the first time in months. A wicked smile curves across his lips, matching the cocky glint in his eyes.

His eyes skim over me with approval, but before he can get too distracted, Ellie hurls herself at him. "Daddy!"

He catches her with his free arm, his shocked eyes looking over her shoulder to my smile, before he buries his face against her. Ellie turns a familiar grin on me. "Were you surprised?"

"So surprised," I admit with a laugh. Apparently, her stage fright was only a ruse to keep me here long enough for Sterling to sneak up on me.

"Not doing this without me, right?" he says.

"What are you doing?" I ask. "Shouldn't you be..."

"Poppy mentioned how you didn't have anyone to walk you down the aisle," he says, "but you do, Lucky. Me."

This one detail had bothered me since we began planning the wedding. I hadn't known until then how much I would wish Felix was with me today. I'd obsessed over my lack of escort for weeks before gathering up the conviction to do it myself.

"Isn't it bad luck?" I ask as he draws closer.

"Nope," Ellie pipes up. "Daddy says we've got all the luck in the world."

"Does he now?" I repeat, my eyes never leaving his handsome face. I don't know how we made it. The road that led me to him is twisted and rocky. It hides behind blind curves in spots. It runs along narrow, terrifying cliffs. It winds through darkness. Navigating it is an act of faith, a test, but what's waiting here at the end is worth the risk.

A family.

A future.

A forever.

Sterling opens the door, steps through onto the porch, then turns to offer his arm. Our eyes meet as Ellie and I join him. I take his arm carefully, looping my small bouquet of magnolias around it. Ellie's hand is warm in mine, and she looks up at us with adoration as our friends and family cheer over the music.

A pathway of magnolia petals blankets the ground leading to an archway that drips with creamy white roses, lilies, and more magnolias. Large pillar candles set in hurricane glass light the way to our friends, waiting for us to join them at the end of the aisle to make our vows.

"You ready?" Sterling asks.

We're finally here. Past the darkness and the despair and the deception, emerging from it into the brightness of endless possibilities.

"I'm all in," I say.

"You got this?" he asks Ellie.

She grabs a handful of petals with a determined focus that makes us both laugh.

"Thank you for your picture," he tells her as he leads us down the stairs.

"What was the surprise on it?" I ask him.

"Actually, I was wondering the same thing." He leans down so she can hear him over the music swelling around us and we move toward our future. "You drew me and mommy with you and Zeus and...?"

She tosses an exasperated look in our direction like she can't believe she has to explain it to us. "My baby brother."

"Oh!" Sterling breaks into a wide grin. "Is that a request?"

"Nope!" She breaks free of us, running ahead to toss even more petals, earning appreciative laughs from our guests.

"I think we've been given an order, Lucky," he says wickedly.

"You have plans later?" I whisper as we reach the minister. Here, surrounded by friends, by one another's side, I can't think of anything I want more.

He takes my hand, bringing it to his lips. "I have plans for the rest of my life. You?"

"I'm all in."

Sterling

I NEVER UNDERSTOOD ALL THE POETRY ABOUT LOVE until I met Adair. In this moment, I can't help feeling every poem ever written is about her. I'd expected her to take my breath away in her wedding gown, but it feels as though an angel walks beside me. Adair steals glances at me as we take the final few steps to the altar. Turning, she hands her bouquet to Poppy and lifts one finger as she bends to kiss Ellie's cheek.

Jack's hand squeezes my shoulder, anchoring me to the moment. Until then, I'd almost believed I'd wandered into a dream.

"You ready?" he asks.

"Hell, yeah," I mutter with a grin

During the rehearsal, we'd gone over the expectation that Ellie would go to sit with Francie. Now that feels all wrong.

"Wait," I say under my breath before Adair sends her off. I hold out my hand. "She should be with us. Would you mind, Ellie?"

Her face splits into a smile that showcases a missing lower tooth. She loops the handle of her basket on her arm and reaches for my outstretched hand. Her own is small, soft and warm, against my skin, and I wish, for a moment, that I never had to let it go.

Adair straightens, lifting tear-filled eyes to mine, as she takes our free hands, completing the circle.

"Is this okay?" I whisper. I know Poppy planned every moment of the ceremony down to a timer, but I'm learning to listen to my heart.

"It's perfect," she murmurs.

The officiant, a minister from the Valmont University chapel, greets us with a wink. We'd gone back and forth on who should marry us. Adair wanted a friend to do it. I was deeply concerned that Luca would decide he was the perfect man for the job and insist on performing the service.

We'd asked for short and sweet, opting for a reading from Song of Songs and to do our own vows. Everyone falls silent as he begins the ceremony:

My beloved speaks and says to me:
'Arise, my love, my fair one,
and come away;
for now the winter is past,
the rain is over and gone.

Arise, my love, my fair one,
and come away.'
Set me as a seal upon your heart,
as a seal upon your arm;
for love is strong as death,
passion fierce as the grave.
Its flashes are flashes of fire,
a raging flame.
Many waters cannot quench love,
neither can floods drown it.
If one offered for love
all the wealth of one's house,
it would be utterly scorned.
My beloved is mine, and I am his..."

I don't have to look at the audience to know everyone is crying. I can sense it. Weddings aren't about making promises —not really. I've made my promises to her. She's made hers to me. We don't need anyone to witness or legal documentation. This wedding is a celebration of love triumphant. We fought to be here today. We chose the hard path even when we couldn't see what lay ahead of us. We chose each other. Just like we did yesterday. Just like we will tomorrow and every day after. Today we win the war. Tomorrow, we wake up and keep fighting for our future.

"Sterling and Adair have chosen to say their own vows," the minister says, giving us our cue.

Adair's eyes meet mine and suddenly, it's just the three of us in our own world. She smiles at me a tad shyly, and I realize pronouncing her love publicly must be torture for a woman who doesn't like to hug—a thought that hadn't occurred to me until now.

"It's not too late to elope, Lucky," I say so only she can hear.

This earns me a laugh and a subtle shake of her head. When she opens her mouth, her voice is clear and certain. She isn't feeling shy, after all.

"I hated Sterling the first time I met him," she proclaims, earning an appreciative chuckle from quite a few guests. "And he hated me—and, as somewhat of an authority on the subject of books, that's how all great love stories begin, don't they? But despite that poor start, you were there for me from the first moment without reservation. You helped me. You protected me. You challenged me. You made me a better version of myself. We made mistakes along the way, I know. We're going to make more mistakes." She pauses to grin at me, and I can't help nodding. I'm glad her expectations are grounded in reality. "And that's okay, because I know, without any doubt, that I want you on every page of my story. You belong in every chapter of my life. The book of my life began the day we met, and it will end with you by my side."

I can't help remembering the first time I saw her. Not the moment we met—that came later. It was just a glimpse of a girl from the doorway of my dorm room. She's right. That's when our lives began. We'd simply been waiting for that first chapter. Adair bites her lower lip as a sudden burst of sunshine breaks free of the clouds. I have to resist the urge to kiss her. It's against the rules. We'd been warned as much during the rehearsal when we'd fallen victim to our own giddy whims one time too many.

The minister must sense I'm about to skip to the end, because he clears his throat. "Sterling?"

What do you say to the woman you owe your life? What do you say to the woman who gave you not only her heart, but a family? To the woman who made you a home? I'd struggled with that for days leading up to this. I'd written down various thoughts, inside jokes, promises. Standing here, though, I don't need to look at the paper I have folded up in my pocket.

"I loved you the moment I saw you," I begin, knowing both sides of our story brought us here. "I don't know why or how. I just looked up and saw the other half of my soul—but then we actually met, and yeah, I hated you." She shakes her head, looking down at our clasped hands with a knowing smile. "But I didn't. I never could. I wasted a long time worrying about being good enough for Adair MacLaine's love, and it turns out that was time wasted. I never had to earn your love. You gave it to me. You gave me everything. So all that I am today, and all that I have, is yours. I kept trying to find the right words this week to tell you how I feel, and I kept coming back to one simple promise: I'm all in. But you know that, Lucky. The truth is that I didn't have to find the words. Someone else found them for me. I read this quote from Fitzgerald years before we met, and I didn't grasp it. The first time I saw you I understood it:

'I fell in love with her courage, her sincerity, and her flaming self-respect. And it's these things I'd believe in, even if the whole world indulged in wild suspicions that she wasn't all she should be.'

He gave me the words I couldn't find to tell you what you mean to me. Adair, I love you, and that is the beginning and end of everything."

Adair's hand tugs away from me to wipe her eyes, smiling up at me from wet lashes. *Everything*. It's what she was from the first moment. It's what she'll be in my last moment on this earth.

"The rings," the minister says gently. I reach down and untie the bow at Zeus's neck. He barks, his tail beginning to wag as if to say *about time.*

"Repeat after me," the minister instructs, and I echo his words as I slip the band on her finger. Adair doesn't even look at the diamond, her eyes are locked with mine. Words are our foreplay, and there's something deeply sensual in the way her gaze lingers on my lips. When it's her turn, she slides my wedding band on with the determined focus of a woman who knows exactly what she's doing and why.

"I now—"

"Hold on." I force myself to break eye contact, reaching in to my breast pocket to find the small white box I'd tucked there this morning. "I have one more vow to make."

Kneeling to the ground, I open the box and show the diamond pendant inside to Ellie. "This goes with your good luck charm," I explain. "May I?"

She nods, her eyes bright saucers as I carefully take off her necklace and thread the diamond onto her chain. "You, Ellie, are the plot twist I never saw coming," I admit to her, "and I never knew how much I needed you until you walked into my story. I promise to be here. No matter what I will always be here for you and your mommy."

"Because we're family?" Her tiny fingers hold up the diamond for inspection as she asks.

"Yes," I say, kissing her forehead.

"Forever?"

I don't miss the hint of fear hiding in her words. It will take time to heal what happened to her. I'm going to be there for every moment of it. "Forever and a day."

She holds up a pinky and I hook my own with hers. We shake on it. I lean closer and whisper to her, "Go sit with Mama Francie, baby. I need to make your mother an honest woman."

Her neck retracts and she stares at me for a split-second as though she fully appreciates the gravitas of this request. She skips over to Francie, who catches her in a big hug and pulls her onto her lap. My eyes meet Francie's just long enough to see she's crying, too. I'd expected that. She smiles widely at me, nodding her head a little as if to urge me forward.

I straighten up and adjust my tuxedo jacket.

"Are we ready?" the minister asks.

"Yes, we are," I say, unable to hold back a smirk. Somehow I'm here, despite everything. I can't help feeling like I've gotten away with something. Because life isn't supposed to be this perfect—and yet, here we are.

"In that case, I now pronounce you husband and wife. You may *finally* kiss your bride."

This is met with cheers all around us, followed by the loud popping of what I suspect is fireworks. I'm not sure because I only have eyes for my wife. My palm reaches to cradle her face, lifting her lips to meet my own. The kiss is slow and sweet like a lingering drop of honey. There's no rush. There's only her and I. There's my beginning, my ending, my everything.

Adair

As soon as Sterling breaks the kiss, the world blurs into well wishes and hugs and laughter—and joy. My heart swells inside me until I think I might crack open from happiness. Sterling's hand stays knit through mine as we maneuver our way back up the aisle. Francie follows with Ellie. Jack and Poppy handle Zeus.

We don't reach the door before Poppy dashes ahead, wagging a finger at us. "No sneaking off. There will be time for that later on your honeymoon!"

Sterling glares at her but shrugs good-naturedly. "Already telling me what to do with my wife."

"Yes," Poppy says, missing his sarcasm entirely, as she points toward the tent that's been erected in the small meadow behind our home. "Dance with her."

"I guess I could do that," he says, allowing my best friend to redirect us. He leans closer. "But later, I'm carrying you over that threshold and consummating this union."

"How medieval of you," I laugh.

"I'm feeling very possessive," he admits.

"I hope so, because you just bought a lifetime package," I tease him as we step inside the tent into another world.

I'd mentioned to Poppy that my dress reminded me of *The Great Gatsby.* She'd run with that tidbit—and then some. Even Sterling is struck silent. Sparkling swags of lights meet at oversized chandeliers that hang over tables laid with decadent gold place settings. In the middle of each, a crystal vase rises four feet into the air, white flowers spilling over its sides and downy white plumes fanning out from the top. A black and white dance floor has been set up in the center. Men in white tuxedo jackets immediately begin offering trays of champagne and hors d'oeuvres. Poppy plucks two coupes from one and passes one to me.

"Can I plan a party or what?" she asks with a smug smile.

"Poppy, this is..." Sterling trails away, taking in more details. "Are those books?"

I follow his eyes to the tables and realize he's right. At each setting, an antique book waits with a white ribbon wrapped around it.

"Not just any books," she says, plucking one off the table closest to her. "Your favorite books. I had to do a little digging, call a few stores."

I stare in wonder at the copy of Pride and Prejudice in her hands. "Maybe I should read this," she says thoughtfully. "Would you recommend it?"

"Yes," we both say at the same time.

Poppy laughs, clinking the rim of her glass to mine. "To happy endings."

I stare at her for a moment, realizing she means it with every fiber of her being. Without thinking, I throw my arms around her, spilling Dom Perignon on both of us in the process. "Thank you," I murmur, hugging her closely, "for always being there."

"I always will be," she says, "but now I think you should dance with your husband."

I take a sip of my champagne and pass it back to her, wrinkling my nose a little.

"What?" she says, instantly on alert.

"A little flat or something. Not a big deal," I say quickly, but she's already off to deal with it as a ten-piece band begins to play. "I hope she doesn't spend all night running around worrying."

"She's Poppy," Sterling says. "Of course, she will." He extends his arm. "Shall we?"

Sterling leads me on to the dance floor, drawing my body

against his as he leads us into a slow waltz. I can't help staring up at him, his dark hair haloed by the sparkling lights overhead.

"Is it everything you dreamed it would be?" he asks.

I give him a sheepish smile. "Honestly, I would have been happy with the courthouse, but this is pretty spectacular."

"You deserve spectacular." He tightens his grip on my hand. "You deserve wonder. You deserve magic."

"You already gave me all of that," I murmur, tucking my head under his chin and relaxing into his embrace.

"Well, a little party never killed anyone," he teases.

I can't help myself, even as I burrow deeper and drink in the woody smoke of his cologne. "Did you read the end of *The Great Gatsby?*"

"You have a point."

The music shifts and a delicate finger taps on my shoulder. I turn my head to find Ellie's toothy grin staring at me. She's in Jack's arms and he flashes me an apologetic, but winning, smile.

"I think it's my turn to dance with Daddy," she proclaims.

"Of course." My gaze meets Sterling's and I melt at the love I find reflected there as he releases me for the only other woman who owns as much of his heart as I do.

"Shall we?" Jack asks, offering his hand.

I nod and we slip into a slow dance, each of us stealing glances at Sterling and Ellie. Her head is pressed to his shoulder, her face tilted up to his as they circle the dance floor.

"I guess there's a father-daughter dance, after all," I murmur absently.

"I'm sorry more of your family didn't come," Jack says in his soothing baritone.

"Oh." I shake my head, realizing he misunderstood me.

"I'm not—sorry they didn't come, I mean. Watching him with her...sometimes, I wish I'd had that, but I'm so thankful Ellie does. I'm so grateful her father loves her."

"Your father loved you," Jack says, cutting me off when I start to protest. "In his twisted way. Some people confuse controlling someone who affection. Believe me."

There's a dark undertone to his words that speaks of secrets and pain of his own. Most of the time, Jack Archer is the life of the party, serving whiskey and keeping the music going, but I know enough about him to suspect he's running from troubles of his own. I also know he doesn't want to talk about them. In some ways, we're more alike than it seems outwardly.

"I'm not sure that's true, but thank you," I say softly. It's not as simple when it comes to my parents. I haven't told anyone about what Ginny told Sterling on that rooftop the night Windfall burned. Sterling's offered to help me look for answers. We'd discussed doing a DNA test, but that would involve telling Malcolm. There's no way to know if Ginny was lying without one. But I'm not certain I want to know the truth, or, more importantly, that I need to know. "Family is the people you choose. They're all here today, and I couldn't ask for more than that."

And I mean it.

"You three against the world, huh?" he asks, shifting to his usual charming self.

"If it comes to that, but for now, I like to think you and Poppy and Kai—even Sutton and Luca—are family." Maybe it's wishful thinking, but today—my wedding day—it seems like every wish I make might come true. So, I'm going to make as many as I can.

Poppy appears at my side. "Can I steal her?"

"If you must." Jack releases me, lifting my hand to his lips. "Congratulations, Adair."

"What is this about?" I ask as Poppy guides me by the elbow out of the tent and into the house.

"You're trailing your train all over the ground. I want to get it bustled before you ruin it."

I roll my eyes. "It's just a dress."

"It's your wedding dress." She stares at me like I'm speaking a foreign language. "And, honestly, I think it's the only one you'll ever wear—"

"—it is," I confirm.

"—so I want to be sure that Ellie can wear it someday if she wants," Poppy finishes.

Something about the idea of Ellie walking down the aisle on her way to her own happily ever after pushes me over the edge, and I burst into tears. "Sorry!" I look around wildly for a tissue before she can lecture me about ruining my make-up. "I'm like a leaky faucet today. I can't seem to turn it off."

"It's your wedding day." Poppy hands me a tissue and smiles warmly before she circles me and begins to hook my train into a bustle. "They're happy tears. We could all use more of those. I was a little surprised, though..."

She's not the only one. I'm not usually the type to wear my emotions so openly. "I know. I thought I might cry, but damn, everything is setting me off."

"At least, there was nothing wrong with the champagne," Poppy tells me, stepping back to inspect her work. "Maybe you drink too much whiskey to appreciate the good stuff."

"I hardly drink at all anymore," I remind her. Sterling didn't buy it, and I didn't want it most of the time.

"Well, tonight be young and happy. Sip champagne

under the stars and dance until your love carries you home," she proclaims.

I take one look at her, my best friend, who's been there through all of this with me. She's here now, watching my dreams come true after her own fell apart. "And next time, it's going to be you."

"Oh, I don't know..." She shakes her head.

"I do. You're going to find someone who walk to hell and back for you—and I'm going to dance at your wedding," I say fiercely.

She squeezes me into a hug. "I hope so."

"I know so." I've never been more sure of anything.

"So, are you finally going to tell me where you two are headed on your honeymoon?" she asks.

I clench my eyes, bracing for her reaction. In the past few months, Poppy floated the Seychelles, Fiji, and the Maldives for potential honeymoons. All of them sounded amazing, but there's one problem. "It's the three of us, actually."

"You're taking Ellie? I thought Francie was going to stay with her!"

"We wanted to take her. We've never had a family vacation and Disney..."

"But this is your honeymoon!"

"And we got a huge suite," I reassure her. "We'll have plenty of *alone* time."

"Your honeymoon is supposed to be one hundred-percent alone time," she says flatly. "Are you sure? I can keep her."

"Francie's taking her tonight, so we can be completely alone," I soothe her. "But, trust me, Sterling and I will have plenty of honeymoon sex."

"Good, because your daughter wants a brother," she tells me.

"So, I've heard." Apparently, I'd been the last one to be informed of Ellie's own wedding wish.

"Do you think Sterling...?" she trails off, her eyes glinting.

"I think if I asked Sterling to knock me up during the cake cutting, he'd do it right then and there," I say with a giggle. "I suspect he wants his own small army."

"He wants his own family," she corrects me softly.

"He has one."

"So Disney World," she says this like she can't quite process it. "You're packed?"

"Mostly." I'd been so caught up in wedding preparation that I'd only started my own bag yesterday. Ellie's is ready and Sterling is handling his own—although I'd discovered a box containing a fair amount of lacy lingerie he obviously felt I was going to need in his bag.

"I'll handle it," she tells me. "You'll be gone for two weeks, so I'll make sure you have sunscreen and plenty of clothes and tampons—stuff like that."

"Seriously, you're the best."

"Let's get you back to your husband before he plans an extraction," she teases. Poppy had seen what Sterling was capable of when they burned Cyrus and still seems to be in total awe of him and his friends.

We make it halfway to the back door when something occurs to me. "It's the third week of April, right?"

"Remind me to put your anniversary on my calendar, so you don't forget it," she says dryly. "It's the fourth Saturday, actually."

Calculations and calendars swirl in my head, landing on one obvious conclusion. "Oh."

"What?" she asks curiously.

"Nothing." I shake my head, unable to keep a faint smile

from my lips as we make our way to the tent. "I'll tell you later."

Sterling

"Total fail," Luca announces, coming up to Adair and me with a half-empty bottle of West's Reserve in his hand. It's as close to sloppy drunk as I've seen him in a while, and I say a silent thank you that we don't have horses on property yet. There's no telling what he'd do.

"Fail?" I repeat as Adair's head leaves it's tucked position under my chin and turns to look at him, too.

"I don't know if you know this, but when a man rents a tuxedo and agrees to be a groomsman, he usually has a pretty good shot with the bridesmaids," he says.

"You own that tuxedo," I say.

"The principal remains the same. Groomsman and bridesmaid. It's a classic combo like cake and ice cream."

"This again?" Jack appears at his side. "There are plenty of gorgeous women here."

I glance around, remembering Poppy's insistence that we invite most of Valmont, likely as a snub to Cyrus, who remains on all of our blacklists permanently. Ava is here with Darcy. Cameron Laird came as well, but she brought a date. There are a few more I don't recognize. "Be careful. Valmont girls are known to bite."

Luca straightens with a smirk, the information perking him up considerably. "Really?" He cracks his neck as though preparing to go into battle. "I guess I'll forgive Sutton."

"Sutton? You're not her type," I remind him. Maybe I'd misread their earlier interaction.

"I know that," he says like I'm being stupid. "But that woman from your office..."

"Trish?" Adair pulls back from my arms and begins scouring the dance floor. Our eyes settle on them at the same time. They're dancing closely together in their matching gowns, Trish's head on Sutton's shoulder.

"How old is she?" I ask.

"I don't think Trish is the one to worry about," Adair says. "Sutton can handle herself, big brother."

So, I'm always told, but that doesn't change the fierce instinct I have to protect my kid sister. Although, Adair is probably right. If one of them walks away with a broken heart, it's far more likely to be Trish.

"That's two bridesmaids down for the count," Luca informs us like he's calling plays on the field. "And unless you changed your mind about Poppy..."

"No," the three of us say in unison. After the year she's had, the last thing she needs is another wolf like Luca in her life. I love him like a brother, but he has a long way to go before he's commitment material.

"Fine," he says, not showing any sign of dejection. "Which one is more likely to bite?"

"All of them," Adair promises him.

Luca turns to Jack and says one word before striding confidently toward my old classmates: Cairo.

"Oh, that's not good. I better go with him," Jack says, hurrying after.

"Are you ever going to explain what happened in Cairo?" Adair asks as we watch them approach the women at the bar.

"You wouldn't believe me," I tell her honestly. And

tonight? It's not about the past. It's about this moment and the one that follows and the one after that.

The stars are out now and Adair is in my arms, and everything is right with the world. Francie packed up Ellie an hour ago after she'd worn herself out spinning for hours on the dance floor, and took her back to the guesthouse at Luca's new estate. After everything that happened with the Eaton and Windfall, I prefer to know my daughter is somewhere with tight security if she's not under the same roof as me.

"I don't think this party is going to be over anytime soon, Lucky," I whisper. "But I've had enough people for the day."

"Does people include me?" she teases.

"Nope," I say, only half-joking. She's more than just my love or my wife. Adair is part of me. She fills in the pieces of myself I didn't know were missing. Having her by my side is as natural as walking on my own two feet.

"Do you think they'll notice if we sneak away?" she asks, her voice heavy with meaning.

"Who cares?" I tug her away from the lingering guests out into the moonlight night. We walk, hand-in-hand, for a moment before I get impatient and sweep her into my arms. I'm vaguely aware of a cheer erupting behind us at the gesture—so much for sneaking away. But it seems no one is going to try to stand in the way of me taking my wife to bed.

"You're really going to drag me, caveman style in the house?" Her protest is weak and undermined when she sighs happily and wraps an arm around my neck.

"I'm told it's for luck," I say, pausing at the threshold.

"Actually, you don't want to know its backstory," she says, laughing. "Trust me, it's primitive."

"In that case." I lower her to her feet and hold out my hand. "We go across together. Equal."

She slips her hand into mine and we cross it together. As soon as we're through, I kick the door shut and pull her roughly to me. "But don't get any ideas, Lucky." My lips cruise along her jaw eliciting a sharp gasp. "You still belong to me."

"And you belong to me," she whispers. "I think it's a pretty fair trade. My heart in exchange for yours."

"If you say so." I'll never quite understand it.

"I know so."

"Now, I know I said we're equals," I begin, licking my lower lip as I imagine all the delicious things I want to do to her, "and I put you down, but..."

She tilts her head. "What are you up to, Sterling Fo—"

She's cut off as I throw her over my shoulder and bound towards the stairs that lead to our bedroom. Dropping her onto the bed, I pounce, my hands trying to understand the complexities of her dress. Adair's mouth crushes to mine, but she manages to wrench her skirt up, breaking the kiss to pant. "I chose this dress for a reason."

"Later, I want to taste every inch of your skin," I say gruffly. "I'm going to take this off you and worship you, Lucky. But now?"

Her fingers fumble with my belt buckle, and I know she feels the same urgency. Later, we'll make love. I'll explore her body like a treasure map, but now, I'm overtaken by the need to be inside her. She manages to undo my zipper, and her soft hand strokes the length of my dick.

Under the layers of tulle and lace, I discover a delicate powder blue garter belt holding up her stockings. My hand slips between her thighs, urging them open only to discover there's nothing more there than that garter belt.

"Wait." I pull back and drink in the lovely sight of her. "Fuck, Lucky. Never mind. You can leave that on."

"As long as it doesn't get in the way," she teases but before she reaches the end, I rock against her, nudging her open. Adair's fingers dig into my shoulders, a low moan spilling from her, as I slide slowly inside her. I want this moment to last forever.

Leaning forward, I press my forehead to hers, my eyes closing as I feel her tighten around me. "I love you, Mrs. Ford."

"Ms. Ford," she corrects me dreamily.

I might give her a new name, but I'll never douse the fire burning inside her—and I wouldn't have it any other way.

"I love you, Sterling," she says softly, brushing her lips across mine. "Thank you for coming back to me."

"I'll never leave you again," I vow, rolling my hips until there is no longer her or me—only us.

I love her. She is my beginning. She is my end. She is my everything.

We tangle together, coaxing one another to the edge until her breath shifts to shallow whimpers. I crush my lips to hers and let us fall. Adair cries out and I swallow her pleasure with my kiss, making it my own as I make her mine.

A few moments later, I roll onto the bed, my hand finding hers. Adair turns to smile at me.

"That was better than I ever dreamed," she murmurs.

"Dreaming of me, huh?" I can't keep a cocky grin off my face at the idea that even asleep, she can't get enough of me. Just like I can't get enough of her.

"Always," she promises, and I know she means it.

I roll to my side and fiddle with the lace wrenched

around her hips. "Now, how do I help you out of this beautiful dress? I want to fully appreciate my wife."

"Already?" She raises an eyebrow, but I see the same hunger I feel burning in her eyes.

"Well, I believe we were given orders earlier, and I'd hate to disappoint," I say, thinking of Ellie's drawing.

"About that..." she trails off, her teeth biting into her lower lip while she waits for me to catch up with her.

I stare a moment as the wheels turn in my head, ratcheting me closer to something just beyond my reach.

"Are you sure?" she asks.

"Lucky, I've never been more certain of anything. I spent all night trying to keep myself from throwing you across a table and getting started." I'd considered it before, wondered when it would feel like the right time to try for another baby. Seeing her in her wedding dress the first time, made me wish we'd started yesterday.

"I don't think that's necessary," she says with a giggle, "especially since..."

"Wait..." The final cog clicks into place, and I stare at her for a moment. Then I roll on top of her, pinning her arms over her head. "What are you saying?"

"I mean, maybe I'm wrong, but..." she starts to list all the reasons my wish might have already come true. "I'll have to test to be sure. Are you happy?"

Despite everything, she's still hesitant, afraid to show how she feels about this until I do. It's going to take her a long time to understand that I will always share her joy and her suffering, that we can build a family better than the ones that hurt us. Until she does, I'll show her every day, starting now.

"I have everything I ever wanted," I whisper. "Of course, I'm happy." I trace the curve of her lower lip and smile wickedly. "I think we really should do everything we can to be sure it takes."

"I don't think it works that way." But she's smiling, too. "But you're probably right. I mean, I'm game to keep working on a baby until we know, if you are."

I lower my face to hers, ready for my real life to begin. "Lucky, I'm all in."

ACKNOWLEDGMENTS

First of all I have to thank you, lovely reader, from coming on this journey with me. I hope you laughed, cried, and swooned as much as I did.

Thanks to Louise, my fabulous agent, and the team at The Bent Agency for always being a source of guidance.

Thank you to my foreign teams for working to bring this new series to readers worldwide. Thank you to my team at Blanvalet for your excitement about The Rivals.

Thank you to my amazing assistants, Natasha and Shelby. I would go nuts without you.

Thanks you to my Loves for recipe swaps and meme posts and everything you do. Special thanks to my Inner Court, who I can count on any day, any time.

To my author friends, thank you for being women who inspire me every damn day.

Thank you to my family for sharing me with fictional people, and only complaining a little.

And to Josh, thank you for always cracking a joke. Thank

you for being my forever. Thank you for being my rainbow after the storm.

ABOUT THE AUTHOR

GENEVA LEE is the *New York Times, USA Today,* and internationally bestselling author of over a dozen novels, including the Royals Saga which has sold two million copies worldwide. She lives in Poulsbo Washington with her husband and three children, and she co-owns Away With Words Bookshop with her sister.

Geneva is married to her high school sweetheart. He's always the first person to read her books. Sometimes, he reads as she writes them. Last year, they were surprised by finding out Geneva was pregnant with their third child. They welcomed a beautiful baby girl in 2020.

When she isn't working or writing, Geneva likes to read, bake ridiculous cakes, run, and binge television seasons. She loves to travel and is always eager to go on a new adventure.

Learn more at GenevaLee.com